THE
LOST
PRINCE

ALSO BY SELDEN EDWARDS

The Little Book

SELDEN EDWARDS

THE
LOST
PRINCE

DUTTON

DUTTON
Published by Penguin Group (USA) Inc.
375 Hudson Street, New York, New York 10014, U.S.A.
Penguin Group (Canada), 90 Eglinton Avenue East, Suite 700, Toronto, Ontario M4P 2Y3, Canada (a division of Pearson Penguin Canada Inc.); Penguin Books Ltd, 80 Strand, London WC2R 0RL, England; Penguin Ireland, 25 St Stephen's Green, Dublin 2, Ireland (a division of Penguin Books Ltd); Penguin Group (Australia), 250 Camberwell Road, Camberwell, Victoria 3124, Australia (a division of Pearson Australia Group Pty Ltd); Penguin Books India Pvt Ltd, 11 Community Centre, Panchsheel Park, New Delhi–110 017, India; Penguin Group (NZ), 67 Apollo Drive, Rosedale, Auckland 0632, New Zealand (a division of Pearson New Zealand Ltd); Penguin Books (South Africa) (Pty) Ltd, 24 Sturdee Avenue, Rosebank, Johannesburg 2196, South Africa

Penguin Books Ltd, Registered Offices: 80 Strand, London WC2R 0RL, England

Published by Dutton, a member of Penguin Group (USA) Inc.

First printing, August 2012
1   3   5   7   9   10   8   6   4   2

LIBRARY OF CONGRESS CATALOGING-IN-PUBLICATION DATA
Edwards, Selden.
The lost prince / Selden Edwards.
p. cm.
ISBN 978-0-525-95294-7
1. Wives—Fiction. 2. Family secrets—Fiction. 3. Time travel—Fiction. I. Title.
PS3605.D8985L67 2012
813'.6—dc22   2011050079

Printed in the United States of America
Designed by Nancy Resnick

PUBLISHER'S NOTE
This book is a work of fiction. Names, characters, places, and incidents either are the product of the author's imagination or are used fictitiously, and any resemblance to actual persons, living or dead, business establishments, events, or locales is entirely coincidental.

For Nan, Bruce, and Paula
My wonderful children

CONTENTS

PART THREE

PART FOUR

PART FIVE

PROLOGUE

ll of those who attended the memorial service in the chapel at St. Gregory's School that May afternoon in 1918 knew well the elegant woman in her midforties who sat up near the front beside her staunch banker husband, one of the school's most prominent alumni and its greatest hero, whom they also knew well. Frank Burden had represented his school splendidly in the classroom and on the playing fields of Harvard College during the early 1890s and had won two gold medals in the first modern Olympic Games in Athens in 1896. His wife, Eleanor, had become over the past two decades one of the most respected and active figures in the social and charitable life of Boston—wife, mother, patroness of the arts, social activist—but no one came even close to guessing her secret life, or the curse she had borne daily for the past twenty years.

A few were aware that it had been entirely Eleanor Burden's doing that the subject of the service, Arnauld Esterhazy, this school's former teacher killed in the war, had come to St. Gregory's School in the first place. Her godfather and confidant, William James, was the only one who knew the whole story. But he was now eight years gone, so no one among those congregated that day for the sad event knew or guessed at the depth of her connection to the man being eulogized or the complex grief she was now barely able to contain.

For her, Arnauld Esterhazy could not be dead. Eleanor Burden was cursed by knowledge of the future, at least part of it. She had known the world war was coming and that Arnauld, safe in Boston, would be swept up in it, and she knew also that a second war was coming in twenty years, one that would also have a profound effect on her life. This death simply did not fit into the ordained future, and yet the word had come from the Italian front and had been verified by her friend Carl Jung, a source she trusted for thoroughness. "Killed in action," he had said, "absolutely no doubt." The news had been devastating to her, not just because she loved the man, but because this fateful turn confounded everything she had been working to promote over the past twenty years, everything for which she had made her fortune, for which she had stood toe-to-toe with powerful men, among them Sigmund Freud, and, yes, even J. P. Morgan.

The school had lost a beloved teacher in the war, and she and her husband were there in the center of the mourners because the man had been a close friend of their family and a guest in their home on innumerable occasions, but no one guessed how much more he had meant to Eleanor, either in the innocent role in which he had arrived in Boston eight years before or in the overpowering earthy connection of his departure, at the end. As Dr. Freud often said, all grief is representational, referring in its power back to some previous more primal event and forward to one's own impermanence on this earth. And now with this quiet desperation, she was reliving the traumatic ordeal of twenty years prior, when she had lost the love of her life and then did not know how she could go on.

She could not accept this death and yet she had to, as it stared her square in the face, here in the words of eulogy of this service and in the certitude in Carl Jung's voice as he told her the fateful news—"unavoidable" was his assessment.

Eleanor Burden, this woman of heroic strength, caught now between the past and an uncertain future, found herself once again not knowing how she could go on.

PART ONE

1

A SECRET DESTINY

hen Weezie Putnam returned from Vienna in 1898 determined now to be known as Eleanor, she brought with her from her ordeal three items of inestimable worth: a manuscript, an exquisite piece of jewelry, and a handwritten journal. Each would change her life, she knew, and each would play a part in determining her destiny.

The manuscript had been written in a cathartic fury at the end of her Vienna time, the completion of the commitment she had made in going there in the first place, to write "something of significance," as her former headmistress called it, to be delivered as promised to the *New York Times* immediately upon her return. She brought the manuscript to the *Times* office in New York City, and the editor Henry Moss, whom she had known from before Vienna, held it in his hand and measured its weightiness with a satisfied smile. "As promised," he said, "a significant body of work."

"That is my hope," Eleanor said. "I am relieved to be done with it." Then she concluded with, "It is to be called *City of Music*," the title that she knew was meant to be.

Mr. Moss also cabled her in the week after her return home to Boston and insisted that she travel back to New York immediately, he and two other editors having just completed reading the manuscript. "We are deeply moved," he said, "by the vibrancy we have seen in these pages."

When she arrived in their offices, the other editors smiled at her as Henry Moss offered with enthusiasm, "You have launched yourself as a serious writer, Miss Putnam. Or, I should say, Mr. Jonathan Trumpp has."

Her response was more sudden than she would have wished, had she not been caught by surprise. "Absolutely not," was what came out, in a burst. "I shall work with you to edit this project," she said, "as I wish it to be as thorough and accurate as it can be, but it will remain the sole long work of Jonathan Trumpp, and Mr. Trumpp has written his last." She said it with such conviction as to leave the *Times* editors speechless.

"That is not the response we expected," Mr. Moss said, disappointment obvious on his face.

"It will be a waste not to follow this up," a second editor said.

"So be it," she said. "It is what it is. I appreciate all that you have done for me, but there will be no more from Mr. Trumpp." She expressed her gratitude even further and then left the *New York Times* office, not seeing fit to mention at that time or later the painful events that had led to the catharsis of writing, nor its fateful inspiration, which could never be replicated.

The second item she brought with her from her Vienna experience was the piece of jewelry, a most extraordinary ring which had belonged to one of the most famous and most tragic figures in recent European history. The ring's value was, she hoped, easily recognizable, as she knew she was meant to set about selling it immediately. She knew nothing of the fine art of selling extraordinary pieces of jewelry, and she knew that for purely emotional reasons parting with this particular piece would be most difficult, but it had to be done.

And the third item, by far the most significant, was a remarkably detailed journal, a leather-bound handwritten volume that recorded in exactness all that had happened to and around her in Vienna. This volume also revealed forthcoming events well into the twentieth century, including events she knew she would have to make happen and others that would come about well beyond any of her doing. She had her own reasons for believing the journal's recordings to be true and for following its prescribed tasks religiously, knowing all the while that Sigmund Freud, back in Vienna, had participated intimately in the journal's origins and had thought it, with a certainty equal to her own, the product of a deranged mind. Because of the sensitive nature of the material in this extraordinary volume, she knew she was required to guard its many secrets with the utmost care, to show it to no one.

And so, because of this journal, whose provenance for the time being shall remain unexplained, whose contents had become for Eleanor inseparable from her very sense of herself, she would know the role she needed to play to ensure the future she knew had to be. It was for her lifelong commitment made during an indelible time to the love of her life.

She knew of the great events coming in the years ahead. She knew she was to marry, for better or worse, Frank Burden, a man she didn't love; to raise with him three beautiful and talented children; to become a great social and cultural force in Boston; to count on the support of two extraordinary men, first William James and then Carl Gustav Jung; to watch helplessly the emergence of two horrific worldwide wars; to suffer great loss; and to die an old woman in the same house she had been born in, on Acorn Street on Boston's Beacon Hill. She even knew the date and time.

And from the pages of this Vienna journal, she foresaw from the time of her return from Vienna that her principal business associate was to be a man named T. Williams Honeycutt, and that this Mr. Honeycutt, whom she had never heard of, was to play a crucial role in coaxing Arnauld Esterhazy to come to Boston and to remain there for the rest of his life. She knew that Arnauld Esterhazy, in his position as revered teacher at St. Gregory's School, well into the twentieth century, was to shape and change the lives of many Bostonians, playing as he did so an indispensable role in the destiny of her family.

These developments concerning Arnauld Esterhazy are the main substance of this story.

THE MAN FROM CHICAGO

s she contemplated the magnitude of what lay ahead, she realized she must abandon her girlish diminutive name Weezie and adopt permanently the adult persona implied by her given name, Eleanor. It was a momentous transition understood by no one but her. And she would set about performing the tasks, of which the most immediately challenging was dealing with the selling of the ring. For advice back then, she had begun with the director of the Boston Museum of Fine Arts, Jackson Peard, a close friend of her family. It was Jackson Peard, this man who had spent a lifetime examining exquisite pieces of art, who gasped upon opening the fine linen handkerchief and recognizing at once the item's significance. "Rather takes one's breath away, doesn't it?" he said, looking at the ring, then at Eleanor. It was beautifully jeweled, white gold, with tiny diamonds and emeralds and a large sapphire in the center, an item of great craftsmanship and inestimable monetary worth. "How ever did you come upon something like this?" he said.

"Extraordinary circumstances," she said calmly.

"You know its history, I assume," he said.

Eleanor nodded. "I do, and I suppose that improves its worth."

"Most definitely. Everyone by now knows of the great tragedy and its mysteries." Then Jackson Peard, an authority on fin de siècle Europe, added, "Scandal increases value, no question. Tragedy increases value. It is a sad but intriguing story." He paused and shook his head, then looked back at the object in his hands. "But an enhancement of the value of such a piece of jewelry as this remarkable one we have before us, no question."

"And the handkerchief?" Eleanor asked.

"And this fine linen handkerchief with its embroidered seal," the director said, "very good. It authenticates things."

"That is my hope," Eleanor said.

"It most certainly does," the director said as he examined both the linen and the ring. "You could donate this item to us," he said, and then seeing from the look of consternation on Eleanor's face the inappropriateness of his remark added quickly, "Or you could sell it at auction." He held the ring up to the light, as if to ascertain if he was in fact holding what he thought he was holding. "Something of this value would merit an auction," he repeated, "in London."

"How does one do that?" she said.

"Oh, we can help. We do it often—discreetly, of course."

Then the director looked at Eleanor seriously. "In order to sell this item," he said slowly, "you must reveal how you came to possess it."

Eleanor rose up in her chair, her back stiffening. "I will not be able to do that," she said.

"Then it is questionable that there can be a sale."

"Then," she said, "I shall have to prepare myself for that eventuality."

With Jackson Peard's help, she went ahead with plans and made contact by cable with the famous auction house of Sotheby's and decided to travel to London herself to accompany her precious acquisition, fully aware that at any time her refusal to provide background on the acquisition might bring an end to any deal.

Then, as she was beginning to make plans for the long and involved trip to London, she received another message from Jackson Peard, another discreet one. "This is not within our usual protocol," he said, pausing respectfully.

"Because of my failure to disclose details?"

"In this case," Mr. Peard said, "disclosure might not be as much of an issue. I am assured that you will treat our involvement with the strictest confidence, but we have someone in New York whom you should see." He handed her a small business card. "There is interest in your object, but it cannot pass through the usual formal channels. It is on Maiden Lane. Are you familiar with it?"

"I am not," Eleanor said.

"Well, it is located in the Financial District. Most cities have such markets in out-of-the-way places, but New York's is right in the heart of things, where it has been for decades. There are booths on the street where you will find diamonds and jewels of all shapes and sizes, quite a show. You will find this office in the midst of it all." He pointed to the card. "I suggest you travel there immediately. You will want to go there yourself, but take a man with you, of course."

"I shall go alone," Eleanor said with conviction.

So, her prized possession in hand, Eleanor headed off to New York on the first train of the following morning, alone. As she sat by the window, watching Massachusetts and then Connecticut roll by, she did her best to overcome the natural nervousness that such a monumental transaction brought with it. The whole business of this unique piece of jewelry brought back painful memories of the extraordinary circumstances in Vienna by which this treasured object had come to be in her possession. Keeping the ring was out of the question. Using its sale to raise monies to establish the fund she was required to begin was not only judicious, but her obligation. As with so many monumental transactions now and in her future, she hoped that what she was doing was right, in keeping with the journal's very general instructions.

Arriving in New York a little after noon, she found her way to the given Maiden Lane address, and did indeed find, as Jackson Peard had described, the small office of a jeweler named Constant Auger in the midst of what looked like hundreds of small booths, all dealers of stones and jewelry, which she, a woman alone, had hurried past to arrive at the prescribed door. The waiting room was decorated with a few large prints of European estates, and many glass cases, all filled with sparkling diamond jewelry. She sat for a time before a short and officious woman came out to greet her. "Mr. Auger will see you now," she said. "You will follow me." She ushered Eleanor into a small office where two men stood beside a table, obviously waiting for her. "This is Mr. Auger," the woman said, and an elegant European-looking gentleman took her hand, and the woman left the room.

"This is my client," the jeweler said. "He is from Chicago and has a keen interest in European objets d'art." Her eyes turned to the man from Chicago, who showed no interest in shaking hands. "He has been greatly looking forward to this meeting," Mr. Auger continued, "and to seeing the object." From the two men's comfort with each other, Eleanor assumed that this was not their first business together.

Eleanor took the offered seat as the two men sat behind the table. She opened her purse and withdrew the handkerchief-wrapped object, handing it to the man from Chicago, who took it and eyed it reverentially for a moment before carefully lifting the folds. She watched his face with care as he pulled away the fine linen wrapping. "My, my," he said, examining it with care, then shifting his attention to the handkerchief, as if he knew exactly what he was looking for. He then handed both the ring and the linen to Mr. Auger beside him, who showed nothing in his face and began examining it with a magnifying eyepiece. He remained silent and passed the ring back with only the hint of a nod.

"The empress's seal," Mr. Auger said, examining the handkerchief again, and the other man nodded his satisfaction, again ever so slightly. "That is certain."

"Authenticated?" the man from Chicago said, clearly taking control. The jeweler nodded. "You know this item's significance, I assume," he said, looking directly at Eleanor.

Eleanor nodded. "I do," she said without hesitation. "Yes."

"Mayerling," he said. "Frightful business. Young Rudolf, the crown prince, and his wife struggled in marriage. He became irritable, drank too much, took opium, and sought consolation with Vienna's young women, even fathered an illegitimate son, they say. Add to that the dreaded affliction of venereal disease. Then the murder and suicide, all by his hand." Then he examined the ring for a moment. "All increasing the value of this ring, I imagine you have been told."

"Yes," Eleanor said. "I have been told."

"And people in Boston tell us that this object is very dear to you for emotional reasons also," the man from Chicago said without looking up.

Eleanor nodded again. "That is correct," she said.

"And it is our understanding that you have not revealed how you obtained such an object," the man from Chicago said.

"That is true," Eleanor said. "I have not."

"You understand that in such a matter, we must know."

Eleanor stood firm. "I understand."

"And?" the man from Chicago said.

"And circumstances forbid my telling."

"We hear that you are a very headstrong woman, Miss Putnam," the man said.

"That may be," she said, "but circumstances do forbid me."

Mr. Auger was about to speak, to explain perhaps the importance of full disclosure in negotiations such as these, and the man from Chicago held out his hand. "It is a personal matter, I gather," he said.

"It is, one of a most personal nature." Eleanor was looking him straight in the eye. "Yes."

The man from Chicago then looked over at the jeweler, who gave a slight nod. "It was obtained through legal means, we can assume?" he said. "Improbable, but legal."

Eleanor did not flinch. "Yes, you have my word on that. This ring came into my hands through completely legal circumstances." The man from Chicago was quite obviously taken by the directness of this woman's manner. "Improbable, but legal," she repeated, "a gift from a cherished friend, making it difficult to part with."

"But you would part with it?" the man said.

"I would," she said, "under the right conditions."

"Would the sum of five thousand dollars constitute the right conditions?" he said.

Eleanor tried her best to show no surprise; she simply nodded. "I think that would," she said.

"A deal-ending bid," Jackson Peard called such a move in preparation for this meeting. "Ready yourself. You will be doing business with a wealthy industrialist, a man who never wishes to be outdone or outbid. If he wishes to go forward, he will do what is necessary to take what he wants off the table."

"I would like, then, to take this very special item off your hands." He held the ring and its handkerchief out toward her.

"That would be possible," Eleanor said, again trying not to show any of her relieved surprise.

"We have an agreement, a most discreet one?"

"We have an agreement," she repeated with conviction, "and, yes, a most discreet one."

"That is good," the man said, and both men nodded their satisfaction.

"And may I hold it one last time?" Eleanor said, and she took the ring into her hands and closed her eyes, allowing herself to be carried back for just a moment to the time at which she had acquired it, feeling the strong pull of complete love and gratification, afraid for just an instant that once back there she would not be able to return. Then she opened her eyes, snapped back to the present, felt her fingers tight on the ring for one last time, and reached out, giving it over to the man from Chicago, never to see it again.

So almost as soon as she had arrived in New York City, Eleanor Putnam the neophyte jewel seller was heading home with a five-thousand-dollar bank draft—a small fortune—for her fund, the Hyperion Fund, she knew she must call it. "Hyperion, one of the mythic Titans, lord of light," a classics-professor friend of William James told her one night at a Harvard Club supper party. "He was one of the precursors of the Olympian gods and goddesses, from prehistory. One of the forebears of it all."

MRS. FRANK BURDEN

lso during that time immediately after her return from Vienna, the newly rechristened Eleanor had begun to seek the company of Frank Burden, the promising young banker and hero of countless athletic events during his school days. Since no one in Boston knew what had transpired in Vienna, the association seemed perfectly natural within the city's well-established social order, an eventuality even, considering the affinity of the attractive couple's two families and the fact that they had known each other all their lives and had both just returned from Europe, where it was known they had spent some time together. No one realized the degree to which the eventuality was in fact another result of Eleanor's strong determination, pursuing what she knew was meant to be. She had to marry Frank Burden in order for the future to be the future. She knew that plain and simple, and falling in love or being in love had nothing to do with it.

Frank was a very forthright and purposeful young man, intelligent, self-assured, and talented in the areas where a banker should be, and he carried himself now with the confidence of one who was formed in such a mold. What was most comforting about Frank Burden was his absolute commitment to "things as they are now and ever shall be," a phrase he used with regularity. "Frank does not like change and did nothing to promote it," one of their common friends said years later. He was not at all introspective and had very little interest in engaging meaningfully with those who were. He knew of the works of Freud and Jung and William James and their kind, especially later, but he said simply that he did not wish to "engage the world at their level," keeping to himself mostly the fact that he saw little or no value in that manner of engagement. "I am very literal," he would say with pride, "and I wish to remain that way." Changing Frank Burden was not part of Eleanor's destiny. In fact, from what the journal told of the necessary future, he was to remain pretty much as he was, unchanged, all his life.

Frank had actually asked for Eleanor's hand before their time in Vienna, it was known, and although Eleanor had not responded then or immediately after their return, they both moved forward, it seemed, with certain assumptions, Eleanor leading the way. Over the weeks following their return, with no actual commitment yet, Eleanor made a number of requests that Frank Burden granted without hesitation.

"Frank, I would like to accompany you to Trinity," she had said in the first weeks. "It would be good for both of us." And he nodded agreement, knowing full well, as did she, what would be assumed by such a public change in their lives, her sitting at his side at Trinity Church on Sunday, up front in the Burden pew.

Eleanor and Frank both attended Trinity Church by family tradition going back generations, but arriving together and sitting side by side was as good as an announcement of their intentions. And Frank, who had recently been appointed to the finance committee of the vestry, a position formerly held by his father and before that his grandfather, agreed to join also the charity committee, a surprising addition to his involvement in the church, and the statement of his willingness to be part of the church's activities in the poorer quarters of the city, a sign perhaps of the influence of the community-minded young woman he had begun sitting beside on Sundays.

Frank also agreed to take part with her in a number of other charitable activities, including those connected with the Boston hospitals. "We can always use a man of finance," one committee member at the Boston Lying-In Hospital said to the staunch young banker, as he appeared at one of their meetings for the first time. Those who had known Frank Burden well would have noticed the change in attitude brought about by his open and willing association with Eleanor Putnam and might have concluded that he was, for some reason, doing penance.

Another change of habit at this time in his life was his accompanying

Eleanor to lectures at various museums and even an alumnae event at her all-female Smith College. "Such visits to a women's college will do a man good," Eleanor said lightly, "in case he finds himself raising daughters." And indeed after his daughters were born, he even made statements, admittedly mild ones, supporting women's suffrage. And once, a few years later, Frank Burden would stop conversation at the annual Symphony Ball by announcing loudly, "By the time my daughters reach adulthood, they will be voting."

Of any dark part of their history together there was simply no mention. Eleanor had chosen to move ahead with her steely resolve, and Frank went about his business with characteristic rectitude, establishing himself in the banking world, especially in areas of international finance, as a young man of promise. Of course there was never any mention of why it would be unwise for him to set foot on the Continent or to go anywhere near Austria or Germany or, more specifically, Vienna. He made it clear to anyone who asked that, for the time being, he would not be returning to Europe. No one at his bank noticed any sudden discomfort and reluctance when associates brought up the subject of European travel, an area in which he had in the past shown great enthusiasm and had in that same past established considerable expertise. He simply made it clear that travel would be the province of others at the bank and that he was going to stay home and mind affairs in Boston for a while. Eleanor was helpful in this regard.

"It is really quite simple," she was heard to say. "Frank and I have declared a five-year moratorium on personal travel," she said. "It is very natural. There is so much to concentrate on at home."

But then, of course, no one knew the full story of their relationship, nor would anyone ever, save two people. In Eleanor's extraordinary destiny, marriage to Frank Burden was just what had to happen.

From the moment of her return, she shared this part of her life, concerning Frank Burden, with her godfather, William James. During her childhood time at Winsor School in Boston or at Smith College or now upon her return from abroad, William James always made it clear that he enjoyed her discourses on her various adventures. Now, more than ever, she enjoyed sharing with her wise godfather her goals and ambitions for her life in Boston. "You seem to have found with Frank a mature compatibility that serves both of you well," Dr. James observed. "It is very satisfying to watch."

"We are very different," Eleanor said, "as if we are of different temperaments."

"Different temperaments can make for good marriages," he said.

"That will be so in our case," she said, and Dr. James smiled knowingly and nodded.

"You, my dear, will make it so." On many occasions the great professor had told her of the high regard he had for her powerful resolve. He who had known well Eleanor's late parents observed often how the daughter had inherited the mother's "strength of character," as he called it.

Dr. James had also known Frank Burden in his recent athletic days at Harvard and had been impressed by how Frank and a group of American college students had traveled to Athens and participated very successfully in the first modern Olympic Games, a few years before in 1896. "Frank is very steadfast," Dr. James said.

Oblivious to most of the way he was being perceived, Frank, having recovered from whatever it was that had subdued him upon his return from Vienna, went about his life with that characteristic steadfastness and began gradually regaining all of his former energy and vigor. The eventual announcement of his forthcoming marriage, by the time of its arrival a surprise to no one, was greeted with universal approval throughout Boston. Those close to him had observed that he had gotten through a mysterious rough patch, a very uncharacteristic period of uncertainty and doubt of unknown origin. And Eleanor, ever silently at his side when he appeared in public, had received much credit, although not as much as she secretly deserved. "It is estimable," a colleague at the bank said years later, "what the support of a good woman can do for a man."

Frank and Eleanor emerged in the new century as leaders in many areas of Boston society, especially those having to do with service to the arts and to the city's needy. In short, Eleanor Putnam was seen as a very positive addition in the life of promising young banker Frank Burden, providing what he needed to ensure that things in his world progressed exactly how he wanted.

And she asked him, in those days directly after her Vienna sojourn, as she called it, to handle her family investments and inheritance at the time of her father's death. She found herself now with responsibility for a small endowment in stocks and bonds along with the house at 6 Acorn Street, the house where she had grown up, and Frank agreed to oversee it all.

"Women do not need to worry about finances," he said to her. "That is what a good marriage is for." He knew nothing then or later of the inner workings of the Hyperion Fund, which Eleanor knew she was intended to handle entirely on her own, independent of her husband.

And so, in a few short years following their return from Vienna, Frank and Eleanor established an equilibrium as one of the highly respected marriages in Boston, well documented in the social columns of the Boston newspapers and well received in the discussions of the professionally successful and the well-to-do when they discussed such things. Few, if any, knew the degree to which both Frank and Eleanor needed time to recover from what had transpired in Vienna and how after a few years they had successfully done so.

Overtly, one fact was clear to all: Frank Burden was now totally devoted to his wife and dependent on her for the strong family and social life he had around him, exactly how he thought things should be, "now and forever in Boston," as he liked to say. Years later, in summing up Frank Burden's life, a close friend would observe, "In Eleanor Putnam, Frank was getting exactly what he wanted. She ran a beautifully organized home, arranged the family's social schedule, saw to all the necessary involvement in the cultural life of the city, presented him with three gifted and successful children, allowing Frank to worry about little more than his very active and demanding life at the bank. Who would not have envied him that?"

This stability at home allowed Frank to become "one of the most prominent bankers in this city that prides itself in great banking," the friend said. "None in Boston could imagine a better life partner for Frank Burden than Eleanor Putnam, or a better financial advisor than young Frank himself."

Frank eventually proposed again, and this time Eleanor accepted, and their plans of marriage had gone exceedingly well, initiated primarily by him it appeared, and had resulted in a wedding date in the fall of 1902. "We shall need to wait for the Jameses to return from England," she said. William James and his wife, Alice, were in England with his brother Henry for over a year during that lengthy courting time, and it was he who would be giving her away. And, not coincidentally, the necessary postponement of the wedding date, waiting for the Jameses to return, would allow her time to pursue the next rather arduous assignment from her Vienna commitment, which she kept in deepest secrecy.

That assignment was the purchase of stock in a company called Cincinnati Soap and Candle Company, one she knew in name only from a single line in the Vienna journal and one, she deduced from that simple reference, in which she was intended to invest the entirety of her new-found fund. This was to be her first foray into the stock market, the specific ins and outs of which she knew virtually nothing about. But who better to advise her than the staunch young banker she was about to marry, Frank Burden, provided that she could keep the very core of it secret? Being very careful not to divulge too much, and certainly not to mention anything having to do with Vienna, she sought his advice on how to begin a conversation with a prospective company.

"All businesses want investors," Frank said very precisely, as if talking to a child, "and of course some more than others, at certain times more than others. The challenge is to choose wisely and not to allow the needs of the company to sway one's decision. A woman should not be making decisions on such matters, of course. You will soon have a husband to handle such affairs for you, should they arise." He smiled and changed the subject to one he thought more appropriate. "That is what we are for," Frank concluded, a theme she had heard from him many times before.

In this and her other conversations with her fiancé, she took what tiny nuggets of advice and perspective she found and disregarded the rest, always concluding with something genuinely gracious. "Oh, thank you, Frank," she said this time. "You are very kind."

Steadfast Frank Burden never, then or later, suspected in such remarks even the slightest bit of irony.

4

OUT WEST

n the time before Eleanor's marriage to Frank Burden, Arnauld Esterhazy was still a university student in Vienna, and although she had begun a correspondence with him, she had not yet even begun the difficult task of talking this talented young intellectual into leaving the comfort and stimulation of his dear city and coming to Boston to pursue an academic life at a boys' school.

Not wishing to overpower her young friend and yet wishing to attract his interest, Eleanor decided to write him in return each time she received from him a letter, thereby allowing him to set the pace, as it were. Because a letter took almost two weeks to travel from Vienna to Boston, the frequency of their correspondence added up to a letter every month or so. Having no family life to report on, Eleanor decided to describe for young Arnauld the historic and cultural life of Boston. Drawing parallels where she could with the life she knew of his Vienna, the strategy accomplished her two goals: first of sharing her life, if only in this general way, and second in making Boston life sound so compelling that he might wish to participate in it, when the time came. And we do know from the existing correspondence that she sent her young friend a copy of *City of Music* shortly after its publication.

It seemed to Eleanor that the young friend became more and more comfortable sharing his inner thoughts. After her death there was found in a trunk a collection of letters and papers assembled with great care over a lifetime by someone wishing for the complete story to be known. Within this considerable assemblage of correspondence is a packet of the letters between Eleanor and her young Viennese friend, the central documentation for this story. Only a few months into the exchange, we notice that young Arnauld Esterhazy ceased addressing her as "Miss Putnam."

My dear Eleanor,

Spring has finally come to our dear Vienna, and glorious clear days have brought with them a euphoria. Everything here seems joyous and fluid, bursting with new life. The outdoor cafés in the Prater are filled with music of all kinds, lovers seem to be strolling by everywhere, and even the written assignments at the university seem filled with insight and lightness.

Alma invited me to join her in the director's box at the opera, and Herr Mahler, who was in exquisite form directing Parsifal, *joined us afterward in the continuance of what was an absolutely electric evening. Of course, whenever Herr M. travels, the most luminary crowd follows. Alma accuses me of being starstruck, and I suppose I am. Our lives, hers and mine, have taken such different paths since our childhood together and she tells me that it is not too late, that a life of celebrity and social stardom lies ahead of me should I pursue it, and I smile and tell her how gracious she is, but that I would rather pursue the quiet life of a scholar. Alma says I am being "a silly boy," and that she is going to have to see to my initiation. Fortunately, her entreaties go no further than those teasing moments, and as soon as we are no longer together she forgets her proposals.*

In the meantime, I am indeed content with my life at the university and in the Café Central. I have received and read with interest the book you sent concerning life in Vienna, the music, and in the cafés, and I have shared it with my friends. We all agree that the author, Mr. Trumpp, has captured beautifully the atmosphere of our city and has added some remarkable perspective and insight. The account paints our progressive Herr Mahler in a very attractive light, one many in this city would benefit from considering, as I fear he is now a prophet without honor in his own territory. I have yet to share the book with Alma.

I appreciate greatly your descriptions of rich life in Boston, and as always I wish that I could come visit you there. Perhaps Herr Mahler will take an appointment someday with your symphony orchestra, and

*Alma will entice me to come join them. That offer would not take much
enticement.*

As always,

*Yours,
Arnauld*

In Boston, Eleanor knew what had to be done, the double life she was
destined to pursue. On the one hand, she busied herself establishing the
beginnings of a life of social prominence, not just marrying the very respectable Frank Burden but also joining activities in cultural life and the
arts expected of her class. All of that working to preserve what Frank
called "the valued status quo," the sacred social practice in that city of, as
he said, "keeping the world exactly as we inherited it for the next generation." At the same time she was mindful of the secret world she was meant
to pursue, the world of change.

Eleanor was expected to make extraordinary investments during her
lifetime. She knew that from the beginning. And all those investments
were laid out for her, all prescribed on one single page of the journal she
had brought from Vienna, a description from the end of her life of all she
had accomplished, would accomplish, the details written out with care on
that one page. She knew what needed to be done the moment she first
read the journal and when she brought it back with her. That was the
uniqueness of her destiny, what was to be the long span of her adult life.
That was the blessing and the curse. She was going to be living out her life
and taking actions based on the details recorded in 1897 from knowledge
of her life from now until its end. The whole long journal was filled with
prescribed actions, many of them in just one simple handwritten line.
Even if she were inclined to share her Vienna knowledge with someone,
which she was not, she knew that no one could understand her position,
and she would be labeled gullible or deluded, just as Dr. Freud had labeled
her years earlier. But of course Eleanor knew that the journal, unbelievable as it might appear, was accurate—it simply was the truth and her
destiny, and that's all there was to it.

Some of the changes were within her control, some, especially general world events, well outside of her doing. But the one page in par-

ticular concerned itself exclusively with the investments she would make, all spectacular ones, it seemed. And it all began with the simple mention of investment in Cincinnati Soap and Candle, a firm she had never heard of but had recently uncovered in, of course, Cincinnati. She assumed that she was intended to invest all of her funds there. And that was that.

Again, alone and uncertain of the wisdom of what she was doing, and still without a business helper and uncertain what role her future husband was to play in her business ventures, she consulted Frank Burden. In financial matters at least, Frank was nothing if not thorough.

"A hypothetical investment," she had told him by way of an introduction.

"I am glad it is only hypothetical," Frank said, and then told with skepticism what he could find about the company and its history, none of it with much enthusiasm, and none with any knowledge of what she had planned. "It is out west," he said dismissively, as if for a Bostonian that explained all that one needed to know. "A very shaky investment."

Afterward, without telling anyone, she planned a trip by train alone to Cincinnati to meet with the president of the company, Homer Smith, with her bank draft for five thousand dollars in hand.

Eleanor found herself on the long train ride to southern Ohio, content to have this time to herself, solitude having become in no way troubling to her since her time in college. She had been accustomed to riding the train while at Smith College in Northampton, Massachusetts. "Smith women are very familiar with trains," her roommate from Philadelphia had observed. "We are all escaping from the strictures of some other world." Her roommate was escaping Main Line Philadelphia. Eleanor believed she fit into that truism, having felt a blessed release every time she traveled "out west," as her Winsor School classmates called it, at the beginning of each school year, always by train. "Boston women feel comfortable traveling to Europe," her grandmother Putnam had observed many times, "but we have never been west of Worcester." Northampton, Massachusetts, the home of Smith College, was west of Worcester and so was New York City, but even Eleanor, as venturesome as she was, in good Bostonian fashion had never traveled west of New York. So now she felt she was headed off to the territory that only a century previous had been the western extremity of the nation. She knew from her experience in

Vienna and from the journal that California with all its boundless freedom figured significantly in her life, but she knew she was not going to
travel there. So Cincinnati was as far out as she was going to go, and she
had to admit a certain anxiousness as she passed the long hours alone on
the train hurtling westward.

She had never minded traveling alone, and she paid no heed to people
who turned up noses realizing that she was. And of course back home she
told no one and no one seemed to notice; she was after all still single and
without immediate family.

On her long train rides she enjoyed being "alone with her thoughts," as
William James called it, and of course she enjoyed reading, often the long
involved European novels of Zola or Flaubert or those of Henry James,
whom she adored, and always when she was not reading her mind wandered. It was on those long train rides, she told her famous godfather, that
she thought her most profound thoughts and, as her roommate from Philadelphia also observed, she found herself "contemplating her place in the
universe outside Boston." Her roommate, a thoroughly practical and com-
monsense woman, was always amused by hearing what Eleanor had been
thinking on her train rides to and from her provincial home. And so on
this long train ride to the western extremity of her universe, Eleanor found
herself thinking about her life over the past two years and wondering how
it all was going to fit together. She was on a mission she did not fully understand, determined to return home having converted the monies gained
from her rather miraculous sale of a piece of jewelry into part ownership of
a company she knew nothing about. She was doing it all because she knew
she had to, and she admitted that the raw feeling in her stomach came
from far more than just her heading out into unfamiliar territory. It came
from her fear that she did not know what she was doing and that she might
fail. She might not end up with what she needed, and then what?

Eleanor, who always prided herself on being a woman of independent
spirit, now found herself acting on instructions she did not understand
written in a journal whose literal authenticity she chose to believe in. She
found herself asking the question she would ask herself many times over
the succeeding years: Was she doing all this as a matter of free will or in
order to fulfill some predetermined destiny? Was this a noble mission or
simply a fool's errand, a blind adherence to some fantastic writings of a
madman and the deluded dream of meeting again the love of her life?

She planned to stay the night at a hotel in Pittsburgh, then catch an early train and be in Cincinnati by early afternoon. From the train station in Cincinnati she learned that a considerable tram ride and a short run by cab would deliver her to the door of Cincinnati Soap and Candle, where the owner would be waiting for her, she hoped, because of a cable she had sent announcing very naïvely her intention of having a meeting and providing financing for his company, Frank's words "all businesses want investors" echoing in her head.

The company office was in the original and formidable pre–Civil War brick factory building, and inside a compound with a large wrought iron gate and the company's initials welded in, in a style familiar from the company's printed materials.

She tried her best to appear totally self-possessed as she approached the imposing edifice and walked through the heavy oak door. She announced herself at the large front desk, and a studious-looking woman, tall and slender and, Eleanor could see from the absence of a wedding band, a spinster, with her gray hair pulled up in a bun, greeted her formally. "My brother is expecting you, Miss Putnam," she said, making it clear that Cincinnati Soap and Candle prided itself on being a family company. "He says you have come at a good time."

Homer Smith, an older man in his late sixties, reminded her, in his robustness and hardy vigor, of Teddy Roosevelt. He had headed the family company since his early adulthood, she knew, and had a reputation as something of a hothead, but a fierce competitor and a demon for details and numbers. "Cincinnati Soap and Candle Company has been successful," he said, "because my family has a long-standing cultivation of the hardworking factory families. They think of us as a vital part of their lives. That is a position and a prestige we are not willing to give up." There was a fierce defiance in his eyes, as if he was looking into the face of a competitor.

"I am here only to invest," Eleanor said quickly. "My fund knows of this area's history and your company's fine place in it, and would like to help."

Early in the century, with the advent of railroads in the Midwest, Cincinnati had been a center for hog slaughter, and the consequent abundance of tallow as a by-product made it a center for the production of candles, and soap as well. In Homer Smith's grandfather's day, the company was formed, first distinguished by candle manufacture and then by soap. By something of an accident, employees began experimenting with the addition of air to the soap bars, which were already large and pure white, making them—quite inadvertently—buoyant. "The floating bars did not sink into the dirty water of coal miners' baths," Homer Smith explained, "and hence a tradition grew and Workman's Soap became a family necessity." The soap appeared in time for the American Civil War, which called for a great volume of both soap and candles, and the company's reputation spread, leading to wide popularity among soldiers, coal miners, and factory workers.

Homer Smith seemed to accept Eleanor's conciliatory offering. "Workman's Soap is not scented or fancy. It is simply inexpensive and pure. It is just what the people know and respect. It has been a solid and dependable product. And now the giant octopus Procter and Gamble wishes to take us over. And you know what?" He slammed down his palm on the rolltop desk. "They're not going to do it. Thousands of small companies, good companies, are being swallowed up by giants all over the country. It is all part of Mr. J. P. Morgan's vision. Big and giant is efficient and good, he says. Well, those big eastern trusts are not efficient and not good for the average American citizen, and I personally am not going to allow it. I'll sell to the Colgate people before I let the giants run us over." There was a fierceness in his eyes beyond what Eleanor thought reasonable and a ruddiness to his complexion that suggested he might explode.

"Then I am here to help."

"Help?" he asked dismissively. "What degree of help can you offer?" He did not refer to her being a woman alone, but Eleanor had no trouble hearing that implication in his voice.

"I have five thousand dollars," she said, doing her best to hide how much she felt out beyond her depth.

He stared at her for a long uncomfortable moment, obviously disappointed. "Pooh," he said. "In your telegram you mentioned the word 'significant.' I misinterpreted."

"You expected more," Eleanor said.

"Yes, we need a lot more, and we need it right now," he said. "I assumed that one presumptuous enough to send such a telegram would know that." He seemed ready to end the conversation as it was for Eleanor just beginning, and without hesitation, as if it was the most natural thing in the world, she took a deep breath and spoke.

"As I told you before, I wish to invest. All companies need investment."

Her assertiveness, she could see, caught the irascible owner off guard, and he eyed her for a long moment. "I appreciate your interest, dear lady, I really do, but there is nothing you can offer this company." He stood to usher her to the door. Immediately she felt regret at not having done more research on this difficult man. Surely there would have been a way to avoid this dismissive impasse.

"Wait," she said suddenly, aware that her moment was slipping away. "What *can* I offer you?"

"Nothing," Homer Smith snapped abruptly. "There is nothing you can offer me." He continued ushering her out, signaling with every ounce of energy in his fierce eyes and ruddy face that as far as he was concerned the meeting was over.

Mr. Smith's spinster sister was conciliatory as she ushered her to the door. "Now you have met my brother," she said. "He either loves you or hates you. I hope his reaction was not too fierce. He finds our company in a predicament and he was perhaps hoping for a rescuer."

"Which he did not find in me."

"Please do not take it personally. I doubt that anyone could help him right now." She smiled benignly as she opened the door. "We all try."

And soon riding the tram back to the train station, alone in an unfamiliar city, very much out of sorts, she was certain that she had lost the contact and the investment she knew from the journal she was required to make. She had come to a dead end, she thought, most definitely, a dead end and a disaster. What a weakling she had been. During the whole first encounter with Homer Smith, an intense one, she had to admit, she had allowed herself to be intimidated, dominated entirely by his pugnacious personality. As swept up as she was by the urgency of the need to buy Cincinnati Soap and Candle stock and the fear of being overrun by this strong, obviously quick-tempered man, she had been barely able to hold herself steady, struggling to see in this man a peculiar but worthy adversary rather than a bully to be avoided.

Throughout his emotional rampage and his insistence in telling her about the outrage of the Procter and Gamble takeover, she found herself— she knew now in retrospect—seeing through to the core of his behavior and seeing how much he was behaving according to a type, one she knew not so much from personal experience as from the literature she had read and the stories she had been told. This man's behavior did not seem to her in his own or his company's best interest.

Homer Smith was a person, she wrote to her friend Jung later, a fiery hotheaded rooster of a man, who was behaving now not as the mature wise head of a family and a family company, but as a wounded combatant, furious at an overpowering tyrant and trapped without adult perspective in primitive ill-formed reaction. "He seemed so stuck within his habitual approach," she wrote, "that he could not see what he was doing. And as much as he kept calling himself a 'sensitive man,' his actions in this time of personal crisis could not have been further from human sensitivity." It was up to her how to not allow this rejection to happen. It was up to her now, although she had no idea at this moment how to pull off such a feat, to become the wise advisor.

Often by surprise, in times of trouble she found coming to her aid a steady perceptive self, her Athena self, "strength when you need it," it had been called, her animus self, as Jung would describe it later. So often in the past, especially in the heat of battle, she could feel herself being taken over by that wise and understanding personage, her late mother watching over her, she liked to think. Whatever it was, she found it with her now, and so it was now as she reconstructed in her mind the rashness of Homer Smith's reaction to what he saw as the takeover by Procter and Gamble, and she decided to act. *It is the man's personality,* she said to herself. *He cannot save himself. It is up to me to save him.* It was at that moment at the doors of the Cincinnati train station that she stopped, turned around, and found a cab. "Take me to the largest bank in your city," she said.

After a short wait in the bank's reception area, she was led to the desk of a bank official, a tidy and punctilious young man, who greeted her with a warm handshake and asked her to sit down. "I am Mr. Cabot," he said.

"I am new to this," she said, suddenly cautious of admitting her naïveté. "I wish to invest, but I have been rebuffed."

"You cannot then," he said. "It seems simple."

"But I must," she said, barely able to contain her exasperation. "How do I turn this five thousand dollars into the fifty that I need?"

The banker looked at her for a long moment's evaluation. "You mean besides alchemy," he said with a condescending smile.

"I am not an alchemist, Mr. Cabot," she said.

Taking in perhaps her erect posture and the fierceness in her eyes, reconsidering his frivolous comment, he became serious. "No, I see that you are not." He paused. "So, in that case you offer up collateral and then borrow the amount you need."

"What collateral?" she said, as if the new term was a totally familiar one.

"Do you own a home?" he said, and she nodded. "Here in the city?" he asked.

"No, in Boston."

"All the better," he said. "You simply go to our sister bank in Boston and secure the loan based on the value of the property, and take this risk."

"And the risk?" Her look of consternation at that moment betrayed her ignorance, but he did not pause again.

"Well, I don't know if there is much of that actually. Loans on property are very common—"

She cut him off. "But what are the risks?" she asked, looking him square in the eye. At first, uncertain about this customer, the young man didn't know what to say. "I am not unintelligent, Mr. Cabot. I am just new to this," she said. "I would appreciate candor."

"Well, in that case, in candor," he began, "if you cannot repay the loan, you lose the property."

"Thank you," she said. "And now, please instruct me on exactly how to proceed."

After Mr. Cabot had finished a rather lengthy, and she assumed complete, set of instructions in the most fundamental principles of investment, she thanked him and set about returning to Mr. Homer Smith.

He barely agreed to see her again and greeted her curtly. "What is it now, Miss Putnam? I thought we understood each other."

"We did understand each other," she said flatly, "and very well. I am sorry to be so persistent, but I really do wish to invest," she said. "You need more than I offered."

"Quite a bit more." He shook his head with impatience. "I made that perfectly clear," he said.

Well prepared for his dismissive tone, she focused on the meaning of his words. "And if I could come up with a larger sum, we would have an agreement?"

Homer Smith was serious now, taking measure of exactly what this obviously green young woman from Boston could possibly offer. "With all due respect, Miss Putnam, I do not see how you and your small fund could help. We need ten times your offer. At least."

This time she did not flinch. "And if I could raise that ten-times amount, we could have an agreement?" She stared at him.

Homer Smith rolled his eyes. "We could have an agreement, yes. But I honestly do not see—"

She cut him off. "That would be fifty thousand dollars," she said precisely. "I can raise that amount," she added with a burst, summoning up every bit of bravado she could muster. "But I will need a few days."

The impulsive Mr. Smith's impatience was not diminished. "We have a week," he said. "I can give you the better part of that."

"I will return within a week," she said. "With the money you need."

So, with something like raw fear in her stomach, wondering what she had allowed herself to get into, Eleanor returned to Boston and ventured into territory she knew nothing of. She knew she could not avoid consulting again with her fiancé, Frank Burden, and his counsel on this matter of finance would be useful. Then and later in their lives he was always absolutely certain about financial matters, a true authority, she heard often from men in his profession. And Frank, always a literalist, rarely looked beneath the surface of things or examined too closely underlying causes, so that at this moment and for the rest of their lives together he never seemed to notice that Eleanor had a financial life of her own. Somehow, she could always seek his advice without his becoming suspicious that there might be something going on. She also surmised that her taking him into her confidence and allowing him to hold forth would bring them closer. And it most definitely did.

"There is great risk borrowing against one's home," Frank said this time, upon hearing his fiancée's concerns. "It would be an extremely ill-advised strategy, even if one could find a lender."

"But what if one needed funds and with maximum haste?" she said. "I am interested hypothetically, of course."

"Well, *hypothetically*, of course, under dire circumstances one could always find a lender and an interest rate, most likely from a Jewish lender, and one less than principled," Frank said. "It is not an indebtedness anyone would wish to incur."

"Hypothetically"—Eleanor pressed on with a show of objective confidence well beyond what she was feeling—"if one wished to proceed with such an emergency investment."

"Well then, again hypothetically, if this soap and candle company of yours should fail or diminish drastically in value," he said sternly, "one would lose the family home or whatever of value had been offered as collateral. Believe me," Frank added, "it is a position you definitely do not wish to be in, with a Jewish banker or any lender. You must not consider this."

"Oh, don't worry, Frank. It is only a whimsical speculation, a self-education, not something to act upon."

So Eleanor went about her business immediately, aware of Frank's admonitions and all the while knowing now more than ever how much she needed an associate who knew the ropes of finance. She did in fact do the research and did find a lender, a kindly old banker on Boylston Street named Lowenstein, and after much careful explanation from the banker she did indeed sign a quick one-year note against the value of her family holdings and 6 Acorn Street, then took the long train back to Cincinnati, with its compulsory stopover in Pittsburgh.

"You could not have come at a better time," Homer Smith said, looking more red-faced than before, showing more relief than amazement that this naïve-seeming young woman had pulled off such a feat of finance. "The giants are closing in."

"Then my fund's investment is timely."

"Indeed," Homer Smith said.

So he took the money and gave her an envelope that he had known through telegrams to prepare ahead of time. "I am being generous with the price," he said. Eleanor opened the offering and did all she could to remain calm as she found herself staring at six thousand shares of Cincinnati Soap and Candle Company, made out in her name.

"I am proud to be an owner," she said, grateful that her hands were not shaking, as if for her looking at such a piece of paper was the most natural thing in the world, more relieved than Homer Smith or anyone could know that she had lived up to her obligations.

"Glad to have you on board," Homer Smith said, more glad for the quick appearance of cash, she deduced, than for the newly minted association with a mysterious young woman from Boston.

TWO WORKS OF SIGNIFICANCE

t was shortly after her return from Cincinnati with the partial ownership of Cincinnati Soap and Candle Company in hand that she shared with William James *City of Music*. Even though reconnecting with him upon her 1898 return was greatly anticipated, she knew there were parts of her new life she would not share with him, at least not then. Those were the parts related to the journal and its mandates.

William James had always been amused by what he called her "spunk" and had appeared around her in the early years, as an interested if somewhat detached protector, always keeping a respectful distance. But since her return from Vienna the bond had somehow deepened and grown, as if he now accepted her more as an adult and colleague, and the new profundity of her situation drew her to the spiritual nature of this extraordinary man. In those meetings with him in Cambridge and telling him of the rich life in Vienna and her encounters with Mahler and Freud and the rest she felt his respect for her. She just needed to be mindful of not telling too much.

Presenting him with a copy of *City of Music* was as close to telling the whole story as she could come. "This book is very important to me," she said, without explaining further.

He read the slim volume with care and commented affectionately, not because he suspected that she had had anything to do with the book's authorship and the extraordinary tale behind it, but because she was sharing with him now adult-to-adult something that obviously meant a great deal to her. "Beautifully written," he said to her. "The observations of this Jonathan Trumpp make one wish to travel to Vienna immediately and to encounter the music of Herr Mahler."

"You would love Vienna and the whole scene, Mahler and all," she said.

"And the author?" he said. "I had not heard of him."

"His is a pseudonym, I believe," she said, offering nothing more.

"Well, his gifts are significant. The book is one of elegance and depth, and it makes one appreciative of the profound experience you had there. I am very glad that you gave it to me, and, by the way, I hope to read more work of this impressive Mr. Trumpp."

That was a theme echoed by the book's publisher, the renowned Mr. Adolph Ochs of the *New York Times*, who met with Eleanor in New York City in the year following publication. "You must be pleased," Ochs said. "People are scrambling to find out the identity of this mysterious Jonathan Trumpp. The book is selling as fast as we can print it, and word from Vienna is that New Yorkers are now traveling there, with the express purpose of listening to waltz music and to visit the Café Central, always with the little book in hand."

"I am pleased," she said with a satisfied smile.

"And your book, single-handedly, has made Gustav Mahler a phenomenon here. There is a clamoring to get him to come to New York."

"I am pleased," she repeated. "I feel greatly honored, actually."

"My friend Mr. Charles Scribner, the book publisher, is eager for us to reveal the identity of the author."

Eleanor gave him a worried look. "You wouldn't tell, would you?"

"Oh, no. Don't be concerned," he assured her. "No one keeps a secret identity secret better than the *Times* of New York. Scribner's would love to take over the publishing of this book and give it a national exposure, with more to follow. Mr. Scribner is convinced that Mr. Trumpp would have quite a following."

"I have told Mr. Moss that Mr. Trumpp has written his last; I thought I made that clear," Eleanor said emphatically. There was no way she could explain the extraordinary circumstances surrounding the writing of this single volume, but her clarity on the matter she could express. "I am certain," she said.

"We all know that here, but still there is demand. The author could have a comfortable life just publishing further books."

"That may be," she said, acknowledging the publisher's point. "And I am flattered, but my opinion is not going to change." She became serious. "*City of Music* was written under special circumstances that the author could not replicate and would never wish to have replicated." She gave a little shiver as if recalling some intense unpleasantness.

"It is a shame," said the publisher. "Mr. Trumpp's is a work of great insight, not to mention popular appeal. But I understand."

"I am grateful for that," she said.

The publisher interrupted. "But I am curious," he said. "How does Mr. Trumpp see it all turning out?"

"How do you mean?"

"What lies in that great city's future?"

"Oh, yes, that," she said. "It is, of course, difficult to predict, but perhaps he would observe that the empire will have trouble sustaining itself."

"With all its political factions?" Mr. Ochs said. "The Czechs wishing to be Czech, the Hungarians wanting to be Hungarian, and so forth. And all without a crown prince to signal the bright future, after that awful Mayerling business."

Eleanor suppressed a frown. "Exactly," she said. "To lose such a prince is to lose the future."

"And what of the politically motivated anti-Semitism?" Her book did not dwell on the phenomenon, but it had described in detail the strategy of the mayor of Vienna, Karl Lueger, using resentment of Jewish control to rally the working classes.

At first Eleanor looked away, not wishing to venture into the territory of future predicting—knowing what she did of the future, the part of her challenge she had assiduously avoided and would continue to avoid. But then she realized she was in the presence of a representative of a major world newspaper, an ultimate realist.

"Horrific" was the single and simple word she chose.

❧

Eleanor could not tell Dr. James until later about the encounter with Mr. Ochs over *City of Music,* since he did not know at that time the identity of the book's author, but she could tell him about her close association with Sigmund Freud, at least a part of it. In 1900, when three copies of the newly published *Interpretation of Dreams* by Sigmund Freud, in the original German, arrived in a package from Ernst Kleist, a friend from her time in Vienna, she made certain that Dr. James received one of them. "Another book to read," he said, repeating his gratitude for her attention.

"I believe you need to know about Dr. Freud."

"I was teasing," he said. "We all know of Dr. Freud, and I have been eagerly awaiting this publication." William James had met Dr. Freud in Europe some years before and had been impressed by his thinking. "You are good to have obtained a copy for me with such speed."

"You are meant to read it," she said decisively. "It is the vital next step."

"You are impressed by Sigmund Freud, aren't you?"

"I am," she said with conviction. "I think his message is one the modern world needs to hear right now."

"Well," the famous professor said, pleased to hear such self-assurance from his young protégé, "I shall put it on the top of my stack. I am eager for the vital next step."

In the following year, 1901, convinced of the book's worth and determined to do all she could to spread its important message—"my mission," she was to call it years later—she arranged for twenty or so copies of the then-obscure work to be sent out, anonymously, to the most prominent German-speaking scholars she could find. "It was in my interests to have Sigmund Freud discovered by American scholars," she also said later.

At the same time she set about having Freud's largely unknown work translated into English. She searched around Harvard until she came upon a German-born graduate student in history who seemed amenable to the task, and in need of the money, and he agreed to work quickly on the project.

"This must be carried out in the greatest secrecy," she said.

"I am German," the young man said. "I have no trouble with secrecy." Later she went to his small office and collected a thick typed manuscript.

"This is beautiful," she said to the young graduate student.

"It is quite a work," he said. "This Dr. Freud is a very profound thinker."

She lifted this stack of papers. "And now, thanks to you, we have at least one copy of his words in English."

"What are you going to do with it?" the young man said.

"It is intended for just one purpose," Eleanor said, "to spread the discoveries of this remarkable man."

6

MR. HONEYCUTT

T he fact that she met Will Honeycutt because of discussions with William James about dreams was, she found later, one of the great ironies of this story. During her many visits with her godfather and confidant after her return from Vienna, she had mentioned a number of times her belief that one could actually engage productively in dialogue with characters from one's own dreams. It was not a practice she had actually employed herself but one dear to the soul mate she met in Vienna and one referred to numerous times in the journal. She remembered Dr. James finding in the idea more fascination, she had to admit, than she found in it herself. "It seems a straight path to the unconscious mind," he had said.

One day, as they were talking, the subject came up again, it seemed to her, quite spontaneously. "Remember your notion of conversations with dreams?" Dr. James said. "You told me of this a few months ago, and it made quite an impression. Now I have something I wish you to read," he said to her, holding up a bound volume of what looked like handwritten pages. "This is a Harvard senior thesis from last year, sent over to me from the physics department. I would not expect you to read the whole thing, but the main idea is fascinating, and apropos of our previous discussions. A former student of mine, a quite eccentric fellow, claiming that he got the idea solely from my lectures, has written a dialogue about physics with a character in his dreams." James handed her the volume, and when she opened it and saw for the first time the name of the Harvard student who had written it, she found herself shaken. There before her was the name

T. Williams Honeycutt, the very name mentioned in the journal as some-one who was to play a major role in her future; "the linchpin," he would be called later.

It was shortly before the whole Cincinnati adventure began, and she was just putting together her approach to the assigned tasks, having just begun the rudiments of a search for someone of that prescribed name: T. Williams Honeycutt. A man with such a name was supposed to become the longtime director of the monetary fund she was to create, she knew, and someone in all likelihood it was her responsibility to find and recruit.

For all she knew this T. Williams Honeycutt might have been in Chi-cago or Omaha or anywhere. As with the rest of her assignments, she had not approached this important part lightly, but she had had little idea how to proceed. Initially, she had not thought to ask William James if he knew of anyone of such a name, and now, totally at random, here he was hand-ing her a senior thesis with that very name inscribed.

"Do you know this T. Williams Honeycutt?" she asked, pointing to the first page of the document.

"Oh, yes," Dr. James said. "I know Honeycutt, Ted as he is called. Sort of a strange fellow, rather bereft of social grace, but, like that document you hold in your hand, his is quite a story."

"And you know how I can find him?"

"Oh, of course. He has a small office not far from here, in the physics department." And he reached over to his own desk and wrote on a small slip of paper the office address at Harvard.

Before the visit to that office in the physics department, also through William James, she found a number of Harvard faculty to interview with regard to the young graduate student's remarkable thesis, his character and performance. Each of his former teachers was cautious in describing the young man and his intelligence, but each referred to him with some-thing like a wince and Dr. James's "quite a story."

Before Eleanor actually contacted this Mr. Honeycutt, William James told her with a smile, "When he was an undergraduate, he took two of my classes. He was immediately memorable for the look of rapt attention he brought to each lecture, and his intense questioning after it. A razor-sharp mind, but without much social moderation to accompany it, quite disarm-ing actually, and he certainly stood out, this Mr. Honeycutt. He is now a graduate student in the physics department. Quite a famous one, or infamous, you might say. That thesis you have seen stirred up quite a commotion. I have found it intriguing, and most imaginative."

The thesis had indeed drawn a great deal of attention within the department. It had been, everyone agreed, a stroke of originality the likes of which few in the department had ever seen. Ted Honeycutt had written an expansive dialogue between himself, called Theodore, and the fourth-century B.C. Greek sage Democritus, the discoverer of the atom. In this lengthy discourse this Honeycutt had summarized—quite brilliantly, it was admitted—the known and theorized world of the atom, including Newton and the newest discoveries, and allowed his Democritus to speculate upon all of it, and the future. The results, called "outrageous and without foundation" by one senior department member, had been heralded as "stunningly bold and prescient" by another.

Years later, it would be noted that Honeycutt's Democritan speculations were a near-pitch-perfect description of what would become known as quantum physics, the theory of connectedness. At first, it was feared that he had plagiarized from some unknown source, and when asked how he, a humble undergraduate, had come up with the bold imaginings, the young physics student said, "I simply allowed a visitation from a historical character and let him do the talking. The method came out of my studies with William James," he offered as some sort of validation. Apparently, it was said, Dr. James had mentioned once or twice in a lecture that dreams were part of the reality of the unconscious mind, and we could carry on revelatory conversation with characters from those dreams in our waking life. "So that's what I did," Honeycutt said. "Democritus came to me in a dream, and I started the next morning writing down my conversations with him. I told him about modern physics, and he took it from there. And it worked, I guess."

When William James was at first shown the thesis, he said he did not remember making the observation in a lecture, but he considered Honeycutt's a fitting application of the idea, if he had said it, "a brilliant piece of parapsychology." Some agreed with Dr. James that the thesis was brilliant, and some thought it the work of a deranged mind. "The young man hears voices," one professor said, and then added dismissively, "We have a Joan of Arc on our hands."

"And what was it that so distinguished the thesis?" Eleanor asked.

"It was a brilliant idea," William James said, "conversations with a character who had come to him in a dream. He got the idea from me. I got the idea from you when you were fresh back from Vienna. You got it from a wise man of your acquaintance there."

"I do remember telling you that," she said. "The idea had made quite an impression on me, and was helpful at the time."

"Well, I don't remember passing it along in a lecture to Harvard students," he said. "Still, Honeycutt here wrote a rather astounding dialogue, and it made a powerful impression. The department asked him to defend himself, which is an uncommon practice for an undergraduate thesis."

"And he did well, I assume."

"It was quite a show," William James said. "Mr. Honeycutt is not exactly normal; he is overly brusque, but brilliant, something of a savant, I am told. He is painfully inept at human interaction."

"What is he like?"

"Well, he is definitely an original specimen. One of the skeptics asked young Honeycutt why he chose this man Democritus, and he answered imperiously, 'I did not choose him, sir. Democritus chose me.'

"When another asked if he often heard voices, the young man answered in the affirmative, which did not help his case. The department has taken him on as a graduate student, some with great reluctance, and they are asking him to give proof to the many radical assertions made out of his extraordinary imaginings. The department is still split, I hear, as to the state of the young man's mind, and whether this defense can be made. But they all are in agreement on one aspect: His is an exceptional mind."

"And you know of no other of the same name?" she asked abruptly, realizing the complexity she was about to step into here by pursuing this young man.

"T. Williams Honeycutt?" William James said, and Eleanor nodded. The great man thought for a long moment. "No," he said, with a kind of certainty. "Not in my ken."

And all other research went nowhere. This controversial young graduate student about her age, in the department of physics, was her only possibility, it turned out, at least in the Boston area. And so, with no other options in front of her, and reasoning that T. Williams Honeycutt was an unusual and perhaps unique name, she made an appointment, which surprised the young man no doubt, since Ted Honeycutt, by his own admission, was not the type who made many outside appointments, certainly not with attractive young women.

They met on the Harvard campus, in the ancient hall that housed the physics department, in a small office cluttered with books and laboratory paraphernalia. As Eleanor engaged him in conversation, she could not help recalling some of the pejorative comments she had heard about him in her researches.

"He talks to himself," a fellow graduate student assigned as his laboratory partner is reported to have complained to his advisor.

"Listen well," the advisor is said to have quipped. "You might learn something."

Even before his famous senior thesis, just as one faculty member was tearing his hair in exasperation another was reporting a conversation with him that showed great vision and clarity. In one famous faculty discussion, one teacher is reported to have said, "Honeycutt is the kind of mind that every university would like to have within its walls."

"There is another institution down the road," a colleague responded, "the state hospital, that specializes in having his kind within its walls."

Whatever talents or future this young graduate student possessed were not immediately apparent to her as she sat with him in his cluttered little room. In fact, her immediate reaction was to wonder how someone this disorganized had earned his strong reputation. Later, she admitted to being suspicious, discouraged even, but she was looking for a T. Williams Honeycutt. What other choice was there?

"Thank you for seeing me," she said after taking his hand. "I know this must be peculiar for you."

"I don't often have visitors in here," he said, gesturing to the clutter in his office and offering a gentle smile that Eleanor, much to her surprise, found reassuring. He was of medium height, lean of build, and only slightly ill at ease having a visitor intrude into the confined space of his office. "I'm not the sort that people come to visit." Almost as an afterthought, he cleared off a chair and offered it. "And just why are you here?" There was a kind of gracelessness to his question.

"I will be direct," Eleanor said. "I have come on a mission, Mr. Honeycutt. I have heard of your brilliance."

"Heavens, no," he said. "Just an eternal predoctorate student, trying to get all of this organized"—again, he gestured around the room with his hand—"into something my betters will accept as a dissertation. The university is waiting for me to produce something of value. I wrote a controversial paper in my senior year that got everyone's attention. Now they want me to prove it."

"I have heard," Eleanor said.

"I guess I stumbled onto some ideas no one else had thought of."

"A dialogue with Democritus, was it not?"

He looked startled for a moment. "You have heard."

"I have," she said. "You caused quite a stir. And I have heard of your method: a dialogue with a character in your dreams. Some call it brilliant."

Honeycutt laughed. "And some called it deranged. *Schizophrenic*, I believe they say, one who hears voices."

"But everyone agrees what came out in this dialogue was brilliant."

"Even if it came from derangement?" He paused, looking suddenly very nervous and distracted. "It is about the atom, you know. Those who believe my dialogue to be of value wish for me to read and research everything known so far and think perhaps that I have said—without knowing it—something new and revolutionary. They wish me to *grow into it*, I believe those who believe say."

"And those who do not believe?"

"They wish to have me committed."

"And what do you say?"

"Somewhere in between, I guess. Democritus really did appear in my dreams, and he spoke for himself within the dream. That is not so demented, is it? To have someone speak in a dream?"

"No," she said. "I would say it is quite normal."

"I was just the scribe. I did not try to explain anything on my own. I just wrote it down. I guess that is the disturbing part for some."

"Disturbing for you?" she asked.

Ted Honeycutt looked away. "Oh, no, I have been living within my head for a long time. I am like the ancient alchemists, my professors say, always looking for the *prima materia*, but it comes with a problem."

"And that is?"

"I seek this *prima materia*, they say, at the expense of my relations with people."

"William James thinks you brilliant."

Suddenly, the young man's mood changed. "You don't know that," he snapped. "It is rumored, but you don't know that."

The words took her aback for an instant. "I do know it," she said, not backing off. "In fact, I know it quite well."

"How could you know such a thing?" There was what seemed like defiance now in his eyes.

"Dr. James told me."

Honeycutt scrutinized her seriously for a moment, then softened. "You know Dr. James?"

"He is my godfather," she said. "He was a great friend of my deceased mother. We confer with some regularity and with some intimacy. In the flesh," she added, trying unsuccessfully for a note of levity. "He had you in class, I believe. I asked him about you, and he has mentioned a very high regard."

Ted Honeycutt looked her over for a long moment, still skeptical. "You know that?" he said. "William James really told you that?"

"I know that. He really told me that. He read your thesis when a friend in the physics department gave it to him, and he gave it to me to read. He told me when I asked that he was very impressed."

"Well, that is something," Honeycutt said, still without humor. Then he stopped and looked suspicious for a long moment. "Why were you asking about me?"

"I told you that I am on a mission. I am looking for someone to come work with me."

"Doing what?" he asked abruptly. "What could someone like me possibly do for someone like you?"

"Quite a bit, actually."

"You are interested in working with atoms?"

"No, it is nothing to do with atoms. It is a business project. Investments, to be precise, stocks and bonds."

The young physics student looked confused. Then he laughed dismissively. "You did not do your homework very carefully, madam. I am a scientist," he said, "I'm not a businessman."

"Actually, I did my homework, and quite thoroughly," she said quickly, wishing not to lose ground or to be put off by his gracelessness, about which she had been warned. "Scientific or not is no concern of mine. I am looking for someone bright and eager—brilliant even—to be my partner in a business venture, and from what I can gather, you are a perfect candidate." She did not let on that it was his name alone that was the source of her present conviction.

"I am difficult," he said, still without an ounce of humor.

"All the better," she said. She was not being completely candid, certainly not where her own misgivings were involved. What she really wished to say was that she knew the name and that was all, and he was the only match she could find. In a way, she was desperate. "I am looking for someone smart, efficient, and discreet," Eleanor said, "and someone named T. Williams Honeycutt. And from what I have been able to discover, you are all of those."

The eccentric physics student looked uncomfortable and eyed his guest suspiciously. "You have investigated me," he said.

"I have indeed. This is an important maneuver on my part. I need to make a series of investments, over the next few years. I am confident that I will know at the time exactly what those investments will be, and I know what returns they will bring. I need an assistant to carry them out."

"And you think that I am that person?"

"I do. In fact, I am quite convinced. And I am willing to offer a year's salary in the form of shares in a stock purchase I have just made. As they increase in value and as you pursue a parallel course to the one I will be tracking, you will become a very wealthy man."

"Has it occurred to you that you have made a mistake in identity?"

"I am well past that uncertainty," she said. "You are T. Williams Honeycutt, are you not?"

"Of course I am," he said with something close to contempt.

"And are you aware of another such T. Williams Honeycutt?" She asked the question on the reasonable assumption that he, having had the name all his life, would know more about the possibility of duplication than anyone else.

"That is a strange question," he said with a pause that she should have noticed with concern. "I am the only one I know. Who else would have such a mouthful of a name?"

"Well, then you are the one I am looking for." There was a finality to her statement that brought the young physics student to silence, which he held for a long moment.

"Well, I am very much afraid that I cannot help you."

"Are you certain of that, absolutely certain?"

"Absolutely certain," he said, yet again gesturing around the room. "I have my job to do here."

She allowed a long, uncomfortable silence to fall between them before she spoke. "I have prepared for this eventuality." She opened her purse and withdrew a small envelope. "I have a reward for your troubles. This is a letter of commitment to give you one share in Cincinnati Soap and Candle Company, the company I have just invested in. The share is worth, by my reckoning, the small sum of twenty-five dollars. One share," she repeated. "I would like you to take it and to keep track of its progress in the stock market. Do you follow the stock market?"

"I can't say that I do. I know a good deal about the periodic tables and about Sir Isaac Newton's basic physical principles, and I have no interest in stocks and bonds. In fact, I find the whole world of finance a bore."

Undeterred by his brusqueness of manner, Eleanor pressed on. "Take this letter and set it aside, wait a few months, and follow this particular stock and you will watch your twenty-five dollars increase in value many-fold."

He eyed the envelope in her hands suspiciously. "All right," he said, "if you insist." Thinking back on the exchange sometime later, she realized that the young man's abrasive manner actually helped her mask her own uncertainty as to how her recent purchase was to fare, and it allowed her to continue with this unlikely recruitment she knew was required of her. "But what is the catch?" he continued without grace.

"There is no catch, I just want you to wait and watch. And then I want you to imagine how your fortunes would have changed had you received from me today a full year's salary in this stock, which I was prepared to offer you." She held out the envelope and kept it extended until the young man, still suspicious, took it from her. "You will contact me when you have seen enough and you are convinced."

"Well, all right," he said, taking the envelope. "But I doubt very much that I shall be calling you."

"You have great strengths, I hear. Remember that Dr. James describes you as brilliant."

Ted Honeycutt's demeanor changed to the closest he could come to civility. "I like you, Miss Putnam. I really do. But I see atoms and molecules in my future, not stocks and bonds. You have just engaged in a complete waste of time."

"Very well," she said, rising. "I fully understand. But you will discover that I am a very determined woman, and that I want very much for you to join me in this effort."

"Again, I do not wish to be offensive," he said. "But I think perhaps that you are the one here not fully in control of your senses."

"That may be," Eleanor said, "but I wanted to bring your attention to bear on my project, and I hope I have done that."

"But how are you on your side so certain that I am the one you are looking for?"

"I am also, as you will further discover, a highly intuitive person, Mr. Honeycutt. I am here on the very strongest of intuitive hunches. I am very definitively certain that you are exactly the one I am looking for, and I greatly hope that you will come around." She pointed to the envelope now in his hand. "And with that envelope I rest my case."

And with that envelope Eleanor had made, unknowingly, a fateful move.

"DISASTER AVERTED,
IT APPEARS"

 ometime after her return from her adventure in Cincin-
nati and her initial meeting with the graduate student
T. Williams Honeycutt, her fiancé, Frank Burden, ever
the serious banker, oblivious to Eleanor's having successfully completed the loan, came to her with an article
he had found among his bank's news resources. "Disaster averted, it appears," he said with a helpful and satisfied smile. "I am exceedingly glad
that your interests were only hypothetical. That soap company you were
inquiring about is going bankrupt." Frank laid an investment news sheet
opened out in front of her. Eleanor could only stare in disbelief.

The article was succinct and highly unflattering. Cincinnati Soap and
Candle was indeed headed for insolvency, it appeared. The company's
owner, a certain Homer Smith, was portrayed as irrational, unable and
unwilling to sell the company to what he perceived as the greedy giant
attempting to take it over. IRASCIBLE OWNER GOING DOWN WITH THE
SHIP, the headline read, a shame, the article concluded, because Workman's Soap was a "superior product," one any company, large or small,
would be happy to call its own, and CS & C was a proud old family company being run to the ground by a stubborn grandson of the founder.

"It is good that you have left the interpretation of the investment world
to those with heads for it," Frank said.

Eleanor managed to maintain a poised façade. "And what if someone
had in fact made such an investment?" she asked with outer calm.

"Well, he would have lost practically everything," Frank said coldly.

"Bankrupt stock has no value." Then after further thought he added, "Or some opportunist sweeps in and buys at a ridiculously low price." Frank Burden always took on a paternal air when explaining any of the rudiments of high-level finance or the stock market or any areas of business to his, he assumed, naïve and inexperienced fiancée. "Again, you see," he added patiently, "it is best to leave the serious decisions to the men of finance. That is what we are for."

And that night Eleanor, feeling cold and alone, was confronted by the reality of ruination, a despondency that stayed with her for days. She sat in her living room on Acorn Street, uncertain of the timing but fully aware that disaster loomed ahead, wondering how she should have played out her assigned hand differently. *What have I done?* she thought as she itemized the details of the decision. *What other choice was there?* There were no easy answers, no easy peace, and no one with whom to share her dejection.

She had lived her entire life in the Acorn Street house, as had her mother before her, and now that her mother and father were both gone, sole ownership had fallen to her and she was supposed to live out her whole life there. She was shocked now to think how easy it had been to sign the deed over to Mr. Lowenstein's bank and to put the fate of the family house into the hands of an impersonal third party. That was what risk was all about, she was now learning painfully as she reviewed her decisions.

And one more troubling thought visited her on that night of despair, an old thought, one she had confronted before. Her father had been a weak man and had never gotten over the death of her mother in Eleanor's eighth year. Because he had been a man of the cloth and a member of one of Boston's oldest families, no one had realized just how much his life and his promise had collapsed when he lost that great strength that marriage and his wife had provided him. At one point, when Eleanor's mother was alive and entertaining so beautifully in this very living room, her father had been considered one of the shining lights of the New England clergy, perhaps a future bishop of Massachusetts, a future Phillips Brooks, some said. But then the bottom had dropped out of his life and the decline began, and people wondered if he could keep his position as rector, let alone ascend to a bishopric. But he had taken to drink and not to financial profligacy. He had ruined family life, but not family finances. Her father had been weak, but he had never compromised that family legacy, his own or her mother's, and when he died, during Eleanor's junior year at Smith College, the title to the property and the other family holdings remained free and clear, as they had since her mother's great-grandparents' day.

As a compensation perhaps, without a strong father model inside her, she had developed a steely determination of her own, one that served her well in moments of crisis, but one that also stepped in when caution would have been a better course, and pushed her resolutely into action. How much better it would have been in this case to use that cautious part of herself in this moment of decision, to have thought things through the way her mother might have. Now, as many times before, too late, she asked herself, what would Mother have done? She had seen what needed to be done and pursued the solution with great inner strength, a kind of blind courage, and that courage, strong as it was, also had a dark consequence that now was going to lead to her ruination.

A more cautious person, a timid person even, would not find herself in this situation, she kept saying to herself. A more cautious person would not have put Acorn Street at risk.

"You will spend your entire life here," her father had said to her in one of their last conversations. "This house is a fine old Boston landmark," he said. "And now you will be its center, raising your family here, as you have been raised, making your mother and her forebears proud."

That was Acorn Street. And now, because of her fevered devotion to the imperious mandate of the journal she had brought back from her fateful encounters in Vienna, she had risked all and had lost her beloved childhood home.

It was during that night of torment that the dream first came to Eleanor. She was alone on a cold and windswept promontory, a high cliff on the edge of a raging ocean. She was drawn to the edge by a distant figure in white, and as she approached, she was aware of the figure falling far below into what now appeared as a bottomless void. Trying to steady herself, digging her fingers into the muddy surface, Eleanor felt herself slipping as she stared into the dark abyss. It was always at this point that she would waken, in a cold sweat, fighting for breath.

She bore the news secretly and alone, waiting for the axe to fall and for the word to come from Cincinnati to her bank, when she would have to tell Frank Burden and the world that she had lost her family home. She put the decision off for days, and then finally one morning, after a sleepless night, she decided she must act. And it was that very morning that she read shocking news in a small column in the *Boston Herald*. At first she could not believe what she saw, that a circumstance so central in her life would appear in her Boston newspaper, but there it was: Homer Smith, prominent Cincinnati businessman, a Harvard alumnus, it turned out, was dead, felled by a heart attack in his office, and now Procter and Gamble, the greedy giant, spread its tentacles over Cincinnati Soap and Candle Company and, in the old patriarch's view, threatened to suck out its life. In the ensuing takeover attempt, which the family had enough sense to ward off, one of Homer Smith's nephews seemed to take control. Eleanor did not travel to Cincinnati this time, but spoke to the young man on the telephone.

"What have you planned?" she said when he asked about her holdings.

"We have contacted Colgate," he said. "They are definitely interested."

That action on the family's part set up a bidding war between the two companies. Procter and Gamble acted aggressively and hastily, "before the Colgate folks could even put together an offer," the nephew said in the second phone call. "They are offering a price that will double in value our holdings in stock. They very much want Workman's Soap."

"And what do you plan to do?" Eleanor asked.

"Why, we'll sell, of course," the nephew said in a burst, not acknowledging any humor in her question. And then he paused. "I hope that is satisfactory with you."

"Thank you for inquiring," she said, registering fully only much later the mature consideration in his tone. "And, yes, it is satisfactory with me."

After the packet arrived special delivery from Cincinnati, Eleanor made the trip back to Mr. Lowenstein's office on Boylston Street. "I trust that I can pay you in Procter and Gamble stock," she said.

"Oh my, yes," the kindly banker said. "That stock is like gold right now."

Eleanor flashed him a look of concern. "For a moment, it looked as if my investment was going to fail, and I was going to lose my family home."

Mr. Lowenstein gave her a long appraising look, then smiled. "Oh my, no. We would have found a way. This bank would never have allowed you to lose your family home."

"That is comforting to know."

"We would have thought of some solution. Our bank was glad to be of service in your enterprise."

So, all the borrowed monies paid back, her holdings now increased not the tenfold caused by the loan, but twentyfold, it became clear that Eleanor, barely knowing what she was doing, had made the purchase of a lifetime and was able to set up the Hyperion Fund as a more-than-significant financial entity.

What she did not realize fully at the time was that she had just discovered, quite by accident, the explosive power—and the risk—of buying on margin.

Of course, she was able to tell none of this to her fiancé, Frank Burden, nor was she able to convey in any way to him her very satisfactory last conversation with the moneylender.

She had accomplished, with the infusion of a good deal of luck, her first two assignments, the selling of Prince Rudolf's ring and the purchase of stock in Cincinnati Soap and Candle Company, at an extraordinary moment in the company's history. The deep satisfaction from this mostly accidental transaction would revisit her, along with the apprehension, from time to time for the rest of her life. *What if I had not acted?* she would think. At one moment, she seemed a puppet, being pulled this way and that by fate and expectations, and the next she seemed to be acting totally on her own initiative, living by her wits, the mistress of her own drama. Was it all predetermined, some massive fate controlling all the details, or did she bear the heavy responsibility of causing events, or having to save the day? Was it, after all, completely up to her? One thing was for certain: She wished never again to make the journey alone.

The assurance that she would not have to came shortly after her return from Cincinnati after the Procter and Gamble buyout, and from a very unlikely quarter. It came in the form of Harvard physics student Ted Honeycutt, whom she judged from the start, in spite of the very specific instructions, an unlikely savior. It was he who arranged to meet with her again.

"You followed the fate of that Cincinnati Soap and Candle stock?" she said to Ted Honeycutt back in Boston.

"I did," he said. "It captured my attention. I observed from my distance that it doubled in value." There seemed to be a new curiosity in him, but his manner remained brusque.

"Are you sorry that you did not accept a year's salary in that stock when it was offered?"

"I am a scientist, but even I deduced that I would have made a bundle," he said. "I have come to hear more about what you are offering."

"What we will say here must be highly confidential."

"Of course," he said. "I am very good with secrets, Miss Putnam. I don't talk to people."

"So I have heard. That is one of the qualities I discovered in seeking you out."

"I want to know what you are looking for."

"I believe that I told you in our first meeting. With the purchase of this stock, in significant number, I need to add, I have created a fund. I will be making other purchases over the years, and the fund will grow in importance and value. I will need someone intelligent and discreet and efficient to manage it. I wish for you to be that person."

"And after our first disagreeable meeting you still wish that?"

"I didn't find our first meeting disagreeable," she said. She was not being completely honest. "I like honesty."

For a second time, he asked, "What makes you so certain that I am the man you want?"

Unable to explain the real reason for her certainty, Eleanor said this time, "Mr. Honeycutt, I am, as I have explained, highly intuitive, a good judge of character."

"Well, I am leaning toward coming on board," he said quickly.

"I do not want *leaning,* Mr. Honeycutt. I wish to have a decision."

Ted Honeycutt paused for a moment, looking away, and then his eyes came to hers. "You are very persistent, Miss Putnam."

"I know what I want," she said, "and I try very hard to get it."

"And . . . ," he said with his head down. "There is something I need to make perfectly clear."

"And what would that be?"

He paused for a moment, then burst forth. "You are a very attractive woman, Miss Putnam, and I know that you are accustomed to getting your way. But I need to make it clear that attractiveness has no effect on me. I am considering joining you because of the offer, nothing else.

I wish to have what you would call a business relationship, nothing more."

At first Eleanor said nothing. Thinking back on it, if there was one moment in which she thought she could not go on, this was it. Later she would admit that she found his brashness refreshing and a departure from Boston propriety, but for now she was aware simply that she had no choice. She took a deep breath. "A business relationship is what I am looking for, Mr. Honeycutt. Nothing more. But, my, you are very direct."

"I think you will find that will always be the case." He looked her in the eye. "I think you will find me a rather blunt fellow," he said. "I am not exactly like others in that regard."

"My goodness," Eleanor said, both stunned and attracted by the frankness. "We must be cautious here to keep things honest, Mr. Honeycutt, even if they seem blunt. We must be clearheaded, dedicated, discreet, efficient. But we must be able to trust each other." She paused to be sure that he was taking her seriously.

For a moment, he looked as if he might wish to explain. "You will find me very trustworthy," he said blankly. "Trustworthiness is one of my strongest attributes."

"You understand that I will be asking you to pursue certain very specific investments, and that your job will be to do exactly what I say."

"I understand that."

"And as a part of your compensation you will always have ten percent of the Hyperion Fund at your disposal to do with as you wish, to use to gain knowledge of how the stock market works."

"That is very generous."

"And also essential for your education," she said, thinking of the discomfort of traveling alone to Cincinnati, reaching out her hand and accepting his. "Now, with regard to that year's salary you did not accept when first offered—"

"You need not apologize," he interrupted. "I had my chance, and I did not avail myself."

"Other opportunities will present themselves. There will be many chances to invest. As I said, you will become a very wealthy man." She paused. "Now, there is something I do need to give you." She withdrew from her purse for the second time an envelope. "I can offer this to you now." She handed it to him.

He opened the envelope and examined its contents carefully, a look of confusion on his face. "It is the year's salary," he said, "purchased six months ago."

"It is," she said. "Cincinnati Soap and Candle stock purchased back then, in your name. Now worth considerably more. Double, actually. All you need to do is redeem it for the highly valued Procter and Gamble stock."

"You knew I would say yes. You knew I was about to lose my position here."

"I did not know—" Eleanor began, then stopped herself. "It had to be," she said. "And now you are on your way, it would appear."

"We are on our way, Miss Putnam."

"Indeed we are," she said, and she rose and extended her hand to say good-bye.

Ted Honeycutt said nothing at first, giving his head only the slightest nod, staring blankly at the envelope he held in his hand. "Tomorrow," he said finally, "I begin. And where are we going to put it all?"

"Northern Pacific," she said. "We put it all into Northern Pacific."

"All of it?"

"All of it," she said. "This will be good for you. You can test your wings and begin to learn how to move around in this brave new world."

"And how on earth do you know to do that?" he said, and then paused to think. "Intuition?"

"Intuition, Mr. Honeycutt. You will become accustomed to such spontaneous and decisive bursts, I fear."

Ted Honeycutt only shook his head in disbelief. "I'm not intuitive," he said, looking quite serious.

"One last detail, Mr. Honeycutt," she added suddenly. "Has anyone ever called you Will?"

"Not for years," he said. "It is the name from my childhood."

"Now, I wish that for the extent of your tenure with the Hyperion Fund, you shall be called Will Honeycutt." And so the last piece of the hiring business was settled.

She did not at this time mention in any way that she would need his help in the most important of her challenges: recruiting Arnauld Esterhazy from the comfort of his life in Vienna to his teaching assignment at St. Gregory's School.

8

PRIMA MATERIA

ittle did Eleanor suspect that she was creating a monster. From the moment of her recruitment of him this newly minted Will Honeycutt took to his new life with great enthusiasm. "I do not enter into anything halfway," he said. From the beginning, she described how he would be fully in charge of the Hyperion Fund.

"You are the executive director," she told him, "but when I tell you to invest, you must invest. Is that absolutely clear?"

"Absolutely clear," her new employee said with certainty.

"And you must follow with your share of the fund. You must invest those as I say. No deviations or gambling with your own funds. Is that also clear?" He nodded. And then she explained again about his 10 percent fund, the monies he could do with what he wished. "I would like you to learn all you can about investing, and therefore you will always have that portion of our holdings to invest as you see fit."

And then she set him on his first project. She pulled out the large stack of papers that was the translation of Dr. Freud's book. "This is the only copy in English of this very important book, and I wish for it to be published in a very limited edition. It will remain quite secret." Being new to his position, Will Honeycutt did not question or object.

Eleanor then told Will Honeycutt of a small publisher and bookbinder in Boston, where he made the arrangements for publishing the book, keeping Eleanor removed from the negotiations, just in case anyone tried to track down the source of the underground edition. Within three months, Will delivered to her four hundred paper-bound copies of *The Interpretation of Dreams*. And this time she set him about wrapping each copy and preparing each for mailing. Before long, the bulk of that number was mailed in unmarked envelopes from numerous post offices in New England to the leading historians, social scientists, and psychologists in the country, and nearly all the major magazines and newspapers.

With no markings of any kind other than title and author on the books themselves and the sworn secrecy of their producers, the origin of the publication became a great mystery. And Sigmund Freud began to be better known in America than he was in Europe outside Vienna. The reason was, of course, the mysterious "White Book," Will Honeycutt's first project for the secret Hyperion Fund.

And then there were the bucket shops. "Master the ticker-tape machine," a friend of his had told him when he first announced his new appointment, "and then master the bucket shops." So, following his friend's advice, at the same time he was pursuing his surreptitious publishing career Will Honeycutt walked into a world he had never known existed and before long was knee-deep in stock speculation.

The bucket shops were essentially betting parlors for the stock market and had been a national rage for two or three decades. They were made possible by the advent of the telegraph and the ticker-tape machine, which provided the minute-by-minute fluctuations in stock prices on Wall Street, almost instantaneously, thanks to Thomas Edison's invention of the quadruplex, which allowed multiple messages to be carried over a single wire.

The name "bucket shop" was derived from a time when boys in London used to drain the remainders of discarded pub beer kegs into buckets and gather in hideaways to drink and gamble. In the betting shops that began to spring up in London first, then America, the city's working folk would gather and make wagers on stock fluctuations that were written in chalk on blackboards as fast as they came off the ticker tape. The bucket shops operated like horse-race parlors.

"If you want a quick lesson in stock speculation, get to know these bucket shops," one old-timer in a bowler hat told Will Honeycutt, sitting beside him in one of the storefront locations. "If you want to know about bucket shops, get to know the Boy Trader. He has been banned from playing here and just about everywhere else in the country."

The Boy Trader was a young man just Will's age named Jesse Livermore, who had grown up in Boston and began placing bets on stocks at age sixteen. From an early age a genius with numbers and memory of them, he kept meticulous notebooks on the behaviors of the many stocks being traded on the New York market in those days. Jesse found that he could keep track of statistics in his head and project with uncanny accuracy the individual stocks that were ready to move, and he could take out bets accordingly, winning with such regularity that the shops refused his business. "It is just the type of mind Jesse has," Will explained to Eleanor. "Mine works a little that way."

Eleanor tried to suppress a laugh. "I would say that your mind works *a lot* that way," she said. Not understanding fully the degree to which her new partner was involved in this new obsession, she watched with amusement. "This is good," she told him. "This is what the ten percent fund is meant for. I wish that you get to know the stock market."

"You think it strange for a physicist, don't you?"

"I am learning not to be surprised by anything you do," she said.

"It is a system," he said quickly. "I like seeing through to the base of things, to the *prima materia,* the medieval alchemists used to say, to the very heart of how things work. Physics was simply my way of doing that, don't you see? Seeing through to the atomic level."

"That is it, isn't it?" Eleanor said, as if a veil had been lifted from her eyes. "You really do see through to this *prima materia.* Like the alchemists."

"I do," Will said seriously. "Yes, I cannot help myself, it seems."

"And that is what you are doing here," Eleanor said in conclusion. "When you read that ticker-tape machine, you are somehow doing that."

"I get lost in the figures, I will admit. I read the tape, and I can see what is happening at that base *prima materia* level, and I can usually predict what will happen next."

"You can see the companies and the people represented in the flow of numbers on the ticker tape?" Eleanor asked, trying to understand. She had seen enough of the stream of paper tape spewing forth from the rapidly clicking machine to know that she would soon be overwhelmed by it.

Will Honeycutt stared at her with a look of incomprehension. "Companies and people?" he said. "I don't see the companies and the people. I see numbers, only numbers."

"But with the stock market the numbers represent human actions, do they not? Complex human actions."

Again, Will Honeycutt stared at her for an uncomfortable moment. "Numbers," he said bluntly. "What is it that you do not understand about numbers?"

At that moment, Eleanor wished very much to ease the tension between them. "Mr. Honeycutt, I do not understand the numbers here. But I do know that I do not wish to in any way discourage you."

"You cannot discourage me," the new associate said. "Remember, I am a very determined fellow."

Will traveled to New York City in search of this Jesse Livermore, and the two men found that they had much in common. At first, Jesse proposed that Will, an unknown face, do his bidding for him, but soon both Will and his new mentor realized that the young scientist needed to take off on his own and develop his own mastery of the numbers.

"Remember," Jesse said, "bucket shops aren't like the real thing. The transactions are too simple. The prices come in on the ticker tape and go up on the chalkboard. It's instantaneous. You put down your money on the stock and keep reading the tape and watch for trends, for the rise or fall. Then you cash in, and you make your profit, no delays, no commissions, no fluctuations. A keen way for a ticker-tape whiz to make money."

"I'll never be as good as you with the *real thing*," Will said, acknowledging Jesse's true genius with what went on in New York, "but I am learning what comes in on the ticker tape."

"Keep your bets small," Jesse advised, "so as you don't call attention to yourself. That way they'll let you stay around while you learn those ropes. My problem was that I made a lot of money and attracted a lot of attention."

So Will Honeycutt went back to Boston and spent part of each day in the bucket shops and began keeping his own copious notes. "You are becoming a ticker-tape expert," Eleanor said to him one day. "I am not certain that is entirely a good thing. We need to watch out for you."

"Say, you're getting the hang of this," Jesse said to him one morning as his apprentice returned to New York and came to him with a handful of bills.

"I'm trying to see the whole canvas, not just the numbers," Will said.

"We make a good team," Jesse said, which Will took as one of the great compliments of his life.

Having moved past the small-stakes world of the bucket shops, Jesse was now investing in the much more complex game of the real New York stock market. "You can come join me here later," he said to his protégé.

"My calling is in Boston," Will said. He had never considered divulging the secret of Eleanor and her Hyperion Fund and the 10 percent he was allowed to gamble with, nor the steadying normalcy he found from reporting in and working beside her every week.

"Still, keep in mind that here is where the big game is," Jesse said, referring to the New York Stock Exchange. "This is where you make the big money. And no one stops you from trading."

Eleanor noticed Will's attention to the shops and some of the near-addiction of his frequenting them, but she did not worry. "I am glad to see that you are learning the investment game," she told him as she noticed the ebb and flow of his 10 percent account. "It is a long way from the physics department of Harvard. I hope you don't mind that I lured you away from there."

"Oh, no," Will said with a satisfied, distracted smile. "I much prefer the excitement of this. It is the real world, not an ivy-walled sanctuary. I'm able to keep my head up among workers," he said, "and I make more money than my professors ever had. Just wait till I get to Jesse's level."

"Be careful," Eleanor admonished him, aware that her new partner seemed to be neither eating nor sleeping. "It is, after all, gambling."

"Gambling with knowledge," Will said. "I am learning to read the ticker tape. That is the secret edge, where the real mastery lies."

The first years of the new century were a perfect time to become involved with investments and speculation. They were years of great national prosperity. Abundant harvests, new supplies of gold, significant world demand for American goods, all added up to a booming American economy. Keeping track of the companies that seemed on the brink of boom times was easy for someone of Will Honeycutt's passion for analysis, and the artificial world of bucket-shop speculations seemed made for him, a perfect place to learn and to expend nervous energy, of which her Will Honeycutt had a great deal.

So Will took funds from the 10 percent of the Hyperion Fund and invested every day, watching his choices pay off or lose, and each day, as he got better and better at Jesse's numbers game, he watched his share of the fund increase. Eleanor would visit him at their small rented office and, marveling at his copious notes, take pleasure in seeing the former physics student showing more and more interest in stocks and bonds.

"You are developing a true expertise," she said.

"It is a fascination," Will said back with a distracted smile. "I wish to make the ticker tape my whole life."

"I know you exaggerate," Eleanor said with a genial smile, and her partner stared at her. What Eleanor did not see at that time was how the new discipline was becoming for Will Honeycutt what it had become previously for Jesse Livermore: a full-blown obsession.

She did not notice fully, perhaps, the change in her new colleague because she had her mind elsewhere, on her developing correspondence with Arnauld in Vienna and her next big project, ensuring that the young Viennese would end up in Boston.

9

THE WRONG MAN

 ust as everything came to a head with the Northern Pacific stock eruption in the spring of 1901, she discovered the truth about Will Honeycutt. It all came to her as an epiphany when she saw the name on a document in her fiancé Frank Burden's office that shook her to her core. Nothing was going to be easy. She had already learned that.

"Who is this?" she said to Frank, pointing to the name in the description of a stock transaction in the portfolio of her family holdings that his bank managed.

Frank, not detecting anything of great significance in her question, answered quickly. "He's the bank's man in Chicago," he said. "He's a brilliant fellow and knows everything about commodities and bonds."

"Is he from Boston?"

"He grew up here, in Milton, and went to Harvard. His whole family has gone to Harvard. He goes by Williams."

"Williams Honeycutt," she said dumbly, running it all through her mind. "Does anyone call him Will Honeycutt?"

"I suppose so. I've never heard it though."

"And he lives here?"

"No, he lives and works in Chicago. He moved out there for the bank. We're trying to get him to come back."

"May I keep this?" she said, holding the stock transaction document. "I'd like to read it."

"Pretty dry stuff," Frank said. "I doubt you'd find anything you can understand in it. It's all financial terms, you know."

"That's all right," she said. "I'd like to get to know this T. Williams Honeycutt of yours."

The shocking discovery came at the same moment when the man from Loeb and Sons had telegraphed with the warning, as she had asked. There had been the anticipated sudden movement in the Northern Pacific stock, and she thought, *This is it. The time has come.* She tried to get in touch with Will Honeycutt, but he was nowhere to be found. *What a time to go missing,* she thought, with little charity.

"When that stock begins to move," she had told him just a week before, "you had better be there in person. When the warning comes, you go immediately. I will follow when you think it right. I'll depend on you." And now the warning from New York had come, and her colleague had disappeared. And there seemed to be no way to contact him. She would have to go herself.

She had held back uneasy feelings about Will ever since the wildness of his bucket-shop obsessions, or from the very start, she would have to admit now. He was a "strange fellow," as William James said, "rather bereft of social grace." And now there was the entry of this second T. Williams Honeycutt, one far better suited for the task she had in mind and probably much easier to get along with. Things were very far from settled in her world, and she intended to do something about it, as soon as she found him.

Now, all the way to New York City on the train herself, she kept looking down at the paper Frank had given her, and the name. And once again, the old question returned: Should she have acted or waited for events to unfold? There was a second T. Williams Honeycutt, one already well versed in the stock market, brilliant, from a Harvard family, probably a relative of her Will's, one he had known well, from birth. Had she waited, perhaps that young man would have come to her. By stepping in early and recruiting the Ted Honeycutt from William James's experience, she had forced matters and had caused the error. Had she been patient and waited, things would have turned out differently.

Will Honeycutt has known all along, she said to herself, as she fumed inwardly, looking out the train window as Connecticut farmland rolled past. *The man, this second T. Williams Honeycutt, was his cousin, after all.* That is what really irked her. She would confront him as soon as she got to New York, and demand an explanation, if she could find him. And she was pretty sure what the outcome was going to be. It was in no way good. Left alone again, she struggled now to get command in her mind of at least the situation with Northern Pacific.

The railroad company's stock where, per instructions from the page in the journal, Eleanor had placed all her funds had been in decline. As a result Will Honeycutt—now at the peak of his bucket-shop trading frenzy—was beginning to feel the investment was a disaster and worse, a product of his employer's total whimsy. The Hyperion Fund, over which he, with his new "expertise" in the market, was supposed to have some oversight, was now invested solely in that one commodity, a large mistake, as any stock speculator knew. Eleanor insisted on holding tight, and losing value by the week.

Will had broached the subject of reconsidering. "I suppose it would do no good," he said, aware of Eleanor's intransigence on certain subjects, "to try to talk you out of what looks like a very unwise investment and into moving at least part of your investment to something with more promise."

"You are correct," she said without flinching. "It would do no good. And it is *our* investment."

"*Our* investment," he said. "And it would do no good?"

"It would do no good, Mr. Honeycutt. Our monies are exactly where they should be."

"I thought as much."

"You are becoming quite confident with analysis of the market, I see. That is very good."

"I am coming along, I guess you would say. And I know enough to know it is not wise to have all eggs in one basket, even if they are good eggs, which these of Northern Pacific are not."

"My dear Mr. Honeycutt, I know your concern and your desire to move our investments about. We will hold. You will just have to trust me. From time to time, you will just have to do that. But this one time I will tell you this: If our position has not at least doubled within the year, I will grant you any wish you want."

"Any wish?" he said. "My, you seem very confident."

"Any wish," Eleanor replied. "And, yes, you are correct in your assessment. About some things, I am supremely confident."

And Will Honeycutt could only shake his head in disbelief.

And then the call had come from Loeb and Sons that the stock had begun to move. "You will have to be in New York City, I fear," she had said to Will in that early May of 1901. They had been working together for over a year. "It might be for only a short time. We shall have to move quickly." From the time of their purchase they had placed the full amount of Northern Pacific stock in the hands of the Loeb investment house, and Eleanor knew that if they made known their intention to sell the whole bundle at five hundred, the good investment bankers would have thought them stark raving mad, but she wished them to be forewarned. If there was any unusual movement, she wished to be informed immediately. Hence the telegram on that May morning when Will Honeycutt was nowhere to be found.

Will Honeycutt had been incredulous when she told him the preposterous idea of holding out for the high figure. "But Northern Pacific started at thirty-five," he had said. "It is a decline from fifty when we bought. Five hundred is ten times what we paid for those holdings six months ago."

"That is correct," Eleanor said with finality, seeing no reason for further explanation. She looked at him for a moment. "And you will keep our strategy confidential."

"Do you think I have learned nothing?" Honeycutt said blankly. "I tell no one anything."

"Good," Eleanor said. "I shall hold to my faith in you." The fewer people who knew of her foreknowledge the better, she knew. Because of its volatile nature, her information derived from the journal must be kept secret.

Now, in Will Honeycutt's absence, having no idea where he was, she would have to be in New York herself. She would have to be present when and if the stock prices began to rise as the journal foretold, and she had just learned of the other T. Williams Honeycutt, a disturbing discovery that was going to require a face-to-face confrontation, and action. Perhaps Will had heard of her discovery and fled.

"I will join you at the Loeb offices," she would have told him had she been able to. He was to introduce her as his secretary, in that world of men. But now, she was forced to travel to New York and represent her holdings herself, alone.

How on earth, she thought on the long train ride, was she ever going to extract herself from this fateful mistake?

◥

When she arrived at the Loeb office on Wall Street, Mr. Loeb Sr.'s secretary welcomed her and said, "They are convening in the conference room." She walked in and saw two Loeb men standing beside a tall, neatly dressed man of finance she nearly did not recognize. It was her partner, Will Honeycutt.

"We have been here for some time," one of the Loeb men said. "Mr. Honeycutt is minding the ticker tape for us. We are waiting."

Will had kept up with the rising action on his own and hustled to New York when he realized what was happening. "I told them to notify you," he apologized. "I see from your consternation that they neglected to tell you that I was already on the job." Eleanor was stunned to see him and stunned to see how firmly in charge he was.

Already, when Eleanor arrived at noon, action had begun, and she had no chance to raise her sensitive subject. Will was busy watching the tape and barely greeted her. "I'm glad you are here," he said. "Something is up. Already this morning we have had ten or twelve inquiries." And she noticed immediately that there was something very different about his bearing. "I am assuming that you want us to hold."

"We hold for five hundred," she said in little more than a whisper, wishing none of the Loeb men to know their outrageous strategy.

"Good," Will Honeycutt said. "As I suspected. It is already over one hundred, and people are wondering why we don't sell off at least a part."

And then it hit.

As with all the specific instructions Eleanor took secretly from her Vienna knowledge, past and future, she would try to investigate ahead of time and determine how the instructed investment would work, how it would end up being the absolute right thing to do. But often there was no clue, and she would just have to go blindly where that knowledge dictated. Such was the case with the Northern Pacific purchase.

From what she could see, the Northern Pacific Railway was to become an important link from the Great Lakes to Puget Sound on the Pacific coast, a northern rival to the great transcontinental railroad completed through Utah and the Sierra Nevada to Sacramento gold country in the late 1860s. There seemed to be no reason why the stock would suddenly shoot up disproportionately to any other railroad stock. All she knew from a note in the journal was that sometime in early May the fund would sell all its holdings for an unbelievable price.

Suddenly, on that fateful morning, a representative from the House of Morgan approached young Honeycutt quietly and explained that he would buy the entire lot that Hyperion was holding for two hundred dollars a share. She noticed the change in him almost immediately. Something had definitely happened. Will tried his best poker face and reported that he would get back. He had been reading the ticker tape. Privately, he told Eleanor, "It's gone to high two hundreds, Miss Putnam," enunciating when she resisted. "That would quadruple the fund."

"We hold for five hundred," Will Honeycutt told the Loeb representative calmly.

"But, Mr. Honeycutt——" he began, incredulous. "Would you at least move *some*?"

"Hold it all," Mr. Honeycutt said, and then, after a pause, he returned to the Morgan man with the answer.

The man's demeanor immediately turned to fury. He fixed his beady eyes on his obviously inexperienced opponent, questioning his very authority. "Mr. Morgan himself wishes this," he continued, as if that would be enough.

"We are holding for five hundred," Will said, staring back at the Morgan man in a long, awkward moment of silence.

"Very well," the man said. "You can report back to your mystery controller that you will certainly regret this." He stared for a moment. "Let me ask you something," he said solemnly.

"You may ask."

"Are you Jewish, Mr. Honeycutt?"

Will Honeycutt paused for a moment, his eyes fixed on the Morgan man without blinking, nowhere near intimidation or panic. And looking back on it later, Eleanor concluded that this was his supreme moment, and if one wished to find the exact instant in which this inexperienced apprentice rose to the demands of the adventure to which he had been called, this was it. "It would seem to me," Will Honeycutt said, again slowly and calmly, looking around the room, at Eleanor and the Loeb man, "that we are all red-blooded American capitalists here." And the

Morgan man, looking apoplectic, as if he might explode, turned and walked out of the room. Eleanor stood back and watched in something like amazement. Seeing her colleague in this new persona had an unexpected effect on her. It was only later that she realized the powerful impact on her. She was being taken care of.

The next offer was three hundred fifty, well above what Will had just read on the ticker tape. The offer was no longer from the Morgans and for only one-half the shares. "This is going wild. We must take it," Will Honeycutt said emphatically. "I do not know a lot about these kinds of panics, but I do know that when the bubble bursts it does so suddenly and is bound to disappear soon. Three fifty is a huge increase. It would be wise to act." There was now a calm urgency in his voice, again, no panic, just a calm urgency.

"We are holding at five hundred, Mr. Honeycutt," Eleanor said.

What neither Eleanor nor Will Honeycutt had any way of knowing until later was that they and the whole investment world had been swept up in a huge competition between the forces of Edward Henry Harriman, head of the Union Pacific Railroad, who was also looking for a road which could connect his company to Chicago, and the house of J. P. Morgan. Harriman was making a bid to buy up enough shares to control the railroad, and Morgan was determined not to let that happen. It was a power struggle between two industrial giants, one totally out of proportion to the worth of the railroad itself. Because so many individuals and houses, seeing the price rise out of control, were short-selling and about to lose it all, the fierce competition began to envelop the whole market and consequently the whole financial system of the country. J. P. Morgan had caused it. Sometimes wise and sometimes impulsive, the great financier playing the part of the dual-natured Zeus on the top of Mount Olympus was now acting purely on ego, determined not to be bettered by any rival, no matter the stakes. And from southern France he had issued the fateful order to his underlings in New York, "Buy at any price."

The entire market was surging out of control, always on the brink of ruinous free-fall, and yet the offers came rolling in. Brokers all over the street thought they had to obtain Northern Pacific shares to protect themselves. The price shot up ever higher and higher, and T. Williams Honeycutt and the Hyperion Fund held tight. By two o'clock that afternoon, with pandemonium reigning, and offers flying in from all corners, they had received many offers at well over five hundred. "Send for the Morgan man," Will said calmly, now fully in charge.

With couriers dashing into the Loeb offices Eleanor watched in awed silence and then said to her partner, "You see why we needed to be here in person."

"I do." He barely had time to respond as the Morgan man rushed into the room, this time with a totally different demeanor, this time with an unmistakable look of panic in his eyes.

"We'll meet your request," Will Honeycutt said bluntly.

"At what price?" the man said.

"At the promised five hundred. But we have offers for a good deal more than that. And the offers keep climbing by the minute." Even as they spoke a messenger entered the room and laid in his hand an offer for half the shares at seven hundred fifty. By the end of the day, before the collapse, offers would rise above one thousand dollars a share.

"We will match any offer you have," the Morgan man said, eyeing the paper. "For the full number of shares."

"There will be no need for that," Will Honeycutt said without emotion, raising himself to his full five feet nine inches and looking calmly at the man from the House of Morgan. "I told you we would sell at five hundred," he said. "We will sell at five hundred." With a firm, confident handshake from the seller's side, the deal was struck and the new persona of T. Williams Honeycutt, experienced fund manager, was firmly established.

"You did magnificently," Eleanor said to her young partner as they left the offices of Loeb, quite forgetting her intention to replace him. There was a clearly evident admiration in her voice. "I cannot believe how calm you were."

"I did what needed to be done," he said, and once again Eleanor was surprised by his poise.

"Did your friend Democritus appear to you?" she said with a touch of whimsy in her voice.

"No, not this time," Will said with total seriousness. "This time it was Alexander Hamilton."

"Alexander Hamilton!" Eleanor exclaimed. "How is that?"

"Alexander Hamilton came to me in a dream, so I began talking to him, writing down our conversation. It turns out that he was the first treasurer of the United States, something I had totally forgotten. He was most helpful."

Eleanor could only shake her head in amazement. *Whatever works,* she heard the pragmatic William James saying in her ear. "This has been a most extraordinary day," she said, revealing a rush of exuberance. "You, Mr. Honeycutt, have handled yourself with great aplomb, coached by Mr. Hamilton or not. We shall retire to my hotel room to celebrate."

10

A CELEBRATION

he mood was ecstatic. "Living on the very edge!" Eleanor exclaimed. "Absolutely magnificent," she reiterated as they were halfway through a ten-year-old bottle of Château Mouton Rothschild. She had her feet up on the coffee table in front of her and had in her hand a thin, discreet Cuban cigar Will had just given her. "But I do not wish to do it often." She had been impressed beyond words by Will Honeycutt and by her own calm. With his strength at her side there in the high-stakes game of powerful men, she felt exhilarated and fearless, so unlike the refined persona of a proper Boston girl, and so caught up in a childlike giddiness, she realized later, she had never experienced in her own sad childhood.

"Wall Street tycoons celebrate with cigars," he had pronounced, then waited in such a way that it sounded very much like a challenge.

"Is that a Hamiltonian suggestion?" she had quipped, accepting the offered victory cigar.

"No doubt, he might have," he said. "But this suggestion was pure Jesse Livermore."

So there she sat now, feet propped up, wineglass and cigar in hand. Will examined the image for a long moment. "That is certainly not the world's image of Eleanor Putnam, refined Boston lady," he said.

"Well, the world had better get used to it," she said with satisfaction. She had taken a large puff and with her head back had attempted a smoke ring, but she coughed and released just a small, formless cloud. "What a disgusting habit," she said with a frown, eyeing the cigar. Her partner smiled and said nothing. Then she gave him a serious look. "You showed nerves of steel, Mr. H. You stood up to the House of Morgan."

"What circumstance dictated," he said. "Your Hyperion Fund is now over five million dollars." He paused, just a little bit tipsy, as if to absorb himself what he had just concluded.

"*Our* Hyperion Fund," she said.

"*Our* Hyperion Fund," he said. "And I fear that *our* Hyperion Fund is not anonymous anymore."

"And of your private funds? You followed suit?"

"As instructed, Miss Putnam. I sold my total holdings for the five hundred." Then he added, "As required by our agreement."

"That makes you a very wealthy man, Mr. H."

"It does indeed."

"And the Special Fund, your allowed ten percent to risk? What of that?"

Ted Honeycutt looked sheepish. "I risked," he said quickly, the ragged look of the bucket-shop veteran coming into his eyes. The Special Fund was indeed, as intended, how he had learned, he rationalized, as he looked at its erratic performance over the time they had worked together. "I am afraid I gambled and did not follow your lead."

"As allowed in our contract."

"Yes, but—"

She interrupted him. "No need to apologize, Mr. Honeycutt. You were learning valuable lessons." She paused and gave him a kind smile. "But now I wish to know the details."

At first, Will said nothing and looked down at the carpet. "I waited for one thousand."

She stared at him, letting the words sink in. "You sold at *one thousand*?"

"It was my speculator self," Will said. "I was playing a hunch."

"And that is what Alexander Hamilton would have done."

Will looked down for a moment, not sure how much to divulge. "It is what he advised."

For just an instant, a look of concern came onto her face, and Will Honeycutt, the man who heard voices, looked at her distractedly. Then a broad smile burst onto his face. "I am just joking," he said. "The decision was all Will Honeycutt, bucket-shop master." He paused and took a puff of his cigar. "Ten percent of our shares, bought at thirty-five and sold at one thousand."

"And the Special Fund is now back in the black," Eleanor said, her eyes wide.

"You could say that," her partner said. He sounded steady and grounded.

She eyed him for a moment of pure admiration, suppressing a smile. "I am delighted for you," she said. "But you have lost your bet."

"Bet?" Will said.

"The Hyperion Fund has more than doubled by year's end."

Will looked puzzled for just a moment. "I had forgotten," he said. "I have indeed lost that bet. A good year has not yet passed and you have more than doubled the Hyperion Fund."

"*We,*" Eleanor corrected him quickly. "You and I. A fateful team. It was meant to be, only one of us didn't realize it."

"*We,*" Will Honeycutt repeated, nodding.

She looked at him for a moment, considering her words. "Something has been worrying me all day," she said, handing him the article from Frank Burden's bank.

Will Honeycutt gave the paper a long look. "Oh," he said suddenly, looking sunk. He was caught. "You have found Cousin Williams. It was bound to happen."

Eleanor nodded slowly, saying nothing.

"He is your stocks and bonds man," Will said, his head down, "an inveterate one. He's quite unlike me; I guess you discovered all that."

Still she waited for more explanation, but none came. "He's brilliant with commodities and bonds," she said, quoting Frank Burden mechanically. "I already know that. Another T. Williams Honeycutt?"

"Only he calls himself Williams, rather pretentious, I always thought. You probably know that too. I was always called Ted," he added, his resignation becoming all the more obvious. "That is, before you changed me to Will." He swallowed hard. "Williams is a little older, grew up in Boston, went to Harvard and all, but lives in Chicago now. I always thought he was an arrogant bully," he added. "He's a commodities trader, a real business type." He paused and let it sink in. "A successful one."

"But where was he when I was looking?"

"Out of town. Away from Chicago, studying in Oxford or some such at the time. Now he's back."

"Studying *economic theory* at Oxford, I am to assume."

"Yes," he said, still looking sheepish. "As I said, a capitalist type through and through."

"And always was a 'capitalist type'?" she said, musing. "And you knew of him when I first found you?"

Suddenly, he stopped rambling and was quiet for a moment, pulling himself up into his new assertive persona. "Of course I knew of him," he said. "He is my cousin."

Eleanor said nothing, her mind whirring with the first inkling of the enormous misstep: that she had chosen the wrong man to fulfill the destiny of the journal. "And?" she said finally.

"He is the one you were looking for," this Will Honeycutt said. "I knew that from the beginning. He's a capitalist and has been since he was a boy, from birth. He's your man." He looked down but seemed relieved that all this was finally coming out. "I knew this day would come. I am prepared to relinquish my position and return to my life in physics research."

Eleanor looked nonplussed. "Why didn't you tell me?"

He still could not bring himself to look at her. "Because I didn't wish to tell you," he said finally. "I wanted you to choose me."

"But why, Will?"

"Because—" He was now about to become emphatic. "I just wanted it—" Another pause. "It was an emotional thing. I am not good at emotions, you know, and I wanted you to choose me. It's as plain as that. I wanted you to choose me." There was now a long silence between them; each looked into the other's eyes. "There, I said it."

"I understand," she said softly, but he was not finished.

"Well, you asked," he said without remorse or embarrassment, retaining that spark of steely resolve. Then it all came out in a burst. "I know you will marry Frank Burden, and I know you will create a perfect Boston family and become a highly respected patron of the arts, and you will be very, very good at it all, and that there is no way I could measure up to any of that. I know all that. I would not have intruded in that in any way, I promise, so you needn't have worried. I don't have much else of value in my life, and I probably was about to be bounced from my position at Harvard, half of them thinking me deranged. I just wanted to be close to you, and I must admit that it meant the world to me whilst I was there." He reached a crescendo, paused again, and looked down. "There again, I said that too!"

Eleanor stared at him for a long moment, running through her head the revelations of the past few hours. "Well," she said, stopping, allowing a long silence to settle in. "I am deeply honored, and what is done is done." And she went to think through this monumental eruption in her careful planning and strategy.

"You would like to replace me." It was more of a statement than a question. The man who had for a moment thought himself destined to be Will Honeycutt, legendary director of the Hyperion Fund, now looked down, waiting for the axe to fall.

"You did magnificently today, you know," was what he heard. "You more than proved yourself." Eleanor paused.

"But?"

"But," she said, eyeing him again with mock seriousness, "that doesn't alter the fact that there is this other T. Williams Honeycutt to consider."

"It does not," Will Honeycutt said, still not certain what was coming.

Eleanor paused and took a puff of her cigar and leaned her head back. She released one single, imperfectly formed cloud of smoke vaguely resembling a ring. Then, admiring her work for a long moment, sitting up and looking him square in the eye, she said, "From today's encounter with Wall Street, I would say that one thing has emerged as perfectly clear."

"And that is?"

"And that is . . ." She paused and leaned back again and this time released a second puff of smoke, this one a perfect ring, and she watched with the greatest satisfaction as it dissipated in the air of the hotel room. "It appears that I have chosen very much the correct T. Williams Honeycutt."

PART
TWO

11

"MOTORCARS, MR. HONEYCUTT"

leanor and Frank Burden were married in the fall of 1902, four years after she returned from Vienna and a good two years into their formal courtship. The wedding took place, as planned, in Trinity Church, and it was an important punctuating event in the Boston social year, although a little subdued since both Eleanor's and Frank's parents were gone and neither had brothers or sisters.

Perhaps the most memorable feature of the wedding ceremony itself was the fact that William James walked the bride down the aisle, and the vision of those two handsome figures in that solemn and significant ritual moment gave the feeling of nobility to the ceremony and brought tears to many eyes. That accompaniment part of the ceremony had been William James's idea actually. As the forthcoming event was being announced, a good eight months in advance, James wrote from England that if no one else had come forward he would consider it a great honor to "accompany you down the aisle," he said. William James and his brother Henry had known her parents well and had been very close to them when they were younger, before Eleanor was born. Although he had never been given such formal designation, Eleanor had always considered him her godfather, and the older man had certainly been, more than expected, a faithful observer of the major events of her life.

His letters of congratulations and encouragement during her young life had always been special to her, and the few times they had a chance to be alone together and talk in those early days had always been for her

memorable. It was he, for example, along with Eleanor's (in those days
called Weezie) headmistress Miss Hewens, who suggested that she attend
Smith College, and his letters while she was there had played a large part
in encouraging her in her pursuit of art history and music. And since her
return from Vienna, her regular meetings with him in his office in Cambridge had become a staple.

So she wrote back to her godfather in England and said that although
the long line of candidates who had asked to perform the duty would be
disappointed—there were no other candidates, actually—she would love
to have him join her in that "very short and very poignant walk to matrimony." Her lightness of expression on this matter was an attempt to mask
the weight she felt concerning the whole issue of being given away, and
how moved she was by the offer by someone of such significance in her
life. She had confidence that William James of all people knew well how
much his offer meant to her.

And Arnauld, in Vienna, recognized the event with a letter, one of
those obviously most cherished in Eleanor's lifelong collection.

> *My dear Eleanor,*
>
> *It is with the greatest sadness that I must acknowledge that I will
> not be able to be with you on your very special wedding day. I know
> that you will be surrounded by friends and admirers from all stages
> of your life, and I hope you know that I take my place among the most
> admiring of those. That the eminent William James will be repre-
> senting your family on that day is momentous. That you will be be-
> ginning the matrimonial phase of your life with great affectionate
> ceremony is fitting and proper, and all the more reason for my great
> sadness in not being able to be present. I know you will be happy on
> that day, and I can only imagine the pride with which Frank Burden
> steps forward into the honored position of your life partner. I do hope
> that you will be able to pause for just an instant and think of your
> friend in far-off Vienna who is overjoyed for you and overcome with
> emotion on this day. Someday I shall join you in Boston, and I look
> forward to that.*
>
> *Yours in affection,*
> *Arnauld*

The letter was important to Eleanor for many reasons; not the least was the fact that it was the first time, after all her efforts, that Arnauld had mentioned his intention to come to Boston.

After the wedding, Eleanor and Frank moved into her family's Acorn Street house near Louisburg Square on Beacon Hill, the house where she had been born and where she knew she was supposed to live out her full life. The young couple set about establishing a proper Boston social life, she continuing her volunteer work in a number of important charitable endeavors, and he continuing his promising career as a Boston banker. It was assumed by everyone that they would set about immediately starting a family. And indeed a little after a year following the wedding, Eleanor announced that she was pregnant, and a few months after that Susan was born, and a little more than a year and a half after that Jane followed. Eleanor, the young mother, found the raising of two bright, young daughters a fulfillment beyond anything she had anticipated, the great compensation of her marriage.

From the point of view of nearly everyone in Boston, Eleanor and Frank Burden played out their parts with a kind of perfection that brought great pleasure to those who wanted to believe that Boston was the ideal way of life, life as it should be. No one even began to suspect the secret life Eleanor lived and the remarkable success she had within it, nor the dark secret of their time together in Vienna.

After the extraordinary success with the Northern Pacific stock, she knew exactly what she and her new colleague Will Honeycutt needed to do with the Hyperion Fund monies, and she broke it to him immediately upon returning to Boston.

"Motorcars," she said when Will, newly confirmed as the Hyperion Fund's permanent associate, met her one morning in their office. "Starting tomorrow we will shift our considerable funds to motorcars, Mr. Honeycutt."

Catching the bumptious Will Honeycutt by surprise was never a good idea, she was to learn over the years. Her directive caused him to stare speechless for a moment. Then he turned suspicious. "You know about motorcars?" he said, the whole idea obviously new to him.

"No, I do not," she said distinctly, with confidence. "But you are going to."

"You are doing this for a reason," he said.

"We are doing this for our next investment."

But he would have none of it. "This is about the bucket shops. You are trying to get me out of the bucket shops." He was grimacing now. "You are worried that I am too obsessive."

Eleanor, never one to jump into an argument, paused, reflecting, herself now caught off guard. "Mr. Will Honeycutt," she said very slowly, "I have told you this before, and I repeat it now. There is much I cannot tell you, and I am sorry for that, but yours is not to question my motives. Yours is to do what I say." There was a new iciness in her tone.

Will Honeycutt, deadly serious, stood for just a moment, as if deciding his entire future. "And you are adamant about this motorcar business?"

"I am," she said.

"Very well," Will Honeycutt said curtly, sensing the discussion was over, never one for poise exactly, but poised enough in this moment to swallow whatever it was that he really wished to say. "We need to do as you wish."

"Good," Eleanor said.

"And what exactly is the appeal of motorcars?" Will asked later, calmed now, both he and Eleanor back to the flush feeling, returned to bathing in the warm glow of their success.

"They are the future, Mr. Honeycutt."

"You are certain of that?"

"I am positive," she said. "Your job will be to find a man by the name of David Dunbar Buick in Detroit, Michigan. We are going to back him." And Eleanor, who had no way of explaining to her partner the certainty of her investment intentions or the reasons for her inability to provide reasons or facts, said simply, "I just know," which was all she said whenever asked. And once she had made those intentions clear one more time, her partner had acquiesced with a resigned sigh.

Moving the Hyperion Fund monies to Detroit and the investment in motorcars was to be a perfect solution, she surmised, which would keep Will Honeycutt busy, out of town mostly, and would allow her time to concentrate on her life with Frank as a successful Boston couple.

So while Eleanor was tending to her personal and social duties, Will Honeycutt traveled alone by train to Detroit and set about his task and within a few days had progress to report and had forgotten, it seemed, any tension that had arisen between them. "Your Mr. Buick is indeed an automobile man," he said on the telephone. "He makes the new internal combustion engines in Flint, Michigan. Fascinating stuff." And Eleanor could feel that Will Honeycutt could barely hold back from telling her about the intricate workings of David Dunbar Buick's new internal combustion engines.

"Have you met him?" she asked, a bit impatiently.

"Yes," Will replied, "of course, and I have seen his engines."

"Well done, Mr. Honeycutt," said Eleanor. "I trust he is glad to hear that we intend to give him what he needs."

"Oh my, yes," Will exclaimed. "We have gotten along quite famously."

Then, apparently having gotten to know this Mr. Buick a little better, Will telegrammed his second thoughts: "Have met Buick several times. Wisdom of investments questionable."

Not really interested in finding out the specifics, Eleanor's return message was short, instructive, and to the required point. "Proceed as planned."

Upon his return to Boston, Will Honeycutt discussed with Eleanor in great detail what he found in Detroit and the surrounding area. And he became convinced that the greatest profit was to be made with investments with the ancillary products. "There is the greatest flurry of automotive energy," he said with passion. "As far as one can tell, it had all begun there because of Buick and a few others, but now things have spread well beyond him and his company. Lots of creative energy. There are all manner of subsidiary producers, wiring devices, electrical batteries, carburetors, and the like. It is very exciting. And the sparking devices," Will said. "We ought to back them."

"Sparking devices?" Eleanor repeated. "I am not familiar with them."

"They are an essential part of the engines," Will Honeycutt said. "At the top of the cylinder." He held up his fist and raised it into the palm of his other hand. "The piston pushes to the top of the cylinder and compresses the gasoline. The device connected to the electrical battery produces a spark that ignites the gasoline and drives the piston down to the bottom of the cylinder. That spark producer needs to be of the highest quality and must be part of every engine. Mr. Albert Le Champ, a Frenchman, has designed the most efficient of these devices. I have met him, he's a highly energetic fellow, and he is in need of investment. My recommendation is to back him. The returns would be manyfold."

Eleanor stared for a moment. "We are not destined for such an invest-ment, Mr. Will Honeycutt. I think you know that."

"But it is a wise one. I have met with Mr. Le Champ, and I have seen his product. It is the wisest—"

She stopped him. "We are not going to invest there, Mr. Honeycutt." And she said no more. "You have your ten percent for such gambles." She paused again. "And you can enlist your friend Jesse Livermore."

"It is not a gamble," Will said, exasperated.

"That may be. But we are not budging from our plan to back Mr. Buick."

But what gave Will pause about this man Buick, it turned out, was his reputed disorganization. "Mr. Buick seems to be of creative mind but without sufficient discipline and direction," he said to Eleanor on his re-turn home. "He is a man of too many ideas. He has been working at it for years and has only one automobile to show for his efforts. But he does need the money, and he was most enthusiastic when I told him of the Hyperion Fund's interest."

"Nonetheless," Eleanor said pointedly, "we shall back him."

Word of the possibility of investment spread as a number of people sought him out; one of them was a man named Henry M. Leland, who represented Mr. Henry Ford, another inventor in the area. "They would very much like our support," Will Honeycutt said. "Given my choice," he said, "I would have pursued this man Henry Ford. He has a fire in his eyes and the organized approach to back it up. You should see the man's plans for production."

Again unmoved, knowing well in advance from a simple journal entry what she was meant to do, Eleanor said simply, "That may be so, but we are backing Mr. Buick. You may do what you wish with your allotted ten percent. That is yours to gamble with, as intended." Again, she gave no further explanation, and Will Honeycutt knew it was pointless to argue.

"We will travel there," Eleanor said, and she told her husband, Frank Burden, that she would be visiting a Smith College friend in the Midwest.

Their trip to Detroit representing the newly empowered Hyperion Fund was a first manifestation of the style that would be serving them, she thought, for the next fifty years. They would be traveling alone to-gether and no one back home would know it. It was decided that when traveling overnight by train she would reserve a first-class sleeper compartment and that he, entirely by his own choosing, would sit up in the coach car. "It reminds me of my student days. I enjoy mixing with the other travelers," he said. "One always learns a great deal."

When they arrived at the hotel, they would engage separate rooms, sometimes in separate hotels, again, he preferring to associate with what he called "the great social mix," she preferring the peace and quiet and security of the best hotels. "We will dine separately or together," she said, "depending on our moods." On this trip, as on trips in the future, their mood and business needs usually dictated that they dine together.

When they arrived in Detroit, she found, as her associate described, a wide variety of businesses relating to the production of automobiles. Separate companies had sprung up producing items that only a few decades before had been unheard of. There were separate plants now for spark plugs and batteries and carburetors and headlights. "This is the place where automobiles are being invented," Will Honeycutt said, "piece by piece. It is extraordinary."

"Why Detroit?" Eleanor said. "Why not Cleveland or Akron or a New England city?"

"Mr. Buick," he said, "Buick and Mr. Ford. They are both from here originally."

And then as they were traveling to meet this David Dunbar Buick she had sent Will Honeycutt to find, she asked him, "Are you absolutely certain that this is our man and that there is not another somewhere in the country?"

"I know why you ask," he said, thinking of his own situation. "But I am as certain as one can be in such circumstances. My investigations turned up no other name even close. And what are the odds that there would be another associated with motorcars with the unusual combination of 'Dunbar' and 'Buick'?"

"You have a point," she said simply, not mentioning that "Williams" and "Honeycutt" seemed similarly unusual in combination.

Buoyed by the sudden infusion of funds from Boston, Mr. Buick and his company began producing automobiles, the Model 17 eventually becoming at one point the highest selling in America, one of which he had shipped to Boston, but neither Will nor Eleanor ever was seen in it. "What we wish for our fund above all else is anonymity," Eleanor declared, and Will Honeycutt at least on this point concurred.

The crisis appeared to them imminent in 1906, when rumor spread that David Dunbar Buick would be separating from his own company. Will Honeycutt returned to Michigan on an emergency trip to investigate and found the rumor to be true. The Hyperion Fund was at a decision point. "Do we stay with the departing Mr. Buick himself?" he asked, this time by telephone, "or do we stay with the company he leaves behind?"

"Oh my," Eleanor said, confronted with a contingency not covered in the journal. "That is a problem. You will have to give me time to think that through."

Moments like this were a test of her conviction, Eleanor conjectured. She knew of this challenge from the journal only in the simple mention that she would find a specific person—David Dunbar Buick—and invest in his company. Now, at this moment, she had no guidelines. What an odd circumstance that the founder and namesake would separate himself and go in his own direction. A similar departure had taken place a few years before, Will Honeycutt pointed out to her, when in 1902 Henry Ford left the company named after him. The original company went its separate way, eventually forming the Cadillac company, and Henry Ford went on to become one of the giants and Buick's main rival. So now what was she to do?

"What do you suggest?" Eleanor asked.

"I still say we should back Mr. Le Champ and his spark plugs, but if that is not a possibility, we should roll the dice," Will said.

"Then we go with the Buick *company*," she said, after only a moment's pause, "not the man."

"Intuition?" Will asked.

"Intuition," she responded confidently, this time, without guidance from the journal, having made the decision on her own.

Will Honeycutt, as director of the Hyperion Fund, arranged for all their monies to be transferred to the new Buick Motor Company, parting ways with the erratic founder David Dunbar Buick himself, who went on to pursue investments with his son, ventures that would amount to very little, especially compared to the company he had founded and now abandoned.

"Once again," Will Honeycutt said to her one day, back in Boston, as the reports from the new Buick Motor Company came in as very positive, "it appears that you have made the opportune choice."

"That one," Eleanor said with a relieved sigh, "was a major part luck."

"And what are the others?" Will asked. Eleanor did not answer.

Some years later, after David Dunbar Buick had been bought out and moved on to other projects, a man named William C. Durant led a move to form a holding company to enfold the Buick Motor Company and then acquire others in quick succession, including Oldsmobile, Cadillac, the Rapid Motor Vehicle Company of nearby Pontiac, Michigan, and Mr. Le Champ's spark plug company.

When the consolidations began, Eleanor and Will both became concerned enough that he traveled once again to Detroit to investigate. "I greatly favor consolidation," Will said on the telephone, "but I fear that this new merged company goes too far. It is too great a risk, and Jesse Livermore advises that we remove our invested funds."

"This new move is as it should be, Mr. Honeycutt," she said decisively. "We will back it."

"We are in a very dangerous position," Will Honeycutt said, objecting, as if she had not heard his advice from Jesse Livermore. "We have no means for judging the wisdom of what we are doing."

"We shall back Mr. Durant's move," she repeated, refusing to give in to the uncertainty she was feeling. "We shall let our investment ride." Things were not as they should be, she knew.

She brooded for most of an afternoon. Things had spun out of control again, way beyond anything the skimpy instructions of the Vienna journal could help with. David Dunbar Buick had failed them and had now disappeared, and Will Honeycutt was a thousand miles away, trying to make order out of their mangled investment plans. She wanted him back home in their office, comfortably in control of things, and she wanted an end to this preoccupying uncertainty and worry. So she took a deep breath and accompanied her children on their daily walk around Louisburg Square, hoping that by the time she returned to the comfort of her own parlor, a way would open up. But as she began the walk, that possibility seemed remote.

As she sat on a bench in the square, watching her children and envying the simplicity of their play, her mind began to drift back to her time in

Vienna and the conversations she had there with the man who had become the love of her life. The exercise, when she allowed it, often brought
clarity and peace of mind. All her fortunes now at sea, she could find no
solution. But as she sat, letting her mind drift, rather miraculously an
answer began to form, a way to bring all this complexity in Detroit into
alignment with the details in the Vienna journal. At first it seemed much
too simple, but as she stayed with it in her mind, the idea began to penetrate the layers of uncertainty. On her walk back home, she realized that
she had what she needed.

She was able to reach Will Honeycutt on the telephone. "What name
have they chosen?" she asked.

"Name?" he said, as if that one detail had little significance at the moment, with all that was whirring around him. "They are calling the new
conglomeration General Automotive Company."

"Unacceptable," she snapped suddenly. "Tell them we will back the
move completely, one hundred percent," she said, and then paused. "But
we insist that the name be changed."

"Those are your only instructions? Change the name?" he said. "That
is it?"

"That is what I wish," she said. "And that alone."

"And if they balk at that?" he said, thinking no doubt of the stubborn,
prideful men he was dealing with. "These are powerful men," he added,
as if she did not know this fact.

"If they do not agree, we shall pull out all our money," she said, her
confidence fully restored.

"Why?" he asked. "Why is a name of such importance?"

"It just is, Mr. Will Honeycutt. It just is."

"And what, pray tell, would that precious new name be?" he asked,
amazed once again by her sudden burst of certitude. She told him the
name, and they hung up.

At the end of the day, he cabled her. "Resistance to name change. How
important?"

"Essential," she cabled in return. "Our name, or we are out." It was, she
knew now, the only way to make things work out, to bring about agreement with the details of the journal. "Close deal and come home."

And once again Will Honeycutt knew that he had no choice in the
matter. After a long agonizing delay, he wired back, "Our name accepted."

And so, after all the twists and turns with Mr. David Dunbar Buick and his whimsies, the Hyperion Fund would become, as predestined, a major stockholder in the new combined company exactly aligned now because of her insistence on the change of name with the minimal instructions from the one line of the Vienna journal. The value of the new company was to expand—Eleanor knew from that one fateful handwritten line—tenfold between then and 1929, at which time the fund's monies were to be withdrawn to avoid another great market crash. Everything was in place.

The new combined motorcar company where the entirety of Hyperion Fund monies now rested would bear the name General Motors.

12

STEADY ROSE

I t was in 1906, during the time of her second pregnancy, that she sent Will Honeycutt to Vienna, and at the time of the culmination of that pregnancy, the birth of her second daughter, Jane, that she found Rose.

The idea of sending Will to Vienna came about because of a simple inspiration. Before the General Motors negotiations, when there was little to do with the Hyperion Fund, she approached Will. "I think it would be good for you to travel to Europe," she said.

"Still worried about the bucket shops?" he said, this time with a wry smile.

"To broaden your mind, Mr. Will Honeycutt," she said, this time returning the smile.

"Who will manage the fund," he said, "when you are in the hospital giving birth?"

"I think the birth and the fund will do well without your attentions," she said. "And there is someone I wish you to meet." The thought of encouraging a budding friendship between Will and Arnauld Esterhazy had come to her in a moment's inspiration. "Increased hormones," Dr. Ballantine had said, "often lead to flashes of inspiration."

So she set about planning a trip to Vienna for Will Honeycutt and she wrote to Arnauld, knowing that he would serve as a congenial host, hoping that the curious Will would like what he found there. The plan was successful beyond her expectations. Shortly before she went to the hospital, she received this very satisfying letter.

My dear Eleanor,

I write this letter from a table at the Café Central, in the heart of Vienna, your friend Arnauld having just left me here to my own devices. He has been the most accommodating of hosts, giving generously of his time, and when his duties at the university call, arranging for one friend or another to serve in that host role. He has introduced me to all manner of friends, poets, and philosophers. Once, he even arranged for us to be the guests of his friend Alma Mahler at her husband's performance at the opera.

One embellishment of our time here is the entry of Arnauld's cousin Miggo. He is the opposite of Arnauld in many ways, and he is forever taking us around and trying to "enhance our experience," as he says. Miggo, as you may remember, is an Esterhazy cousin, through Arnauld's aunt, son of an Italian count, and grandson of the Vanderbilts. He has three cultures, as he is proud to say, and he benefits from the best traits of all three. In private Arnauld quips that he has also the worst traits of the three—decadence, arrogance, and craftiness. But that summary, humorous as it is, slights the fact that he is absolutely great company.

Arnauld and I have discussed many times the possibility of his coming to Boston, and I have reinforced the idea that he would enjoy it there greatly, while privately wondering if any city in America could match the stimulation of what he has grown up with and become accustomed to.

Your faithful servant,
Will

As for the fateful addition of a new housekeeper, one of the reasons Eleanor was able to conduct her complicated life with such seeming grace and calm, both the public and highly secret parts, was the presence of Rose Spurgeon. She had met Rose in 1906, at the time of the birth of her second daughter, Jane. Eleanor had elected to have her children at the Boston Lying-In Hospital, the institution where she had given so much of her energy over the years. "With the common folk," Frank Burden had said of the decision.

Among the women who had given birth were those who were recovering from the loss of their child. And as Eleanor walked the halls sharing a good word and good cheer with these women, she encountered a young woman sitting in a chair by her bed doubled up in what looked like grief and pain. In talking with her, Eleanor learned that the young woman was an unwed factory worker from Fall River, one of the poor who benefited from the hospital's welfare. Her name was Rose Duffy, and having given up her baby for adoption, she had seen it whisked away from the delivery room before she could do more than hold it for an instant. "It is painful, ma'am," she said finally as Eleanor remained at her side, determined to have a conversation.

"And your people at home," Eleanor asked, "are they able to accept?"

The young woman only looked up with sad eyes. "My father will perhaps recover from it someday," she said," but right now—" She stopped and shook her head.

Eleanor noticed the young woman's careful diction and remarked on a copy of *Pride and Prejudice* beside the bed. "I read, ma'am," the young woman said. "It's my tenth time through. Dreams of a more perfect world, I fear."

"You could come to Acorn Street," Eleanor said. Mrs. Thomas, the Burdens' aged housekeeper, had recently become, as Frank said, a bit questionable of mind. "I shall need help with the baby," Eleanor said with great conviction. "If you could bear it, your services would be invaluable to me and to the household."

Rose came to work in the Burden home, caring for the infant and her two-year-old sister, and a year later took over the housekeeper role and soon after that married Tom Spurgeon, who came into the house as gardener and handyman, then responsible driver and mechanic when the Burdens acquired their first auto car.

One day, Eleanor, shortly after the wedding, asked if she and Tom might someday wish to move on. "We all shall understand if a young couple would wish to leave and start a life of their own somewhere."

Rose looked startled. "Oh, no, ma'am," Rose said with the firm determination of hers that matched well that of her mistress. "Tom and I shall never wish to leave you and Acorn Street."

So Eleanor had Rose as a permanent presence. "Steady Rose," Frank Burden called her. "We shall always have Rose."

13

"WE ARE NOT GAMBLERS"

n early 1906, when Will Honeycutt had returned from Detroit with the General Motors decision, he had expressed vociferously one objection. "I do not think it wise to have so much money tied up in this one source," he said, arguing vainly.

Eleanor listened as she always did, then delivered the message she had long known she would have to deliver. "Next year, 1907, will be a disastrous one in the stock market."

"And how, pray tell, do we know this?" Will asked.

"I just know," she said, as she always said, with no further explanation. "We shall be removing all our funds."

Long past asking what on earth she was thinking, Will Honeycutt did ask, "And where now do we put them?"

She knew she would be relying on her partner's ability to learn yet another financial complexity. Without hesitation she replied, "Chicago real estate. You must travel to Chicago at once and establish a home base for investment."

When a more thorough explanation was required, she elaborated that investments in Chicago would serve them well over the long haul, the city being one of the fastest-growing in the country and a very safe place to store funds while the stock market appeared vulnerable.

"And how do you know the stock market might be vulnerable?" Will asked.

"I just know," she said. "And now is the time to make this move. And besides," she said, "you will be closer to Detroit. We will keep some of our investments there, as they will not be affected by the market fall."

"You want out of the market," Will said, still incredulous.

"*We*," she said. "We will need to be out of the stock market as 1907 begins."

"And just when will this calamity take place?"

As with so many other events, she did not know the exact timing, just that the journal entry cited sometime in 1907 as the time for a calamitous crash. "We do not know when, Mr. Honeycutt, just sometime in the year. That is good enough for action, is it not?"

"It is," Will Honeycutt said, in total resignation. "It certainly is."

So Will Honeycutt set up a makeshift office in Chicago and from there began removing all Hyperion funds from the stock market and placing them into commercial real estate in that city, in a way that would attract as little attention as possible, the Hyperion Fund having become a significant enough player as to cause market fluctuation by any sudden investments or dramatic withdrawals.

"You will have a full year to withdraw funds discreetly and slowly," Eleanor said. "That should prevent any adverse reaction."

And as he had done so many times before, Will Honeycutt took on his new challenge with an obsessive intensity that deprived him of sleep and gave him the look of one deranged. He soon knew more about Chicago real estate than Eleanor thought possible.

On one of his visits back in Boston, Eleanor asked him, "And just what is it that you find so compelling in Chicago? Surely it cannot be simply the buying of buildings."

He looked at her with wildness in his eyes and then laughed. "I know you think me possessed," he said. "But I have found the futures market, and I must admit that I spend a good deal of time at the board of trade."

"It is like the bucket shops, I gather," Eleanor said.

"It is my new addiction, you would no doubt observe, speculating in pork bellies and wheat."

"Buying and selling?" she asked, genuinely curious.

"Yes," Will said. "There is a logic to it, all its own, and some people are good at it, instinctively, I believe you would say."

"And you are one of those who are good at it, *instinctively*."

"Yes," Will said humorously. "Yes, I am. But you don't need to worry. I have it all well within my control, and within my ten percent."

"I never worry about you, Mr. Honeycutt. I know you will always return to sanity." And she reached out and patted his arm.

"Speculation *is* my sanity," he said. "I read the ticker tape and I take my notes and the patterns always appear to me. Now I follow the futures market."

"I do not understand it, for sure, but I think it is where your genius lies," she said. "I do not understand, and I can live with that."

"To the world, I know, it appears to be a great game," Will said, "but actually it is science, just very fast-moving science."

"My talents are not in the sciences," Eleanor said, "but I know we must be out of the market for 1907."

"And I know my assignment," Will said. "Move the Hyperion monies to real estate." Then he stopped and looked straight at her. "But for the life of me I do not know where *your* genius lies." And then, before she could respond, he said, "I truly do not." In the long silence that followed, Eleanor found herself wondering where indeed her true talents did lie. Certainly not in the intricacies of managing a monetary fund, a far cry from the music and literature that had consumed her interests just a few years before.

But the moment passed, and she felt Will Honeycutt look away. "You are not going to tell me what really drives this fierce purpose in your life," he said, "are you?"

"I can't, Will," she said.

"That's all right," Will Honeycutt concluded. "I can live with that."

About six months into what Will Honeycutt had begun to call their "Chicago strategy," the buying up of downtown commercial properties as they became available, he was evaluating their position. He enjoyed the life of a prudent investor in real estate, but the life lacked the excitement of watching stocks rise and fall. He came to Eleanor with a proposal. "I have been talking with Jesse Livermore," he began.

She had grown to expect something dramatic when the conversation began with that preamble. "Yes?" she said, fully attentive. "And what has the esteemed Mr. Livermore said?"

"I have been so convincing in telling him my strong hunch that next year there will be a collapse that he has already devised a set of preconditions for instability, as he calls them. He insists that the conditions are indeed in place, and a collapse of the markets is indeed a possibility, perhaps even likely. He suggests a strategy."

"And what does your Mr. Livermore recommend that we do with our money?"

"Not getting out, but selling short," Will Honeycutt said succinctly. "Jesse agrees now that the market is ripe for a fall. He has already begun plans for borrowing large amounts of stock on margin, with a promise to pay back at the going rate on January 1, 1908, one year after the purchase and after the crash. I think we ought to follow suit. One borrows when the stock is riding high and then pays it back when the stock is considerably lowered in value."

"And what if the market does not collapse and continues to boom?"

"Then the stock will be *called*, as they say, and Jesse Livermore will lose his shirt." Will Honeycutt paused and looked at her for a long appraising moment. "But that will not happen."

"How do you know?" Eleanor asked pointedly, forgetting perhaps how this whole turn began.

For a moment, Will Honeycutt stared in consternation, as if not believing the question. "But it was you who declared that it will collapse in 1907."

"You are correct. I have predicted that."

"And when will this collapse happen?"

"I do not know exactly. I only know that it will collapse, within the year 1907. And we shall be prepared."

"And we should borrow against that fact."

Eleanor sat up with an erect posture that signaled the end of the discussion. "We shall not. We are not gamblers, Mr. Honeycutt. We shall not be engaging in gamblers' practices. We shall not benefit from the misery of others." She did not bother to add that he had his ten percent to do with what he wished. That was his to deduce.

And so Will Honeycutt proceeded with the Chicago strategy and by the first months of 1907, the Hyperion Fund had no money remaining in the stock market. In its place, the fund now owned significant holdings in downtown Chicago, where Will Honeycutt had opened a small office.

"There is nothing to do now but wait," he said to Eleanor.

As 1907 arrived, there was general agreement in the financial world that the country was sinking into financial recession, a condition that had concerned Frank Burden all year. "Now is not the time to do anything venturesome," he told Eleanor one evening at dinner when she asked how his bank intended to proceed. "We shall hold tight," he said, *hold tight* being a favored phrase of his.

"He has nothing to worry about," Will Honeycutt said. "Boston banks are too conservative to speculate."

It was not so with some of the biggest New York banks, Knickerbocker Trust being the most extreme. Most of the year 1907 passed without incident, and Will Honeycutt began to wonder aloud if perhaps the whole elaborate maneuver with Chicago real estate might have been a colossal waste of their time.

"Have patience, Mr. Honeycutt," she said, her confidence never faltering. "We shall see."

Then in October the wildness began when a group of speculators tried to corner the market in a Montana copper mining company.

"We have seen that before," Eleanor said to Will Honeycutt, and they both agreed they were glad not to be in the middle of this one. By late October, a full-fledged panic ensued, and people all over the country were withdrawing their savings from banks large and small. Eleanor watched Frank's reactions each morning as he read the newspapers. "What is happening?" she said.

"It is complicated," Frank said. "I cannot explain, but Knickerbocker bank has made a colossal mistake, and it is not good. Boston banks would never do that."

Then a few mornings later, he announced, "The crisis is over; Mr. Morgan has stepped in once again, as he did in the 1890s. He has gotten all the powerful financiers together, it seems, and forced an elaborate buyout, arranging for enough money to be pumped into the banks to keep them afloat. It will take time," he concluded, "but we will survive."

By early 1908, Frank's words bore out, and the crisis seemed past. In the meantime, as soon as the stock prices tumbled, Jesse Livermore was able to pay off his huge borrowings for next to nothing, and he made a fortune, as well as winning a reputation as the man who predicted the Crash of 1907. No one ever suspected the role Eleanor and the Hyperion Fund had played in his sensational and seemingly clairvoyant strategy.

"How did Jesse Livermore know what was coming?" Eleanor asked Will Honeycutt one morning.

"I told him," Will said, "and he believed me." Then he stared at her hard.

"And did you follow his lead and sell short with your own shares?" They both knew that was against the rules. Will had promised in the beginning to keep his own holdings within the Hyperion Fund, to gamble with only his ten percent.

"I did."

"And you made a great deal of money?"

"I did." He stared for a moment, then he asked point-blank, "How did you know?"

"I just did," she said quickly. "I cannot say that I understand you, but I did know that." And this time Will Honeycutt looked visibly shaken. "And that will not happen again, Mr. Honeycutt. You will not gamble with your own future again. Can I have your word on that?"

Will Honeycutt looked defiant for a moment, but remained silent, then said finally, "You can." And that was that.

"And now," Eleanor said again quickly, breaking the spell, "we have our work to do. We can begin reinvesting our Chicago money. We shall continue with motorcars. Again, it will be exclusively the new General Motors."

"Shouldn't we just leave it in Chicago?" Will said, very comfortable with the new investment skills he had acquired.

"No," she said, "there is greater margin back in General Motors."

And then after the crash of 1907 had run its course, both Eleanor and Will Honeycutt marveled, as did the whole country, at the omnipotence of Mr. J. P. Morgan. "I shall meet that man someday," Eleanor said seriously, and Will Honeycutt shook his head again.

"I am sure you will," he said.

"You will help me," she said. She made no mention that the meeting, one she knew she was destined to arrange, would concern not investments but Eleanor's foreknowledge of the fate of Mr. Morgan's great ship the *Titanic*.

14

DR. HALL'S CONFERENCE

t was in 1906 that, sensing the seriousness of his heart condition, Eleanor decided to share with William James the first of her many secrets. "There is something I wish to tell you," she said on one of their walks along the Charles River near Harvard.

"I am always glad for that," he said.

"It concerns the book *City of Music*," she said. "Jonathan Trumpp is a nom de plume."

"I gathered," James said. "An artistic young man not far removed from my brother's crowd perhaps, although I was never able to discover who it might be."

"Mr. Trumpp is a young woman."

The great professor looked perplexed as if he, the one who considered every possibility, had not considered that possibility. "A young woman?" he repeated. "And just how would you know such a thing?"

"A young woman," she said, "and one you know quite well." She gazed out at the river until the message sank in.

"Oh my," he said, with something like a gasp.

"I'm afraid so," she said. "My nom de plume."

"Goodness," the great man said. "That is a matter for some consideration."

"I know," she said with a soft smile. "It takes some getting used to, even for me, I must admit, and after all this time. It began when I was in my last year at Smith. I had been to hear the New York Philharmonic and had penned a critique to the *New York Times*. I used the name of the janitor at our house." William James shook his head slowly. "My letter was published, and the editors asked for more, which I wrote, two or three more pieces, using the same pen name. Then, after graduation my dear headmistress Miss Hewens, who knew of Mr. Trumpp's true identity, suggested I travel to Vienna and write more. You were one who counseled that, I believe."

He smiled warmly and nodded his agreement. "I do remember that part," he said. "I thought it an excellent idea, to give you the breadth of experience. But I did not know of your writing."

"I had quite a moving experience there in Vienna, and *City of Music* was the resultant work."

William James gazed at her, taking in the import of what he had just learned. "This book caused quite a stir," he said. "It is a poignant account of that city's magical powers." He smiled at the thought, then wrinkled his brow. "And its vulnerability," he added. "And I believe it is credited for much of Gustav Mahler's initial reputation in this country. A considerable reputation."

"Yes." She nodded. "He has changed how people look at music, I believe."

"Well, well," he said, beaming at her. "I enjoyed it the first time I read it, but I shall reread it with greater care. And with, I must admit, considerable pride," he added, still shaking his head in disbelief, piecing it all together. "And that is why you went to Vienna in the first place," he said.

"My dear El," the professor said to her one morning shortly after that, "you have introduced me to the most interesting ideas and people." He gazed at her again in amazement. "Since your sojourn in Vienna, you have changed dramatically. You seem to have developed a maturity beyond your years." He searched for the word. "A gravity, as if you returned with some sort of mission. It has appeared that you have seen the world and know what is important and what is not."

"Do you think I have become—" She paused, searching for the word. "Do you think I have become *worldly*?" she said.

He thought for a moment on the word. "Yes, *worldly* would be one way to describe the change I noticed, in the best sense, I would add," he reassured her.

"My experience in Vienna was all-consuming. I became swept up in a situation that was both wonderful and horrible. I gave all to it and held back nothing. It has come at some price, I fear." It was the first time that she had revealed to anyone some of the darker parts of this newfound worldliness.

"When you returned, you were different," he said, a look of concern on his face.

"It is an old story, you know: the loss of innocence. Haven't you observed that as a universal theme in literature?"

"That was my brother," Dr. James said. "It was Henry who made that observation that the central theme in all world literature is the loss of innocence." He gave her a look of genuine concern. "I suppose we ought to talk more about that," he said.

"Perhaps we shall," she said. "There is more I have to tell you."

"As have I to tell you," he said with a look of seriousness.

It was also on another of their long walks that he mentioned his friend Stanley Hall's plans for a conference in 1909. "I would like to talk with Dr. Hall about that," she said with an urgency that surprised William James. "I would like to make certain that he invites Sigmund Freud."

Regardless of any troubling memories of her encounters with Sigmund Freud in Vienna, she knew the importance of his ideas. She knew from the journal the arrangements she needed to make in order for him to be introduced in America, and she knew it was her lot to pursue those moves with maximum effort and enthusiasm.

"Dr. Freud's ideas are timely right now," she said to William James. "There is something of vital importance in his talking cure, something the world needs."

"Unconscious motivations," her mentor said with a burst. "Dr. Freud's talking cure is the key to understanding the unconscious mind. We have all heard much about him and his young colleague Carl Jung. Perhaps at Stanley's conference we could meet them."

When the original Austrian editions of his *Interpretation of Dreams* had arrived some years before, sent from Vienna by her friend Ernst

Kleist, she had given two to Dr. James, knowing he would find some appropriate use for the extra copy, and the recipient had been G. Stanley Hall, a former student of James's who had been founding president at Clark University in Worcester, Massachusetts. And Dr. James had conveyed to her how grateful Dr. Hall was for the gift. "He has found much to be impressed with," James said.

Then, some weeks later, when Eleanor heard how Dr. Hall had followed up with correspondences to the Viennese doctor, she said to Dr. James, "I wish to meet him. I think we have much to talk about." So Professor James paved the way for the visit by informing his former student and old friend Stanley Hall in Worcester of Eleanor's exposure to Sigmund Freud's ideas on her trip to Vienna.

"You are unusually well informed, Mrs. Burden," the famously brilliant Hall said to her in that first conversation about psychology and Sigmund Freud.

"Psychology is one of my keen interests."

"Eleanor met Sigmund Freud when she was in Vienna in 1897," James added proudly.

"I am impressed," Hall said. "And I think you will appreciate this." He reached into a drawer in his desk and produced a paper-bound book, its white cover intact, although extremely well-worn and browned with use and age. "This is a most prized possession." He ran a hand over the cover. "It is a copy of 'the White Book,' the now very rare translation of *The Interpretation of Dreams,* Freud's most important exploration of the unconscious mind. It was found in a book dealer's shop and bought for a handsome sum. It is a gift from one of my students. These English translations have become collectors' items. You can see how tattered it is."

"I am familiar with the book," Eleanor said, her surprise barely noticeable. "I am impressed that you possess such a copy."

Dr. James took the book and turned it over in his hands before passing it to Eleanor, who took the volume and also turned it over a number of times, examining it with care, before handing it back to Dr. Hall, letting on nothing of her intimate knowledge of the volume's origins.

"Dr. Freud has set us on a new course," Dr. James said.

"And you find that course an important one?" she said.

"Oh my, yes," Dr. Hall said, and Dr. James nodded.

Then, after a respectful silence, Eleanor added, "You are about to celebrate a great anniversary of this university, I believe." Dr. James had already mentioned that Hall was thinking of putting together a conference to mark the twentieth anniversary of the founding of Clark's graduate school in 1889. "You could invite Professor Freud here as a commemoration."

"Oh, goodness, I fear we do not have sufficient funds for such a grand idea."

"That can be remedied," she said with remarkable forthrightness. "I know of people with funds who would be interested in underwriting the project."

"How interesting," Dr. Hall said with a politely dismissive tone, until he saw the look of seriousness on James's face and the earnestness in Eleanor's. "What degree of underwriting?" he said.

"Whatever is needed," she said. "It would be the conference of your greatest imaginings. Completely underwritten."

Stanley Hall was silent for a long moment. "Dr. Freud and his colleagues from Europe," Eleanor continued, confident with the full weight of the Hyperion Fund behind her, "and those you think appropriate from this country." She paused as Hall only stammered, and then looked over at Dr. James, who simply nodded, with a suppressed smile of pride. "This conference will be of major significance in bringing this new and deeply important subject of psychoanalysis and exploration of the unconscious mind to the American public and thus to the world," Eleanor said in conclusion. She spoke now with such authority that it took most of the air out of the room. "The gift would be commensurately significant and absolutely anonymous."

Both men sat in silence for a moment, surprised by such words from this unassuming young woman. Hall pulled himself together enough to speak. "I would be interested in exploring this subject with your sources," he said quietly, not a man accustomed to modesty.

"It will be arranged," Eleanor said. "Dr. James will see to that."

In the following months Eleanor traveled to Worcester by herself, to meet again with Dr. Hall. "Is Dr. Freud able to come?" she asked, and learned that Dr. Freud had declined, saying that a trip was too extravagant, and too much of a financial burden on himself and on his hosts.

"Please write him back and explain that all expenses will be covered in total, plus handsome honorariums for him and his colleagues. His presence at this conference is of the utmost importance to this proposed event and to the American psychological community." Dr. Hall did not speak. "Do you doubt my sincerity on this?" Eleanor said. "You have received the funds you need so far, I assume."

"I have indeed," he said quickly, having good reason to take her at her word since he had already received two large checks from the Hyperion Fund. "I shall write Dr. Freud and do whatever persuading is necessary."

15

MAHLER

n meeting Stanley Hall, Eleanor had initiated the first of the great instigations required by the Vienna journal. The second had been the mandate to bring Gustav Mahler to New York, one that had started with the popularity of the pseudonymous book *City of Music*. She had gone to Heinrich Conried, the director of the Metropolitan Opera, and made the offer, and he had, like Dr. Hall, been eager to receive the support.

"I will arrange for a gift to make it happen," she said. "Of course it will remain anonymous."

"People in New York are calling for this," the flamboyant director said to her. "The man has become quite the rage, because of that book." Then he reflected for a moment. "And what is the size of this offer you can arrange?"

And again, Eleanor, well accustomed to others' difficulty in believing that she could guarantee such things, said, "Whatever your needs. My source wishes Herr Mahler to come to New York. That is the intention." And she removed from her purse a check, which she handed to the director. He took the check, eyed it suspiciously, and then looked again.

"Will that suffice for starters?" Eleanor said.

"Yes," Mr. Conried said. "This will do quite well for starters."

"And you understand that there will be more to follow, considering your needs in persuading Herr Mahler and his wife to come to your company?"

The director nodded. "Yes, I understand this," he said.

Heinrich Conried's offer to come to New York arrived in Vienna at a most crucial moment, it turned out, just as Mahler was experiencing an intense controversy and vitriolic anti-Semitic attack. So, as Conried suspected, the timing was opportune, and, the funding secured, a deal was struck.

When the Mahlers first arrived in late December 1907, Eleanor had visited Arnauld's friend Alma in the couple's New York hotel room and had welcomed her, when her husband was off touring his new facilities. Recalling their first meeting in 1897, the two women rekindled their friendship, and they rediscovered an immediate rapport, with much affectionate talk of Arnauld. Alma had just lost her daughter, and Eleanor was able to be very comforting. Eleanor had expressed her hope that the couple would come to Boston and stay on Acorn Street. Alma had said graciously that she did not know the schedule that had been laid out for them in this new land.

One can only imagine what Eleanor experienced only a few weeks later, after all she had been through, when she actually heard her first Mahler performance in New York. How she must have been stunned when she first heard what was to be on the schedule in that first season, the opera she had last heard in Vienna ten years earlier, in the heart of her intensely emotional time.

"It is to be Wagner's *Tristan and Isolde*," she told Rose Spurgeon, excusing her second trip to New York in as many weeks. "I have deep feelings about that opera," she said without explaining. "I don't know if I can bear it."

Rose, who had become indispensable to the household and was becoming the closest Eleanor had now to a true soul mate, offered to help. "I could accompany you, ma'am," she said, and Eleanor thanked her for the kindness but said she was up to going it alone. Rose, who knew nothing of what had happened in Vienna, had come to know much about her mistress's heart.

The performance, Mahler's American debut, was to be the night of January 1, the dawning of 1908. She had arranged, with Rose's help, to be alone and away, which was not easy since it was New Year's, but she did indeed get herself onto the train and into the city, amid all the celebration. Mr. Conried had seen to it that she had been given a ticket in a discreet position in the fifteenth row, and she sat by herself and watched breathlessly as the energetic conductor entered, acknowledged the applause, took his position, raised his baton, and signaled the commencement of the powerful overture. Later, she admitted to Rose that it had been one of the most difficult and most powerful moments of her life. "Someday, I shall tell you about it, Rose," she said. "It is music of a whole new order for me, and Herr Mahler conducting is something to behold."

Then, it was not until a year later, during Mahler's second season in America, that she first heard one of his symphonies, with or without his conducting. The actual selection was Mahler's first, the one she had seen in score form in 1896, the spring of her senior year, the introduction that had launched her remarkable story, but she had never actually *heard* the music. A friend had visited Budapest and heard the exciting young conductor and had arranged to have a complete score brought back to the Smith College music department. Weezie Putnam had sat with it for hours following the cello part and trying to hear in her head how the whole piece sounded with a full orchestra.

It was from this experience that she wrote her critique of the New York Philharmonic that the *New York Times* published under the pseudonym she had invented from the name of the dormitory janitor Johnny Trumpp, and it was from the publication of that article and the subsequent invitation from the *Times* to keep writing that the idea of her going to Vienna had sprung.

Her Vienna sojourn had begun later the next year, 1897, after her graduation, when she had gone there to write something of significance about music and to meet and hear this new conductor who had recently moved from Budapest. She did in fact attend a performance of Mahler conducting Wagner's *Tristan and Isolde* at the Vienna opera with the man she met there who changed her life forever. For years, she thought that she would never be able to attend a similar musical event, and she avoided Wagner whenever played by the Boston Symphony.

And so, here she was years later, during Mahler's first visit to Boston, a visit she had herself made possible, hosting the Mahlers, as she had offered, at Acorn Street. Now she was to hear for the first time the symphony that had started it all, and she wished to experience it alone, not certain what her reaction would be, but she knew she would be sitting beside her husband, Frank, of course, among the Boston Symphony's major donors, all of whom she knew well.

She watched the energetic conductor enter once again; take applause that seemed even greater than in New York, this time in her native city; and then rise to the podium, lift his baton, and pause. Her heart stopped. Then the first strains of this symphony she knew well in theory filled the air of the symphony hall she had known since childhood. She fought to show no emotion as the music transported her, whether she wished it or not, back to an unimaginable place, back again to that city that had filled so many of her dreams and back to that moment of utter fulfillment of a love she had never known before and would not know again.

Of course neither Mahler nor Alma ever knew that it was her Hyperion Fund that had caused the invitation in the first place. That gift would remain forever anonymous. Always, if Gustav Mahler was aware of her significance at all, he saw her as a respected patron of the Boston music scene, one he always met with the beneficent smile he used for supporters. She heard him conduct a few more times over the years of his visits.

Ironically, Arnauld met up with the Mahlers only once during his first year in Boston, as the great conductor's last season was in the winter of 1910 and 1911, Arnauld's first in America. He gave what was to be his last performance at Carnegie Hall on February 21, 1911, an event Arnauld regretted missing due to obligations of his new teaching role, not realizing the event's significance.

Mahler returned home shortly after that concert, in April. More gravely ill than people in New York or Boston realized, he died in Vienna on May 18, 1911.

16

PUTNAM CAMP

he Stanley Hall offer came to fruition in the early fall of 1909, with Sigmund Freud's arrival in America, as planned. He and Carl Jung landed in New York on the German steamship *George Washington* and immersed themselves in the life of the city. It is rumored that Freud said to his young disciple as the ship entered New York Harbor, "If the Americans had any idea of the sexual underpinnings to the ideas we are bringing with us, we would not be permitted to disembark."

It was to be the first and last visit to America by the famous Viennese doctor, who would claim later that he had hated his time there. But it was to be the first of many American visits for the younger Dr. Jung, and many Americans traveled to Zurich over the years to seek his counsel.

At the time of the visit of the two European psychologists, William James was ill and limited in his mobility, but he attended the Clark University lectures with enthusiasm, listening with especial attentiveness to Freud's carefully chosen words and responding encouragingly. By 1909, William James was well established as the most prominent of American pioneers in psychology, the one at the conference everyone had traveled to see, the one whom everyone wanted to impress. His few conversations with Freud were brief and weighty, but those with Jung were more animated, and it was easy to see from the tall, young Swiss doctor's face that he took the attention as a deeply affecting compliment.

After two days at the Worcester conference, his diminished energies spent, James was ready to return home. Sigmund Freud accompanied him on his walk to the railroad station, and on the way James was stopped suddenly with debilitating chest pains and handed his companion the bag he was carrying, asking Freud to go ahead without him, offering that he would catch up as soon as the attack of angina passed. Freud commented later on the remarkably unruffled manner in which the older man handled the serious situation. "It is my hope that I can handle my own end time, when it comes, with the same mature dispatch."

From the start Eleanor knew she was going to be reintroduced to Sigmund Freud, whom she had met in Vienna ten years before, and introduced for the first time to the young Swiss physician, who was by coincidence exactly her age. She was greatly looking forward to the opportunity. It was clear to her even before it occurred that the first meeting would be enjoyable, but what was not clear from the beginning was that there was to be an immediate and vibrant attraction between these two magnetic personalities.

At that time, Carl Jung found himself strongly affiliated with the brilliant Dr. Freud, so much so that few observers knew where Dr. Freud ended and Dr. Jung began, the father-and-son analogy obvious to everyone who saw the two together or knew of their correspondence. Even though the younger man had already developed for himself a strong reputation in Zurich, Jung had fallen under the sway of Freud and his Vienna movement, and Freud had chosen him to head the newly formed International Psychoanalytic Association, the vehicle by which Freud expected the study of the unconscious to spread, precisely according to his directions.

Nineteen years apart in age, Jung and Freud had met in 1906, when the younger man sent Freud his book about word associations. Their first conversation, one that according to legend had lasted over fifteen hours, proved a sign of an intense bond. For a period of six years, Freud considered the immensely talented and energetic Jung his heir apparent, and the two of them shared a strong belief in the power of the unconscious mind and its effect on everyday life.

From the beginning of their relationship, it was clear to everyone in the movement that Freud was the patriarch and Jung was to be his disciple, a perception the younger man tolerated willingly but at which he quite obviously chafed a bit. And as close as the two German-speaking doctors were there were always signs of tension, including a number of times when Freud actually accused Jung of wanting him dead and out of the way, citing the ancient Greek myths in which sons killed their fathers.

From the first moment of their arrival in America, Jung was in no way overshadowed, at least in Eleanor's mind, by the older Freud. On his own Jung was tall and lean and energetic, and he took her hand and held it for just a moment longer than customary, looking straight into her eyes with an intensity of focus that would bind them for the next fifty years.

During the conference, she had stood as much as she could in the background, asking Dr. Hall to keep her significant role anonymous. It was not until the group had moved to Putnam Camp, Eleanor's family retreat in the Adirondacks, that she came forward.

In the days following the conference, at the invitation of Eleanor's older cousin James Jackson Putnam, a Harvard colleague of William James, the eminent group had taken up a few days' residence in the guesthouses at the family camp, which Eleanor knew well and where she had been an eager participant during the summers of her childhood and adolescence.

The two visitors traveled by train and stayed in a hotel on Lake Placid the night before, then were transported by horse-drawn carriage along the remote road to Keene Valley and the camp. Quite according to character Dr. Freud was reserved about the whole experience, and Jung was exuberant.

"To get to the remote family camp," Putnam had warned, "you will be subjected to a long carriage ride from the ramshackle hotel at Lake Placid through splendid Adirondack wilderness. I think you will find the experience an exhilarating one."

And those who knew the two visitors well could have predicted their separate reactions. It was not difficult to call up the image of diminutive, soberly outfitted, fifty-three-year-old Sigmund Freud rattling along in a two-horse buggy over a pitted dirt road into the heart of the American wilderness, fretting about whether he'd brought the right walking shoes or wondering about how he would manage his rustic toiletries. Freud, who was temperamental and predisposed to dislike things American, would have cast a skeptical eye on the surroundings, unfit, it would seem, for the work ahead. Jung, on the other hand, famously emotive and expansive, would most likely have been awed.

How could the exuberant Jung not love the American grandeur of scale? It was closer to his own personality. He must have relished the whole scene. In fact, the whole adventure to the American Northeast carried for Jung delightful overtones of the Wild West fantasies of his youth. When they arrived at the camp, Freud, again in keeping with his character, was reserved and cautious, and the younger doctor was effusive in describing the vastness of American scenery and potential he had just absorbed in the long carriage ride.

The camp was like nothing the two Europeans had ever seen before. The participants, most all relatives of the founders, dressed in Alpine costume, the men in lederhosen and the women in dirndls. Upon the two European guests' arrival, one extroverted and self-possessed Putnam child challenged them to a game of tetherball. Both men were delighted with what they described later as "the distinctly American scene."

The first night at dinner in the communal lodge, Eleanor had allowed herself to be introduced, and she was not certain that Dr. Freud recalled their encounter ten years earlier. She made no mention of it, and he did not seem to take any special notice. During the evening she noticed the young Swiss professor's attentions to her. After dinner, after her two young daughters had been taken off to bed by an older cousin as was camp custom, it was Jung who approached with the proposal. "You are the authority on the wilderness trails in this region, I have heard, Mrs. Burden."

"I don't know about being an authority, but I have been coming here since I was a little girl." Putnam Camp and the Adirondack wilderness had been the solace of her childhood after her mother died and she was left alone with her severe aunt Prudence and her grieving father Joshua Putnam. Invited to the camp where her overly serious father and aunt never came, she could hike and romp about with cousins of all ages. Long walks on the trails with their many stream crossings were part of her cherished summer routine.

"Perhaps you will serve as our guide tomorrow. Dr. Freud is an avid hiker, as am I. We would relish being escorted by one who knows the way." It was the young doctor at his most charming.

"There are others who know the terrain better than I," Eleanor said. "But I would be honored to serve as your guide."

The next morning, Eleanor sat at a breakfast table some distance from the two visiting doctors, and she took great delight in seeing them dive into the rich offerings of eggs, bacon, biscuits, and the pancakes that were a camp specialty. Afterward, when they met outside the dining hall, ready to depart, Jung caught Eleanor with a surprise.

"I'm afraid Dr. Freud has been stricken with a stomach ailment and will not be able to join us."

The announcement came suddenly, at a time when Eleanor could not modify the day's plan, no matter how uneasy she felt. The tall, confident Dr. Jung allowed his robust enthusiasm to carry the decision. "I do not think that the good doctor's incapacity will dampen our appreciation of a day in the mountains. What do you think?"

"I think we should carry on," she said, perhaps too hastily and against what would have been thought at home as better judgment. And so that is how the two of them ended up spending the afternoon alone together in the Adirondacks wilderness.

Dr. Freud had indeed missed some of the strenuous parts of the Putnam Camp visit, having been famously indisposed, some stomach ailment he blamed on American food. Since she was the one quite familiar with the mountainscape, Eleanor chose the more strenuous course, but also the one that left the two hikers quite alone, which, considering the young doctor's demeanor and their obvious attraction to each other, Eleanor recognized only afterward as potentially dangerous. It was, as expected, on that long arduous walk in the New York wilds, far away from the other guests, that the attraction became manifest, and the potential danger heightened.

17

A ROMANTIC IDYLL

ot giving much thought to the fact that now the two hikers would be alone together and how that might be perceived, Eleanor and her guest charged off, following the course of the brook bordering one side of camp up a hill, straight into what Jung called "a northern primeval forest." It didn't take long for the guest to realize he had entered a whole new way of hiking, with a whole new way of leading and being led, the Putnam way. Again, without much thought, Eleanor was simply modeling what uncles and aunts and cousins had modeled before, entering the expansive wilderness of their family camp with gusto and total commitment of personal energy. From earliest girlhood, she remembered one lederhosen-clad elder or another bursting forth with, "Follow me," and striding up some steep path to a waterfall or a meadow she had not seen before. "Look at this beauty," she would hear from earliest age, and look around in wonder at what family heritage had caused to be her own.

Carl Jung seemed overcome with the joy of being out in the American vastness, and at such a pace, with such a vibrant woman. He had been effusive ever since stepping off the train at the Lake Placid railway station, the scale of the country's wilderness having been in his imagination from childhood, this "Wild West." Now actually finding himself in the center of it made him explode with appreciation, even while finding himself catching his breath.

"Look at this," he would say, waving his arms out at the magnificent pines and shrubs he saw all around. At one point they startled a pair of deer from a small meadow, and at another they saw a bald eagle off in the distance. "This is everything one would hope for," he said. Eleanor found herself absorbing his enthusiasm with a vicarious delight.

Rain had been falling intermittently for days, with wind still lightly gusting as they scrambled along narrow trails, over tree roots and black mire, and scaled a series of rude wooden ladders propped against boulders.

"I love showing all this off," Eleanor said at one of their infrequent pauses along the familiar trail.

"It is a unique opportunity," the energetic Jung said, catching his breath. "A unique opportunity of becoming acquainted with the utter wildness of this formidable landscape."

Always ahead of him the vision of Eleanor, spry and cheerful, skipping forward in her long hiking skirt, expounding on the natural histories of their surroundings without a pause for breath, filled him with energy of his own.

"I used to come here as a girl," she said. "It was my salvation." She rattled off the names of flora and fauna and the mountain peaks as if she had been an Adirondack mountain tour guide all her life. They struggled up one last slope to reach finally a cliff edge where Eleanor announced, "Here it is, the view I wanted so much for you to see."

And the Swiss doctor looked out at nothing but further layers of thick foliage, huge moss-covered boulders, and tall trees with endless other chains of remote, seemingly uninhabited mountains beyond mountains, stretching off to infinity, or at least to Canada.

"A wild glacial landscape," he exclaimed. "Virgin forest as far as the eye can see." And he took in also the image of the woman beside him, one that stayed with him indelibly for the next fifty years. "A breathtaking life force," he concluded later on, giving the captivation of this first impression considerable thought.

᠙

The skies cleared and the wind stopped as if by command as they sat beside a stream and watched small trout darting about in a clear pool. Eleanor could not remember feeling so free or so animated. And further along, on a grassy flat beside another pool, she signaled that they would stop and sit again.

"I am sorry that your friend Dr. Freud is not seeing this," Eleanor said, wondering how it might affect his dour nature. "I gather that he is something of a city dweller."

"Actually, Dr. Freud loves his vacations in the mountains around Vienna," Jung said. "His children find him hard to keep up with."

"He seems not terribly fond of our mountains."

"Oh, he finds much to like here. He is not feeling at his best—stomach ailments, you know. It is just that he is by nature a little cautious in his expression."

"A caution that you do not seem to share," Eleanor said with a smile.

"Dr. Freud finds me a bit unrestrained."

"A little less restraint would be good for all of us," Eleanor said, noticing her own comfort with this conversation. "I think Dr. James finds Dr. Freud a bit rigid and serious."

"He seemed very pleased at meeting him."

"Oh, yes. He believes Dr. Freud's influence very significant and his lectures historic. He came to the conference especially to hear Dr. Freud's ideas, and still—" She paused.

"He was not as impressed as he wanted to be?"

"Perhaps not as much as he expected to be. Dr. James found the lectures a little dry and mechanical. But he has said many times that he has no doubt that they will become the cornerstone of the new movement in psychology, here and in Europe, and that Dr. Freud will be thought of as one of the great innovators of the twentieth century."

"Is that a prophecy?"

Eleanor laughed. "Oh my, I have been presumptuous in speaking for Dr. James."

"And of my lectures?"

"You too will have your appeal, but perhaps after—" She stopped herself.

"After?" he said without taking any form of offense.

Eleanor looked down. "I didn't mean to be judgmental."

"No, no," Jung interrupted. "I understand, and it has been said before. After I separate my ideas from Dr. Freud's influence?"

Eleanor looked uncomfortable for just a moment, as if she had said too much. "Oh, I hope I have not been too forward. I did not mean to imply—"

He cut her off again. "You seem to have a very authoritative perspective on Dr. James, Mrs. Burden. And on the future."

"Oh goodness," she said. "I don't mean to be all that. I am certainly sorry if I have been inappropriate."

"Oh, no, it is quite appropriate. I enjoy the frankness. Dr. Freud and I have been very close. On this trip alone we will spend seven weeks together. And yet we do indeed have our differences. Ones that Dr. Freud feels uncomfortable with, I fear. We agree on most matters, you realize. It is just that there exist some fundamental disagreements, ones we have not entirely worked out."

"And what are those?"

"One superficial matter. In his treatment, for instance, Dr. Freud's patients lie on a couch while he sits behind them silently, out of sight. I prefer a face-to-face method on chairs placed close together, more a dialogue between two interesting people."

"And how is that so different?" Eleanor said.

"Dr. Freud believes the physician should intrude in no way on his patients' free flow of thoughts. That distance is very important to him."

"And you?"

"I do not wish to lose any facial expressions or physical manifestations." Jung laughed. "I suppose you could say I cannot help myself."

Even now in their conversation beside an Adirondack stream Eleanor could see that more passionate style at work, the doctor's eyes studying her face, observing inflections in her voice, drawing her into the conversation with the intensity of those eyes. Dr. Freud she knew to be far more detached and objective.

"And there is a problem with that personal approach?" she asked.

"Dr. Freud would tell you that I contaminate the process," Jung said, then laughed again.

"I think Dr. James would have more sympathy with your methods."

"I am gratified to hear you say that. You seem to know well the man's mind."

"Dr. James and I have become very close over the years, perhaps you know."

"I envy you that."

"He served as something of a godfather to me as I was growing up. He was a friend of my mother, who died when I was eight, and I think he saw himself as one of my protectors, a bit formal and distant perhaps, but one I very much needed. He gave away my hand at my wedding, you know."

"So I understand. And now?"

"Now we are very close, and he is more a confidant. Upon my return from Vienna in 1898, I told him of my encounter with Dr. Freud and his ideas, and I made sure that he received *The Interpretation of Dreams* the following year. I knew they would find much of value in each other."

"Dr. James must have been deeply impressed, seeing you no longer as a bright-eyed college girl."

"Yes, I think he found that I had grown more worldly, for better or worse. He has taken me in more as a colleague in thought, and I have greatly appreciated the changing role."

"And his impression of me?"

"Dr. James was very impressed with your ideas. I think you and he have a greater interest in the less formal aspects of the human mind," Eleanor said. "He is at heart, as are you, I believe, a pantheist."

Jung looked surprised. "You find me a pantheist?"

"Perhaps I exaggerate—"

"Oh, no," Jung interrupted. "Please finish."

"Have you read Dr. James's Edinburgh lectures?"

"*The Varieties of Religious Experience,*" he said, "yes, I have read them and have found them very much to my liking."

"That is his very broad definition of the religious experience, one which you would find very similar to your views, it would seem." She looked to see that he was following and took heart. "It is just that you and Dr. James, like the ancient Greeks, seem to see the spiritual in many forms and in all things, in a broad spectrum of humanity and in nature all around you."

"That is another way of describing it. I have come to think of myself as a Gnostic. And I think I should include Dr. James within that description."

"A Gnostic?" Eleanor said, musing on the idea. "I fear I am not totally familiar with the Gnostics."

"They were at the time of the early Christians, you know. A Gnostic, one who pursues gnosis, the fullness of knowing. It is one dedicated to knowing the reality of the inner life through direct experience and personal revelation. It was this quest for gnosis which led me to grant fundamental importance to dreams, fantasies, and visions, to attempt to understand them through the study of literature, philosophy, and religion, and, ultimately, to adopt psychiatry as a career."

"And that is a unique calling?" Eleanor said.

Jung paused and gave the question more weight than perhaps the questioner intended. "You know I have for a long time thought of myself as made up of two separate personalities. Number one was the son of my parents who went to school and coped with life as well as he could, while number two was much older, remote from the world of human society, but close to nature and animals, to dreams, and to, yes, God. Number two has no definable character at all. Born, living, dead, everything in one, a total vision of life. As a psychiatrist I came to understand that these two personalities were not unique to me but present in everyone. Only I was for some reason more aware of them than most, particularly of number two. In my life number two has been of prime importance, and I have always tried to make room for anything that wanted to come from within."

"The earthbound self and the universal self," she said. "And you see Dr. Freud as too much number one."

"Well, that is putting too fine a point on it perhaps, but, yes, I suppose so."

"And Dr. James as a fellow number two."

"Intriguing," Jung said. "And how do you see Dr. James as number two?"

Eleanor frowned slightly and gave the question some thought. "Defining *that* is a tall order," she said. She paused again before offering, "Dr. James's definition of the mind's work is broad enough to encompass the transcendentalists and the Buddhists and the Hindus. We know that much. He would say that our normal waking, rational consciousness is but one kind, while all about it lie potential forms that are entirely different."

"And he encourages us," Jung said, continuing her thought, "to spend our energy exploring those other potential forms?"

"Exactly. We may go through life without suspecting the existence of those alternate forms of consciousness, but if we apply the proper stimulus, they will appear to us in their completeness."

"That is where we find his interest in meditation and the pursuit of mystical experience, taking certain drugs perhaps, the realms of what Dr. James calls parapsychology?"

"Yes, exactly. Here is where he found Dr. Freud interesting and definitely provocative. His controversial theories have caused a sensation, to be sure, and perhaps set the stage for what he calls psychoanalysis. That is Dr. Freud's great contribution, I am certain Dr. James would say, but at the same time that it is all too literal and restricting."

"His sexual theories?"

"Yes," Eleanor said, looking down again. "A Boston lady does not speak of such things, you know."

"Oh, I am sorry to be so bold."

Eleanor smiled. "You do not need to worry, Dr. Jung. We are very far from Boston out here. And besides, I am one who wishes to be bold in such matters."

"I am glad that I am not offending," he said, pausing. "Sexual theory, seen as bold even in Vienna and Zurich, is the very source of our disagreement," Jung said quickly, rushing past any embarrassment. "Dr. Freud considers the cause of repression always to be sexual. For me, the causes are much broader than that. The narrowness is highly unsatisfactory to me."

"Dr. James would find agreement with you, I believe."

"Does he think me literal and restricted by Dr. Freud's ideas?"

"I believe he sees your ideas as more in agreement with his, as they begin to consider more of those parapsychological elements."

"Such as séances and mystical experiences?"

"Yes."

"And are there other occurrences?" Jung asked.

Eleanor paused, thinking. She had wanted to tell him of Will Honeycutt's thesis and now found the moment. "A former student of Dr. James wrote a remarkable senior thesis in the physics department at Harvard College, and Dr. James took it seriously, as I think you would have."

"And Dr. Freud would not have?"

"Perhaps," Eleanor said. "This student carried on a discussion with a character who appeared in his dreams. The revelations in this imagined conversation were thought brilliantly accurate by some, and—"

"And demented by others," Jung said, finishing her thought, as if familiar with the phenomenon.

"Exactly. He was, after all, hearing voices. Dr. James mentioned on a number of occasions that he thought you would have been among those who found the consultation with dreams brilliant. In matters like this, he finds you capable of a great, expansive future, if only—"

Again, the young doctor cut her off. "And he sees my close association with Dr. Freud limiting in that regard? In this case of what we could call active participation in one's dreams?"

"Again, I do not wish to be presumptuous in speaking for Dr. James," Eleanor said, pausing.

"But he does see me as being restricted?"

"Yes. I do not wish to be blunt," she said, pausing again. "But, yes, I believe Dr. James sees you as held back from areas like this *active imagination*," she added, using a term she had learned from the Vienna journal.

"And Dr. Freud would not be interested in this—" He paused. "This *active imagination*," he said slowly, repeating the term.

"Yes," she said. "I think he would not find my Harvard friend's thesis interesting and would find the practice of conversing with characters in dreams outside his interest."

Then the two hikers sat in silence, absorbing the beauty around them and reflecting on what had been said. "Dr. James is not well, you know," Eleanor said after a time, her mood shifting suddenly. "In the past he would have been on this walk with us, leading the way up the mountain with his great strides. You would have heard from him directly. He is a man of great vitality—or was. But his heart is not strong now, and he is taken frequently by bouts of angina."

"What a shame," Jung said. "That is not a good symptom, you know."

"He struggles through bravely."

"You may have to speak for his ideas after he is gone. Are you intimidated by that role?"

The observation caught her by surprise. "Oh," she said, "I hope the condition is not that serious."

"Nevertheless, you are a good surrogate." Carl Jung had a way of staring intently into the eyes during a conversation, a habit Eleanor, like most of his associates, became accustomed to over time, but now in this first meeting it made her self-conscious. She looked away. "You do him honor," Jung said, with what Eleanor was beginning to find a very appealing directness. In fact, it was around this time that she began to realize how much she was loving this depth of exchange.

"I have enjoyed these conversations," she said, returning his gaze.

"We must find a way to continue them," he said. "Across oceans and continents."

That made Eleanor laugh. "Across oceans and continents," she repeated. "How grand."

"Grand"—he paused, now he the one looking down at his feet—"and fitting."

"Quite fitting," she repeated, acknowledging for the first time that it might have been unwise for them to come this far alone.

"What advice would Dr. James give?" he said quickly.

"I can hardly speak for him," she protested again.

The young doctor smiled and looked around. "I notice that the eminent professor is not here, and I was hoping that someone might represent him in this idyllic moment."

She released a laugh. "Well, in that case, in this idyllic moment, as you say, I suppose I ought to try again."

"I suppose also," he said with the same smile.

Eleanor took a deep breath and looked up at her hiking partner. "I believe that Dr. James would suggest, as we have discussed, that you loosen the ties to Dr. Freud and his Viennese colleagues." The directness of her words surprised them both.

Jung paused. "Dr. Freud and I agree on much, but there is much unspoken on which we do not agree. There is a tension. At the beginning of this trip, while we were still in Bremen, Dr. Freud accused me of wishing him dead."

"Oh my," Eleanor said.

"We are a bit too close. I feel a responsibility to remain near to him in thinking and to avoid any differences, and yet I do feel a kinship with Dr. James and the less literal aspects of psychology. Dr. Freud's interpretations, his Oedipus complex and others, seem to both of us too narrow. To those interested not only in the scientific but also in the spiritual approaches, they seem only part of the story. There are astrology and medieval alchemy and the whole world of Eastern religions to consider."

She nodded and paused to consider her words. "And Dr. James has a deep interest in those unscientific sources," she said very deliberately. "The unconscious speaks through images, I think he would say to you. And I think he would encourage you to explore those images more than the literalness of childhood impulses."

The young doctor looked as if he had seen a vision. "He really would say that?"

"I believe he would. He has said that he finds you gifted in recognizing the full wonder of the unconscious mind." She paused, giving thought to what she just said. "Yes, that is it. He would suggest that you pay more attention to the signs of the unconscious mind that emerge in all cultures." Later, she would wonder where the words had come from, but she was not unhappy that she had said them.

"Dr. James has sent quite a representative," Jung said. "We must discuss these matters further."

"Yes," she said suddenly, looking up, and quickly moved to rise, "but not now. Now we need to return to the camp. The others will worry." She held up her hand. "We would not want your hosts to think that I had lost you in the wilds."

"I certainly would not," the Swiss doctor said with enthusiasm, rising to his feet and helping her to hers. "But at your pace, we will be back in no time."

And when they arrived at the compound at least one of the elder Putnams remarked upon their late return.

"We were about to send out a search patrol," he said.

"Oh, that was not necessary," Eleanor Burden said with an unapologetic enthusiasm, smiling and keeping to herself the rush of affectionate connection she was feeling with this new friend, a connectedness and intellectual intimacy she had not felt for more than ten years, since her return from Vienna.

⟋

The next morning, as the two European visitors boarded the two-horse carriage that would take them along the rustic road to the Lake Placid train station, the whole Putnam Camp assembled for the traditional farewell ceremony. Jung stepped toward Eleanor, now joined by her two young daughters, and extended his hand. "Thank you for what will remain in my mind as a thoroughly delightful afternoon, an important one."

She held out her hand and took his. "I too shall cherish it."

"We shared an idyll, the romantic poets would say."

"We did indeed." And she looked up into his fierce blue eyes. "I enjoyed it immensely."

"There will be more opportunities for such conversations," he said.

"That is my hope also," Eleanor said.

As the carriage pulled away and the Putnam family group began to sing its farewell, as was the long-standing tradition of the camp, the children threw crab apples, the Adirondack sign of affection and respect, Freud wrote later in a letter home. Jung looked back at Eleanor and smiled warmly. And thus in that moment, wordlessly, the covenant of a lifetime was sealed. Shortly after that, when Jung had returned to Zurich, the letters began with an immediate intimacy and affection, and the deep friendship became manifest.

She did not know at that time the important role this new friendship would play in what was to come.

18

A COMPANION
OF THE SOUL

he finally shared with William James the whole story. He had been in increasingly ill health, the moments of incapacitation due to angina a great concern to those around him. During the 1909 Clark University visit of Freud and Jung, it was clear to all participants that William James had great interest in the themes of the conference, but was unable to participate fully because of ill health.

It was a year later, early in 1910, the year of Arnauld Esterhazy's entry into Boston and life at St. Gregory's School, that Eleanor held her fateful meeting. William James was sitting up on the sun porch of his Cambridge house, with a blanket enfolding his lap. "Oh, my dear," he said as Eleanor approached and kissed him on the cheek. "I have not much energy this morning, I fear," he added, excusing his not rising to greet her.

"You look fit and ready for the day," she said with a burst of her usual enthusiasm, but she knew she was convincing no one. He looked weakened and tired, and Eleanor had been filled recently with the dread that she might soon lose him. "And you are traveling to Europe?"

"Henry is not well. It is those dark moods of his, you know. He is despondent and needs the comforting perspective of his older brother. We leave in three days for his home in East Sussex."

"Are you sure you are strong enough to make such a trip?" The deep concern she felt was obvious on her face.

"Oh, yes," William James said, nodding as if to acknowledge that he was famous for making do, carrying on, going the extra mile. "It will be quite restful, actually. Alice and I love ocean travel, and Henry's England is magnificent this time of year."

"Am I wrong then to worry about you?" She suppressed a shudder, thinking for just an instant of his obvious fallibility.

"You needn't worry, dear Eleanor," he said with a warm smile that attempted reassurance. "I shall miss you though. You brighten my day so with your visits."

"They mean the world to me. You know that." She had long since grown accustomed to the closeness they shared. Earlier, she had been uneasy about his reputation of being attracted to younger women. There was the example of the young and brilliant Pauline Goldmark, a Bryn Mawr student with whom, around the time of Eleanor's Vienna visit, he entered into a three-year correspondence, and who seemed to enter his conversations regularly in a way that certainly caused speculation and talk, whether there was anything but platonic attachment. And, it was rumored, such behavior certainly caused a strain on his marriage, whether anything showed on the surface.

He had always showed a great loyalty to her, one she could never fully account for. No matter how busy he was, he always dropped everything when she visited him, listening to her intently, genuinely interested in what was on her mind.

In her youth she tended to take his attentions for granted, enjoying the small gifts and occasional attendances at significant events of her life, like school ceremonies and graduations. That he had been a close friend of her parents was Eleanor's explanation. "Dr. James had been empathetic to a young girl losing her mother," she told her Winsor School friends when they would ask how she was so fortunate as to have the attentions of such a famous man. But later, as her interests began to broaden and deepen, he was someone with whom to share ideas. However it was, she cherished her visits to him now, as she had all her life.

On the eve of her wedding to Frank Burden in 1902, when Dr. James agreed enthusiastically to stand in at the ceremony, in a rare moment of affectionate candor, he admitted to his feelings of guilt at allowing her severe and puritanical aunt, her father's sister Prudence, to take over the duties of her upbringing. "I and others should have interceded on your behalf," he had said then without elaboration, words she treasured then and for the rest of her life.

"There is much I need to tell you, before my trip," he said on this visit, leaving out any mention of what might happen during the strain of travel abroad. But it became clear to her in retrospect that a certain foreboding caused him to choose that particular moment for what he was about to reveal. She pulled a chair up close to his and leaned forward, taking his hand in hers.

He smiled at her characteristic eagerness and took a deep breath, allowing his tired eyes to sweep over her face. "What I will tell you now, I have not told another soul for over thirty years."

"I am ready to listen," Eleanor said, her usual enthusiasm diminished only slightly by his solemn tone.

"Before Alice and I married," he began, "before we met even, when I was still in my twenties and very much at sea as to my vocation, I fell quite deeply in love with my cousin Minnie Temple, a very forceful young woman of great vitality. And for a time she was the world to me, but she had tuberculosis, which proved to be fatal. I almost died myself of grief. I was deeply moved by a friend, a married woman my age, who reached out to me with comfort and solace."

He paused then, making it clear that this might be a lengthy narrative.

In 1872, William James, new to his teaching position at Harvard, was thirty years old and very much adrift. His health was not good, his professional future was not in any way certain, and he was subject to recurring bouts of depression. Charles W. Eliot, Harvard's bright new president, had begun a renaissance at the college and had very much wanted James to be a part of it. The young scholar with a very scattered academic background had taken his first teaching job and had loved it, his true calling, he realized. But what to teach?

The position was in medical science and physiology, but young James really wanted to teach philosophy and what he called "mental science." Minnie Temple's death that year from tuberculosis had taken the wind out of his sails in the most profound of ways, and with his poor health he doubted that he could ever be a husband or a father, let alone an energetic teacher of college students.

His younger brother Henry, one of the pillars of his life, had moved to Italy first, then England, a departure that benefited Henry's writing, but a blow to their brotherly closeness. And thus, in many ways, William James was indeed adrift, and alone.

Before Henry left for Italy, he had introduced William to a young married couple, two of his acquaintances in Boston. The husband was a young man of promise, and his young wife was a beautiful and vivacious hostess, in their beautiful home. Their living room, her "salon," as Henry called it, was a stimulating and restful place to settle on a weekday evening, as Henry had done often before his departure for Europe, and William had continued in his brother's absence. The young wife, it turned out, an unusually insightful and compassionate counsel and comfort, had known Minnie Temple and had mourned her loss along with many of William's friends. She had also a deep interest in the ideas of the transcendentalists, having met, like the Jameses, many of the Concord group in her parents' home. In short, she was a compelling companion for William at this time in his life, and she possessed what William called "a remarkable ability to listen." He had never met, he admitted to his brother, a woman of such beauty and energy for ideas and a depth of knowledge and understanding. "It seemed that every time I began on an idea or a complex sentence," he said, "she anticipated its direction and became ready to absorb the thought and enrich it.

"Somehow during discussions with this beautiful and sensitive woman, both the grief I was feeling and the ambivalence about my life at Harvard seemed to come to calm and resolution," he said. "It was during these conversations that I began to form confidence in both my professional and personal beliefs." At her side, he began discovering what he really wanted in his life, focusing on philosophy more in his teaching with a vigor and energy that had been lacking before. "What had been scattered," he said, "became connected, what was vague and amorphous became crystal clear." More than any other influence in his life until then, this remarkable woman caused him to gain perspective and to bring about change. The feminine strength she radiated became infused in him. "I was discovering new dimensions of my very being."

There was, however, unanticipated consequence. What had begun as comfort in a great loss blossomed into mutual and passionate attraction. The two friends both became deeply conflicted about what was emerging, and in the fall of 1873, he bearing the worst of the guilt, it seemed, still fretting over his discomfort with teaching medicine at Harvard, William decided to travel to Europe, to meet up with Henry in Italy, to rest and sort matters out.

But not far from his reasoning was the substantial fear that his attachment to this attractive young Boston wife had gone much too far and needed interces-

sion. She had become for him, he feared, like Coleridge's opiate, and he needed an escape.

His time with Henry in Italy proved to be unsettling rather than restorative. His own ill health seemed to have returned, he found the grimmer and grittier sides of European poverty distressing, and he admitted to being deeply homesick, longing for the inspiration of the married and respectable young woman back home. Then Henry became ill, and William tended to him, leading his younger brother to call him his "ministering angel who nursed and tended" him "throughout with inexpressible devotion." Somehow, helping his brother seemed to work wonders with his own illness, and he began to feel stronger. In March, he sailed for home, writing a very simple and respectful letter to the young matron advising her of his return.

Upon that announced return, guarded as they were against such a reaction, the two met with an ardor that stunned them both, "a wondrous meeting of souls, minds, and bodies," William described it privately to his sister, Alice, without naming the subject of his emotional outpouring.

After his return, William began working with the medical school, and he began recognizing his significant debt to Ralph Waldo Emerson, the great friend of his father who was now in his seventies. The two friends shared a poem by Emerson: "Give all to love. Obey thy heart. Nothing refuse. 'T is a brave master," the great transcendentalist said. "Let it have scope. It requireth courage stout. Souls above doubt, valor unbending. It will reward." Sharing these words, the two clandestine lovers fell into each other's arms. And, as desperate and passionate as they were, realized from almost the beginning that they had to cease and desist.

With the most painful of resolutions, they agreed to part and not see each other again. It was during that resolute period of parting that they discovered that she was pregnant.

✎

As he approached the end of this telling to Eleanor the story, in which William had avoided using names, a heavy silence fell now between them. "She was one of the most beautiful beings I have ever known," he said. "A total companion of the soul. Giving her up was almost my undoing, and I fear that even today she occupies, after all these years, a significant place in my heart."

"What happened to her?" Eleanor breathed, barely able to utter the words, for fear of what she would hear.

"We avoided each other as well as one could in tight-knit Boston society. It was a matter of high resolve on both parts. I found Alice, the second dear Alice in my life, and, most happily, we married."

"And the woman?" Eleanor repeated, still breathless.

"Nine years later she died," he said, and the two of them could only stare into each other's eyes. "Diphtheria," he added softly. "She died with her young son, leaving behind her eight-year-old daughter."

A profound silence fell between them in that moment. When she spoke finally, it was in little more than a whisper. "It was Mother."

19

"WE SHALL MEET AGAIN"

he first of her most precious letters, the one from William James, was obviously written in the long hours of his Atlantic crossing and was mailed from England back to Boston as soon as the ship docked.

Before he left, she and William James had a number of conversations about his monumental revelation and about something new she wished to share with him.

Upon hearing Dr. James's revelation about her mother, Eleanor had been speechless. "Why did I not know?" she said when she had collected herself.

The old philosopher had paused. "Because from the start it was thought better that you not, that no one know."

Neither spoke, these great believers in words. "I am glad to know now," Eleanor said finally. "And I have something I must share with you."

~

She returned the next day and found him sitting in the same spot with the same blanket in his lap. She looked greatly touched. During that night of her hearing the details of her birth, sorting through all the implications, she had decided to share with the great philosopher the Vienna journal. She had been able to share it and the details of her time in Vienna with no one. Now she decided to include this special man in her secret.

"There is something else about me that nobody knows," she said. "I must now share something deeper with you." She held out toward him an offering. "This journal tells a complicated story, one it will take much time and rumination to understand. You will have time on shipboard. I shall entrust it to your care."

He took the offering from her and from the look of concern on her face knew immediately that it was important.

"I will protect it," he said immediately.

"When you read it, you will understand my whole story."

"I shall cherish the opportunity," he said, having no idea the significance of what he held in his hand, this volume from Eleanor's time in Vienna that explained all.

"Be warned," she said. "It is a complex and troubling tale."

"I am good with complexity," he said with a gentle smile, his hand on the journal, "and with trouble."

His letter arrived back in Boston a few weeks after his departure.

My dear Eleanor,

 As you can imagine, I have given much thought to our poignant conversations on the eve of my departure. While shipboard with much idle time I have read several times the fateful volume you gave me and spent hours trying to absorb its contents, as you anticipated, quite a task to occupy myself in the long hours at sea. I know full well the monumental revelation on my part that caused you to share your monumental contribution with me. I conjecture that you have had, as I have had, much quiet time to sort through the multiple and varied implications. I look forward to my return when we will have opportunity to sit and talk about the many layers of your extraordinary tale.

 Above all, you must know the great weight of responsibility I feel for not being attentive to your childhood. I knew that while your dear mother was alive you were the most fortunate of children, given the very best of caring nurturance with no need for anything that my attention could have provided, and the circumstance required that I stay far removed. But, as I have told you, at the time of her passing I should have interceded and prevented the atmosphere provided by your overly austere aunt and your disconsolate father, some of which I did not real-

ize until reading this extraordinary volume. That was a grievous error on my part, one for which I find it difficult to forgive myself.

As to the journal, it explains much and leaves much open to contemplation. Primarily, on your return from Vienna in 1898, one close to you, caring as much as I did, could not help noticing the change in your very demeanor and carriage. Now I realize the depth of that change. You had suddenly grown up and gained an almost unearthly maturity and perspective, a "loss of innocence," I believe you called it, "the great theme of all literature," a phrase from my brother Henry that you attributed originally to me. Now I know and appreciate the cause. You saw much and felt much, more than many people could have borne. And yet you carried it with such dignity and grace that no one, I included, suspected the depth and poignancy of what you had experienced.

Although I do not know yet all the details, as they were not within my purview, I sense that you are engaged in finance in an uncommon way and that your involvement with the Hyperion Fund, as prescribed in the journal, is more than passing. Your financial help with Stanley's conference in 1909, with its invitation to Sigmund Freud and Carl Jung, and the remarkable luring of Gustav Mahler to New York were your assigned tasks, carried out efficiently and executed well, in all secrecy. Your prescribed participation in those events is remarkable, as has been your influence on me and my thinking. Taken literally, your contributions, my dear Eleanor, might change the course of history.

You have known investments to make and world events to anticipate. I had no knowledge of any ship christened the Titanic, *but our captain here, when asked, has observed that the White Star Line, owned by Mr. J. P. Morgan, I believe, is now in the process of building an extraordinary pair of ships in Ireland, one with that mythic name. They will not be completed for two years. The thought that such a ship would sink on its maiden voyage, and that you—and I now, if I am alive then—are aware of that awful fact in advance is staggering, a great weight to bear. The fact that our current century is to bear two devastating wars is unthinkable, and, one hopes, not accurately foretold.*

I have been ruminating on a most profound notion: that, because of what in it has already come to pass, some by your intervention, some not, this journal is the source of your strong faith in the future. It is your holy scripture. Is it not? It is the foundation for your faith just as the Gospels are the foundation of fundamental Christianity or the Upanishads are to devout Hindus. Is it not? For you, as for the most devout fundamentalist, it is a literal document, the determined fate, the future laid out in certainty as an absolute. It is determinism, and yet you have lived as an independent woman within it, your faith strong and purposeful, your independence admirable.

And for Dr. Freud the contents of this journal were and remain metaphoric, impossible to accept as literal truth, and open to the broadest interpretations. Just as the great doctor believed the author to be delusional, you believed him to be the bearer of truth. And for you it is all as real as this moment we share across continents. I suspect that in this remarkable situation I would have sided with you. I am grateful that you have shared all this with me.

You know that since the death of our infant son, Alice and I have sought out many sources of spiritual interaction with what we call reality. That has been a lifelong study of mine, never believing one way or another that such forces are or are not present in our world. You may recall that I had much in common with your friend Dr. Jung on this score, and that I found disappointment in his colleague Dr. Freud's unwillingness to accept the mere possibility of what we call parapsychology.

What I wish to communicate to you more than anything else, now that we have both shared our auspicious secrets and their consequences, is that parapsychology or no, spiritual intervention or no, the burden you carried away from Vienna in the form of this journal is staggering and not for the faint of heart. Since your childhood, I have had the greatest respect for an inner strength I have always believed you acquired from your extraordinary mother.

Your experience in Vienna has put that inner strength to a monumental test, and I could not be more proud of you. Be well until we can meet heart-to-heart. You know how much my heart, flawed as it is, is with you.

I look forward to long conversation with you, my beloved daughter.

William

William and Alice returned by ship to Quebec, not Boston, arriving in mid-August, and by the end of his time in England, he had to be carried on board. They passed directly to their summer home in Chocorua, New Hampshire, to recuperate and regain strength. And that is where Eleanor was summoned to see him. She made the long journey from Boston, first by train, then by carriage. He was so weakened from the England journey that he could no longer hold his head up. He was taking both digitalis and morphine.

"I hate for you to see me like this," he said to Eleanor. "I wanted you to wait until I had my strength back and to remember me always as a vibrant man."

"Oh my," she said with authority. "You will always be in my mind the most vibrant of men." She paused.

"And when this frailty passes, we will have time for long discussions. I regret so—"

She stopped him with a gently upraised hand. "You were always a pillar for me."

He had too little strength to object. "Oh, there is so much still to account for," he whispered.

"We shall have time," she said, not knowing if that was true.

"You must go tend to your family and to Arnauld Esterhazy, your guest from Vienna. He has a big job to do," he said, this being the only reference he made then to his knowledge of the journal's predictions. "He is the linchpin of it all."

She nodded without saying anything, finding comfort in the fact that now at least one other person shared her knowledge of what was to be. "You know about that now, don't you?" she said.

And William James barely nodded. "Yours is a powerful story," he said. "We will have time to discuss it all at length, when this weakness passes and Alice and I have returned to Cambridge."

"I will return to Boston, but I shall wait for you. You will come." He nodded his head slowly. "Do you promise?"

"I promise," he said, his voice barely audible. "We shall have time to discuss at length the whole remarkable story."

"You don't think it preposterous then?"

"I think it intriguing."

"Dr. Freud heard the whole thing, as you now know, and he found it preposterous, the work of a madman."

"Dr. Freud's is an important voice, and he will force mankind to revise its view of itself, not unlike Copernicus and Columbus and Charles Darwin. And you were absolutely right to promote his ideas as you did. But on some matters Dr. Freud has no imagination. Your friend Jung sees possibilities. Dr. Freud sees certainties."

"And you too see those possibilities in the journal?"

"Yes, I do," he said weakly. Then he paused a moment to gather his strength. "In a few years you will give birth to a son who will grow up to be a great hero at Harvard and elsewhere. That son—my grandson, I might add—will have a son and give him his name. That boy will in turn grow up to be a famous personage and eighty years from now, dislocating in time to Vienna twenty years ago and meeting you, will write this journal. That is quite a conception, is it not?"

"It is indeed," she said.

"Then you will return to Boston when I am still vigorous and we will begin long wonderful conversations." He paused again for breath and strength. "The greatest fulfillment of my life," he continued. "Reminding me so much of your dear mother."

"It has been great fulfillment for me also," Eleanor said then.

William James was now conserving breath, choosing his words with great care. "In eighty years," he said, "this Wheeler will find you in Vienna. At that point, you will return once again, and we shall reopen our connection. And all this."

"That is so," she said.

"You see, my dear daughter, we shall meet again." And he paused again. "I greatly look forward to that."

Then she prepared herself to return to Boston, saying her farewells to Alice and then to William James, who had not moved from his bed.

She leaned down to kiss him good-bye on the forehead. Then the great man looked into her eyes, too tired now to lift his head off the pillow. They exchanged a few last words, and then they parted, she indeed returning to her responsibilities.

Opportunity for further talk never arrived. William James died a few days after her departure, on August 26, 1910, in his beloved summer home in New Hampshire, his head resting in his wife's arms. Afterward, the autopsy showed acute enlargement of the heart. It was noted later that the great philosopher had drawn from that weary heart, right up until the end, every ounce of available energy.

For the rest of her life it meant the world to Eleanor Burden that among his last words to his daughter had been "We shall meet again."

20

ARNAULD ARRIVES

A fter all her efforts getting Arnauld to think of coming to Boston, none of them easy—the steady use of letters, first making brief suggestions that he might consider short visits during his days as an undergraduate at the University of Vienna, then gradually becoming more and more specific— the feat was actually accomplished and Arnauld Esterhazy had actually accepted a position teaching young boys at St. Gregory's. Eleanor found herself relieved beyond words and amazed. But like so many other details prescribed by her fate, she had worked hard and then found herself surprised by exactly the predicted outcome she had been working toward all along.

The connection with Will Honeycutt at Harvard and Cambridge had become a vitally important element. She had thought the strategy up as a way of giving Arnauld the possibility of an intellectual life to compensate for the one he had given up in Vienna. The promise of invitation to Boston homes, she concluded, might help him see perhaps that life in Boston could be a reality he would greatly enjoy. And, of course, the frequent visits to her own home would be the icing on the cake. She knew that her grand scheme to bring him to Boston was a great intrusion into his life in Vienna, but she knew also that his arrival was a necessary step in the destiny that was to be for him in the end a great fulfillment: his becoming the great and legendary teacher of young men that he was meant to be.

Finally, one late summer afternoon, as she stood on the platform at Back Bay Station and waited for the afternoon train from New York— Will Honeycutt had traveled to Hoboken to meet Arnauld's steamer—she realized that the whole plan really might work out as intended. Then there he was, standing beside his new American friend Will Honeycutt, smiling broadly, and happy to be in what he called "this brave new world."

"I do so appreciate the work you have done to bring about this happy occurrence in my life," the shy Arnauld said a little stiffly in greeting her and accepting her kiss on each cheek.

"And I hope that it lives up to your greatest expectation," Eleanor said. "This is a happy day for me. That is for sure."

"I hope to prove worthy," he added.

"I think you will adapt quickly," Eleanor told him.

"If eagerness plays a part, I shall," Arnauld Esterhazy said, "as my eagerness to be here is without bounds. I feel, at least for the moment, as if destiny has called me here to Boston."

"It is an eagerness that you will find reciprocal," Eleanor said. "Here and elsewhere. Your arrival has been greatly anticipated."

Arnauld did in fact adjust to it all well. He was a generous and entertaining guest in responding to all manner of invitation, always the center of much anticipation and attention, always a much-sought-after guest, "quite the rage," a friend called him, "there is something in his shy manner that makes everyone want your cultured Viennese friend on her guest list." Sometimes Frank and Eleanor Burden accompanied him on these social outings, and sometimes not. Arnauld, ever comfortable and gracious, didn't seem to mind.

His adaptation to teacher of young boys at St. Gregory's School was not quite as effortless, but in time even that went well. At first, the young teacher's "European" demeanor was perceived as "an air of superiority," as the headmaster reported, but soon the boys began to realize that his bottomless and boundless command of history and geography would serve them well. It was the younger boys, the fifth classmen, the thirteen-year-olds, who discovered it first in their geography class, and then the older boys in world history, the second classmen, always the harder to win over, came around. By winter term, Arnauld Esterhazy was a fixture, and no one could remember why they had not warmed up to him in the first place. Arnauld, for his part, seemed captivated by what he called "the American boy's independence of spirit, like the country." And, perhaps predictably, he fell in love with the peculiar sport of American football. "There are adults in Boston," he told Eleanor, "who actually believe it of capital importance that St. Gregory's defeat its rival in sport."

And, of course, Eleanor, secret engineer of it all, found great relief in the degree to which Arnauld found amusement in the new life he was accommodating. It could so easily have turned the other way, she thought. But then she admitted that in her anxiousness about his adaptation she did not take enough into consideration her new guest's unusual appreciation of newness and of life itself. "You are a wonder," she said one chilly Saturday afternoon in November, as she stood beside him—he wearing the school colors in the wool scarf at his neck—at one of the older boys' football games. "You have thrown yourself into the life of the school with admirable forbearance."

"I forbear nothing," he said with a broad smile. "I love the vitality of it all; in fact, I have found myself wishing that I had been an American schoolboy."

In his moment of arrival in the new country, with all its stimulations and adjustments, Arnauld's letters home to his mother and father began in earnest. It was because of these letters, Eleanor discovered later, that for his parents there was little question that Arnauld had taken to the surprising new teaching position in a foreign land with relish because of his continued attraction, to the point of adoration, to this woman they had never met, Eleanor Burden. There were in these letters home descriptions of the minutest detail of how he loved the thought of being in this Boston woman's presence, of being invited to spend time in her home, of watching her two girls grow and flourish that would be, it was concluded later, worthy of a book.

> *My dear parents,*
> *I have absolutely fallen in love with the American autumn. The contrast between the hot humid days of September and the crisp cold mornings of November is worthy of a poem by one of their poets—John Greenleaf Whittier or Walt Whitman, whom I have discovered—and of course the change in colors from the intense green to the famed oranges, reds, and yellows is the advertised spectacle. There is a quiet seriousness to the school day, which I quite enjoy, and a boisterous celebration of every weekend, much of it centered on one sporting event or another, usually their unique sport of football, in which the ball is passed from hand to hand and hurled through the air, so different from our game of feet. I joked when I first saw it that it ought to be called handball, but no one saw the humor in it.*
> *I am being treated as something of a guest of state and have no*

paucity of opportunity as a dinner guest and an occasional evening of music. All meals are provided by the school, if one wishes them, and some are part of my required duties, so that sometimes a quiet evening by myself is a relief. The advent of the American Thanksgiving is upon us with the promise of vacation on every boy's mind and what I gather is to be a rich family gathering. The two Burden daughters, who are ages six and four, have prepared me by saying that it is "better than Christmas." I will spend the entire time with the Burden family on Beacon Hill, and I must admit to a certain quivering of anticipation. Frank Burden has invited me to the annual football game between his Harvard and the rival Yale, and he has warned me that it is "quite a stirring event." I will admit there also is a keen anticipation.

So you can see that my Americanization has gone well. One of my youngsters said to me the other day, "Mr. Esterhazy, you are never going to wish to leave." Fear not that my conversion is that extreme, but I did have to admit to my students that I have found their way of life most compelling.

Yours ever,
Arnauld

As time passed and one year led to two, and two led to three and four, everywhere he went in Boston people of all ages loved his warm personality and cultured manner. Parents from the school would invite him for dinner, friends of Frank and Eleanor would invite him for weekends on Cape Cod or north to Gloucester and Portsmouth, New Hampshire. He grew up to enjoy the life of a bachelor teacher at a fashionable boys' school, and Eleanor smiled inwardly as she witnessed, sometimes from afar, sometimes up close, the success of her bold experiment.

Since the idea of his coming to Boston to teach at her husband's alma mater was again completely at Eleanor's instigation, a wild departure for an introspective Viennese intellectual, it was nevertheless one he claimed he wished to take on, for a short time at least, "to do something new and different." That was the part he admitted, but also there was his adolescent dream of being close to the woman he adored, the part he kept entirely to himself, and the part Eleanor knew she would be exploiting to fulfill what she knew of destiny.

21

GRANDIOSE CONJECTURES

From the beginning, long before she had any idea what it meant, she knew from a number of references in the journal she kept such a dark secret that a ship named the *Titanic* would sink on its maiden voyage in 1912, and that the famous J. P. Morgan would not be on board only because of a warning he was to receive from her. That one single journal prediction weighed as heavily on her as any.

Like so many details that would eventually appear on her path, she had to keep an eye out for mention of that fateful name *Titanic*. There was nothing. Then, in April 1908, a few years after her marriage, she noticed a small reference in the *Boston Globe*. White Star Line, the great English shipping company owned by Mr. Morgan, was planning the construction of three enormous luxury liners, the biggest ever built, each more than over eight hundred feet in length. They were to be built in a shipyard in Belfast, Ireland, named Harland and Wolff. The first two would be called the *Olympic* and the *Titanic*, both names fittingly derived from Greek mythology. She followed the construction as she could and learned just how the ships would be "unsinkable," with separate sealable compartments within their massive hulls. She watched with the rest of the world as first the *Olympic* was launched in 1911, with its sister ship, the *Titanic*, soon to follow.

She could see in hindsight how the whole business had led to the unraveling of her partnership with Will Honeycutt, as had, again in hindsight, the events of 1907, four years previous.

She had brought the challenge of unsinkability to Will early on, back in 1910, when she first read of the two gigantic ships being constructed in Ireland. And her questions had lured him into the drama, she concluded later, although at the time she had thought the gesture on her part one caused by genuine curiosity rather than acquiring a partner in her new task of worrying about the ship.

"Unsinkable," he said immediately and with authority upon hearing her question. "Unsinkable is unsinkable. It's all in the design, the science," he said, as he too had read of the forthcoming miracle ships, and in greater detail than she. "There are separate compartments within the hull, each controlled by automatic doors. Beautiful and expensive engineering." But when she insisted on asking just how the "unsinkable" could sink, impossible as it was, he took the question on with surprising thoroughness, as a challenge, and said he would take some time with it. The next day, applying his tenacious energy for research to the task, Will Honeycutt made his report.

"Well, here is how it would be, as I see it, the highest improbability, mind you, but here it is. First, there is the steel—impregnable, they say. Then there are the watertight compartments. Struck from the side, even hit by a huge wave, the ship would remain upright and afloat. But let's add a little imagination. If the ship steams across near-freezing water, which it will in the North Atlantic, we can assume, the hull is exposed to near thirty-two degrees Fahrenheit. At that unusual temperature some steels, depending on their components, become very brittle, as do the steel rivets that fasten them. If only one compartment is ruptured and floods, the ship remains upright and stable, but if a number of compartments flood—three or four, say—and the ship tilts . . ." He gestured by tilting one flattened hand. "Look at this. The compartments, secured as they are by automatic doors, are not sealed at the top. The water spills over the top of each bulkhead into the next compartment. The ship keeps tilting until all the compartments flood. The unsinkable sinks." He paused to see that she understood, and Eleanor, hearing far more than she wished, grimaced her acknowledgment.

"In *Moby-Dick*, Ahab's ship, the *Pequod*, is sunk by a great white whale, based on a real incident, I hear, the whaling ship the *Essex*, in 1820 or something. The whale rams it with one giant head-on blow, breaks open a hole in the hull, and the ship sinks. For the *Titanic* that could not happen because of the compartments. Brilliant design, and they are thus saying, 'Unsinkable.'"

Eleanor nodded. "That is what they say."

As with many other times when Will Honeycutt was engrossed, he barely paused to see if his audience was listening. "Unless the giant whale strikes a glancing blow and the brittle steel tears open in a number of compartments. That would be a different story."

"That would be quite a monstrous whale," Eleanor said.

"Right. But there is another ship, the sister *Olympic,* say, or any ship, even a small one. The massive object strikes a glancing blow; the frozen steel now brittle from the cold, the rivets compromised also from the extreme cold, rends, tears open three or four compartments; they flood, tilt the ship; the remaining compartments flood; and there you have it— the ship is doomed."

"But what are the chances of two ships colliding in the open ocean?"

"Not much, but there is the example of the *Republic.*"

"Remind me," Eleanor said. "I remember only a bit of the story."

"The *Republic* of the very same White Star Line, same as your ship. And also, like your ship, built by Harland and Wolff in Belfast, and lost off Nantucket, rammed by another ship in heavy fog in 1909. An 'all stations' distress, CQD, call was issued on the new Marconi radio device, the first such broadcast ever recorded. It stayed afloat until all passengers were removed, then it sank, in two hundred and fifty feet of water. At the time, the *Republic* was one of the largest and most luxurious liners afloat, though she was designed more for safety and sturdiness, they said, rather than beauty. It happens." He paused and thought. "But it is still highly unlikely."

"But it could happen again."

"Highly unlikely. But you asked me what would sink the unsinkable ship. It's a theoretical question, I assume."

"Of course." She nodded. "So it is unlikely?"

Will Honeycutt paused again. "Another ship, an anarchist's bomb, a rocky shoal—which is hard to imagine—an enemy torpedo, or an iceberg. But since we're not at war, and since a large luxury liner is an unlikely target for anarchists, I'd rule out the bomb and the torpedo."

This took her a moment to absorb. "Fog, crowded sea lanes, a glancing blow from another ship?" she said suddenly. "How do you deduce such things?"

"What else is there?" Will Honeycutt said in conclusion. "This is scientific analysis, remember?"

So Will Honeycutt, having already done a good deal of research and speculation, wrote an article for the *New England Maritime Quarterly* entitled "How the Unsinkable Would Sink," not referring to the great ship specifically, but making clear the implication. The editor wrote him back and thanked him for the "well-thought-out submission" but noted that its grandiose conjectures were too wild and too demoralizing to print in a serious maritime magazine.

Then a few months later Will Honeycutt rushed to her with a copy of the *Boston Globe*. "Look at this," he said excitedly. "The *Olympic*. That is the sister ship of your *Titanic*, the one about to be launched." The article described how the *Olympic*, the largest ship in the world, had been rammed off the coast of Southampton and a huge hole rent in the stern. "It didn't sink," Will said. "Why? Because of the engineering, the compartments. That's why. That's the unsinkable part."

"It must be reassuring to the White Star Line."

"Yes," Will said. "But it wasn't the glancing blow I described, and it was not in freezing water. The steel held. The ship remained upright. In my scenario, remember, the offending ship grazes the side and tears into four or five of the supposedly sealed compartments. That would be an entirely different story."

"Still improbable? Are you changing your opinion?"

"Absolutely not. It is still the highest of improbabilities," Will said distinctly. He looked at her suspiciously. "Are you predicting something here?" he said.

"Oh my, no," she said quickly, cringing for a moment. "Nothing as sure as that."

"Good," Will Honeycutt said. "Because if you were predicting, with your record, I would want to tell Jesse Livermore immediately. He would want to place a large wager on it."

22

A MOST AUSPICIOUS MEETING

ecretly, almost obsessively, Eleanor kept track of all the details of the launch in Ireland of this monstrous ship whose fate she knew, its elaborate outfitting, and the proposed sailing date, one eagerly awaited now by all of America and Europe. The *Titanic* would sail on its magnificent maiden voyage on April 10, 1912. *How,* she ran through her head over and over, *could such a ship ever be sunk, especially on the maiden voyage?* This bit of foretelling seemed so improbable as to cause her doubt about the accuracy of all information in the journal. If this one predicted event did not happen, which seemed now highly likely, what then? And if it did happen, what an awful tragedy that would be, one she perhaps could have prevented.

And what of the supposed warning of J. P. Morgan? He was only the wealthiest, most powerful, and most easily recognized man in America. In 1912, at seventy-five years old and near the end of his life, he still wielded power and majesty, the mighty Zeus of the banking world. Although he was often seen publicly in New York and Europe, he was very difficult to see privately. For any ordinary mortal, getting any sort of message to him would indeed be a difficult, virtually impossible, task. Was she really supposed to warn him not to sail on his own magnificent luxury ship?

But with this as with many other events over a lifetime, Eleanor knew she must. She had no choice. So, in the winter of 1912, she began with Will Honeycutt. "I have an assignment for you," she said with the kind of seriousness he had come to expect. "I need to meet with Pierpont Morgan."

"Impossible," Will said without thinking. "Why would he meet with a mortal such as you?" And then, seeing the determination on her face and adjusting, he changed to "I will begin working on it."

And a few days later he came back to report that Jesse Livermore had been an invaluable help, with his connections on Wall Street. "It is nigh unto impossible, but there is a chance. You will probably get nowhere with your efforts, but I know what you are like when you set your mind to a task, and if anyone could make it happen it would be you." And he laid out for her the details of what Jesse Livermore suggested.

She began exploiting that slight chance with a letter, not asking for an appointment, but announcing rather that she would be in his office on a Monday morning, a moment her research told her he would be in residence. Admitting to a great deal of nervousness that she hoped she was able to conceal, she arrived and announced her presence and sat in a reception area for well over half an hour before an assistant, a short, slight, neatly dressed man with slicked-back hair and a rather large mole on his cheek, came out to state with dismissive formality that Mr. Morgan was not available. She handed over a letter. "Please deliver this to Mr. Morgan," she said confidently. "This is for his consideration only. It is an extremely private and an extremely urgent matter."

The letter introduced her as the representative of the Hyperion Fund, a name that would perhaps—because of the whole Northern Pacific business—resonate with members of the Morgan camp. In it she said, "I have personal knowledge of an extremely confidential nature to share with you and you alone."

One more hour passed before the assistant returned. "A representative from Mr. Morgan will see you," he said.

"But I must see Mr. Morgan himself," she said.

"Be grateful for what you receive," he said solicitously, turning to escort her. "This is very much closer than most people get." And he ushered her into an inner wood-paneled room that looked very much like the library where Mr. Morgan met from time to time with important men of finance to browbeat them into seeing things his way. She sat for what must have been twenty minutes, although her heart was racing so that recalling accurate time was a near impossibility.

After whatever time had passed, a side door opened and a man walked in. He was almost like a shadow, sliding soundlessly across the carpet with a surprising suppleness and grace, approaching the chair where she sat. Suddenly, Eleanor found herself looking into the face of the most powerful and most intimidating man she had ever met.

She rose and extended her hand. "Mr. Morgan," she said, struggling mightily to look him square in the eye, "I am honored to meet you." She had prepared well, yet still found herself nonplussed in the presence of this Olympian figure. He was a large man, a "whale of a presence," as a United States senator had once called him. The boldest of men were likely to become humble under his piercing gaze, she had heard, the imperious ground to humility. And she knew to expect the nose.

J. P. Morgan's rosacea, a condition in which certain facial blood vessels enlarge, had given him the most unsightly and bulbous outcropping of a nose, about which he was very sensitive. She had prepared herself to take not even the slightest notice of the ugly protuberance, and somehow she held fast and made sure that her eyes did not budge from his, as if looking into the most handsome face in the world.

"You have something you deem very important to tell me," he said coldly, his eyes taking in her full presence. She had heard that Mr. Morgan would grant an audience with some ease but that the recipient had better have something significant to offer.

"I do," she said. "A matter of great importance. I feel it my duty."

"Well, you may now perform that duty." Morgan gave a barely noticeable smirk and waited. "You may have noticed that you have my full attention."

"You may know that the Hyperion Fund I represent made some dramatic predictions," she said, and now she waited. "If you will remember, our fund predicted the Northern Pacific corner and the crash of 1907."

"The Hyperion Fund," Morgan repeated noncommittally, nodding to signal that he knew exactly her reference.

"Yes, the Hyperion Fund." She continued with confidence, positive Mr. Morgan had done his research before admitting her to his inner sanctum. "Discretion is of utmost importance, I am sure you realize. I do not wish any of this known. In fact, I come here at great risk to the privacy of my fund. But what only you may know, a fact most urgently protected, is that it is I alone who have made the predictions."

"You, Mrs. Burden?" Morgan said, eyeing her with suspicion.

"I know," she said. "It is in your experience unlikely for a woman. I know certain details of the future. And I know something about you that you must accept and must act upon."

Morgan, a man not accustomed to hearing "you must" in his presence, gave a small harrumph but did not turn away, allowing his guest to continue.

"It regards your ship the *Titanic*. I know you are planning to be on board for its luxurious maiden voyage." Morgan nodded ever so slightly. "I know that you have built for yourself and those who travel as your guests a most beautiful stateroom. Well, I have traveled from Boston just to tell you this." She paused, taking a breath, her eyes still fixed on his. "If you sail on that voyage, you will die."

There followed a most awkward silence. For the first moment, the famous J. P. Morgan reacted. "Good lord, madam. What on earth causes you to say that? Are you suggesting some anarchist on shipboard?"

"It is just fact, Mr. Morgan. And it is my role to warn you of it as directly as possible, not to describe to you how it will happen."

Morgan thought for a long moment. "If I do not sail on this voyage, I will never know what might have befallen me."

"You will know," she said emphatically. "You will know and you will be grateful for the warning."

"And—"

"When you know," she said, "you must promise me that before the voyage and then after it you will hold this information in the greatest confidence. If you discover that what I say is true, then you will tell no one." She paused. "Ever."

"If I do not sail with the ship and if nothing manifests itself, what then?"

She said nothing for a moment, her eyes not moving from his. "If nothing manifests itself, then you may do with me and my information as you will." She paused, considering her words, her eyes still not faltering.

"You are a startlingly convincing woman, Mrs. Burden." The powerful man was accustomed to using unsettling candor to his advantage.

Eleanor did not flinch. She stood her ground, and her response was near instantaneous. "My purpose here is to be convincing, Mr. Morgan."

"After the forthcoming voyage we will perhaps meet again."

"Perhaps," she said, releasing him from her gaze. "But if what I say manifests itself, as you say, then there will be absolutely no follow-up to this conversation. Can I be assured of that?" Mr. Morgan did not budge, which Eleanor interpreted as permission to proceed.

She softened. "You will see that I come to you at great risk," she said, "and with confidence—well founded I hope—that none of this will leave this room. You must promise me that you will keep my secret."

J. P. Morgan gave another harrumph and only the slightest nod that might have been construed as the sole affirmation Eleanor was going to get. With a kind of suddenness, the door through which she had entered opened, and the assistant with the mole appeared and stood formally while Mr. Morgan finished. "And now, Mr. Prescott will see to your needs." The great whale of a man stepped forward and shook Eleanor's hand, and he turned and left.

The assistant showed her to the reception area. "That is longer than most people get," he said, still solicitous, aware of the unusual nature of her appearance without an appointment. "Under the circumstances." She thanked him for his kindness and left the Morgan office. It was not until she was out on the street hailing a cab that she realized she was shaking and felt positively ill.

When she arrived at Grand Central Station and sat in the cavernous waiting room, she began to unwind from the tensions of what had just transpired. She had prepared for the meeting with mental exercises so as to remain unruffled and assertive in the presence of the most powerful man in the world, and that had gone as well as could be expected. She had known of his reputation of withering his opposition in the personal meetings, and she had stood firm well enough to deliver a message without appearing either weak or vacillating or, for that matter, strident or presumptuous. Now, sitting alone in the vast station waiting room, she found herself able to evaluate her own performance from what she was now able to recall in the blur of her memory, and she deduced that she had probably managed to appear calm, and she had said the rehearsed words without stuttering or stammering or showing any obvious signs of being well beyond her point of social ease. She had done her job.

And then as she sat alone in that vast space, the old thought came back

to haunt her. Why, if she could warn Mr. Morgan—as prescribed by the
Vienna journal—should she not issue the specifics of the warning and tell
him of an awful tragedy that was about to happen, if it was about to happen? Why warn only Mr. Morgan? she asked herself. Why not warn
everyone? And then there was the old thought that came as just a hint in
this moment but had waited there in the background over the years: What
a relief it would be if nothing happened and she could be freed from the
journal and its obligations. Now, as with other visits from such troubling
thoughts, she told herself first that she had no choice in the matter and
second that nothing was assured to happen. Those two thoughts comforted her now, as they had in the past and would in the future. They were,
as her friend Carl Jung would say many times, pure denial.

Finally, by the time she rose and headed for her train back to Boston,
she had convinced herself that she had carried out the Herculean task
with as much grace as was within her abilities, and perhaps well enough
to be convincing. Whether J. P. Morgan would heed her admonition and
avoid sailing on his great ship's maiden voyage she might never know.

On the train ride back to Boston, she continued going over and over
what had just transpired with her meeting until she had exhausted every
strand of possibility and explored every memory until she fell asleep, again
watching the Connecticut countryside roll by. By the time she arrived
back in Boston, her disposition had returned to near normal.

"And what of your meeting with Mr. Morgan?" Will Honeycutt asked
her the next morning in their office.

"Most satisfactory," she said. "And auspicious."

23

THE UNSPEAKABLE AVERTED

s the maiden voyage of the great ship approached, its scale and magnificence had pushed its way into the foreground of all world news. The whole world seemed to be aware that on April 10, the *Titanic,* the largest, most elaborately appointed ship in the world, was to sail from England on its way to New York. And not everyone thought it a positive accomplishment for civilization. "Shameful opulence," Frank Burden, ever the conservative Boston banker, had announced over breakfast one morning in May as he read in the *Boston Herald* the details of the approaching voyage date. "This kind of display of wealth is unseemly. It is the curse of our age," he added.

But still, the world watched with fascination and not a small portion of awe. "People enjoy watching the extravagantly wealthy throw around their money," Will Honeycutt reported Jesse Livermore as saying. "It's like female peacocks in the thrall of elegant plumage."

From its earliest days of construction in the dry docks of Harland and Wolff in Belfast, Eleanor had had trouble getting the ship's progress out of her mind. *How,* she kept running around in her head, *could the biggest, grandest, safest, most expensive monstrosity, this perfect symbol of the opulence of the age, this great triumph of industrial imagination and engineering brilliance, sink?* The thought was so astounding as to cause her once again to doubt the veracity of the journal. Up until this point in 1912, the predictions in the journal had been correct, even those that began as improbable, and she had the grandiose success of the Hyperion Fund to prove its accuracy. But now this one seemed absolutely preposterous, as Will Honeycutt kept insisting it was highly improbable that such a magnificent ship could sink.

She found herself wishing then that at least parts of the predicted future from the journal had been inaccurately recorded and would definitely not be coming to pass, that history would unfold this time in a different way, take a different path, that the ship would not sink, that the two horrible world conflagrations would not come about, even that her son and grandson would not be involved, even if that meant the future described in the journal to be inaccurate. *Yes,* she thought, wishing that the whole cursed deal of the Vienna journal was off and she could assume the simple life of status quo in Frank Burden's world of Boston as it had always been and ever shall be.

She kept an eye on the ship's progress without sharing her dread with anyone. She knew of its moment of departure and charted its course across the North Atlantic. In the middle of the first day, she telephoned the *Boston Globe* and asked if there was by chance any unusual news from the White Star Line's prized *Titanic*; there was nothing unusual the first day, or the second, or the third, fourth, or fifth. Without wishing to attract attention, she said simply that she always felt nervous about big events. The young reporter on the other end of the line told her to relax, that they were talking about the safest ship that had ever set sail.

Then on the morning of April 15, the sixth day after departure, rumors began. During the previous night, ships well beyond the two-hundred-fifty-mile normal transmission range of the new Marconi radios had heard an unmistakable call of distress from the luxury ship *Titanic*. The great ship's radio, it was boasted, had a three-hundred-fifty-mile range in daytime and a range of one thousand miles at night. "CQD," the message said, which was the international maritime code for the ultimate distress, "MGY," the code for the mighty ship, and "41.46 N, 50.14 W. HAVE STRUCK A BERG. COME QUICK."

Eleanor learned it in her morning call to the *Boston Globe*. "We have heard no more," the reporter said. "Call back in a few hours."

"What about rescue ships?" Eleanor asked.

"It seems that there are some in the area," the reporter said. "We still know nothing of them. Call back in a few hours."

Eleanor remembered Will Honeycutt's description of the White Star ship *Republic*, struck by another ship, and sinking; it had taken long hours, but all passengers had been transferred to rescue ships and a coast guard vessel called to the site by a heroic Marconi operator.

When she called back an hour later, the details were available. The *Titanic* had struck an iceberg in the night. *An iceberg!* she thought; of all the scenarios, that was a possibility Will Honeycutt had presented to her only in passing. This was the glancing blow in freezing water. At first, no one could believe that the huge ship would actually sink. "News is that the *Titanic* is still afloat and that all lives are saved," the reporter said. "It seems that the unspeakable has been averted."

Frank Burden would be following the news from the bank, she knew, as the damage to such a shamefully opulent ship of the line would involve significant financial impact. "No reliable details as of yet," he said when she telephoned him in his office. "Grim rumors persist. There is a report that the vessel remains afloat, and all passengers have been transferred safely to another ship, like the *Republic*. The *Titanic* will be towed into Halifax, the nearest landfall. But the *Republic* was struck only fifty miles from New York Harbor. This accident is in the middle of the North Atlantic."

At noon, Eleanor arranged a motorcar to take her to the auxiliary meeting at the Museum of Fine Arts. The disaster was all the ladies wished to talk about. In old Boston society, there was almost no one who did not know or know of someone who had chosen to sail on the maiden voyage of the opulent new ship. And, hence, in the wake of such horrendous news, there was no one who was not personally attentive to the bits of news and rumor that had been drifting in all morning.

"So often in these situations," said one matron, "everything turns out just fine."

"It is the miracle of wireless radio," said another. "It has meant that rescue ships could be on almost any scene in no time." Everyone in the world who had heard of the distress call and the foundering took solace in the hope that in a matter of hours all passengers would be transferred to other vessels.

"But I've heard that suddenly all went to silence," said another.

"Yes, I've heard something more dire. That the great ship has sunk and some passengers had found safety on an iceberg before being rescued."

At this point Eleanor added what she had heard from Will Honeycutt earlier in the day, that she feared that no news was not good news. "If there were anything good to report," Will had said, "they would be telling us." And most of the ladies agreed.

"I hear there were lots of famous people on board, and they have gone down with the ship."

"Yes, Astor, Guggenheim, and J. P. Morgan."

"J. P. Morgan?" Eleanor said with a gasp.

"Yes, he owns the ship, and he was on board."

"Are you sure?" Eleanor asked.

"Yes. I'm certain. My husband knows the Morgans, and he told me directly."

Eleanor steadied herself and gave no sign that anything was amiss but said nothing for the rest of the meeting, as more and more details were speculated on, most of them without foundation. On the ride back to Beacon Hill, she felt ill.

Then, at the end of the day, after the girls came home from school, filled with wild stories, Frank Burden called to say that the fully awful news was confirmed. "The whole story is in," he said with characteristic finality. "The *Titanic* has sunk, and there weren't enough lifeboats. Only a few hundred of the passengers, mostly women and children, have been saved."

Eleanor felt stabbed in the heart. "And what of J. P. Morgan?" she asked her serious husband.

"And what of him?"

"Was he on board?"

"I have not heard of that," he said. And then he added condescendingly, "Not every famous financier was on board, you know."

Once again, and this time in horrendous proportions, the power of the journal was confirmed, once and for all. She could tell no one. If the world had known of her foreknowledge, she would have been a pariah. Living through Will Honeycutt's suspicions was bad enough. He came to her ashen-faced shortly after he heard the news. "You knew," he said, obviously disturbed. She should have deflected the remark with some quick retort, but this time she said nothing and looked away.

He followed with, "How did you know?" and then, realizing he would receive no answer, he said, "The iceberg. I keep thinking of the iceberg and the article I wrote." He was staring again. "You suggested it."

"I did not," she said quickly. "Not the iceberg."

"But you did, with your hypothetical questions. Only it wasn't hypothetical, was it?"

"I only wondered," she said. "I only asked—"

He interrupted her. "It *was* impossible. The ship *was* unsinkable." Then he paused, thinking. "It is hard to take it all in, the size of it all, the numbers, the scale. You warned J. P. Morgan, didn't you? That was the purpose of your meeting."

Eleanor said nothing, only offering the slightest nod. And her young colleague looked shaken. She could see in his eyes a wildness that suggested more than just eccentricity.

Suddenly, he said, "Did you cause it?"

The question was so bizarre that even coming from Will Honeycutt it stopped her in her tracks. "No, I did not cause it," she said as if answering the most mundane question. "I simply knew it was going to happen."

Will looked for a moment, then said, "Oh," as if it were likewise the most mundane answer. "And you, I suppose, will not tell me what oracle you consult."

"Intuition, Mr. Honeycutt," she said quickly, but this time there was a flat defensiveness in her voice, and she made it clear with her eyes that she was not going to reveal more.

He stared at her hard for a moment, then began, "One would think that after all this time we would trust each other." Then he stopped, shook his head, and turned toward the office door, clearly exasperated by her unwillingness to share her secrets and eager to leave. And she thought in that moment that a great mythic event of enormous magnitude had happened in their world, and everyone would respond differently, but no one she knew would avoid being shaken to the core. No one, that is, except Frank Burden.

In the morning at breakfast, Frank did not notice her dark mood and continued on his tack of "shameful opulence." He had felt for a long time that the excesses of the new century were unhealthy and would lead to no good. "The end of this ridiculous trend," he said while breaking open the top of his hard-boiled egg with a spoon. "It is time that everyone learned a lesson. The builders of such a monstrosity had it coming," he added with cold dispatch. He continued without noticing the look on his wife's face for the remainder of the breakfast.

And it did not help matters that Will Honeycutt, ever the scientist, kept mulling over and over the details. It had been the worst of her Cassandra dilemma, knowing the future but, by the very nature of her fate, being powerless to do anything about it. The sheer size of what was to happen with the *Titanic*—that such a monumental ship was to sink in mid-voyage—made it unthinkable, impossible to believe.

"What they ran into out there was bigger than the ship itself," he said that first day, when everyone was still adjusting to the enormity of what had happened, "much bigger, and you know, only one-ninth of an iceberg rises above the surface. Eight-ninths below the surface, down into the icy inky black." He stopped, his mind working. "Then there is the depth. The ocean at that point is two miles deep. It is my figuring that it took that great ship something like ten minutes to fall to the bottom." He made a sinking gesture with his hand. "Imagine being trapped inside the hull, as many were, I'm sure, sinking to the bottom—"

"Please," she burst out finally, stopping him. "I have to sit down." The observation made her swoon and left her with a feeling of great emptiness.

He stared wildly, not noticing or caring about her dismay. "How did you know?" he repeated, this time with complete scientific detachment.

As reports came in over the next few days, it became obvious that J. P. Morgan had not been on board. In the years that followed, no reason for his not sailing leaked out. The great banker had simply changed his plans and not sailed on his opulent ship's maiden voyage. Obviously, Mr. Morgan would have realized immediately and completely the full import of Eleanor's warning to him, or perhaps, although not likely, the whole incident had slipped from his mind in the confrontation of such enormous loss. He died a year later in Rome, of natural causes, apparently intending to keep secret forever his reason for making the fateful change. As agreed, Eleanor Burden had not heard from him again.

She read about his death in the *Boston Globe* on April 1, 1913, a year almost to the day after the *Titanic* tragedy. A few weeks later, she received in the mail an envelope posted from Italy, with no return address. Inside, on a sheet of stationery headed by the name John Pierpont Morgan, was a handwritten note and an illegible scrawl of a signature that looked, she discovered after some investigation, very much like Morgan's. "If ever you should need a return favor," the letter read, "contact my son, Jack. He knows of your intervention on my behalf."

24

HEART OF DARKNESS

he weeks around the *Titanic* tragedy were a quiet time of action on her part for maintenance of the Hyperion Fund. That was a good thing. Will Honeycutt, now, thanks to his friendship with Jesse Livermore, returned for some time from Chicago, where he had become adept at buying and selling real properties.

"You amaze me, Mr. Honeycutt," she said to him as he showed her his figuring on profits from selling a twenty-story building on Wacker Drive, by the Chicago River.

"I tend to become bedeviled by the details," he said, "to the exclusion of all else."

She nodded with a knowing smile. "And I am grateful for that," she said, "and glad that I do not have to worry about those details."

"Or about me?"

"Mr. Honeycutt," she said with a sigh, "I have long since given up the futile effort of worrying about you."

She had other things, bigger things, to worry about, she thought. Ever since the death of William James, she had been revisited by recurring dreams of vastness, like the one of falling off the cliff or another one that involved being a little girl out alone on an endless expanse of ice. But ever since the *Titanic* tragedy, one dream in particular recurred with regularity, "the Big Dream," Carl Jung later called it when she described it to him in a letter. And now as time passed and she began writing parts of it down in her notebook, it began to make more and more sense.

In the dream, she found herself perched on the top of a huge iceberg, in the middle of a dark and glassy sea. She sat precariously, fearful that she would slide off. Below her, on the waterline, she could see a large long swath of red paint, and below that she was aware of the huge mass extending way down into the deep, beyond where she could see. The depth of ocean beneath her, the two miles that Will had described, gave her an even greater feeling of dread. As she began to slide, desperately digging in with her heels and fingernails, she always woke up, perspiring and gasping for breath. At night when she had to get up and walk around, she could feel nothing but a deep dread, the feeling of vastness. She wrote of it in one of her monthly letters to Carl Jung, and two weeks later she received a telegram from him. "We shall discuss it," it said, "when I come to Fordham."

In the fall of 1912, a few months after the tragedy, Jung had been invited to Fordham University in New York City. It would be his third trip to America and an excellent opportunity for the two friends to meet. The visit would do them both good. The Swiss doctor wanted to talk about Sigmund Freud, and Eleanor wanted very much to talk about the dream.

During that time in 1912, the disagreement between the two psychologists over the origins of hysteria had not yet grown into a full-blown feud and its eventual rancorous and permanent estrangement. The two were extremely close, perhaps too close. Although Jung had established an independent reputation and was highly regarded in the psychological community of Zurich, the great Viennese doctor and his following thought of the younger Swiss doctor as a disciple. Freud appointed the younger man president of the International Psychoanalytical Association, and expected him to lead with authority and eventually rise to replace Freud himself. Tensions arose over a number of technical points, ones that William James had noted in 1909 at Clark University. Freud began to imagine jealousy in his younger colleague, where Jung insisted there was none, and he became critical of Jung's leadership, first in letters, then in personal encounters. Eventually tensions would rise and lead to disagreements and disagreements to hostility, but in the fall of 1912, both men trying to minimize the common strands of what they believed, there was a nervous peace. It was the Fordham lectures, delivered far from either Zurich or Vienna, an ocean and continent away, that caused the beginning of the end.

Because he shared some of all this with Eleanor in letters, she knew before their meeting in New York that his disagreements with Dr. Freud had become more apparent since their conversations at Putnam Camp three years before. She found herself flattered by how much he shared with her, yet shocked and disappointed that these two giants of the new thinking in psychology were behaving with such childish peevishness.

In a way, the disagreements between Freud and Jung were as inevitable as their initial infatuations. The Viennese doctor was nineteen years the senior and considered himself the founder of the psychoanalytic movement now seeking an heir apparent, "the crown prince," as a colleague described him.

Jung fell into that role willingly in the beginning because of his strong affinity for the older man. "Dr. Freud was far wiser and more experienced than I," said Jung. "In the beginning I knew I must simply listen to what he had to say and learn from him." But it did not take the younger man long to begin to chafe at the subservient role, as he began to find the formality of his position an impediment to his own development. In many ways it could be noted that the position of heir apparent was one to which Jung's robust questioning nature and spontaneity made him unsuited.

During their trip to America together in 1909, when they spent long hours on shipboard talking and analyzing each other's dreams, a number of tensions rose to the surface, including one moment when Freud actually accused Jung of wishing him dead, in solid oedipal tradition. "His friendship meant a great deal to me. I had no reason for wishing him dead," Jung reflected later. "But it was possible that the dreams that I shared with him willingly on that trip could be regarded as a corrective, not as a negative wish but as a compensation, an antidote to my conscious high opinion and admiration of him. Therefore the dream recommended a rather more critical attitude."

Freud was obviously more concerned about usurpation than he admitted, and Jung was more worried about the patriarchal dominance than he admitted.

Jung began straining at the strict ideas in Freud's speeches and writing. "It is mostly a disagreement with Freud's views of libido, the primal drive at the heart of all human impulse," he wrote to Eleanor. "For Freud, the libido is purely sexual; for me it is the much broader derivation." When Freud heard of these views from his supposed disciple, he began criticiz-

ing him directly in letters and indirectly to others. Soon Jung was responding to the criticism, not by acquiescing but by snapping back.

Jung had also written to Eleanor about a dream he had shared with Dr.
Freud on the 1909 trip.

> *I found myself in an unfamiliar two-storied house, on the upper
> story, where there was a kind of salon furnished with fine old pieces of
> rococo style, a number of precious old paintings on the walls. It all seemed
> vaguely familiar. Descending the stairs, I reached the ground floor. There
> everything was much older. The furnishings were medieval. The floors
> were redbrick. Everywhere it was rather dark. I came to a heavy door
> and opened it, discovering a stone stairway that led down into the cellar.
> Descending, I found myself in a beautiful vaulted room that looked ex-
> ceedingly ancient, dating from Roman times. I came to another stone
> stairway and descended, leading down into the depths. Thick dust lay on
> the floor, and on the dust were scattered bones and broken pottery, like
> remains of the primitive culture. I discovered two human skulls, obvi-
> ously very old and half disintegrated. Then I awoke.*
>
> *Dr. Freud became convinced that the skulls represented somehow
> my desire to have him dead, an opinion from which he could not be
> shaken. I did not believe any part of that interpretation.*
>
> *It was plain to me that the house represented a kind of image of the
> psyche—that is to say, of my then–state of consciousness, with hitherto
> unconscious additions. Consciousness was represented by the upper-
> floor salon. The ground floor stood for the first level of the unconscious,
> and the deeper floors, the ones of primitive culture, represented a prim-
> itive psyche of the animal soul, just as the caves of prehistoric times were
> usually inhabited by animals before men laid claim to them. It was
> during this time that I became aware of how keenly I felt the difference
> between Dr. Freud's intellectual attitude and mine.*
>
> *That dream which Sigmund Freud was so certain represented my
> contention with him was for me the first inkling of a collective existence
> beneath the personal psyche. It is when I first became convinced of the
> collective unconscious.*

One month before Jung's visit, she received a letter explaining the details of his forthcoming visit to Fordham University that included the following note: "When we are in New York together, we shall dine alone. Grand theatrical attire required, of course."

Grand and theatrical, she found herself thinking with a good deal of awe and amusement. *I am sure that the evening will be one to remember.*

After making careful arrangements and the usual explanations, she traveled alone to New York by train to a room she had booked at the Waldorf-Astoria Hotel. She packed for the occasion a beautiful black silk evening dress she had worn to the New Year's ball that January. It was bare at the shoulders and cut in a way she knew he would enjoy, being prepared by this time in their relationship for Jung's highly developed sense of drama—albeit with healthy suspicions.

On the chosen evening, alone in her room, she received from room service a box containing a book by Joseph Conrad and a very plain cardboard box containing a gaudy diamond necklace that she guessed from its luster to be made of ordinary glass. By then, Eleanor knew her Swiss friend to be purposeful when it came to details of ritual and ceremony, so she could not wait to hear what it all meant.

She put on the dress and the necklace and stood transfixed before the mirror, transported suddenly and for a long moment to an image of herself fifteen years before on an evening in Vienna, preparing to attend the opera to see for the first time the magnificence of Gustav Mahler conducting in the company of the great love of her life.

She stood now surprisingly comforted by the image of herself that she took in, not the proper Boston wife and mother, but a seductive woman of elegance, an object of desire. Though bemused and certainly suspicious, she felt herself overtaken first by a desire to end the charade, whatever it was, and to cancel the evening, and then by a second and stronger impulse simply to submit and cross the threshold to whatever was the intention, and she could imagine herself now descending with stunning effect the grand staircase of an opulent ocean liner.

Jung's time in New York was busy, his days and nights filled with appointments, but he had set aside this evening. His nine speeches at Fordham University were indeed about to set him apart and become the deciding factor in his inevitable rend with his colleague and mentor. It was a time for him of great moment and great exhilaration, a chance to be alone in the

New World, without Sigmund Freud looking over his shoulder expressing eloquently and clearly his own views on the new science of psychoanalysis.

When Eleanor arrived at the entrance to the dining room, she saw none of the seriousness of Jung's professional dilemma: She found her Swiss friend in complementary evening dress of white tie and tails, beaming at the image he saw before him. "My, what a strikingly handsome specimen," she said quickly before he could speak, awed by the sight of her old friend so handsomely attired. "I am greatly honored."

"The honor is all mine," Jung said, bowing elegantly as he offered her his arm and led her into the dining room, where the maître d', as if well rehearsed, seemed to know exactly who they were and which table would be theirs. It was not entirely in her imagination that the other diners stopped their conversations and watched the elegant couple being escorted to their table.

"Did you fear that I would not go along with all this?" she asked after he had taken his seat, aware of his eyes on her, taking in with pleasure the image he had created.

"I knew that a Salome was within, crying for recognition."

"So that is your intention? For me to release my inner Salome?"

He smiled. "It is so."

"And whose head was to be on the platter?"

"To be determined," he said, retaining the smile.

"And you are not intimidated in such a presence?"

"I welcome the release of that aspect of your character. No matter the consequence."

"Well, I am grateful that you do."

And they both paused.

"Tonight's wine is Austrian," he said, "and the meal is Viennese." Then he stopped and stared at her neck. "And that is a stunning necklace for the purposes of the evening," he said, shaking his head.

"It isn't real, is it?" she said.

"Tonight it is."

"And its intention?"

"Its intention is simply its stunning effect."

"One assumes that the intention is honorable, Herr Doctor . . . ," she said, looking up and eyeing him seriously, then with only the hint of a smile said, "Salome herself is feeling actually quite vulnerable."

"Tonight's intentions are totally honorable, I assure you," Jung said, returning her smile. "Tonight we are after a large prize." He raised his glass to her. "You have traveled far for this special night. We shall not waste it. Tonight we talk about the dreams. Yours have done me a great service. In fact, you yourself have been doing me great service ever since we met at your family's Putnam Camp. You have caused me to think, and to change."

"I too have done a great deal of thinking as a result of our conversations."

"They are precious to me."

"Like a diamond necklace?" She smiled appreciatively, letting him know that the symbolism was not lost on her.

"Precisely. Our conversations then and in the letters have helped me clarify what I really wish for, and where my ideas are headed."

"And you have come to New York to tell the world?"

"I have," he said. "What I am going to say here will set me apart."

"The direction you wish to go, I assume."

"Yes, that." He paused.

"And your vast differences with Dr. Freud," she filled in for him.

"I suppose," he said with a slight grimace. "And we must discuss your dream."

"My dream?" she asked.

"Yes," he said. "I am greatly interested in the iceberg. The part above the water." He gestured toward her. "The personality."

"The part in which we all play a role for the world," Eleanor said.

"Exactly," Jung said. "The persona."

"And the part of the iceberg below the waterline?"

"That too. The ninety percent below, the secret self, our famous unconscious that Dr. Freud has made so apparent. Above the surface we have our public selves." He held out one hand. "The masks of classical drama. The tragic." He held out the other hand. "And the comic. The persona, the Romans called the mask each actor wore."

"Costume jewelry and a revealing dress."

"In this case a charming and radiant beauty. The part of us above the surface, even the seductive part."

"And your reason for the celebration tonight?" she asked.

"That persona," he said decisively. "So much for me seems to be examining and describing the workings of personality, while Dr. Freud is after quite a different description. And each of us has the underwater part, some near the surface where we know of it, and some deep below, out of reach. That underwater part fascinates me, yes, but so does the visible part. Each of us has a unique persona above the waterline and our entire personal unconscious below. An iceberg there," he said, gesturing to Eleanor, "and an iceberg here." He tapped his own chest. "But what of the deep ocean beneath, the terrifying depth that now holds the *Titanic* in its dark and silent grave, the vast depth that has so overtaken you?" A look of concern settled on Eleanor. "It is the ocean depth that connects us all."

"A common depth."

"It is our collective unconscious."

"And that is the meaning of your own dream," Eleanor said, "the old bones and skulls in the dark cavern beneath your house?"

"It is. And you are good to remember my dream."

"Your dream that Dr. Freud misinterpreted, I believe."

"Yes," Jung said. "That is correct."

"And the mythical Titans, what of them?"

"And the Titans—" He paused and looked into her eyes. "The predecessors of the gods. Are they not the primal mythic connection of all culture for all time?" Eleanor said nothing and only shook her head slightly, then released a small sigh. "The parapsychology and the spiritual that Dr. James talked about," he said.

"And that Dr. Freud has little interest in?"

Jung stared at her for a moment, surprised that she could absorb all this so quickly. "Dr. Freud is concerned primarily with the iceberg, the drives that rise up from the majority of the mass, the deep and profound nine-tenths below in the darkness, the underwater part, and the control it exerts on the surface."

"And you are concerned with the depth even below the iceberg."

"Yes."

"And the two of you disagree, as Dr. James pointed out."

"Perhaps." Carl Jung looked at her with a smile of concern. "That is what my current lectures are about."

"The part that Sigmund Freud would not like to hear?"

"Yes, that."

"And in my dream, it is I, on the surface, clinging desperately, terrified of sliding off into that depth." She shivered at the mere thought.

He paused for a long moment, holding the seriousness. "You, my dear friend, have had the most profound encounter with that depth, and it has ruined, for the moment, your equilibrium." He paused again. "What if you simply let go?"

"I could never—" she began, and stopped, shaking her head. "I could never just let go. There is a whole life force."

"There is immense fear of the depth, propelled by the 'life force,' as you call it. We will need to bring you back to the surface. That is our task for your time here."

"That is the reason for the extraordinary costumes, I gather," she said.

"Partly, and partly just to enjoy the evening."

"The larger task will take time," she said seriously.

"We have time." He raised his glass. "We begin with the easier part." And both of them stopped to watch the waiter delivering the Wiener schnitzel and *Kartoffelpfannkuchen*, the potato pancakes everyone remembers from Vienna.

◥◣

"And the Joseph Conrad book," she said later, as they were waiting for the dessert course. "What of that?"

"It is *Heart of Darkness*, a story Conrad published a few years ago. Have you read it?"

"I have enjoyed Joseph Conrad, especially his *Victory*. For months, I imagined myself a cello player in a traveling women's ensemble," she said. "But I have not read this one. I understand that its contents are rather disturbing."

"It is an intentionally dark tale. Herr Conrad is a remarkable writer," Jung said. "A Polish seaman, you know, and yet he writes in his recently acquired English better than most Englishmen write in their own."

"I have heard this," she said, suspecting a wish on her host's part to be acknowledged in a similar light, as one who wrote surprisingly well outside of his native Swiss German.

"In this tale of great depth," Jung continued, "the narrator, Mr. Marlow, travels into the darkest jungle to find the military and school hero Kurtz," Jung said. "Kurtz has been trading ivory, surrounded by natives in the Congo, far removed from European civilization. He has descended to the depths, so far that he cannot escape, into 'the horror,' as he calls it.

Marlow witnesses the horror, but he is able to extract himself and come back to civilization, alive, but a changed man. He has been on the edge of the abyss that Kurtz has descended into. He has looked into the abyss, and it threatens to make him mad."

"You believe that I have looked into the abyss, and it threatens to make me mad."

"There is still much darkness ahead for both of us, but we need to remember to come back to the world of surface." There was now a look of deep concern on his face. "I wanted you, my dear friend, to come here, to come back to life."

"And are you perhaps addressing your own self?" She fixed him in her gaze, and he responded with a return gaze and only the slightest nod. "To use the experience but not to be drawn down by it," she said. "To descend to the heart of darkness and return to this bright world of costumes, slightly bloodied but unbowed, and the wiser for it."

"Precisely," Jung said with a contented smile, having made his point. "My thoughts, to the letter."

"Well then," Eleanor said, taking in a deep breath and raising her wineglass. "In that case, let us thoroughly enjoy the evening."

The waiter appeared with two dishes of chocolate cake and whipped cream. "Sacher torte," Carl Jung said with great pleasure.

"And *mit schlag*," Eleanor added, "the crowning Viennese touch. You have thought of everything."

"I wanted you to be content with the meal."

"Oh, I *am* content," she said dreamily. Suddenly, a look of concern came onto her face. "I am very content now. But where do we go from this?"

"We go our separate ways," Jung said, barely pausing. "We exchange letters, and then you come to see me in Zurich."

"And my coach turns back into a pumpkin."

Her dinner partner paused now, as if he had totally missed her concern. "Oh, I see," he said seriously, as if he was only now understanding how much his partner had invested in the ritual of the evening. "You do not have to lose all this, my dear Eleanor. You simply hold the moment."

"Hold the moment," she repeated blankly. She closed her eyes, then opened them slowly and looked about the dining room, allowing a contented smile to return. "Yes, I see," she said. "I shall hold the moment, but that will take some practice."

"This is the lesson of the evening. You can always recall all this—the jewelry, the fine dress, the music, the food—they are the world of the persona, and they are always there for you to revisit and to bring a smile."

They agreed to meet the following morning for an early breakfast at her hotel. He was to be up early to refine his lecture for that evening, the fourth in the series of nine, and she had a train to catch.

The tone of this part of their encounter was affectionate but business-like.

"That was a delightful evening," Eleanor said, smiling warmly, "grand and theatrical, as promised."

"One in which we both learned a great deal, I think."

"Yes, I learned," she said. "I always learn when we are together."

"Another rare moment of connection," Dr. Jung added, which made Eleanor smile. "Our fellow diners must have thought us lovers."

25

MOVING OUT

he morning following her return from New York and meeting with Carl Jung, the warm glow stayed with her as she greeted her family at Acorn Street. The night before she had received the report from Rose that all had gone well in her absence. At breakfast the girls were eager to tell all that had happened at school, and Frank nodded seriously his confirmation that he had heard the stories the day before. He added after the girls had left the table that a crucial meeting of the Trinity Church building committee with the city council had gone well. Frank knew of her meeting with Dr. Jung and showed polite interest. "Is all as it should be with your doctor friend?" he said, and Eleanor nodded and stated simply that all was well with him. "Good," Frank said, folding his napkin into its ring.

The feeling of well-being stayed with her all the way to the Hyperion Fund office and as she opened the small amount of mail that had accumulated in her three days of absence.

However, one thing was different. Now Will avoided lingering in the office in those moments at the end of the day Eleanor had grown to enjoy, when, the comfort of boundaries firmly in place, they had shared the details of their business and their lives. She almost asked him if something had occurred to upset him, but the opportunity never arose, and he had always seemed to be of such an unusually even temperament that nothing unsettled him. She hoped against hope that whatever it was, it would pass, and the ship would be righted.

Then one afternoon she arrived at the office and found Will removing items from his desk to a large wooden crate.

"Moving out, Mr. Honeycutt?" she said to him lightly.

Caught by surprise, he swung around and simply stared at her, unable to speak at first. "Actually, I am," he said, looking awkward and uncomfortable. "I am leaving," he said finally.

"Leaving?" At first, she could not believe what she was hearing.

"I'm going with Jesse Livermore. He is moving me to New York."

Eleanor waited quietly for him to break into that smile she found charming, signaling an eccentric's ironic twist. But none came. "You are joking," she said.

"I am not joking," he said. "I am moving to New York."

"This cannot be."

"Well, this *is*," he said with a bitter finality that shocked her.

"Leaving just like that. No warning, no discussion, no—"

"I am going where I am needed."

"Where you are needed?" she said, incredulous. "You are needed here. The Hyperion Fund needs you." He only stared hard at her. "I need you."

"You can find a replacement. You can find someone you don't need to invent, to fulfill some twisted sense of destiny."

The words and the biting tone took her breath away. "I didn't need to *invent*," she said. "I found you—"

"Well now you can *find* my cousin," he interrupted curtly. "Remember? He is the one you were looking for in the first place. I was a mistake."

"You have been the savior. I have told you that, many times. You are an indispensable part of all this."

"That will be remedied soon. You can get Arnauld to take my place."

"Arnauld?" She couldn't believe what she was hearing. "Arnauld is a history and German teacher."

"I was a Harvard physicist. You are excellent at transformations."

"Mr. Honeycutt," she said decisively, as if to shake him out of some spell he had fallen under. Then she paused. "Arnauld," she said. "Is that it? Is this about Arnauld Esterhazy? Do you think that I favor him over you? Is that what you think?"

"Quite frankly I do not care. You can fawn over him all you want. I am accepting Mr. Livermore's offer to move me to New York. You can do with yourself and your own affairs as you wish."

"Have you signed a contract?"

That stopped him for a moment. "I have. I have signed a contract and have begun looking for an apartment."

Now it was Eleanor who was staring hard. "Mr. Honeycutt—" she began, then stopped herself. "Will," she said emphatically, "is it that smitten business again? Is that the cause of all this?"

He put his head down, unable to look at her. "It is a business decision," he said quickly.

"I thought you were a scientist, above emotion." She was now on the attack, still trying to shake him loose from this attitude she had never seen before.

"I am moving to New York."

"It is jealousy, isn't it?" she repeated. He still wouldn't look at her. "Isn't this taking things just a little too far?"

Will Honeycutt looked up, and a coldness came into his eyes. "Emotion has nothing to do with it."

"Oh, Will," she repeated, now trying desperately to break through this wall she had never seen before. "I am so sorry. I have neglected you, and you are so very important to me."

"Save that for someone else," he snapped, and he placed the last items in the box. "I shall finish packing when I can be alone here. I think you need time to collect your thoughts and absorb the fact that I am leaving. You will not have me to take for granted anymore."

"Oh, Will," she repeated in a burst, as if finally understanding. "I have taken you for granted. That is what is happening here."

"It doesn't matter. I am leaving." He carried the box with him and approached the door. "I shall return later to finish the packing." He opened the door, stepped out into the hallway. The door closed behind him, and Eleanor stood deathly still for a long moment. Will Honeycutt was gone.

〜

After a sleepless night, she returned to the office, hoping to find him sitting at his desk, smiling and signaling that it had all been a grotesque mistake. His desk was empty. There was no sign of him left in the office. He was really gone.

She spent one day and part of the next sitting alone in the office, trying to clear her mind and think through what to do next, but a stream of questions ran through that thinking, ruining her equilibrium. Had she really been so overtly attentive to Arnauld as to be an affront? Had Will Honeycutt's affection for her risen so far beyond the gentle mutual respect that they both shared that he could no longer endure it? Had watching Arnauld triggered some deep insecurity in him? Had she said some one thing to offend him, or had it been an accumulation over time?

As if to assuage at least some of the desolation she was feeling, she rose and moved across the office to Will's desk and sat staring at the now-cleared surface, then opened each of the emptied-out drawers. But one, the large broad central one, was not emptied. Without touching it, she stared for a long moment at the large, thick coil-bound artist's sketchbook she saw there. Then carefully, respectfully, she reached for it and slowly removed it to the desk surface.

Almost afraid to move, she lifted the front cover and revealed the first page, a colored ink drawing of such intricate complexity that it took her a few minutes even to begin to make out what it might be.

Then she turned the page to the next intricate drawing, and then to the next, and then the next. Her attention became so rapt by what she was seeing that she lost total track of time, and a full hour passed before she completed a cursory review of the book's contents.

On the front sides of each page were the drawings, most of them in India ink, colored in with pastels or watercolors, occasionally crayon, but a few were executed in brilliantly colored thick tempera paint.

The drawings were executed with surprising skill, and there seemed to be no practice sketches. The contents were varied, mostly representations of mythic characters or dragonlike creatures and complicated designs with a distinct Chinese or Tibetan look, some of recognizable human forms even. One series of smaller drawings, some two or three to a page, depicted a woman in white robes, a temple priestess, with the name Isis written carefully beneath them. The figure looked remarkably like Eleanor herself.

≈

Later, she wrote Jung about her losing Will Honeycutt, "an unexpected and great blow," she called it. Jung did not know all the details of her secret source of knowledge, but he knew that she had had a complicated relationship with investments that had allowed her to have access to a great deal of money, and he knew at least the bare bones of her dependence on her young colleague Honeycutt. He knew also, through Eleanor's accounts, of Will Honeycutt's remarkable relationship to dreams and his recording of them that had led to his Harvard College dissertation dialogues on atomic structure with an ancient Greek, recorded in the slim paper-bound volume Eleanor had given him. "Now he is gone," Eleanor wrote with finality. "I hope the situation is resolved by the time you read this, but I am not hopeful that it will be resolved satisfactorily."

And she told him about the remarkable sketchbook she had found left behind in the desk drawer, described the drawings and paintings and the elegant cursive descriptions on the backs of pages. "His ancient Greek sage Democritus does appear many times, often surrounded by abstract drawings of atomic structures. And there is a character labeled Isis, with the look and robes of an ancient temple priestess. She is quite attractive, actually. It is artwork and elegant language beyond anything I knew him capable of," she said. "And that is evidenced nowhere else in his life, at least that I know of."

"That book is his world of dreams, the powerful language of the unconscious. Democritus, this is the wise old man," Jung said. "An archetype for sure, and Isis, of course, is the Egyptian goddess, the divinity, mother, lover, magician at the center of life. She is probably the most comprehensive figure in all of mythology, but one senses here that your Mr. Will Honeycutt is calling her up in her more sensual aspects. And his forgetfulness, that was no accident, you realize. He wanted you to see it." The thought had occurred to her, she admitted.

And one observation by her great Swiss friend stood out for Eleanor. "And this Isis character he draws," Jung wrote. "No doubt she resembles you."

She had no idea that she was losing Will Honeycutt until it was too late and he had moved his personal items out of their office. In retrospect, she could see how much she had counted on him and how unrealistic that had been, how because he had seemed able to take on any task, undaunted by any challenge—in fact, he seemed to thrive under what she gave him, gaining strength with every new assignment—she had depended too much, leaned too hard, to the breaking point. She could see now, in retrospect, that it was the part of her story she kept from him—compared to what he saw happening—that had put the fatal strain on their working together.

He was from the beginning unflagging in his loyalty—he had, after all, given up his career as a university scientist for her—and he kept their dealings in the strictest confidence, as was their explicit understanding from the start. There was never a problem with confidentiality, as she knew in her bones the moment she met him. As he said back then, "I don't have anyone I talk to." And then, with time, that changed to "You are the only one I talk to."

But each time after one of her extraordinary predictions had come to pass, after he had carried out his part of the bargain, as she herself was recovering from and adjusting to the shock that it brought with it, he would approach her with more or less the same questions: How did you know this? How did you predict such a thing?

And each time she would give him an evasive answer, something like her standard "Intuition, Mr. Honeycutt, intuition," and each time consider telling him the whole story, trusting him with the depth of her secret, she would invariably pull back from the idea, deciding once again that it was her fate to keep the secret of the journal to herself. And each time he asked and each time she pulled away with an evasion, she could see later with the power of hindsight how it chipped away at his goodwill and his willingness to continue in his role as her indispensable assistant and invaluable colleague.

She had not been good at reading potential catastrophe into his moods and mannerisms because—she reasoned afterward—he was always filled with nervous energy. That seemed his very nature. The strain came from those moments when he attempted to discover her secret. An incidence of this came in the fall of 1912, with details around the whole *Titanic* matter. Arnauld had been at St. Gregory's for nearly two years by that time and was settling in. He seemed to enjoy teaching young boys, although Eleanor was not certain how long that would last, but his invitations to Harvard and the rowing on the Charles River appeared to be more deeply gratifying, as was his great friendship with Edith Hamilton, whom he had met through Eleanor's planning, and his visits to various Boston homes.

All in all, Eleanor felt quite reassured, and relieved. Things with regard to Arnauld were going as they should. With all that she did in her high-profile external life as mother, wife, and community leader, Will Honeycutt like everyone else never even came close to guessing at the significant role she had played for years, putting in place the details that would lure this Viennese scholar to Boston, and then arranging things so that he would wish to stay. Her husband, Frank Burden, remarked on a number of occasions, "It is impressive to see the ease with which Esterhazy has fit in," and Eleanor would breathe a sigh of relief every time she heard him pronounce it.

Nor could Will Honeycutt or anyone else guess at the other secretive activities that nonetheless laid upon her shoulders not-insignificant demands. On some matters she knew that she had no choice but to act, to do as the journal directed. But at all times, she depended on Will Honeycutt, her partner in logistics and business. And now he was gone.

She held Will Honeycutt's sketchbook in her hands for a long time, reexamining each exquisite page, letting the significance of each sink in, trying to absorb the pathways into the unconscious the entries represented, trying to explore the world of dreams, allowing the pages to remind her of her own vivid dreams that had visited her since the awful moment of discovering the *Titanic* tragedy. Then she put down Will Honeycutt's sketchbook, replacing it in its drawer, and picked up the black-covered notebook of her own that had been sitting on her desk, unused, for months. She opened it to the first blank page, picked up a pen, and began to write, recalling not a recent dream but one that had recurred from her childhood and had stayed vivid ever since.

26

THE LADY IN WHITE

ill Honeycutt's departure had thrown Eleanor into a darker depression than one would have expected had she been able to share it with anyone. She went about her daily routine with outward poise and calm, but inside she was filled with anxiety and doubt. At times like these, her friend Jung would say, be especially mindful of dreams.

The black college notebook found among Eleanor's papers contains a mixture of impressions of dreams and the beginnings of dialogues, all written in pen, in her careful handwriting, notations added in pencil. A number of the descriptions are of a recurring dream of her childhood, one she was especially eager to encounter now. In her writing she introduces the detail that a woman in a long white dress, a character identified as Eleanor's late mother, sitting on a blanket in a large expansive meadow, a picnic basket beside her, invites young Weezie to come sit beside her. The first dialogue of real substance with this figure from her dreams is dated the day after Will Honeycutt's departure, and obviously inspired by Will's elaborate renderings of his own dreams. From her notes and stage directions added in pencil, it is possible to reconstruct the scene with a good deal of completeness.

⟋

"I don't know what to say," the grown Eleanor says, approaching the figure in white. "I am pleased and surprised that you have appeared in my dreams. Now, I hope that we may talk."

"Of course, you may talk to me," the lady in white says. "That is how things work. That is what I am here for."

"I am new at this, and I don't know where to begin. Are you real, or are you part of my imaginings?"

"I am both. I am both new information and what you already know, but are not aware that you know."

"Do we begin with Vienna?" Eleanor says.

"That is a good place to start."

"There is much I wish to say about Vienna. There is the journal."

"But for now, mustn't we concern ourselves with your present state of mind? I can see from your appearance that you have gone without sleep, and you have been distracted by the departure of your friend Mr. Honeycutt."

"His leaving has upended my world. I have grown to depend on him to make the assigned tasks less onerous. And facing his departure leaves me alone again."

"Reminding you of other losses."

"That is so," Eleanor says, amazed at how naturally the woman speaks of great loss.

"Do you know why he left?"

"Yes, he said I was too attentive to Arnauld Esterhazy. But I do not believe that I was. Mr. Honeycutt is a bit impulsive. He has projected much onto me, and that makes him vulnerable, beyond his own understanding. He was perhaps more in need of my attention than I knew. And when I could not meet his unrealistic demands, he overreacted and left."

"My, that is a predicament," the woman says.

"There is little I can do except be aware of his deficiencies."

"But still his hasty departure leaves you in a state of seeming desperation."

"You say 'seeming,'" Eleanor says. "To me it appears as *real* desperation."

"You are strong, my dear, like your mother and your father."

"I have learned about my father," Eleanor says, as if it is a revelation.

The woman smiles knowingly, without being ruffled. "You are strong like him. That is the gift. You now know, and you will always know, you are strong like him."

"That is what you have come to tell me?"

"You have always had great power within, even when you were a little girl and suffered the greatest loss. You will manage now, and you will find help as needed."

"But what of the journal?" Eleanor asks. "What of the need to have Will Honeycutt as my colleague years from now? That is what is foretold."

"You need to have faith. I know that you believe that your actions are necessary, and they are, but meanwhile things will evolve as they should. That is my main message to you."

"I do not always have that faith."

"That, my dear, is completely natural," the woman in white says. "You have not failed yet, have you? All has worked out, has it not? You face a dilemma that you can manage." She laughs gently. "It is as if you are at bicycle pedals, and someone has attached an electrical generator."

Now Eleanor laughs. "That sounds like something Will would devise. As I pedal, the energy is supplied for what needs to happen."

"That is correct, my dear. You see, you are very wise in the ways of the world."

"And I must keep pedaling or nothing will happen, even if it seems hopeless, as it does right now?"

"That is correct. You must keep going, and if you keep going, everything will happen as it should. It is a combination."

"Free will and destiny."

The woman looks for a long moment. "Oh my, you sound like your father."

"You are here to tell me that, aren't you?"

"Oh, my dear, I am here to show you what you already know. You are the one who will do the work. You are the strong one. I am only the helper."

"And that is for always?"

"Always, of course. It is purely the nature of things." She smiles. "Now, go home to Frank and your girls. They love you and need you. Go home and, for goodness' sake, get some sleep."

"And keep pedaling," Eleanor says.

"And keep pedaling." The woman in white stops for a moment to admire her daughter, and smiles again at what she sees. "You do it so well."

And that is the end of the dialogue.

27

A HIGHER CALLING

She sat at her desk and tried not to notice Will Honeycutt's empty desk on the other side of the room. But soon even her best intentions did no good, and she turned and stared at the empty space where his stack of books used to sit.

Suddenly, she was back running the old questions through her head. What had caused the precipitous eruption to a situation—not without its problems, granted—that seemed to have weathered all the storms and remained stable for so long? Was it something she had said or done? Could it have been avoided or was it inevitable? Did he really mean to give up his position to his cousin in Chicago? Was the other Honeycutt, the serious and businesslike T. Williams, really the one for the job in the first place and the gods or fates or whoever was controlling this whole thing simply making it possible to insert the right man? Was it all in fact just pure jealousy of the special place Arnauld Esterhazy held in all of her dealings? Was that it?

She began to wonder how she would ever get in touch with the second Will Honeycutt, and she was just about ready to find a Chicago telephone directory, when she heard the key in the lock and the door swung open.

Standing before her was someone who looked vaguely like her young, energetic colleague Will Honeycutt, only this apparition had deep shadows under his reddened eyes, and he had not shaved for a day or two. He did not see her at first.

"Oh," he said, looking up with surprise. "I didn't think you would be here so early."

The distraught look on his face warded off any rush of relief she might have felt by seeing him. "I have been away," she said. "I had to come early."

"I forgot something," he said. "I returned for it."

"Your sketchbook," she said. "It is in the drawer where you left it."

"You saw it?" he said with apprehension.

"I did," she said without apology, as if anything left behind was fair game. "I know it is private, but I did see it, and I am very touched and impressed by it."

"It is my dreams," he said apologetically now. "My dialogues."

"I know. They are beautiful and complex and profound. I had no idea that you were such an artist."

"You do not think it the work of a madman?"

"I do not. I think it is the work of a man who has had very profound encounters with his unconscious mind."

Will Honeycutt looked down and said nothing. "I came back for the sketchbook, but there is more."

"What, Will?" she said in little more than a whisper.

"I look awful," he said. "It happens when I don't sleep or eat or even go home for two days."

She wanted to go to him, to hold him in her embrace for a long time, but she stayed in her chair without moving, holding her ground. She read the look of total resignation on his face and barely needed to say, "What is it?"

"There is a change," he said quietly.

For a moment she continued trying to read the face of this young man she had come to know, she thought, so well. "Does this mean by chance that you are not going to New York with Jesse Livermore?" she said, cutting through the layers.

"No New York," he said, now fighting for breath. "I have had a terrible time, wrestling with demons, I guess you would say. I know why I reacted as I did, and I am not proud of it. In fact, I fear I have been very dreadfully immature. I am ashamed—"

She cut him off. "Did you consult your Democritus about this?"

The question, intended lightly perhaps, caught Will Honeycutt by surprise. He did not look at her, trying to hide what looked from the outside like embarrassment. Eleanor was stepping over a line in asking the question. "No," he said suddenly, looking into her eyes and finding no sign of anything but respect. "William James."

"Oh my, Will, I think you had better sit down." She gestured toward the chair at his former desk and smiled in a concerned way that erased all doubt.

Reading the smile, Will Honeycutt walked to the desk chair and sat, issuing a huge sigh of relief. Then he looked back to her. "He appeared in my dream last night, and I entered a dialogue—" He stopped, seeing the stunned look on her face. "I mean I began writing, and he spoke to me. It was a great relief."

"And . . . ," she said hesitantly. "And what did Dr. James say?" There was now a hush in the room.

"He said that I most definitely needed to stay with you," he began, feeling his way cautiously, "that you needed me, that you were answering to a higher calling, one I could not understand. And that I had a role to play."

Eleanor looked at him with a reverence in her eyes. "And what is that higher calling?"

"I do not know. He would not say. He just said that it was beyond my knowing, and that I needed to return to your cause and to serve without question. He said that you had spent enormous effort bringing about the work we do here and getting Arnauld to come to Boston, and now it was of ultimate importance that he wish to stay, and that I could be of service in that cause. He said it needed to be for me a holy mission and that I should put aside any petty concerns of my own."

"Oh my," Eleanor said, and then was silent for a moment.

"And he said more," Will Honeycutt continued, still cautious.

"Yes?" she said again, in little more than a whisper.

"He said that I would have an important part to play in the story later, and that I needed to be patient and not expect to understand, to stop being so demanding."

She remained silent for a long time, looking away, but feeling his eyes on her. "Oh my," she repeated, shaking her head slowly. "That is very much to consider, isn't it?" Slowly, she looked up, collecting herself, and a gentle smile came to her lips. "Does this mean that you will be moving your things back into the desk?"

"If I am allowed."

"I would be greatly honored," she said.

"Then it will be so. I have informed Jesse Livermore."

"Honored and relieved," she added. "More than words can express, actually."

Will Honeycutt looked down at his feet. "I am too," he said. "Actually."

She said nothing for a long moment. "I should have been more attentive—" she began softly.

"None of that is important now," he said abruptly, cutting her off. "I know my role now." Then upon thought, he added, "I am certain of it."

"Can you live with what is?"

"I can," he said, his eyes downcast.

She looked at him until his eyes met hers. "Do you have any idea how important you are to me?"

Will Honeycutt said nothing. "Perhaps," came out finally. He was looking down, giving the matter thought. "Yes," he said, gaining conviction. "Yes, I think I do." Then he added, "William James has told me."

She paused and stared again. "Good," she said with her famous *well that settles that* certitude, and then rose and moved back toward the office cupboard. "Here," she said, opening the cupboard door and removing a cardboard box. "There is something I wish to show you."

The box was sealed with paper tape, and she opened it with a pair of scissors from her own desk. He watched, without moving, as she withdrew from the packing material a pair of crystal glasses. "I requisitioned these, I believe they say in the military."

"From the New York hotel," he said with a smile, "ten years ago."

Eleanor nodded. "I packed them away in this special box." She placed the two glasses on the table and then dug further into the packing. She withdrew a bottle of red wine. The label was familiar to both of them, the now-twenty-year-old bottle of Château Mouton Rothschild. "Will you sit down?" she said.

There was a plan for contingencies on Acorn Street, one rarely employed, but put in place if Eleanor needed to stay overly long at a meeting, and Rose knew exactly what to do. For once the needs of her family were not foremost in Eleanor's mind in this late afternoon; in fact, they were far from foremost in her mind. "Do you recognize the wine?" she said calmly to the disheveled man in front of her.

"How could I not?" he replied.

"I have been saving these for the right occasion," she said. Her smile was warm and gentle. "I believe we have arrived at that occasion."

The disheveled Will Honeycutt looked back at her with epic relief on his face. And then she dug down into the packing and found the last items, which she began to withdraw. "There is something more."

Will Honeycutt saw what she withdrew, and a huge smile broke out on his face and the shadows seemed to disappear from under his eyes. The items were a pair of familiar, thin Cuban cigars, which she laid carefully beside the two glasses, then held up and examined. "This time I think we shall forgo these," she said.

Will Honeycutt looked enormously relieved. "I take it that this means that I have not ruined everything," he said.

"I'd say that you most definitely have not," she said, taking on a feigned seriousness, allowing for a dramatic pause. "You did come close, I will admit." And she began opening the bottle. "But you have not."

Neither spoke then as Eleanor opened the bottle with a corkscrew she had pulled from the box, and then after she poured two glasses, she rose and brought him one of them, then held up hers to his. "I do hope that our expensive claret has not turned to vinegar." Then they said nothing, but her eyes held his for a long moment, allowing him to read in hers whatever intimacy he needed in that moment of communion.

"Now," she said, returning to her desk chair. "I would like you to show me the sketchbook."

"I did not mean to leave it behind. It is very private."

"It is extremely moving, Will. I know it is very private, but I am glad that I had a chance to see it, and now I look forward to reading through it with you."

He moved toward her, overcoming any hesitation. "I would be honored," he said with a smile.

"And then I need to tell you about Arnauld," Eleanor said.

PART
THREE

28

SOMETHING UNPREDICTABLE

here is no record of how much of the story Eleanor told Will Honeycutt that day, but it is certain from what follows that she withheld parts at that time. The whole of Arnauld Esterhazy's story can be pieced together, with some interpreting, from the letters and journals, and it is as follows.

Life for him changed forever one spring morning in 1897 in his native Vienna, at age eighteen, when he saw an attractive young American woman—a "compellingly attractive bright-eyed goddess," he would write later—standing beside his childhood friend Alma Schindler in a public park near the Hofburg, where he was meeting a group of friends to take in an afternoon in the Wienerwald. "Arnauld, there is someone I would so like you to meet!" Alma, ever the perverse matchmaker, exclaimed loudly so that he had no choice but to look directly into her beautiful face and hold out his hand. "This is Miss Putnam," Alma continued. "She is visiting us from Boston."

And so, in that one fateful moment, the young American woman from Boston extended her hand in what was for her a most natural act and for him a total disruption of equilibrium. "I am happy to meet you," she said cheerfully, as if the meeting were nothing more special than a dozen others she had made with the same outgoing smile—"outgoing and totally captivating" was how the later description went—since her arrival in Vienna on a secret mission to write something of significance about music and cultural life for the *New York Times,* to be published under a pseudonym.

And, his fate sealed, Arnauld had met the love of his life, the woman he would compare over and over again to Dante's venerated Beatrice. "I hope you are enjoying our city" were the inelegant words out of his mouth, and rather than reply with something equally perfunctory, she held his hand for just an extra moment and said with great earnestness, "Why, yes I am, and you are kind to wish it. I have found my new Vienna friends to be gracious and generous with their time." She looked over at Alma, who smiled happily. "Perhaps you will join us on one of our regular outings."

"Oh, you would love having Arnauld all to yourself," Alma said to her new American friend without an ounce of sarcasm. "He is the one full of historical knowledge. Our great teacher," she added, now teasing a bit.

"That makes it easy," Weezie Putnam said then. "We shall invite you along from now on. I am much in need of history lessons."

The die that was cast with the handshake had now rolled fatefully, and Arnauld found himself on many occasions not only in the presence of this distinctively beautiful woman, but being asked question after question about history and local customs. What is the origin of the term *Biedermeier*? How many languages are official in the empire? Is Beethoven still being played in the symphony halls? Does one ever see the empress in Vienna? Arnauld seemed to know the answer to everything. The more he answered, the more her questioning persisted.

From time to time, Alma, ever the provocateur, would smile at her creation. "I have given you an assignment, Arnauld," she said, now definitely teasing. "You have become Miss Putnam's private tutor." And she smiled her wry sophisticated smile. "And I think she is quite sweet on you, my friend." Then she sat back and enjoyed seeing her sensitive young Viennese friend blush.

And Arnauld remembered the morning of the first meeting sometime later, when the older American visitor first came into that same park by the Hofburg and he heard him give his name, Mr. Truman, and heard Miss Putnam—for some mysterious reason—give hers in return as Emily James. Why she had done that he had no idea, and, his encounters with her never being of a sufficiently candid nature, he never asked. But he did notice that there was an immediate attraction between these two Americans, an older man and a younger woman, a fatal attraction he was to learn later.

The older American's attentions began to draw Weezie Putnam away from the group of friends, a fact that made Arnauld more sad than envious. He liked this man Truman from the very first, although he was of another generation and his reasons for being in Vienna were not altogether clear; in fact, he remained throughout something of a mystery. Arnauld even found himself on occasion sitting in conversation with the man in the presence of his old friend Ernst Kleist and his artistic crowd at the Café Central. But again, his conversations were never candid enough for him to query the man about his intentions, and Arnauld did admit to feeling a bit protective of Miss Putnam as he saw this Mr. Truman, from San Francisco he said, moving closer and closer to her. And then they both began appearing less in public, causing Kleist only to smile knowingly.

"You need not worry, Arnauld," Kleist said, but Arnauld guessed that his friend's idea for what should cause worry was quite different from his own.

The older American and Miss Putnam were seen at the opera together and out walking in the Prater and waltzing at the Sperl. And Alma too only smiled and patted his arm when Arnauld asked if she was concerned, and he knew that Alma's standards—and experiences—also were far different from his in these matters. "Someday you will have your own affairs of the heart," she said, smiling, again with nothing ironic in her voice. "You will learn to trust the feelings."

So Arnauld tried not to notice and decided to enjoy the moments when Miss Putnam was beside him asking her endless questions, and to enjoy the occasional times when he found himself alone or in a small café group with the older Mr. Truman.

There was even a time, near the fateful end, when he sat alone in the Café Central and the American visitor joined him. For some reason he could not explain, Arnauld began divulging his despondency over his intense attraction to the very woman to whom his listener had quite obviously become attached. Rather than take offense or chide him in any way, the older American took him into his confidence and in the calmest and most reassuring voice told him something quite extraordinary, that he knew with some assurance that Miss Putnam did indeed hold him in the highest regard and that rather than retreat or cease his attentions, Arnauld ought to press on with confidence, assured that the future held for him a certain brightness and fulfillment. The calm reassurance, coming as a complete surprise, especially considering what was about to transpire, had such a powerful and lasting effect on Arnauld that he committed himself, pretty much then and there, to a life course of total devotion to this beautiful woman, whom he continued to call his Beatrice.

Then shortly after his surprisingly poignant conversation with the American, the tragedy struck.

Even years later it was clear that Arnauld never fully understood what happened, but somehow the older American was struck down mysteriously, in the very presence of Weezie Putnam, Kleist told him. And since no witnesses could identify the perpetrator, no one ever knew exactly what had transpired, or why. It was rumored that Sigmund Freud had witnessed the awful event, but Arnauld had never been able to confirm that detail, and Dr. Freud never came forward.

"There remain a number of peculiar details," Kleist told him grimly after it was all over. "No one has been able to determine just who the older American fellow Mr. Truman was or what he was doing in Vienna. Some in our café crowd suspect that his name was not Truman at all, and that he was some sort of secret agent."

However it was, the events had had a devastating effect on Miss Putnam, who remained secluded in her room at her boardinghouse where she had lived her entire time in Vienna, the owner, Fräulein Tatlock, being, by complete coincidence, an old friend of Arnauld's family. Encouraged by Alma, Arnauld actually paid a call on her there, not really knowing what else to do.

She seemed enormously relieved to see him. "I am being required to stay here for a time by the police," she said, obviously distraught. "Until this highly regrettable situation is cleared up." Her face was pale and drawn, her hair mussed; there were dark shadows under her eyes, and there was little of her former radiance, a plight that if anything only endeared her to him all the more.

"If there is anything I can do . . . ?" he began with an obvious helplessness.

"Oh, Arnauld," she said, "I am greatly appreciative just knowing you are nearby. I have received a shock, but I will survive, and I do want you to remain my dear friend." And then she added with what seemed a sudden spontaneity, "And perhaps even come to Boston at some point."

He would follow her anywhere, he wished to say, but of course he did not. "I would consider that an honor," was all he could think of saying. "At some point."

"But right now I need to recover some modicum of equilibrium," she said. "I hope you understand." He left her alone then, but before they parted, she took his hand and pressed it with a surprising vitality. "What I have proposed is of utmost importance to me, and I wish most vehemently to engage you in correspondence. I shall be writing you."

He visited her each morning at Fräulein Tatlock's pension, until the day of her departure. He would sit with her quietly in the parlor, sometimes saying nothing, watching her busy herself with the writing project she seemed now intent on completing. "You are my historical source," she would say to him, referring to what she was writing, and then she would continue asking her endless questions. "It is all written here." She was writing her reminiscence of her time in Vienna, it seemed, and although she shared none of its contents with him then, he could see that she was writing with considerable passion. "I wish to get the facts right. When I am finished," she said once with a compelling smile, "the world will not know if this is my work or yours."

"You exaggerate," Arnauld said, "but I do appreciate being of use."

"Dear Arnauld," she said then, putting down her pen and looking deep into his eyes, a gesture he would remember and hold dear always, "you are indispensable to me, and I do not want to lose you."

Then one morning she announced boldly, "I am being allowed to leave, and I shall be traveling home with this at least." She held up a stack of handwritten pages.

"Your reflections on your time here?" he said.

"At least a start," she said. "I learned much about Vienna and culture from him." She stopped, about to be overcome. "And from your history lessons," she said quickly, pulling herself back.

"You have learned much from your American friend, I think."

"Oh my, yes," she said. "There is much from both of you in these pages. I hope to finish on shipboard."

"The writing has been a good curative, I hope."

"At least a start," she repeated. Already she looked better.

Years later Arnauld remembered and held most dear the intensity with which she spoke those last words and the emptiness he felt the following weeks as he walked past places in his dear city where they had met on so many occasions, an indescribable emptiness, he recalled, emptiness and hopelessness that stayed with him for many days. And then her first letter arrived.

As depleted as he felt by the tragedy that had befallen her—most of which he could only guess at—he was just beginning, in spite of his despair at her leaving, to understand that this woman, this Weezie Putnam from Boston, was to be the permanent love of his life. Like some chivalrous knight of old or a romantic poet of the last century, he was ready to devote himself to the adoration of this lady. The letters, of course, encouraged that.

After the events of Weezie Putnam's time in Vienna, Arnauld found himself a changed man, filled with a romantic vision of his own future and a purpose he could not really define. Somehow throwing himself into study seemed to be the outcome. He was always considered a serious student, but now he pursued scholarship with an energy and a passion that earned him quite a reputation within the university and among the crowd that gathered at the Café Central. However it was, being a serious scholar and being perceived as such stuck with him. The role lasted the better part of a decade, as he pursued first his undergraduate work, the commission in the imperial army required by family tradition, and then the elevation to graduate status. He was on the way to becoming a full-fledged professor of history, "a distinguished one," his professors told him on at least one occasion.

When military duty interrupted his academic career, as he accepted the obligation of the family name, his friends were more amused than surprised. "Arnauld is not exactly the military type," one friend said. "Perhaps he will have more effect on them than they on him." He was an Esterhazy after all, no matter how many generations of low birth order had separated him from any real significance, and Esterhazys were trained as officers in the emperor's army. His own obligation upon receiving his commission was two years of active service as an officer. First, he served as a candidate, then as a lieutenant at an outpost in Galicia, with a colorful regimental uniform to show for it. After the initial service, he was then given the freedom to leave, which no one seemed to object to in a family appointment such as his, and resume his university life with the respectable title "reserve" attached to his name. Throughout it all, he retained the right to wear the uniform to formal occasions such as operas and balls, should he wish, though he never did.

"You really ought to wear your uniform," the disappointed Alma told him. "You look princely and dashing in it."

"I do not wish to look princely and dashing," Arnauld replied.

"But you could win your way into the hearts and beds of beautiful women," Alma said. "That is a fine old Viennese tradition."

"But I do not wish to win my way into the hearts and beds of beautiful women," Arnauld said.

"For shame," she said with feigned disapproval. "You would enjoy it, as would the beautiful women."

Arnauld looked into his friend's eyes and smiled. "Yours is the only heart I wish to win," he said. "And yours is already taken, many times over."

Alma reached out and touched his cheek affectionately, then released a resigned sigh. "Oh, Arnauld, I know where your heart is. It was taken from you, I fear, that day I introduced you to Miss Putnam in the Hofburg park."

Arnauld said nothing but returned to his old friend a look of contented resignation.

"I will still not stop looking out for you," she said, and he smiled again.

During those student days, he kept up his correspondence with Miss Putnam, who had returned to Boston and assumed her given name, Eleanor, and then in 1902 the formal married name of Mrs. Frank Burden. Her letters were always chatty and informative and affectionate, and she never seemed to be holding anything back, although most of the references concerned her social life in the beginning and then in 1904, the details of young motherhood. Whatever it was, he had the impression that she was sharing with him in the most warmly candid manner the intimate details of her life, and he responded by sharing the same of his.

From the start, Arnauld was aware of her close relationship with William James, and, of course, he had read the great man's major works both in English and in German translation. From time to time he would write with questions about the eminent Dr. James, and she would always answer, "Of course, I could not speak for him, but . . . ," and then follow with a very concise and probably very accurate summary of Dr. James's view of one subject or another. Over the years, through her letters and her many references to Dr. James's thoughts and ideas and their times together, Arnauld had come to believe that Eleanor was one of the great philosopher's best-informed interpreters, without knowing or acknowledging the role.

The suggestions that Arnauld come to Boston to teach did not begin until nearly ten years after their fateful meeting in Vienna, as Arnauld was finishing his studies and scholarly apprenticeship at the university and beginning to wonder aloud what to do with his life. The future as a stuffy old university professor seemed to him a bit deflating, but his own reserved nature, he feared, was keeping him where he was. In one letter he actually said, "My life is so awfully staid. I would love to see myself as someone who would do something unpredictable." The unpredictable, she began writing him, ought to be to come to Boston "for a few years," and accept a teaching position at her husband's former school, St. Gregory's.

In 1907, when his childhood friend Alma Schindler, now married to Gustav Mahler, the renowned director of the Vienna opera, moved with her husband to New York City, Arnauld listened to her descriptions of America and was enticed, as if the insistent invitations from his beloved Eleanor were not enough. So at the end of 1909, he abandoned all caution and said yes to an offer from St. Gregory's School. In August 1910, he moved to Boston and took up a position teaching geography to the younger boys, a position that was designed to grow in stature, moving up to the older boys, "when he gained his sea legs," as the headmaster said.

Arnauld Esterhazy's adjustment to Boston and St. Gregory's was fueled first by his fascination with the early history of the American republic. He had never been to America, and he found his initial impression, despite the obvious challenges of being in a new land, to be exhilarating. All his life he had loved traveling to new cities, and in his twenties he assigned himself to the grand tour that seemed de rigueur for young men of university age. "See how the rest of the world works," one of his language professors had said to him. From early years he loved the feeling of abstraction that one received in someone else's culture, how what seemed ordinary and everyday to the denizens seemed magical to visitors. And so, like so many of Europe's upper-class young gentlemen, he had traveled to all the cities of the empire and the cities of Europe and even to India and Africa. But he had never been to America.

In preparing for his new assignment, teaching geography to young boys, he committed to learning their country's history along with them. And from the start, what he found fascinating was that whereas the culture he had grown up in, beneficiary now of a parliamentary monarchy, stretched back over centuries of aristocracy and ruling families, a vast and varied collection of countries knitted together by loyalty to an emperor, America grew up over a much shorter time from a group of cities and states united by a continent rich in undeveloped resources and dedicated to democratic rule. By entering in Boston, he was acquainting himself with the very site of the country's birth, a thought that enthralled. Upon his arrival in the strange new city, he walked through the historic neighborhoods, visiting sites of the great American Revolution, and he began to familiarize himself with such places as Faneuil Hall, Bunker Hill, and the Old North Church, from whose steeple Paul Revere received his lanterned message that the British troops were coming. He relished in absorbing the names and events that formed the revolution from British rule and the origins of the democratic republic that served as a model for the world.

Soon after his arrival, he reacquainted himself with a young man named Will Honeycutt, who in turn introduced him to the library at Harvard College. He had first met Mr. Will Honeycutt when he visited Vienna at the instigation of Eleanor Burden some years before.

And so whenever his duties at his new school would permit, Arnauld would travel to Cambridge, and, often with Will Honeycutt at his side, he would read the papers and letters of John Adams, Benjamin Franklin, Thomas Jefferson, and the rest, and begin to understand how the young republic was born. "This is where you will find the evidence of the birth of democracy for which you have been searching," his energetic host would say with relish.

"It is greatly different from the birth of Vienna," he said. "And that difference is for a foreigner simply fascinating." What the Bostonians took for granted, just as the Viennese took for granted the complexities of the empire, this new visitor found boundlessly interesting. And he began to convey to his young students what he could of those interests.

29

ARNAULD AND WILL

hen Eleanor finished telling Will Honeycutt what she thought appropriate in this story, she paused and waited for his response. "Well?" she said.

Her disheveled partner gave her a long appraising look. "Thank you for telling me that," he said flatly. "It is the thoroughness of detail I desire."

"And that you have deserved. I am sorry that I did not confide in you sooner." He nodded, and smiled his gratitude. "Now you know that Arnauld is very special to me," she continued, "and his continued success here, which you have helped to ensure, is of utmost significance."

"I now know," he said. "And I am glad for it."

Eleanor took a deep breath before continuing. "As you have gathered over our time together," she began, "I have certain instincts about the future, instincts that have been proven right in wonderful and terrible ways, as you know, and by now you may have guessed that it is what I brought back from that extraordinary time in Vienna, including the fact that Arnauld is to play a major role in my future and the future of St. Gregory's School. I can tell no one, save you. It is comforting to know that I can count on your help."

"You could always count on my help."

"You were leaving for New York," she said in an involuntary and sudden burst. "I was devastated."

Will Honeycutt hung his head. "I am sorry. I don't know what to say. It will not happen again."

"Let us hope not," she snapped, then she collected herself and smiled at him for a moment.

He looked up and smiled back weakly. "It won't happen again," he repeated.

She waited a moment, then nodded, dissolving any tension. "Well, there was one good outcome," she said. "It made me aware once and for all of how much I depend on you and how I need to take you more into my confidence."

"And I too have learned from my impetuousness. I will be from now on, you can be assured, worthy of that confidence."

"We shall drink to that," she said, raising the crystal glass appropriated from a New York hotel room ten years before, "with this fine expensive claret."

"That one hopes has not turned to vinegar," Will said, raising his glass in response, watching her take the first sip. He tasted the wine, paused, and then nodded and smiled.

She sipped again. "Very satisfactory," she said, and returned his smile. "Like a good partnership, it has survived over time, and is made all the better by age."

"At first Arnauld found his teaching job at St. Gregory's demanding and difficult," Eleanor said to Will the next morning, as they continued their conversation, after she was sure to mention how relieved and happy she was to have her business partner back in place. "I think he found it at first more a curiosity than a calling," she added. Arnauld had explained to her how his young students had mistaken his Viennese manner as stiffness and arrogance, but gradually, as he became accustomed to their style and they to his, they began to accept him. "But now I think he is on his way to becoming a full-fledged and popular teacher of German and history. The headmaster gives him very good reports."

"I have enjoyed watching him adjust," Will offered. "I must admit. And it seems that Frank has also."

Eleanor's husband, Frank Burden, the staunch and traditional Boston banker, a few years senior to Arnauld, took a liking to the young Viennese intellectual, and joined in introducing him to his alma mater Harvard College, first to the extensive resources of Widener Library, and then to the single sculls of the Charles River boathouse. Within his first year in Boston, Arnauld became an eager and passionate rower, "a passion that could serve one," Frank Burden observed, "for the rest of one's life."

As Arnauld settled in to enjoying the life of a master at a prestigious Boston school, his letters began to take on an easy elegance, describing the life of a popular teacher and a very eligible bachelor, invited—through the instigation of the very well-connected Eleanor Burden—to the social engagements of the very best families. "I find myself greatly stimulated by the social scene," he wrote his parents. "Boston is vastly different from Vienna or any other European city, but then again very much the same. I find the brashness of these Americans very refreshing, while not being completely devoid of Continental sophistication."

Intellectually, he had the resources of Harvard; socially, he had the life of his colleagues; and for exercise he had the Charles River and his new-found passion for rowing, all of which he described in letters with articulate grace. Obviously, he found it a very agreeable life, and one he would have continued gladly forever, had it not been for the awful intrusion of European war.

The rowing had begun in earnest when Frank had introduced Arnauld to the Harvard boathouse in Cambridge. Arnauld had expressed an interest in single sculling, which he had begun briefly while visiting his great and flamboyant friend Miggo in Italy during his university days. Michelangelo Alphonso Sabatini was actually an Esterhazy cousin, the son of one of Arnauld's Esterhazy aunts who married an Italian count in Genoa. The count's mother just happened to be an American industrialist's daughter, so Miggo felt at home in Saratoga, New York, and Genoa and was comfortable in the coffeehouses of Vienna. "He is the son of my father's sister," Arnauld would explain with delight. "His grandmother is a Vanderbilt. Miggo is aristocracy in three languages." To which the effervescent Miggo would respond, "Or scoundrel."

He had a wonderful panache and likened himself to Theodore Roosevelt and the swashbuckling writer Rafael Sabatini, whom he asserted was a relative, a dubious claim.

"Miggo considers himself more American than Italian," Arnauld told Eleanor on one of the two occasions when his cousin visited him at St. Gregory's. "When he is in America. He likes the flamboyant life."

There is evidence in notes and letters that both Eleanor and Frank Burden were impressed by "our young Italo-American," as Frank called him.

"He thinks of himself as a Rough Rider," Arnauld said.

It was Miggo who introduced him to rowing, and Frank Burden who saw that he was instructed properly, in the right places, once he heard by way of one of the exuberant Miggo's visits, that it was an interest, if even a distant one, Frank being a great supporter of all physical exercise. So Arnauld began his career as a Charles River rower, and "one of some little renown," Frank said.

Will Honeycutt, even before his desertion and return, would take Arnauld down to the boathouse, help him carry the shell and oars to the water, and then watch him settle into the single-seated boat and push himself out onto the river, rowing away in smooth synchronized strokes. But after his conversion, Will performed the service with greater frequency and relish. "I want to encourage you in this endeavor," he told his new friend. "I think you have a future in it."

And Arnauld said, "I don't know about a future, but I do love it greatly."

And to Eleanor Will said, "Arnauld is a phenomenon. People around here can't get over it. 'There are some former college rowers who don't have the power and smoothness of that man,' they keep saying."

"I would like very much to see him rowing," Eleanor said.

"You can join us at the boathouse someday. You will be impressed."

And the young Austrian's punctuality impressed everyone. He would pull away from the dock and exactly forty-five minutes later, "to the second," observers insisted, he would be back.

"How do you do it?" Will Honeycutt asked. "You carry no timepiece."

"Internal timing, I suppose," Arnauld said. "The rowing for me is my deep connection. I lose myself in it, like Klimt when he is painting."

"And yet you arrive back at the boathouse with exactly the same timing, every outing."

"I am just in a flow, I guess."

"A flow," Will Honeycutt said, musing over the word. "I guess you could call it that."

One day in Arnauld's first year in Boston, Will told Eleanor at the Hyperion Fund office that that day would be a good day. "He will leave at two," Will said. "He is always very precise, and he will be back at two forty-five. You can set your watch by it."

"I will be there," Eleanor said.

So at a little after two o'clock, Eleanor arranged to be driven to the Harvard boathouse, where she joined Will on the dock, and they both looked downriver toward Boston Harbor. "There," Will said finally, pointing. "That speck."

And they both watched as the distant speck turned into the two beating oars of a single-scull rower and then into a form they both could recognize as Arnauld. "Look at how smooth he is," Will said, "and the power he brings to each stroke. One would never guess all that athletic aesthetic was hidden within our scholarly friend. It is all in the timing, they say."

They watched in silence as the rower glided between the strong smooth strokes of his double oars, the muscles in his back straining as his seat slid back and his oars dug into the Charles River water, rowing, as was his regular practice, up the river past their position, totally unaware of being watched. Eleanor's husband, Frank Burden, was a fine strong athlete, but he was a large-framed man, taut and muscular. Arnauld was light in build and subtly muscled, supple more than powerful, not imposing physically, but somehow as he rowed he called up something from the mythic past. And since athletics had played no part in his intellectual past, one would never have expected it. She had prepared herself to be impressed, but still what she saw was for her somehow overpowering.

"Beautiful," she said with an exhalation. "How does he know how to do it so well?"

"I don't know. He communicates with some subatomic energy force, I think. It was that way the first moment he sat in a boat, as far as I can tell."

"He knew rowing from Europe?"

"Not really," Will Honeycutt said. "He had rowed only a few times in Italy with his cousin Miggo, and here he was inspired to athleticism by America, he says. Here, it became for him a passion."

Eleanor watched in awed silence as Arnauld's shell, having stopped and turned and now gliding back toward them, slowed to approach the dock. She was unable to suppress her smile of wonder.

It had always seemed to her peculiar, and a bit unfair, that athletics were the province of men, and when women were allowed to engage in sport they had to do so with the encumbrance of long dresses. There were those among her Smith College friends, even in her time there in the 1890s, who predicted a forthcoming surge of women's rights, beginning with the right to vote and evolving to the right to play tennis in pants, like men, or to swim in something brief and less obtrusive. Both men and women covered their bodies when they played sports and swam, the exceptions being track and rowing, "where the contestants are next to naked," another of her sophisticated Smith friends observed with a knowing smile.

Back in those Smith College days, Eleanor had seen the man who was to be her husband "virtually naked," as her roommate at Smith said, because he had trained in track at Harvard and was planning to throw the discus at the newly invented Olympic Games in Athens in the summer of 1896, her graduation year. "You must admit," her roommate said, "it causes a certain arousal to see so much of the male physique," and Eleanor did have to admit that Frank Burden was a very handsome man fully clothed or in the short pants and bare shoulders of his track jersey.

But of all the scanty uniforms of athletics, the scantiest were those of the rowers. And scantiness of uniform was the main reason, other than the demand for raw strength in the pulling of the oars, that women would never be allowed to row crew. "Just as they could never throw the discus," Frank Burden said. "There is simply too much demand for raw muscle power."

Had she not received reports from both her husband and her partner, Will Honeycutt, she never would have guessed that Arnauld Esterhazy was athletic. The picture of Arnauld clad in a team uniform coming sweaty and muddied off an athletic field, as she had seen Frank Burden do so many times in his boyhood and early adulthood, would simply not form in her mind. That is why the scene of his rowing toward her on the dock, his muscles straining at the oars, and then lifting himself out of the single-seated shell, the smooth roundness of his bare shoulders and the sinews of his legs plainly in view, sweat droplets on his brow, made the powerful impression it did.

As he pulled his oars in and reached out with a hand to the dock, he looked up for the first time.

"I brought a surprise observer," Will said. "She wanted to see how it is done, firsthand."

Pulling himself back from wherever he had been, startled by the vision before him, the surprised rower gave his observer a tentative smile, as if uncomfortable with having been observed, and then his face broke into a huge grin. And then he blushed.

Suddenly there he stood beside her, nearly naked, looking so very much like a Roman marble that she found herself overcome in that moment in what her Smith College roommate would have called a state of "arousal," unable to think clearly or to speak, even if the exhilarated rower had found the presence of mind in that moment to say something of substance, which he did not.

"I am honored that you came," Arnauld said.

"That was beautiful, Arnauld," she heard herself saying, and he looked up. "It is absolutely beautiful, Arnauld," Eleanor repeated. "You have the grace of the gods out there." Not accustomed to such flattery, from such a source, Arnauld only looked down.

Will helped him lift the shell out of the water and carry it toward the boathouse. "You can bring the oars," he said to Eleanor. And she followed behind, carrying the oars into the boathouse, her face still flushed with wonder, still relishing the memory of what she had seen out on the water, now barely able to keep her eyes off the half-naked man only a few paces from her. It was a moment, she recalled later, when things changed, a moment that made enough of an impression on her at the time that she mentioned it in a letter to her friend Jung. "It is truly sublime," she wrote. "I found myself transfixed. I don't fully understand. It is as if this quiet, unassuming, and gentle man has transcended himself and made contact with some rich mythic past, a study in grace."

⟍⟋

Arnauld did not yet feel anything like grace at St. Gregory's. The teaching did not come as naturally for him as the rowing suddenly did, especially not the teaching of American thirteen-year-old boys. "Teaching German to the older boys is more what I am accustomed to. I fear that I bore the younger ones," he told Eleanor. "They are not as interested as I am."

"They are more interested than you think," Eleanor said with a reassuring smile. "I hear good reports."

"But they are full of energy. In Vienna, we were taught to respect our teachers and to sit quietly and observe, on pain of corporal punishments.

We saved our rambunctiousness for outside of class. Here it seems to be quite the opposite. The boys are forever erupting in class, and outside they are quite sedate and respectful."

"They respect you. I know that."

"I think they wish to help me teach. Where I come from that would be preposterous."

And not wishing to bore his students, he learned slowly how to modulate his passions. Arnauld Esterhazy and the St. Gregory's boys took some time to get to know one another, it was said, but once they did it would be, as Will Honeycutt predicted, "smooth sailing."

"Do not worry," Eleanor said with a great and unusual confidence. "They will come around. You will become very successful. I know that in my bones."

"You sound very certain," Arnauld said.

"Oh, I am certain, Arnauld," Eleanor said. "There is nothing about which I am more confident." And that confidence from her did much to give Arnauld reassurance in moving forward.

Eleanor could not fully account for her feeling of confidence. Some of it came from what she knew of the future, her sense of destiny, but some of it came from the simple fact that she had loved being in Arnauld's company from the beginning, even back in Vienna, when he was eighteen. It began as simple enjoyment and evolved over the years into something deeper. "He has knowledge," William James had said to her upon hearing her descriptions of the young man from her past she was planning to bring to Boston. "Knowledge is great power, and greatly compelling."

When William James was himself a young man, he had accompanied the famous professor Louis Agassiz to the Amazon. "Professor Agassiz knew the names of every species on earth, or so it seemed. Accompanying him into the wilds of the Amazon was a wondrous experience. 'Knowledge is the greatest of aphrodisiacs,' he used to say, 'when applied discreetly.'"

Eleanor smiled and agreed and thought back on how much her young friend had grown on her during their time together in his Vienna, and how greatly she was looking forward to his arrival in Boston all these years later. "Arnauld's applications are always discreet," she said, reflecting on how even though getting Arnauld to come to Boston was her very demanding assignment, certainly not without anxious moments, the anticipation of his arrival and its actually coming to pass now caused her heart to soar. "He is quite shy, actually, a very compelling quality."

"It sounds as if you will enjoy very much his presence here," William James observed on hearing of her plans to bring about his appointment at St. Gregory's.

"You too will enjoy his company," she said then to Dr. James. And later it always seemed sadly ironic that the great professor had died just as Arnauld was making his entry into Boston and St. Gregory's. "He carries the history of European culture in his head," Eleanor had said once to her great mentor.

Of course, William James knew the whole story eventually, but that was at the very end, when it became clear that he would not be able to meet this man who was to play such a very important role in her life. The great professor left, and the young teacher arrived. Grief that settled upon her at the one loss was ameliorated by the pleasure she took in watching her friend from the past adjust to his new role as visitor in a strange land.

During Arnauld's frequent evenings at the Burden house on Acorn Street, Eleanor would grin inwardly with pleasure whenever she saw him in conversation with one of her friends. "His knowledge of things cultural is exquisite," the rector of Trinity Church said to her one evening before the symphony. "He could do a whole treatise on the difference between Brahms and Haydn."

"Or Poussin and David," the wife of one of Frank's partners, who was listening in, contributed.

"Or Flaubert and George Sand," offered a third observer, the rector's wife, a woman Eleanor had known since childhood. "And he does so with such eloquence, with that wonderful accent of his," she added, with a smile of obvious relish. "And he carries himself with such a princely bearing."

Such observations would always bring a proud smile to Eleanor's lips, since Arnauld's recruitment had been her idea, and hers alone. "Young Esterhazy is settling in. I think he just might be here for the long haul," the headmaster said to her, then admitted to a feeling of great satisfaction in the success, as did everyone else at St. Gregory's. "He is very amiable, you know," the headmaster concluded. "Those of us in the school business are quite taken by amiability." By Eleanor's lights, everything had arrived at a very agreeable status.

But all of this was before her moment of "arousal" on the Harvard

College boathouse dock when she saw the near-naked elegance of the rowing for the first time, that moment that changed everything, especially considering what she knew was to come.

"And how are you enjoying your new life in Boston?" she asked Arnauld one evening soon after, before a gala for the Museum of Fine Arts, to which she had secured Arnauld an invitation.

"I am liking it very much," Arnauld said, a little too quickly and glibly for Eleanor's purposes.

She pressed him. "No, I mean really. I do wish to know."

With this, Arnauld paused and gave the question consideration. "Really," he said. "I find much to amuse myself, and I am adjusting to teaching. I find myself each evening wondering how I might present my lessons more effectively tomorrow. I find myself watching the older teachers with admiration and a certain envy. And, of course, I enjoy very much also my evenings like this away from school in your salon, and my life in Cambridge. They have much in common with my former life in Vienna." And he did not add, although he must have been tempted, *and everything is so very American.*

She pressed again. "And for the future?"

"As for the future," Arnauld said, "we shall see."

And in a rare moment of candor she found herself confiding, "I want so for you to be happy here, Arnauld. And I worry."

And returning the rare candor, Arnauld looked into her face and saw the worry. "I do not wish to cause you concern. Being beside you means the world to me. You know that I will do whatever is necessary to continue being there."

And then Eleanor caught herself. "Well," she said. "We shall just have to work all the harder to make sure that you are totally entertained." And she smiled and patted his arm before leading him away toward the others in their party.

⬎

During this whole time, Eleanor depended heavily on Will Honeycutt as a factor in the entertainment of Arnauld, and from the beginning she marveled at the way the two men found mutual attraction.

"We argue," Will said to her one day, with a great smile. "Each thinks of the other as his equal."

"In your case," Eleanor said, "that is saying something. And what do you argue about?"

"Descartes and the Enlightenment," Will said. "The validity of psychology as a science. You know, grand ideas like that."

"I would love to listen in."

"Oh," Will said with a smile, "I fear we generated more heat than light. But we both enjoy the exchange. Arnauld is such a respectful man, I think he enjoys our moments of irreverence."

"You serve as a good provocateur," she said with a smile, thinking of those two minds ranging over the course of European philosophy, Arnauld the devout classicist and Will Honeycutt the upstart American scientist, an introvert and an extrovert, her friend Jung would point out, each fully able to keep up with the other.

It was at Eleanor's instigation that Will first invited the young Viennese to visit Cambridge with him. "He will appreciate getting to know the Harvard you know," Eleanor said, always thinking of how to make Arnauld's new American life more compelling. "And it would mean a great deal to me. Cambridge will remind him of his university days in Vienna perhaps. He will feel very much at home." And so he did, so much so that he solicited further invitations, and soon the two new friends made regular visits to Cambridge a part of life. The two young men grew accustomed to sitting in cafés and walking along the Charles.

"Arnauld is exceedingly good company," Will reported back, "although a little idealistic."

"And what would he say about that?" Eleanor asked, amused.

"Oh, he might say that I am a bit obstreperous." Then he paused and laughed, "We balance each other well, actually, the poet and the iconoclast."

And Arnauld reported in his own way how he liked very much Will's common sense and practical manner. "An American pragmatist," he said. "I find him refreshing. He would liven up our coffeehouse discussions back in Vienna, that is for sure."

"And not too abrasively?" Eleanor asked.

"Oh my, no," Arnauld said. "It is good for us stuffy Europeans to get a taste of true practicality."

It was clear to Eleanor after a time that the two men had become quite fond of each other and fond of their "discursives," as they called them, those "discursives" accounting for the difference in tone. If there was any discussion between the two men of a certain deep and unsatisfied emotion that they had in common, it was never mentioned to Eleanor, to her great relief.

Then the horrible unrest in Europe intruded. For months, the two friends Arnauld and Will Honeycutt would talk and argue about the rivalries of the various European countries.

"An unhealthy tension," Will Honeycutt would say, pointing a finger at the German kaiser, as if the kaiser's very demeanor were Arnauld's responsibility.

"Business as usual," Arnauld would counter, "just saber rattling. Nothing out of the ordinary. The German people are actually very peaceful, but the kaiser and the generals are like peacocks parading in their uniforms, taking themselves too seriously. They have built up a war machine, but I think they and the French will hold each other at bay."

"One hears that the kaiser is a belligerent bully," Will said, trying to get a rise out of his friend.

Arnauld grimaced. "It is difficult to think of fate in the hands of such a character, is it not? He was a Hapsburg cousin, and Prince Rudolf couldn't stand him. It is said that the dread of seeing this artless, graceless cousin succeeding was one of the despairs that drove him to his act at Mayerling."

"Let's hope that he calms himself down," Will said.

"Let us hope," Arnauld repeated.

"It doesn't look very good to me."

"Nor to me," Arnauld finally admitted.

30

JUST THIS ONCE

ach summer, Arnauld would travel home to Austria, as was perfectly natural. Often during these summers some Boston families would schedule visits to see him in Vienna on their European tours. He returned the favor of their hospitality in Boston, with introduction to café life and to the theater and the opera, always saying how much he was looking forward to his return at summer's end to his life at St. Gregory's and Boston.

Each time she would hear from one of the returning families, Eleanor would smile inwardly and marvel at how, in spite of the ups and downs, things had worked out exactly as they should have, all the time aware of the coming war and Arnauld Esterhazy's fateful role in it.

So Arnauld's decision to leave Boston for Vienna in the summer of 1914 was nothing unusual or dramatic, and nothing to do with the international tension in Europe. He had left each of the three previous summers during his time teaching at St. Gregory's, and this time he had even asked Will Honeycutt to join him for part of the summer, which Will initially agreed to until at the last minute demands of the Hyperion Fund intruded. "Next summer then," Arnauld said with confidence. But that was in April. By the June departure date, he had lost some of that confidence.

"You will be sailing into a hornet's nest, my friend," Will Honeycutt said.

"I tend to agree with you," Arnauld said, adding, "This time it is my premonition."

"You are sounding downright fatalistic," Will said. "Not unlike your host, Mrs. Burden."

"She is indeed somewhat fatalistic," Arnauld reflected. "It is as if she knows something of the future that we do not." Will Honeycutt did not respond.

He would sail for Europe shortly after classes ended for the spring term, spend the summer in Vienna and with his parents at their nearby vineyard, and then return in time for the opening of school in early September. But this time, with the palpable tension that seemed to have spread throughout Europe, at least a few people were apprehensive. "What if you got over there and couldn't get back?" one friend on the St. Gregory's faculty said.

But Arnauld always dismissed the concern with what had become for him a quick and always good-natured retort, "Oh, I don't think German belligerence is all it is made out to be."

"And what of Austria's tensions with Serbia?" his knowledgeable friend responded. And that too Arnauld dismissed as overreaction. He would sail in mid-June and be "back in time for football season," he said with a good deal of amusement, as American football seemed to him the most curious of national passions, one he greatly enjoyed nonetheless. "If I were to be reborn," he announced after his second fall at St. Gregory's, "I would want to be an American football hero."

Eleanor Burden had made a point of increasing his invitations to Acorn Street as his departure date approached. From the moment of his coming to Boston to teach, he had loved his time at the Burden home; in fact, he had written home to his parents on a number of occasions describing exactly his impression of the warm and cultured reception he found there.

> *Eleanor Burden is the most beautiful hostess, elegant and receptive, always poised and ever willing to lead discussions on French painting, Italian cuisine, voting rights for women, transcendentalism, or any of a number of interesting topics. She manages her family with an efficient grace and warmth. Her daughters are delicately well mannered and yet full of life. Her husband, Frank Burden, a serious and formal*

banker, a bit stiff and gruff perhaps outside the home, warms to her attentions and is also a splendid and welcoming host. It is he, by the way, who has encouraged my rowing on the Charles River, the single scull to which I have become so attentively fixed. But it is Eleanor Burden herself who fills my life here in Boston with positive energy. The thought of being in her presence anywhere in this city is for me the pleasure that sustains me during my week of teaching, and the actuality of being in her home is a pleasure complete enough to sustain thoughts of living in Boston for a long time.

To his old friend Alma, recently widowed by the tragic death of Gustav Mahler in 1911, knowing her interest in intrigues of the heart, he wrote something even more emotionally specific:

Only to you would I ever admit such a thing, but I absolutely worship the ground she walks on. I see her in her daily life, so full of organizational poise and confidence, and I come away each time newly inspired. She is a social leader in Boston, for sure. Everyone at the school thinks the world of her. She is a kind and dedicated parent of her two girls. And in the evenings at her beautiful home, she is so serene and gracious that one would think she had not a care or responsibility in the world, knowing full well that quite the opposite is true. She is indeed the vision of loveliness of my dreams.

So it was that Arnauld had become accustomed to spending occasional evenings in her home and staying the night in the guest room on Acorn Street instead of being driven home late. His last night in Boston that June would be no different. He would spend it in the Burden home on the eve of his train trip to New York City and the steamship from Hoboken, New Jersey, to Bremen, Germany, the next day. "We will send you off in good fashion so you will remember to return," Eleanor said lightly in offering the invitation.

"Oh, I shall always remember to return," Arnauld replied, with an assurance that betrayed the rather desperate feelings he would encounter on occasion when thinking of somehow losing her presence in his life.

"You mustn't be so serious," Eleanor said this time on the eve of this parting. "You will never lose us, Arnauld." And as always when she talked of the future, he noticed something very firm and reassuring in her voice.

"You always sound so confident when talking of things to come," he said.

She knew what had to be done and had begun planning weeks in advance, carrying out her tasks with her usual thoroughness, making certain that the girls were spending the night away and that Frank would seize an opportunity to be in New York, even noticing in the cycle of her own biology that her body would be perfectly ready. Then just as the final pieces of her planning all fell into place, Arnauld discovered that due to unexpected repairs necessary to his steamer his departure date was to be postponed a week, and the whole business seemed to go disastrously awry, causing her to fall into a secret despair she knew well from so many times before.

And then, by some miracle, Arnauld received word that, the repairs made, his sailing date had been moved back to its original time, and as had happened also so many times before, everything fell miraculously into place. On that early summer night of 1914, she carried out the final details of her assignment with a careful sense of ritual, like a temple priestess, she told herself. But she did not realize in advance the intensity with which the experience would catch her by total surprise and leave her filled with desire and longing, and, four years later, unspeakable grief.

That fateful night of Arnauld's departure in 1914, she knew at least part of the story. She knew that calamity awaited him in what looked to others like a harmless return to Vienna for his summer vacation, and she knew of the coming outbreak of war in Europe and Arnauld's entanglement in it. She alone had foreknowledge of, and could do nothing to prevent, what was to be the forthcoming world conflagration, an all-consuming world war that would destroy a whole generation, and she knew that somehow— she knew not how—Arnauld would be swept up by it with devastating consequences. That knowledge weighed heavily on her as she prepared for his departure.

But she also knew the outcome and knew that somehow Arnauld would survive, return to Boston, and play a major role in the life of St. Gregory's and her family. In fact, she had absolute faith at this time that Arnauld, the man with whom she was destined to share the deepest of connections, no matter what he would endure in war, would emerge safely and to renew his life as a legendary teacher there.

As so many times before she knew what destiny would dictate, but she knew also that she had to act. It was once again that strange dance of her life, between the predestined and free will, between knowing what would happen in the future and knowing what she had to do to make it happen. So she knew well in advance exactly what outcome she was obligated to orchestrate on that evening in June 1914, on the eve of Arnauld's departure.

\N

He arrived with his bags that evening and laid out his tickets and travel papers on the bed to assure himself that he had everything in order. He would leave directly from the Burdens' home on Beacon Hill to the Back Bay train station in the morning.

"Reports are that it is not easy crossing borders these days," he said to Eleanor. "Every country seems to be suspicious of its neighbor."

"Luckily, you will be crossing directly into Austria-Hungary. That is a relief, I suppose. At least the nations of the empire are friendly."

"So far it seems so," he said with a smile. "Although one can never tell with the Czechs." Czechoslovakia lay between his arrival point in Bremen and his destination in Vienna.

It was not until after he had arrived on Acorn Street in the late afternoon and was preparing for the cocktail hour before dinner that he realized that Frank Burden was away on business, the girls were spending the night with a Putnam cousin in Cambridge, and Rose Spurgeon and the cook had been given the evening off. At first, he thought that Will Honeycutt might be joining them for dinner, but that too turned out not to be the case.

"Tonight, I have you all to myself," Eleanor said, and Arnauld admitted to a rush of euphoria at the thought. Being alone with this woman who had sustained his definition of feminine perfection for almost twenty years was an elation like no other he could imagine. After all this time, he could think of no greater pleasure than sitting with her and her other guests in the Acorn Street living room—where William and Henry James had sat years before, during her parents' time. He doubted that Eleanor, with all her elegant detachment, had any idea how much she actually meant to him.

"I am glad for it," was all he said, and then offered, "We have much of my travels to review," as an attempt to mask his true feelings.

On Eleanor's part, in preparing for the evening, with its fateful implications, she had struggled for the proper attitude and approach, until, that is, she recalled the one image in Will Honeycutt's sketchbook, the one she had shared with Carl Jung. Having been introduced to the goddess Isis of Will Honeycutt's drawings and realizing the likeness to her, and the significance of that, she found that she now had a new and highly useful image of herself.

With a great sense of ceremony she had completed the preparation of the meal—the beef bourguignon and baked new potatoes she knew to be among her guest's favorites—and had set the table and arranged each room, each decorated with flowers, with special care.

At dinner, she carried each dish to the table herself and laid each carefully in its place with the ceremonial attention of sacred ritual. "This meal is special, Arnauld," she said, "the anointed sustenance for a proper send-off."

"I am only going for two months," he said.

"Still, I wish you to remember this moment."

As much as they tried to avoid it, they seemed to fill the time talking about the situation in Europe, how alliances seemed to be forming in the most peculiar places, former bitter enemies evolving into allies, and former allies evolving into bitter enemies. Eleanor seemed to have a better-than-expected understanding of the specifics of the situation, how the powder keg might be set off by any one small action, with all parties joining sides in all-out war.

"Let us hope that the saber rattling remains just that, saber rattling," Arnauld said.

"But it rarely does," she said, with obvious skepticism in her voice.

"We need not sound so grim," he said.

"Perhaps you have a greater acceptance of the posturing," she said, "having been raised within it."

"Perhaps I do. The Prussian military temperament seems to contain a good deal of that which you call *posturing*. Lots of military peacocks strutting around. And, yes, we are accustomed to it."

"I am particularly worried about your country and the Serbs," she said at one point, surprising Arnauld with her directness.

"That too is merely bravado," Arnauld said, repeating what he often said. "Nothing will come of it."

"I wish I believed that," she said with surprising coldness. Later, he remembered a fatefulness in her voice, as if she knew what was in store for him and the world. Then she paused and looked deeply into his eyes. "We must not waste this precious time." She held out her hand across the table where they dined alone, and, laying her hand on his, she said, "Dear Arnauld, you must promise me that you will take care of yourself, and that you will return to me."

He felt uncomfortable in her gaze and was about to say something reassuring. "You do not know how important that is to me," she continued, and squeezed his hand with a fierceness that surprised him. "You do not know how important you are to me."

He could think of nothing near equal in weight to say. Then he looked down, and she allowed the moment to pass. "Well," she said, withdrawing her hand, "that being said, I think we shall move on to dessert."

It was after dessert when they had moved into the living room and she guided him to the couch. "Sit here," she said, pointing to the exact spot she wished him to occupy, as if it were part of a divine plan, "and I shall sit beside you. And no more talk of Europe," she said with authority.

They sat beside each other, enjoying the ritual of demitasse that reminded them both of Vienna, their knees nearly touching. She spoke softly and with an added warmth that dissolved any of his discomfort at the sudden closeness. "I shall miss you immeasurably," she said, "and I do worry about the political tensions you are taking yourself into."

"I thought there was to be no more talk of Europe," he said lightly, but stopped when he saw the look of deep concern on her face.

"Arnauld. There is more," she said, and slowly she leaned even closer. Her hand reached out and touched his face ever so gently.

"But—" he began, inching away until her hand dropped to his shoulder, stopping him with the lightest touch and pulling him back toward her, she understanding completely his instinct for reserve.

"This is as it should be, Arnauld," she whispered, and then she leaned forward and returned the soft touch to his cheek. "Just this once, dear Arnauld," she whispered softly, in a way that would stay with him vividly for the next four years during the horror that was coming. He never told anyone, but those words and those that followed in this evening on Acorn

Street were the most beautiful, the most unexpected, and the most welcome ever spoken to him by anyone, ever.

"Now, come with me," she said, and she took him by the hand and led him wordlessly to the guest room, where he watched transfixed as she, now fully in her Isis role, lit candles.

"Just this once," she repeated.

How could he ever come close to describing it all?

31

A YEARNING FOR THE FIGHT

s she stood with Arnauld on the platform of Back Bay Station the following morning, she felt in her heart a sinking heaviness she could not fully account for. Like so much of her future, Eleanor knew that this trip of Arnauld's would not end well, although she knew few particulars.

"Take care of yourself, dear Arnauld," she had said, touching his cheek, "and come back to me."

"You must not worry," he had said as they parted, hearing the concern in her voice.

"It is in my nature to worry," she said. But that part of her nature he had never seen before, and he had no way of knowing its derivation or depth, although he sensed from just her present demeanor that things had changed between them forever.

"I am gone only for two months," he said with a reassuring smile, not entirely comfortable in his new role, failing entirely to notice the depth of the change in Eleanor. "You will see me again in September, right here."

"Nonetheless," she said simply, "remember that you are loved here."

"You must not worry," he repeated, again trying to shake her from this apprehension he felt from her but had no way of understanding.

"I shall write," he said, as he pulled away from her embrace and climbed onto the steps of the train car.

"I shall expect you to," she said, regaining the outer show of strength she knew he expected and depended upon.

From his seat by the window, he watched her as long as he could as the train pulled away. She stood all that time in place until well after the two could no longer see each other, each heart aching, beyond words, each for its own separate reasons.

N

He passed by train to New York and then Hoboken, New Jersey, to board the steamship *George Washington,* confident that the tensions he was heading for in Europe would lead to nothing more than belligerent diplomacy and the arming of borders. "You will be sailing on the same ship that brought Herr Freud and Herr Jung to this country five years ago," Eleanor had said as they were leaving Acorn Street, trying to lighten the inevitable farewell.

And while on shipboard, in his daily entries to the long letter he would mail to her as soon as the ship docked—more descriptive of his thoughts than chatty—he gave no indication of things being any different in his mind from the confidence he struggled to express on that station platform. It was the heartache of parting amplified by what had transpired on that magical last evening that he wished to express, not any uncertainty about European peace.

But while he was at sea, still two days out of Bremen, Germany, news came in on the Marconi wireless that threw the ship into an ecstasy of anxious buzzing. The archduke Franz Ferdinand, aged emperor Franz Joseph's arrogant nephew and—because of the tragedy of the crown prince Rudolf at Mayerling—heir to the throne of the Hapsburg Empire, had been assassinated along with his wife, Sophie, in Sarajevo, the tension-filled capital of Bosnia and Herzegovina. "Serbian anarchists suspected," the wireless report said.

The long concluding entry he added to his letter to Eleanor the following day, on the eve of his arrival in Germany, reveals a sense of foreboding he had been feeling all along perhaps but now, given the dramatic occurrence in the Balkan states, he felt free to express.

We heard the shocking news from Sarajevo. This horrible event, I fear, will serve as the match that will ignite the powder keg you so dreaded. There is an irony to the extreme reaction because no one admired the officious and contentious Franz Ferdinand, so different from

his aged uncle in demeanor and temperament. But popular opinion
will blame the rebellious Serbs, and the outraged Austrians will de-
mand revenge. It is not a good situation. Fated, I fear.

Even in Germany, after he had mailed the letter, as Arnauld made his
way to the train station, the newspapers were full of the outrage, and from
street corners people were shouting for revenge. "How long has this been
going on?" he asked his cab driver.

"Two days now," the driver said. "It is all anyone wants to talk about.
The French and the Belgians are behind the anarchists on this. They will
pay." And Arnauld noted in his next letter the absurdity of bringing in the
French and the Belgians, especially the Belgians, who had offended no
one but had the sad geographical position of lying between Germany and
France.

On the train and along the route to Vienna, he could see signs of the
news everywhere and could see that the egregious assassination was on
everyone's mind. By the time, after Dresden, he crossed the border into
Czechoslovakia, outrage filled the air, and when, after Brno, he crossed
into Austria, a positive mania had grabbed hold of the populace. "I fear
that no one knows or remembers the horrors of war. This unfortunate
incident in Sarajevo may be the cause of a great outbreak," he wrote to
Eleanor, by now abandoning all attempts to sound as if he was reassuring
her of peace. "Nobody admired the archduke, and yet all are outraged, as
if he had been a beloved family member."

It was then that he wrote with detail both to Eleanor and to his parents
of the wild jubilation that swept Vienna. "Staid academics at the university are saying that even they are feeling for the first time pride for their
country. The whole city feels like an American one on the eve of one of
the great football games of the fall. There is a yearning for the fight."

When Arnauld had left New York for home in late June 1914, war seemed
a far-off possibility. When he arrived in Germany ten days later, it seemed
inevitable. The assassination had changed everything. "I fear that a great
imbalance has been thrown into the precariously balanced works," he
wrote.

Arnauld's acceptance of the idea of war began gradually and innocently, until even he became susceptible to the patriotic fervor. Eleanor wondered how he could be swept up in the war mania and worried in the depth of her consciousness that her necessary but aggressive overtures on the night before his departure had been somehow the cause. They had said their good-byes on that fateful day at Back Bay Station, and then, in the following months, after war had begun to rage, his letters, sent through neutral Switzerland, began to arrive. From the first, he explained that he had access to the diplomatic channels that allowed uncensored mail. His letters were filled with the specifics that were from the very start the cause of both a great comfort and a great anxiety. At first, they told of the absolute exuberance and desire for war that had swept Vienna and all of Austria. His fears and sensitivities always rendered him an astute observer, but now his powers of observation were being severely taxed.

> *I cannot believe the change that has taken over my beloved city, the absolute hysteria that has everyone in its grip: professors, intellectuals in the cafés, shop owners, house servants. Everyone is consumed by a desire for war, as if it were the noblest of enterprises to hurl the city's and the country's young men into its jaws, heeding nothing of the possible consequences. Everywhere in the city, and throughout the empire, I am told, there exists the most rapid immersion into war fever, as if it were the most romantic, most manly adventure.*
>
> *The young people seem honestly afraid that they might miss out on this most exciting experience of their lives. Arguing or speaking out in any way disparagingly, or pleading any kind of caution, is considered immediately either calumny or treason. And protesting that only months ago many of us had been in France, in England, in Belgium and had found there our friends who were just as peace-loving and accepting of us as we of them does no good.*
>
> *Retreating from the furor, finding oneself alone for objective contemplation, one cannot help feeling that the past two decades in Europe have been a golden age, and that this fierce loyalty to the nation and contempt for the other nations as enemies will result in the loss of so much of the brotherly spirit we have come to cherish over the years.*
>
> *One wonders from where all this hatred has sprung, from what dark shadow. The excessive nationalism is at times comforting and reassuring, like the spirit of an athletic team on the brink of some historic*

*and significant game, sweeping along with it even the most circumspect
of citizens.*

*As I mentioned before, I have been asked a number of times to take
up my military commission and join the general staff in helping with
railway transportations, a high interest of mine in my previous service.
Duty calls with a surprisingly strong pull, although that will mean
passing up for the moment my return to Boston. I have always felt a
desire to serve. I will be far from the guns and the charge of cavalry,
but I will be serving.*

*I regret that the current situation forbids my return to Boston and
to the school, but I carry always the extreme optimism that affairs will
be resolved by Christmas.*

His letters to his friend Will Honeycutt always took a markedly different tone, more starkly realistic. The two had shared an affectionately
contentious friendship from almost the moment of Arnauld's arrival in
Boston in 1910. And like their relationship, the tone of their letters was
different from the one that Eleanor and Arnauld had established.

*You inquire as to the mood of the city. There is a fervor all around
that drowns out any voices of calm and reason. The anger at the rude
and disrespectful Serbs is palpable. That is the starting point. And everyone is itching to mobilize the army and attack, oblivious to the fierce
Russian resistance that would accompany such a move. Everyone is
convinced now that the English and French are our traditional bitter
enemies, forgetting that just weeks ago this city welcomed visitors from
those lands with open arms.*

*Having Germany as a spiritual ally, of course, fuels the national-
istic confidence. The Russian Bear, fearsome as he sees himself, would
think twice before offending the belligerent Germans, or so popular
opinion goes. The nightmare, of course, would be a tumbling of one
domino into another, and then another and another and another, leading to a huge collapse of everything we consider civilized.*

*But this furor in the streets of my city does not fill one with confi-
dence in the triumph of rational powers. I think that you would be
woefully apprehensive, not that your abrasive influence would be allowed any sway. I will admit to fearing the worst, my friend.*

I surprise myself with the sudden sense of duty I am feeling—I cannot account for it at all. I have indeed decided to postpone my return to take up a position on the army's general staff, to help out temporarily. I have written to St. Gregory's and requested a year's leave of absence and I regret that this will keep us apart for some little time, but I feel that for once I can serve in a meaningful way, and for a short and manageable duration.

32

THE HORRORS OF WAR

ndeed, Arnauld found himself swept up in the fervor when his old regiment began calling up reserves and asking former officers to step forward. It was then that he wrote one of his most remarkable letters back to Eleanor in Boston:

> *Shortly after my decision, as the tensions and furor for war reached fever pitch in Vienna, a series of dreams seized me with a most powerful effect. For some nights in sequence I had been visited by a gallant figure on horseback who rides up to me in a state of some urgency, sword drawn, his horse greatly agitated and he gesturing that I should come near. Always it is the same figure, and after the second or third night, I began to realize that it was Eugene of Savoy, the great eighteenth-century savior of the empire, the one who built the magnificent Belvedere Palace. Only as I approached did I realize that he looked very much like me; as Herr Dr. Freud would say, my doppelgänger, my twin.*
>
> *Each night I awoke from the dream with a good deal of apprehension. Finally, a few nights ago, the third and fourth appearances, the figure of Prince Eugene appeared for such an extended visit that the next morning I had no trouble writing down details in great profusion, and soon, I found myself, through my writing, engaging in a dialogue with this mythic and grandiose double. As you know, I had numerous conversations with our dear Honeycutt in Cambridge about*

his dialogues from dreams, and I have read his splendid thesis from Harvard that you provided.

The other day I took the trolley up to the Upper Belvedere and sat beside the marvelous reflecting pool and fountain, pen in hand, writing out my encounters with this character from my unconscious, as Dr. James would call him. I write this here with a good deal of lightness, but I assure you that the whole experience—the apprehensions of nighttime and the encounters with the writing in daylight—has had a deep and unsettling effect on me.

I asked the prince why he was coming to me, and at first I received no response, or at least I could not call up a response with my writing or from my memory. Then the following night the figure came to me and made himself absolutely clear. He said that the empire was without its prince because of the tragedy of Mayerling and that someone—some charismatic figure—needed to step forward in this time of chaos.

"But I am not that person," I objected feebly.

"If not you, who?" the prince offered as if part of a litany.

"But I am not the one," I argued in my dream, and Eugene only stared at me as if there was some truth I was not admitting.

"I have come," he said loudly, raising his sword, "not to threaten but to anoint. It is your destiny," were his final words, before he dissolved before me. "It is your destiny" echoed after he had vanished.

I awoke in an agitated state and could not fall back into sleep, and as I rose in the morning, I found myself in a continued fitfulness, which stayed with me until that afternoon, when I visited the commander of my old regiment, and he explained the need for officers in service of the railroads. It was after that meeting that I decided to revive my commission and that I wrote my letter to St. Gregory's. I hope you understand.

Arnauld did indeed accept a posting on the general staff, feeling, he admitted, something of the patriotic, with the call to duty of his inherited commission. "It all happened too quickly for proper reflection," he admitted later. Suddenly, he found himself in a position of authority over the national railroads, a position that drew his attention through the immediate and almost overwhelming demands of the mobilization. "There was a sudden need for planning," he said, "and I stepped in. Working with the

complexity of movements and railroads, I must admit, was both demanding and fascinating."

He wrote to Eleanor,

> *Every cavalry officer travels with at least one horse, and every horse*
> *travels with at least one week's food, and then there are the guns and the*
> *munitions. It is a huge challenge, one unlike anything in peacetime. And*
> *that is why the general staff requires many logistics officers like me. We*
> *work day and night and still find ourselves needy of more time for plan-*
> *ning. And I must admit that, so unlike anything else I have done in my*
> *life, it is compelling work of compelling interest. I cannot tell you the*
> *number of trips I have taken to the railroad yards to count boxcars and*
> *to the train stations to count seats on the antiquated passenger cars. Ev-*
> *eryone it seems is being pressed into service, regardless of age, even old*
> *officers who thought themselves long retired. This is a far cry from teach-*
> *ing American schoolboys on the quiet banks of the Charles River.*

Arnauld expressed his fear that the huge energy of mobilization would
lead inevitably to deployment and that deployment with all its mass movement would lead inevitably to war: "I do not see and no one asks how what
we have done will ever be reversed." With all the intricacies of planning,
he noted, there seemed to be no word for demobilization. Later, after the
massive war was fully engaged, it was observed that no one of the par-
ticipating countries, Austria included, had a plan for demobilization.
"What is done cannot be undone," one general said.

When on July 28 the declaration of war was issued by Austria against
Serbia, with wild tumult in the streets, men and horses and equipment
began marching toward the railroad cars that Arnauld and his fellow staff
officers had assembled all over the country. "With great pride," Arnauld
wrote, "we watched the lines of young men marching off to war. We were
very pleased with what we had accomplished. It could not have been done
without us, we told ourselves. Of course there are those who are predicting horrible effects, but they are dismissed quickly as misguided and not
knowing what they are talking about. In this, I feel we are reliving Mark
Twain's very cynical 'War Prayer.'"

As Arnauld had feared, the huge energy of mobilization by his Austria-Hungary and by all the European powers set in motion the inevitable. Tensions that were building up between Austria and Serbia burst into flame when Austria declared war, setting off a firestorm of reactive war declarations: Russia on Austria, Germany on Russia and France, England on Germany, and so on, eventually involving all major powers. Austria's first encounters, with Russia in Galicia, turned out to set the tone quickly. It was from the first day a horrible and bloody affair. The devastation of the first few months of war on the eastern front produced shocking results at home. As Arnauld described it, "Our trains that departed carrying the materials of war now returned carrying the near-dead, the maimed, the senseless, pouring back from the eastern front, from the confrontations with Russian artillery." And Arnauld, the officer in charge of the scheduling, often found himself among them, seeing the bloodied bandages, the stumps of lost limbs, the haggard faces, and hearing the unceasing moans of pain from young men unaccustomed to war. "It is an introduction. Now you are experiencing the horrors of war," an old officer said to Arnauld as they watched stretchers being unloaded at the Nordbahnhof. "Accustom yourself to it."

It was during the time of these first grim war letters from Vienna in August and September 1914 that the world watched in horror as one country after another hurled itself into the fray.

And it was also at that time when Eleanor, watching safely from the remove of Boston, became certain that she was pregnant.

33

"IF NOT YOU, WHO?"

e felt such elation," Arnauld wrote, "before such foreboding. We watched our trains pull out from the Nordbahnhof on their way to Galicia and the Russian front, with men and horses and supplies, and we marveled at our modern world and our new role in it, with no idea of what was to come. That was before one of our number, a gloomy son of the aristocracy from Salzburg, pointed out that the same trains would be 'bringing back the wounded and the dead.'"

During the mobilization and even in the aftermath of the outbreak of the fighting, Arnauld was of two minds about returning to Boston and the nearness to his beloved Eleanor. He admitted to being consumed by the popular mania fueled by the belief that the whole troublesome matter would be over by Christmas, as soon as the enormous army he and his fellow officers had transported to the eastern front reigned victorious, but he also admitted to a dark pessimism that swept over him, especially in the dead of night, that saw the horror of the battle they had made possible raging on indefinitely.

The dream came to him nearly every night of fevered sleep, the heroic prince Eugene rising up before him, asking not for war, but for sanity. "You didn't warn of the horror," Arnauld said.

"It is war," the prince said, as if it was the most natural thing in the world. "That is what happens in war."

"It is insanity."

"It can be stopped, you know."

"But how?" Arnauld would ask.

"What if all sides simply stopped the trains?" he asked Arnauld. "What if someone—someone charismatic like you—rose up princelike on a tabletop in the general headquarters and commanded it?"

"But I am not a prince," Arnauld repeated each time, feebly. "I am not charismatic."

And always the heroic Eugene, his doppelgänger, responded the same as he did each time he appeared. "If not you, who?" the prince would say. And Arnauld would awake each time with a deep sense of despair and dread.

Part of him wished simply to return to Boston, to be done with this whole business of war. He carried with him always and everywhere the image of Eleanor's beautiful presence, and now with the almost overpowering memory of that last night. He cherished it now above all other memories, as he knew the circumstances would not be possible ever again. And over time, in the midst of the anguish that followed the initial enthusiasms for Austria, he longed for a return to the peaceful life of a teacher in a New England boys' school and the nearness to his Beatrice. But something kept drawing him to war, and the dream kept returning.

His position took him from staff headquarters out to Galicia, to the Russian front, to inspect the supply lines and to oversee the initial stages of the new challenges of transporting human fare: soldiers to the front and then indeed prisoners of war and the wounded and dead on the return trip.

On these trips to the battlefields, visits by rail to work out transportation logistics, where he traveled with new recruits—some, having heard now of the horrors there, vomiting from apprehension and fear—and back to Vienna with the countless wounded, so many of them moaning in pain and crying out that it was difficult to concentrate, he saw for himself the evidence that these engagements with both the Russians and the Serbs were so substantial in nature that only the misinformed and the hopelessly jingoistic could believe that this war would be over soon, or that war had been a good idea. His letters to Eleanor took on a pessimistic tone. "I fear that I shall not be returning," he actually said once. "My great inextinguishable fear, haunting me nightly with this specter of war, is that I shall never see you again."

Eleanor never faltered in her confidence in his safe return. Once, she wrote, "It will be hard for you, dear Arnauld, but I know, know as surely as I know any part of life, that you will return to St. Gregory's and to your friends here."

Reading these words seemed to transfer that confidence to him, as for the remainder of the first year of the war he never mentioned the dark thoughts again; in fact, he began to sound, at least in writing, positive and optimistic.

Then in 1915, when the Italians, wishing to better themselves by acquiring new territory, worked out a deal with the Allies—Winston Churchill would later call them "the whores of Europe"—and entered the war on the side of the English and French, Arnauld reflected, along with the Austrian sense of betrayal, a renewed gloom. "Imagine," he wrote, "being enemies now with old friends with whom we have shared so much literature and culture over the centuries, and only months ago a beer." And he noted that the opening of a whole new front in northern Italy, all around Trieste, put an entirely new strain on the railroads and gave him a demanding new challenge, pulling him deeper and deeper into the daily logistics, so that resigning his commission and returning to Boston, as he had planned, now seemed "a remote dream."

That Arnauld had friends in Italy, as he had friends all over Europe; that he had visited Italy countless times as a young man; that he could walk the streets of Florence, Venice, Verona, and Rome nearly as well as the Ringstrasse, made this whole conflict absurd. As an officer in the Hapsburg army doing his part to make sure that supplies and munitions traveled speedily and efficiently along the railroads, he tried not to think about the possibility that the specific supplies and munitions he sent along their way would lead to the deaths and injuries of his friends and their loved ones.

When the Italians decided to enter the war on the side of the Allies and began their military campaign to take over Trieste, the principal seaport of the empire, one of his favorite cities in the world, his transportation efforts took on the greatest irony. Arnauld simply could not imagine that those Italians he knew well and whose coffeehouses he had frequented with regularity would think that attacking the Austrian Empire was a good idea.

Most difficult in this rapid adjustment to Italy's declaration of war was the tragic consequence for his great friend and cousin Miggo.

"Remember, he thinks he's a Rough Rider," Arnauld said, trying to explain to Alma how, back in Genoa, hearing the call of gallantry and war, Miggo had accepted an officer position in the army. But unlike Arnauld, his cousin Miggo, his father's nephew, *did* love the look of an officer's uniform and the entrée into hearts and beds it brought with it. "Especially the latter," Arnauld told Alma. "You would have preferred him as your childhood friend," he added.

Alma had met Miggo on a number of occasions and admitted to being quite taken, as Eleanor had been, by his panache and flair. "He is for you," she told her introverted friend Arnauld, "what our Herr Dr. Freud would call a good alter ego." And then she added, rolling her eyes with her famous license, "Were I not taken . . ."

In 1914, while Italy and Austria were still allies, and Arnauld had been sent to Rome to discuss railroad matters with the Italian high command, Miggo had met him and had escorted him around the city, introducing him to every manner of artist and coffeehouse eccentric, using their respective uniforms for maximum effect. He had even tried to arrange for Arnauld a tryst with an exotic Romanian violinist. "We'll send you back to Vienna," the irrepressible Miggo said, "with your blood a little more Romanian and your stature a few centimeters taller."

And so it was that in his newly activated position in the Italian army, being swept up, Arnauld was sure, in nationalistic fervor—not giving much thought that it would be Austrians and Hungarians and Czechs he would be shooting at—Miggo embraced with vigor the thought of racing across southern Tyrol and into Trieste in a "quick war." Later, Arnauld wondered how even his brash and impulsive Italo-American cousin could have thought the proud Austrians capable of sitting idly by and watching the pretentious and deceitful takeover.

And now, adding to the grinding negative effect of watching the wounded pouring back from the Russian front on his trains for all those months, word reached him. Because, this southern war being sudden and new, communication between Genoa and Vienna had not fully terminated, the news arrived almost immediately. It was just as the Italians approached the Isonzo River, on the first day of combat on the plains of Friuli, that an artillery shell burst from an unknown quarter, both sides not yet knowing fully how to coordinate firings with troop movements, and fell into the center of the advanced convoy in which Major Michelangelo Sabatini was riding. Miggo was dead. And Arnauld's decline into emotional chaos was under way.

34

THE BATTLE OF CAPORETTO

E xactly why Arnauld's posting had been shifted to the Italian front is never made clear in the various sources. We can only guess. His original assignment of organizing the priorities of the railroad lines from general headquarters in Vienna, "far from harm," as he described it, had evolved to assignments at stations on the actual fronts, first and temporarily in the east, against the stubborn Russians in Galicia, then what appeared to be permanent placement on the Italian front, securing delivery of supplies and transporting wounded and prisoners away from the war zone. Perhaps as movement of supplies and men became more and more overburdened, it became essential for officers of Arnauld's experience to be in the center of the action.

What is certain is that by 1917, the two huge armies had been locked in a two-year stalemate the whole length of the Isonzo River, from the high and rugged Dolomites down to the flatlands of the Adriatic coast, seen from the start by both sides as crucial for capture or defense of the great prize: the port of Trieste.

The fateful stalemate was punctuated by twelve separate battles, in which one million soldiers died. Since the Austrian defenses featured mountain gun emplacements along the whole expanse of the Isonzo front, Italian attacks required charging up perilously steep mountainsides, encountering barbed wire two and three lines deep and withering machine-gun fire. Occasionally the attackers would break through, leading to hand-to-hand combat and violent counterattack.

In the first battle alone, there were tens of thousands of casualties on each side.

The Italian strategy was based on faith in superior numbers in constant attack, wearing down the enemy and allowing no chance of rest.

Wars are fought with yesterday's strategies and tomorrow's technologies, it is said. And so it was on the Isonzo, where the strategies of the nineteenth century met the barbed wire, machine guns, and artillery shells of the twentieth. The Italian high command believed implacably that an enemy who uses mountainous positions is always vulnerable to undercover advancement at the inevitable weak points unexpected by the defender. The Austrians would defend both the Tyrolean and Isonzo regions by holding such high positions, and the Italians would attack uphill with overwhelming numbers, after devastating artillery barrages. The result of this hopelessly antiquated strategy was a total advance of less than ten miles in twelve battles over two years, with too many casualties to count accurately.

For the Italians, it was to have been a quick acquisition of territory, and the occupation of the ancient seaport. For the outnumbered Austrians, it was simply a fierce resistance to the takeover by the treacherous former allies.

Life in the trenches on all sections of the stalemated Isonzo was grim. There was little ground on either side of the river that had not been subjected to artillery shelling, machine-gun fire, and carnage. Bodies that had been hastily buried during one part of the campaign were blown out of the ground in the next. The rainwater that accumulated at the bottom of most trenches was rendered fetid by the decomposed flesh and human waste. There were rats everywhere and lice the size of pebbles. The armies of both sides had no choice but to dig in and wait for an enemy offensive or one of its own.

The change in tone in Arnauld's letters and journal entries appeared gradually in 1917, a year or so before the armistice and about the time he found himself permanently assigned to a regiment in the heart of the war zone on the Isonzo River. Earlier, in 1915, Arnauld's letters to Eleanor and his parents bore the rational and objective tone of a university intellectual, his writings to Eleanor more restrained perhaps than those to his parents, such as the following:

> *Life along the front, mostly along the Isonzo River, is bleak, and*
> *after months of fighting and five separate battles, the soldiers of the*

empire are resigned to the most wretched of conditions. My journeys
there accompanying supply trains through countryside and seeing the
effects of deprivation on towns and villages that depended on our
trains for food and supplies is shocking. Townspeople stand beside the
tracks and at the stations and watch us pass through without stopping.
One feels a hopelessness, feeling everything, able to do nothing. Then on
the return trip, our train cars filled with wounded and prisoners, no
one appears trackside.

Conditions are even worse in the enemy trenches. Captured Italian
soldiers describe the prospects of spending the duration of the war in
Austrian prison camps, regardless of how grim they might be, as far
better than serving in General Cadorna's army.

And then this passage from Arnauld's war journal. Written now with
shaky hand, his sketchy and stark notations tell of the appalling conditions mostly omitted from his letters to his parents and Eleanor.

Enemy soldiers poorly trained know not how to avoid exploding
artillery or to keep heads down—they have been issued wool caps, not
helmets. Our snipers know when new recruits arrive in the trenches as
heads keep popping up—easy target practice. "We lop off the heads of
Italians we would have shared a beer with at a street café a few years
ago," says one of our officers. "Not unless you shared a beer with igno-
rant peasants," says another. "These are not the university students you
consorted with in Trastevere."

Because Arnauld continued to send his letters out through the special
courier reserved for officers with connections, he continued his surprising
candor and with Will Honeycutt seemed to hold back nothing. In those
letters we can see the grim life he had settled into. One in particular suggests what lay ahead for Arnauld and those of his sensitive colleagues who
might survive.

Trench life is deplorable and a new experience in war for both sides.
Soldiers eat, sleep, and take care of bodily needs all in the confined space
of the trench, with predictable results. Tents leak, clothes are sodden and
reeking, and most everything smells of rot and discharge. These are the

daily conditions, and the soldiers tolerate it all because it is better than going over the top and facing the barb wire and raking of enemy machine guns. At least, hunkered down in trenches, there is safety from sniper fire and the overhead bursting of shells.

But even in the trenches, debilitating explosions are not uncommon. One hears the distant percussion, then the approaching whistle of the shell and the concussion that tears into the protecting earth and rips into bodies, sending parts flying and covering the faces and hands of neighbors with bits of flesh and bone. Those who were alive and laughing and singing to pass the time one moment are blown into grotesque fragments in another. The infantryman keeps watch with his rifle while a shell smashes the trench a few meters away. Someone is screaming because a poor soul has lost his leg, or his stomach is split open. And always there is the moaning of the wounded and dying and the quick survey of bodies to see if there is perhaps a jacket or trousers or socks or boots that could be of use to the living. No wonder men become deranged.

Usually the wounded are already dead or writhing in their last throes, but occasionally it becomes apparent that there is still the hope of life, sometimes with a limb gone or a stomach ruptured or a face torn away, in which case a comrade bends over the body until a priest arrives or the medics with a stretcher.

Times were hard on both sides. The Italians had proven to be ineffective and poorly organized, plagued, even a casual observer could see, by outdated and incompetent leadership, ruling out from the start the quick campaign to capture Trieste they had once envisioned. The Austrians, although much better off in morale and leadership, had supply difficulties, and their troops had to endure the devastating cold of the mountain regions, with poor equipment and a desperate shortage of rations.

The Austrian countryside between this area on the Adriatic and the heartland around Vienna was brought to near starvation as the railroads they depended on for food were commandeered for the military. It was a brutal time for everyone, soldier and civilian alike, and the seemingly pointless offensives launched by the Italians in an attempt to cross the river took a great toll.

N

The decisive move, the now-infamous Battle of Caporetto, came in the fall of 1917. Because of significant reinforcement from the German army, the Austrians were able to overrun the Italian positions and send the hapless Italians in humiliating and disorganized retreat westward toward the plains near the Piave River and Venice. After more than two years of grim stalemate, the Austrians were victorious.

The battle had begun with a gas attack, the shells landing among the Italians causing mayhem and panic. So when the Austrians descended from the mountains and eventually crossed the prized Isonzo River and overran trenches and gun emplacements along the way, the first sights they saw were enemy soldiers dead and dying from the ravages of gas, their faces contorted in the most awful grimaces, "a journey through hell," the soldiers called it. For Arnauld, already having seen too much death and suffering, the scenes were unspeakable. It was his and his men's assignments to search through the carnage for soldiers still alive to be taken prisoner. He wrote a number of entries in his war journal before the final event in the rail yard that brought about his end.

These entries become more erratic and spotty, evidence that a sensitive and poetic man was witness to too much. Finally, after the letters had ceased, the almost illegible journal entries descend into the near-deranged.

N

And then came the experience with the Italian prisoners at the rail yard that is described not by Arnauld himself but by the accounts that Eleanor demanded and Dr. Jung commissioned from his inside sources after the armistice.

The last war journal entry is almost unintelligible, the shaky hand almost illegible, the page stained with what one could assume was human blood.

> *Descending from Caporetto. Bodies torn mangled. Faces yellow—gasping for air screaming agony lungs ruined.*
> *Company of gunners dead in place—like statues—gas! We pass through quickly survivors calling out to us man torn in two, still breathing—"water!"*

Czech officer with me, he faints "keep moving" officer yells and
yells "keep moving" chaos! Italians running surrendering in droves
with handkerchiefs anything white too many to count how to collect
them all?

Austrian batteries still firing won't stop "it's over—" someone
yells at the sky—"stop the firing!" No avail—chaos!

From the later descriptions, one can imagine the scene that followed. In the chaos of fleeing Italian soldiers, many were taken prisoner, some against their will, some too wounded to know or care, some convinced that their chances were better as Austrian prisoners than retreating Italians. Only hours, perhaps minutes, after the last hasty entry in his war journal, one assumes, the chaos unabated, Arnauld organized a group of officers to handle the roundup and prevent the soldiers on his side from shooting the men coming at them with hands in the air. "We haven't time to stop for them," one corporal yelled, waving his carbine, his intentions made clear by that and the urgency in his voice, and Arnauld yelled, "Nonsense. We are not barbarians," and he waded into the middle of the surrendering group, so as to protect them and to make clear their status as prisoners. "Leave all weapons," he yelled. "We will form orderly lines," he said, and the young Czech officer, Arnauld's friend, the one who read his own poetry during the long nights, stepped forward to assist.

The group, sides and nationalities indistinguishable perhaps, was clustered together for protection, surrounded by witnesses, when the shell exploded directly above them.

35

UNDENIABLE NEWS

leanor first received word of Arnauld's death in a telegram from Ernst Kleist from Vienna. It was on a gray Boston morning in late 1917, shortly before the time of the dreaded influenza. Not willing to accept the news at first, she placed a transatlantic telephone call to her friend Carl Jung in Zurich and set in motion an elaborate and not-inexpensive plan to have the matter investigated, the first news having left, as she said, room for question.

After a number of weeks there was a second telegram, this time from Jung, and it struck the final blow, one that threw everything into ruin. Over the years, nothing had been easy, granted, and there had certainly been moments of doubt, despair even, but then, in spite of all the ups and downs, at day's end, all that was supposed to happen had happened. For twenty years, all the Vienna journal's predicted events had come to be. Somehow, she had kept her part of the bargain. Until this second telegram, this one from her friend Jung, as trusted a source as could be, a shocking reversal of the future.

At first, staring in disbelief at the pasted strips of teletyped text that she held in her hand, she was thrust into another short-lived period of denial. It simply could not be true. Then after a good deal of waiting, she heard Jung's muffled, crackly telephone voice coming in over the transatlantic cable from Zurich, authenticating the details.

"I'm afraid so," Jung said distinctly, with his thick Germanic accent, "confirmed, regrettably. No room for question, from the three witnesses you demanded."

"Are you absolutely positive?" she said with a kind of firmness her Swiss friend had become accustomed to.

"Absolutely," he said with corresponding directness. She knew Carl Jung and his conviction well enough to find little room for hope in what he was now telling her. "Undeniable. It was on the Italian front, as you know, on the Isonzo River. An artillery shell among a group of Italian prisoners. He was in charge. There was horrible carnage." He paused. "Dismemberment even." Then he paused again. "Word has come from Vienna that finality has been fully accepted by Arnauld's parents and friends there."

"No chance that anyone escaped—" She stopped, unable to continue.

"I am sorry," the Swiss doctor said with his famous decisiveness.

So finally the unavoidable sank in. Arnauld Esterhazy was dead.

The confirmation enveloped her in a new despondency. For twenty years now she had been living with the belief that her life was predetermined and that Arnauld was to play a major part in it. She knew also of the important role Arnauld Esterhazy was supposed to play in the life of St. Gregory's and her son's education, and the belief that he was now dead in the war was a bewildering deviation from what was supposed to be. Up until this very moment in the devastating war everything had gone as preordained. Enough of the predictions had proven accurate for her to have total faith that all would come to pass. Her curse was an accurate and active one: She did in fact know the future. Arnauld's departure in 1914 had been expected, though his volunteering to return to his old commission in the imperial army had been a surprise. Now the fact that he was dead, killed in the war, destroyed her understanding of life as she was supposed to live it.

The shock had been one she could share with no one, not her husband Frank Burden, nor her Boston friends, nor her children. In this one fateful stroke, the events in that predicted and preordained future that she had grown to trust had dissolved into total randomness, a randomness in which anything could happen, a randomness that the rest of the world considered the normal course of events. Only William James would have understood. More than ever now she missed him and his avuncular wisdom, the only one who had known the full story—in the end at least—the only one she could really talk to.

~

She would not have elected to attend the memorial service at St. Gregory's School had not Frank, oblivious to the intensity of her shock and grief, accepted for them. "I liked young Esterhazy," he said with characteristic bullish certitude. "Princely fellow. He was a good conversationalist, and he contributed well to the life of the St. Gregory's boys."

The memorial service, not held until the spring following the first rumors of Arnauld's death in battle, drew a surprisingly large group of former students, fellow teachers, and friends in attendance at the school chapel, in spite of warnings about public gatherings. The dreaded influenza that had recently established its terrifying grip on Boston and the entire East Coast was so very much on everyone's mind, but the large gathering was, in the words of the school chaplain, "a testament to this man's great appeal and effect. He was with us for only four years and yet his sensitive presence touched us all deeply."

As Eleanor sat beside her husband now, listening to the eulogies in praise of Arnauld Esterhazy, the beloved and talented young teacher from Austria-Hungary now lost in the war, celebrating the life of this bright and cultured man who had spent so many evenings in their home, she gave little outward sign of the devastation that consumed her. No one knew the depth of her despair, or how she fought for composure as the school's Anglican chaplain read inspiring words about the nobility and sacrifice of war. And no one in that congregation or elsewhere in Boston even began to suspect the secret identity she worked to preserve or the secret bond she shared with this man being eulogized.

As the chaplain spoke, she felt more and more in the grip of the darkness, and she could barely pull herself to her feet and return, when the service was over, to her family. She sat in secret anguish, carrying deep within her the one inextinguishable and inexpressible fear. She could not help thinking that this whole miserable turn of events had come about because of her actions on Arnauld's last night in Boston four years before and some unknown and unpredicted effect on him.

The chaplain pieced together what he knew of Arnauld's life before he came to Boston in 1910. He had grown up the son of an aristocratic family and had been part of the intellectual life of the cafés, had gone on to a distinguished life at the university, had become a military officer, then a teacher. In summarizing this life, the chaplain cited passages from the popular book *City of Music,* pointing out how aptly the passages portrayed the culture and intellectual life Arnauld had led in his beloved Vienna. And then he told how the artistic young Viennese had graced the school for four years, giving so much of himself, inspiring all the boys. "There is so very much loss in war," he said, "but each individual loss reverberates in us with poignancy, this loss especially because of the lives this fine good man touched."

During the whole St. Gregory's service, she did not dare look at Rose Spurgeon, who sat near the back of the chapel, but as always she felt her presence, and before the service the two women had communicated only through eye contact. "He was such a fine man," Rose had said, Rose who had just suffered a great loss herself. No one knew what Eleanor was going through, except Rose. Without a word being exchanged, Rose always seemed to know what Eleanor was thinking.

And she had barely been able to look at Will Honeycutt, who was there as one of Arnauld's great friends. As abrupt and abrasive as he was, he had become over the years her close ally, the only person in Boston, since the death of William James in 1910, who knew at least part of her story.

Will and Arnauld, these two unlikely friends, "the pure scientist and the poet," a Harvard friend had called them, had been introduced originally by Eleanor, again, no accident, and had been in the habit of meeting with regularity at their favorite café on Brattle Street in Cambridge, struggling to replicate, Arnauld would admit in his journals, at least in part, the café ambiance of his native city he had given up to come to Boston. "This will do you good," Will had said, continuing the introduction of his sensitive European friend to his Harvard colleagues, "some good old American pragmatism."

But Arnauld had a way of making everyone feel right, and he would smile and insist that Harvard and Harvard Square had much to offer and were indeed a fitting substitute for the stimulating café life of Vienna.

After the service Will approached Eleanor with uncharacteristic stoic reserve. She forced herself to match his demeanor with a stoicism she was in no way feeling. "I was really attached to your man Arnauld," he said solemnly, and Eleanor offered a wordless nod.

"I know, Will," she said.

"He worshipped you, you know," he offered suddenly, as if it even needed to be said. Eleanor, caught by surprise but accustomed to Will's manner, only nodded and looked away. "I found it impossible to accept—" His voice broke and he paused, and she reached out and touched his arm and held firm.

"I know, Will," she said.

She too had struggled with the reality, even after the second phone call, and then the letter had arrived from Jung just before the memorial service, and it had been the report from the man he hired in Vienna to do the requested research, a retired Viennese policeman named Franz Jodl who wrote with the grim details.

"He is gone," Will had said upon reading the letter. "There is no room for question."

Even Frank, not one to show emotion, had been moved. "One had hoped it wasn't true," he said, shaking his head slowly when he read it. "Young Esterhazy was easy to be fond of."

<hr>

Arnauld was indeed easy to become fond of. "He was sensitive, thoughtful," the school chaplain had eulogized, "and he carried himself with an elegant grace, with what would have to be called a regal bearing," and then he paused and added to the theme, "Arnauld was to us a visiting prince of the empire."

The chaplain conjectured how Arnauld had become that way. "What forces had shaped such a man?" he said. "Raised in one of Europe's most cultured cities, of notable and aristocratic Hungarian birth, seasoned in the fertile intellectual ground of fin de siècle café life. Arnauld Esterhazy studied philosophy and history at the university, but, having accepted the hereditary commission expected of his family," he said, accounting for his being in the war, "he became an unlikely warrior, this encyclopedia of a man, this natural nurturer of our youngest and most senior minds, this gracious guest in our homes, this quiet student of Ovid and Homer. A great jolt of sadness has hit his colleagues, those many students who had considered him among their best teachers, all of us who knew and loved this sensitive man of ideas, this man of peace."

In all that was said of Arnauld Esterhazy on that day in the St. Gregory's chapel, there emerged one absolute certainty, that, considering his intelligent sensitivity and gentle grace, the horrors of this particular war would have had on him—as it would have on so many sensitive young men on all sides—the most terrifying effect. And, as a sign of the enormous respect for this man, in the service in the St. Gregory's chapel that day in 1918, there was no mention during the eulogies that he had died fighting for the enemy.

36

EDITH

he bore her grief alone. She had lost her link to the predestined future, granted, and that was bad enough, but there was so much more. Her immediate devastation came from the visceral, from the loss of this man she had known for so long, whose letters she had come to depend on, whose company she had cherished, and finally, whose very essence she had known in full forbidden intimacy, the man she knew was the father of her child. For three years, while he was away at war, she had found herself at times unable to stop thinking of him in ways no one would suspect, and now she could not stop feeling unexplainable loss.

Only a few people knew of her close association with Arnauld Esterhazy, the man departed. No one knew the completeness of her loss. The only letter of condolence on record, and one she prized most in a lifetime of letters, came from Baltimore, from her friend Edith Hamilton.

Eleanor had met Edith Hamilton in the spring of 1910. From the moment of her return from Vienna, as she pursued the steps that needed to be taken to create the Hyperion Fund and the other demands of her prescribed life, Eleanor in the back of her mind knew to search for Edith Hamilton, aware of little about the woman other than the name and the fact that later in her life a woman of that name was to write a book about Greek mythology that was to figure prominently later in her story and the story of her family.

Finding this Edith Hamilton seemed crucial in the unfolding of the future she knew was to be, an essential part of her strange and unusual assignment, and from time to time she would ask friends in Boston if they had ever heard of a woman of that name, an academic and a classicist, Eleanor figured early on. She had asked William James if he knew such an academic, and he said that he did not. And she asked others. No one seemed to know or know of an Edith Hamilton at Harvard or elsewhere.

She had not brought up her search with her former headmistress at Winsor School, Isabel Hewens, one of the great sources of inspiration in her life. Why she didn't she could not remember. It was in 1909, right around the time of the Clark University conference, that the subject did come up, and Miss Hewens answered quickly, "I think you mean my old friend Edith, who is headmistress of the Bryn Mawr School in Baltimore. You must have met her on one of her many visits to me here in Boston."

"I think I am looking for a classics professor," Eleanor said.

"Oh, Edith is a classicist, all right. She knows about as much about the ancient world as anyone I know." She paused and looked at Eleanor with mock umbrage. "Headmistresses can have academic interests, you know."

Eleanor laughed at her own error. "Of course," she said apologetically. "Has she written a book about mythology?"

"No," her old headmistress said, "but I am sure she could. You can ask her the next time she visits."

So in the early summer of 1910, Eleanor Burden first met Edith Hamilton, the future author of the book that would change many lives and figure prominently in her own. Miss Hamilton was traveling to Maine, where she spent her summers in her family's house and was staying over at Winsor School on her way from Baltimore, as was her habit.

When Eleanor told William James of the visit, he said, "Oh, I know Edith. I know her family from Philadelphia and Maine. But she is a headmistress. I thought you were searching for an academic."

"Headmistresses can have academic interests, you know," Eleanor said, imitating the look of her dear Miss Hewens.

"Of course," William James said, "I certainly did not mean to imply otherwise."

Eleanor did indeed meet her old headmistress's friend and was charmed by the older woman's command of the ancient world. But she had written no books. "I wouldn't write about mythology per se," she told Eleanor. "If I were to write a book, it would be about the Greek way of life. I believe that is my passion." Miss Hamilton smiled wistfully. "I find that running a school and ministering to the intellectual and spiritual lives of so many girls takes my full concentration and energy." Miss Hewens nodded wisely as if to concur. "There is not much left for personal writing," Miss Hamilton said.

Eleanor smiled but refused to give in. "Well, maybe when you retire."

Miss Hamilton looked wistful again. Then she paused and gestured to her fellow headmistress, and both women smiled and held a moment of silence, thinking of their responsibilities to young minds.

"Edith," Isabel Hewens said, "Eleanor wishes you to write a book about mythology, and when Eleanor wishes something she usually gets it. She was remarkably strong and persuasive as a schoolgirl and has continued to be so, if not even more so, as an adult." Miss Hewens smiled, admiring one of her most prized former students.

When Eleanor told Professor James about the encounter, he threw his head back and laughed. *"A remarkably strong and persuasive schoolgirl,* indeed," he said with relish. "If you wish it to happen, we all know it will happen."

Shortly after Arnauld's arrival that fall, as a beginning teacher at St. Gregory's School, at dinner at Miss Hewens's house, Eleanor took great delight in introducing him to Edith, who was returning to Baltimore from her summer sojourn in Maine. "You have much in common," she said to her friend Edith, in what turned out to be an understatement. And that evening the five of them, she, Edith, Arnauld, Frank, and Isabel Hewens, discussed many matters of ancient history and literature, all with great enthusiasm. Arnauld told of his boyhood rapture when reading Heinrich Schliemann's account of discovering Troy, and it was Frank who nodded most in agreement. "Do you believe that it really was Priam's Troy that he found?" Edith asked, adding a touch of skepticism.

"Absolutely authentic," Arnauld said. "It is such a romantic story that we all will it to be true."

"That simplifies the matter," Edith said. "If it is a good story then it must be true." The she turned to her friend Isabel. "I like this man's reasoning."

"I think you have found a match," Miss Hewens said with a smile to Eleanor a few weeks later. "Edith has already invited your Arnauld up to the family house in Maine, and she does not do that often. It is her time for quiet thought and solitary reflection, she always says. Do you suppose that those two will ever pause in their reading Greek to each other and sharing Ovid and Pindar and Homer?" And then she added, "And they have begun a catalogue of every myth they encounter, and every mythological character they can recall. I am certain, knowing Edith and your Austrian friend, that it is as thorough a collection as one will find anywhere."

Eleanor admitted at that time to feeling some relief that this new friendship might serve as a further inducement for Arnauld to remain in America. But now that Arnauld was gone and Eleanor had read and reread Edith's letter, the immediate and natural affinity that those two lovers of antiquity had shown for each other, that at the time had seemed so amusing, she now found heartbreaking.

> *My dear Eleanor,*
>
> *I have just heard the very sad news of Arnauld Esterhazy's death on the Italian front some months ago. I cannot tell you the devastation this news brings with it. So many young men have perished in this endless and seemingly pointless struggle that it is difficult to single out any one, but somehow Arnauld's death brings with it a poignancy that is lost in the news of the abundance of others. He was one about whom great words have been and will be written. Losing him is a loss of an epic scale. I know the closeness you felt with this extraordinary and kind man, and I believe that you knew of mine.*
>
> *It was you who introduced him to me at Isabel Hewens's home in Boston eight years ago, and I believe that you knew at the time how much the two of us would find in common and how his interests and sensibilities would coincide with my own. Of course, he could read Latin and Greek, and that ability in a man is enough to cause a blush of affection from the start. I suppose it is prejudice to point out that such abilities are rare in men in our country but less rare among Europeans. But there was so much more common interest. I cannot recall the company of male companionship more cherished than when he and I would read Homer or Ovid or Hesiod or Pindar to each other and go over each retelling of mythology with wonder and complete absorption. Of course, we loved reading Chapman's Homer to each other, but it was the Greek Homer especially that he read so beautifully. And although I never called him on it, I always suspected that he knew the Greek of the*

Odyssey *by heart. He could certainly cite many passages from memory. I would listen transfixed.*

Having spent long hours with this man in such enterprise, I know well the high regard in which he held you, dear Eleanor. You were indeed his inspiration and his muse, his Beatrice, as he said so many times with reverence. He came to Boston because of you, and it was because of you that he intended to stay. Were any woman desirous of being first in his heart, that would be a futile enterprise, the position already firmly and permanently established by his beloved Beatrice. Of course you know that, but I felt compelled to put it in writing to you now as I sort through the details of my own great sadness.

As I sit now in the presence of this sorrow, I can only tell you that I understand your grief and your loss. We were fortunate beyond recounting to have had this extraordinary man in our lives.

Yours with affection,
Edith

37

INFLUENZA

he future was ruined. There would be no maturing Arnauld Esterhazy at St. Gregory's School, no legendary Venerable Haze in the lives of the schoolboys. Young Standish, born in 1915 and now approaching four years old, would not become the famous war hero Dilly Burden, would not develop a love for Vienna, would turn out to be a banker like his father, and there would be no Wheeler Burden.

Such anguish she had not felt for twenty years, since those sorrowful days at the end of her time in Vienna. She could no longer trust events to turn out as foretold in the journal she had brought with her from that time. Life as she had grown to accept it was over. All because of a simple telegram.

What a fool she had been to believe the prepostcrousness of the journal's preordination anyway. Granted, over the twenty years there had been events and details she had known of in advance: the incredible investments, tasks she needed to perform, the tragedy of the *Titanic*, in all of which she had had no choice or control, and all of which she had been able to tell no one. But now everything had come to an end, with this one death in war, in the midst of so many deaths in war.

That was when Eleanor was revisited by the dream, "The Big Dream," Carl Jung had called it some years before when she first wrote to him of it. It came to her again, leaving her suddenly awake in the cold sweat of panic. In the dream that first night, she found herself perched on the top of a huge iceberg, in the middle of a glassy sea. She sat precariously, fearful that she would slide off. Below her, at the waterline, she could see a large long swath of red paint, and below that she was aware of the huge mass extending far below into the deep. The depth of ocean beneath her, thousands of feet, gave her an even greater feeling of dread. As she began to slide, desperately digging in with her heels and fingernails, she always woke up, sweating and gasping for breath.

She was barely holding on, barely holding herself together, barely coping with this unpredictable and undeniable turn of events. She went about her life on Acorn Street without animation, like a ghost. She could tell no one of her immense shock, and no one except Rose Spurgeon, who had just lost her husband in the early throes of what was to become a terrible pandemic, seemed to notice. "What is the matter, ma'am?" Rose asked, she who herself had just lost so grievously. "You aren't getting sick, are you?"

"Nothing, Rose. I seem to have a touch of something, that's all. Nothing to worry about."

And then Susan became ill.

For twenty years, Eleanor's faith had been tested, for sure, but always affirmed in the end. What was supposed to happen somehow always happened, but now this fateful turn. She had believed from reading the journal that she and her family would be spared, but now with Arnauld dead, killed in the war, anything was possible. The future was wide open.

That the news of his death had come at the time of the dreaded influenza, with Boston one of the most severely affected of American cities, only added to Eleanor's consternation. The epidemic had begun on an army base in Kansas, in the spring of 1918, generated suddenly, it was conjectured, from the widespread burning of pig manure, and emanated to other army bases throughout the country. A dark unnatural cloud settled on the area, it was remembered, and then the sicknesses began. American soldiers carried the pestilence to Europe, where it spread and grew in virulence, then came back with a vengeance, spreading quickly to army bases, Camp Devens near Boston being one of the hardest hit. It was not long before the dreadful pestilence distributed itself in the civilian populations, especially in the big cities of the East Coast, attacking— uncharacteristic of flus in general—the youngest and healthiest, giving it more the appearance of plague than flu.

Wherever it arrived, hospitals and clinics were overwhelmed, medical staffs—already depleted by war service in Europe—were stretched to the breaking point, and emergency tents were set up to care for the affected. Flu victims were encouraged to move to large makeshift infirmaries, for reasons of both treatment and quarantine, lying in hallways, waiting for the dying to relinquish their beds. There were so many deaths, such inevitability, that nurses actually wrapped patients in sheets and affixed toe tags even before they died.

Eventually, in the span of less than a year, the influenza would kill some five hundred thousand Americans. The pandemic spread just as the country had decided to join the conflict in Europe. It was President Wilson's decision to put thousands of soldiers together in the tight quarters of troopships. The disease spread among them and then to soldiers on both sides in the European theater, war and microbes being in collusion.

The American influenza led eventually to fifty million deaths worldwide, becoming a major part of the casualties for both sides in the war. It was the worst epidemic in American history, and the most demoralizing because of its attack on the most vigorous and robust. As their lungs filled with fluid, influenza victims simply drowned. In October 1918, when American soldiers were fully invested in joining the fight and making their impact in the European war, the death toll hit its peak.

There were peculiarities. For some reason, the epidemic, probably begun in Kansas, bore the name Spanish Flu, most likely, because Spain, not at war, did not censor its press and was the only nation to admit up front the pervasive devastation of the illness. In the late fall and winter of 1918 and 1919, only months after its most devastating entry, about the time of the great armistice, the impact waned dramatically.

"The flu ran out of vulnerable victims," said Tom Ballantine, the Burdens' longtime Boston doctor. "We had no idea how it got here or how to stop it. It just arrived, killed off everyone it could, then moved on." It seemed to be over as quickly as it had arrived. But not before it entered the sanctuary of the Burdens' Acorn Street home.

It was Tom Spurgeon who became sick first. One afternoon he complained of pain in his abdomen and by nightfall he was in bed in the Spurgeons' quarters off the kitchen. By the next day, he had become unable to move and Eleanor called Tom Ballantine, who had already become alarmed by cases he had seen around the city. He only shook his head when he told Rose what he had found, and a day later Tom was struggling with his breathing and high fever, and he died.

The family had hardly had time to grieve or plan the service when Susan came down with the symptoms, and Tom Ballantine found himself again called to the Burden house, and again shaking his head. Rose did not falter. "You go be with your family," Eleanor had said to Rose after Tom's funeral, when the dreaded illness paid its second visit to Acorn.

"I shall stay. I shall be the one to sit with her," Rose said. "I am already exposed." Eleanor was impressed then, as she would be many times, by the strength the woman received from her Catholic faith.

Against Tom Ballantine's advice, Rose and Eleanor took turns beside Susan in the child's bedroom, administering to her needs as the young girl began burning up with fever. The family became frantic with worry, and Rose Spurgeon argued with her mistress: "Let me stay beside her," she said. "You take care of the others."

But Eleanor would have none of it. She took up her place beside Susan's bed. "I will sit with my daughter," she said with that fierce conviction of hers that no one in the household would argue with, not even the staunch Frank Burden.

Even in their neighborhood there were cases of children dying from the dreaded flu. The wife of a colleague of Frank's at the bank, another Smith College alumna, was one of the first in their circle of acquaintances to contract the disease and succumb to it, she the mother of three young children. The milkman who had included the Acorn Street house on his morning route for more than twenty years did not show up one morning, and a few days later they heard that he too was dead. One young mother in their neighborhood had heard of the cautions being spread about and had pronounced boldly that she did not intend to "live in fear," took her infant daughter out onto the Boston streets in her baby carriage with no protective mask, and had lost her within two days.

Eleanor knew of the terrible impact of the loss of a child from sharing grief with Alma Mahler, Arnauld's childhood friend in Vienna, whom she had befriended when the famous musician came to New York in 1907. Just before their departure for America back then, the Mahlers' five-year-old daughter, Maria, had died painfully of diphtheria. It was an agonizing experience for both Alma and Gustav, one that neither of them ever got over and that caused Gustav to write some of his most haunting and poignant music. Now the specter of childhood death was at the Burdens' door.

The wise and kindly Tom Ballantine came and shook his head. "It has gone to her lungs," he said with solemnity, and everyone knew what that meant. They made the decision to keep Susan at home, knowing full well the consequences, the risks of infection to the whole family.

Frank Burden, hero of countless athletic contests, including the first modern Olympics of 1896, extensive European traveler, international businessman of youthful promise, who had spent a lifetime perfecting a banker's steely persona, hiding from the surface all the emotions of the weaker sex, was adamant. "You tend to Susan," he said, affirming his wife's decision to stay with her daughter. "The rest of us will fend as we must. You give Susan what she needs."

Then Eleanor herself became ill, and fell into a deep fever, slipping away to join her mother, she thought in her fevered state, losing contact with the world.

"You must prepare for the worst," Tom Ballantine told the staunch Frank Burden. And prepare he did, with a countenance grim even for him, deciding to stay at his wife's side, in spite of the risk to his own health.

And this time Rose argued with the master of the house. "Let me be the one, Mr. Burden," she said. She had just returned after being gone for two days, to take the body of her husband, Tom, back to Fall River for his funeral. "If we lost you, the children would be in a terrible way."

But now Frank was the adamant one. "Thank you, Rose, but I shall stay by my wife's side. If I take ill, so be it."

Eleanor's fever increased, and she could feel the searing pain invading her lungs. *This now is how it ends,* she thought, passing in and out of delirium, aware of her husband sitting beside her bed, her steadfast and loyal guardian, she now totally unable to care for her family as they had all become accustomed. She could only lie there in high fever, too weak to protest this further departure from the future that needed to be, imagining herself being transported to Vienna, the city of so many of her dreams.

In her delirium she became aware that Susan's bed was empty and stripped beside hers. "What of Susan?" she would have asked had she been able. Racked with the pain of coughing, almost completely out of her mind, she was aware that everything was lost, but she herself now was too far gone to care. She lost all connection to the world of the living.

When she awoke finally, it was as if from a deep, fitful anesthesia. She saw the empty bed beside hers, and she knew the worst. "What of Susan?" she asked finally, barely able to form words. No answer came to spare her, and she stopped asking. Barely back to life herself, she was still too weak to care or to make herself understood. She passed back into the deepest of sleeps, as if dropping back into an underworld, this time peaceful and relieved of concern.

And she dreamed. The one she recalled later with great vividness was a return of the dream of her mother, dressed all in white, on a picnic blanket. She gestured for Eleanor, then the girl Weezie, to come sit down beside her. She was accompanied by a stranger, a handsome man, this time, also dressed in white, a bearded man who resembled Dr. James. They were lovers, and they welcomed her together. Each time the dream recurred, she tried to join her mother but never quite could.

Then one night, in the dream state, she became aware of another presence in the room, off in a recessed corner at first, almost unnoticeable, where she had been for a long time perhaps, then stepping out, unmistakable for the faint rattle of armor. It was the familiar guardian of her past come to stand watch, she of the fierce gray eyes and the Medusa medallion. "Have you always been there?" Eleanor asked, and the goddess only nodded and stood her ground. It was then that Eleanor fell again into the most peaceful sleep.

Her fever had broken, and she awoke to an unearthly, almost blissful calm. She rose from her bed, weak, and in her nightdress, she stepped out into the hallway, filled with dread at what she would find.

She walked like a ghost. Everyone was gone from the house, and she had the rooms and hallways to herself. Everything seemed to be in a haze, like the border area of a dream. At first there was only silence, then she heard music and drifted down the stairs to the living room, toward the sun porch, where the upright piano stood.

The music came to her more and more clearly and she recognized its probable source, but still not fully aware if she was imagining this or not, she came to the door of the sunroom and stood motionless. There before her were two young girls in white dresses, one before a music stand, playing an alto recorder, the other seated at the piano, her hands roaming over the keys. The sunlight spilled over them as they played, unaware of being watched. Beside them, in its case, was a cello, Eleanor's cello. Many times she had sat in that chair beside the piano, music stand in front of her, and played first with Susan, as she learned piano, and then adding Jane, as she began learning the recorder. The two girls looked up at the ghostlike figure in the doorway, and for a moment all three figures remained frozen, then they all burst into life.

"Mother!" the older of the two said, leaping to her feet. She then exclaimed, "You are well!"

"Oh, Susan!" burst out of her, and Eleanor's two daughters rushed to her and buried themselves in their mother's arms and the folds of her nightdress. "You are saved," the mother said with what little energy she could call up, joy and relief on her face. "We have survived after all," she said.

Rose walked in on the end of the scene, when she heard the commotion, and watched from the side, her eyes filling with tears. "I don't know what I would have done, ma'am," she said to Eleanor later. "You are so much in my life."

And that night Frank Burden came into the bedroom where she still slept alone and sat beside her on the bed. He too had tears in his eyes for the first time she could recall. "I thought I had lost you," he said with great gravity, looking shaken and for just a moment uncharacteristically helpless, in a manner she had never seen before. He expressed in a moment something she had known secretly for years, something she would know forever. In spite of all his bullish self-confidence and rectitude, Frank Burden loved her and needed her. Her presence at the center of his life had been paramount for a long time. "You are my very life to me," he said. "To lose our girls would shake me to the core," the staunch Frank Burden said, now unable to hide his deep concern. "But to have lost you would have been for me life-ending devastation."

"I know, Frank," she said with conviction, reaching out and placing her hand on his, knowing full well what needed to be said at this moment. "You will not lose me. Now or at any time."

And in the middle of the next night, still sleeping alone, she rose up, weak but no longer aching or fighting for breath, the fever now totally gone, the words "We have survived after all" repeating in her now-lucid mind, which the Athena strength had reclaimed, and she spoke aloud.

"Arnauld is not dead," she found herself saying. "I shall go to the war and find him."

PART
FOUR

38

ARMISTICE

The end of the war came with a surprising suddenness in the fall of 1918. What had seemed to those watching from Boston, an ocean away, like a hopeless stalemate ended with first rumors of requests for peace from various parties and then the news of the armistice on November 11.

Of course, for Eleanor the war was inseparably linked now with the devastating arrival of the influenza and the separate peace its equally abrupt departure had brought her household.

"It was worse than the war," Will Honeycutt said with his usual bluntness the first day she was strong enough to pay a visit to the Hyperion office. "I thought I had lost you."

"We were fortunate to be spared," Eleanor said.

"War and pestilence," he said, "a terrible combination of horsemen."

Some claimed that the spread of that dreaded plague on both sides had caused the war's sudden end, although others claimed it was the American entry or Germany's inability to press on. However it was, the Germanic alliance began falling apart, and the Allied countries, including now the American forces, were emerging devastatingly victorious in France and northern Italy.

Throughout the year 1918, there had been in Boston first a great anxiety about the pandemic and the endless European war, and then an enormous sense of relief at the possibility of hostilities ending. There was wild jubilation when that peace became fact.

On the other side of the Atlantic Ocean, as the bloody stalemate of northern France began to swing in favor of the Allies after the Battle of Amiens, the German populace went into revolt, and eventually the Germans had no choice but to end fighting. The result was the mutual end of hostilities and the armistice.

The Austro-Hungarians had lost their will to fight months before, it was said, and were interested in suing for peace, which the German kaiser did everything to thwart. Because of Arnauld's letters that had come through the diplomatic channels without censorship throughout the war, as well as her fated foreknowledge, Eleanor felt that she had a better understanding of the Austrian side of things. But then after the letters stopped and the report of his death came, she was left with only impersonal news sources for her information.

Now, in early November, she read with relief and surprise how the armies of the Austro-Hungarian Empire simply fell apart on their Italian front, the signal of war's end. Rumor was that hundreds of thousands of Austrian soldiers were taken captive in the final days, a detail that gave her at least slim hope that somehow in the confusion mistakes had been made, even confirmed reports of death in battle might be somehow overturned.

So, in early November, with the armistice a near certainty, and the influenza subsiding, Eleanor wired her friend Carl Jung that she was planning on traveling to Zurich as soon as possible. Jung was at first amazed at the audacity of his American friend, then pleased that she would be attempting such an unexpected visit. So happy was he to think of the end of Swiss isolation that war had brought that he put aside any natural wariness about the dangers such a trip so shortly after the end of fighting might entail. It never occurred to him that she meant she was coming alone, with her almost four-year-old son.

Insulated for the four years of European war, the Swiss doctor was glad to have his first visitor from America, and Eleanor was happy that she would be able to see him. She had known for some time from his letters that her friend was having a very difficult time with the great rend in his life, his separation from Sigmund Freud, and she had wanted to help somehow, but after the release of the dogs of war, as he called it, in August 1914, there had been no way she or any other American could travel to neutral Switzerland.

When she first told Will Honeycutt her intentions, he pointed out that by all accounts Arnauld was dead, and it was a sad fact that they all had to accept.

"But I know that he cannot be. It is something of which I am absolutely positive."

"Have you been given some new information?"

"No," she said. "Nothing new."

"But what we learned already from the letter was decisive. You and I both read the report from Jung's Herr Jodl. There were the three witnesses you required. The evidence is unavoidable. You said as much yourself."

"I am going, Mr. Honeycutt," she said with unmistakable conviction.

"You are quite convinced?"

"I am quite convinced."

"Just as you were quite convinced about Cincinnati Soap and Candle and the Northern Pacific stock and the other miraculous tips?"

Eleanor nodded ever so slightly, with as little commitment as possible.

"From the same intuition?"

Again, she nodded, even more slightly. "The same."

And Will Honeycutt shook his head again. "Well, since I know about that intuition of yours, I should be the last one to doubt. But still, there is no evidence that there is any chance he is alive. He's dead."

"Still, I plan to go," she said.

"Arnauld was my friend," Will Honeycutt began. "If there were a possibility, I'd go—"

"I know that of you, Mr. Honeycutt, and Arnauld knows the depth of your loyalty."

"I know of no possibility, but if you go, I'd better come with you."

"I am going," she said with conviction. "And I intend to go alone."

"Then, that is that," he said. "At least I can help you find a way. Jesse will know."

"If I can just get to Zurich, Carl Jung can get me to Vienna, and from there I can manage what is necessary."

The next day, Will reported back to her. "Jesse says it can be done," he said. "He says to ask a banker. Men of finance let no logistics stand in their way."

So she turned to her husband, Frank Burden, as she was planning to do anyway, whose expertise in the ways of European banking might prove invaluable. "Of course, it could be done, theoretically," Frank said without emotion. "But I don't know what man in his right mind would wish to do it right now. The negotiations of the travel would be difficult, not to mention dangerous. I do know some who accomplished travel to Switzerland, financial advisors and such, even before the war's end. Finance must move on, you know. But it is too dangerous to take on right now. Perhaps after the armistice has been formalized a venturesome man could give it a try."

"This is not theoretical, Frank. I wish to go, and I wish to go now," she said.

Frank was startled of course, but then could see from that look he knew well that she was indeed serious. "That is preposterous," he said. "What man would go with you right now?"

"I wish to go alone."

"Now, that *is* ridiculous," Frank said with a dismissive laugh. "You exaggerate, I know, but it simply cannot be done." He gave every sign that he wished the conversation to be ended with his declaration.

"I am not hyperbolizing, Frank. I am planning to travel to Switzerland, and I am heartened by the fact that you know people who have done it. I shall simply replicate their journeys. I would like your help."

Up until that point in their marriage, they had disagreed on nothing, or so it seemed to Frank. Eleanor made most of the domestic decisions, "running an organized household," Frank called it, but on the few occasions when he wished something done or not done, he simply stated it, in the positive or negative, and it was either done or not done, according to his will. It was his wife who always acquiesced quietly, as things ought to be. Of course, Frank had no way of knowing that in the secret matters of her life as a financier, his wife did what she alone willed and her husband had neither influence nor knowledge.

"I am not sure that such a trip would be wise so shortly after the hostilities," he said, softening his usual style. His tone was cautious and respectful, giving her the benefit of the doubt, but expecting agreement.

"Frank," she said, looking him square in the eye, "I am going. First to Switzerland." She paused. "And then to Vienna. And then"—she paused again—"to wherever I must. But definitely to Vienna."

The words stopped her husband in his tracks. The mention of that city they had shared twenty years before and not mentioned since hit him with great force. Accustomed to expressing himself robustly, Frank instead swallowed hard and then stared at her. His wife had just played her emotional trump card and the discussion was over. He managed a brusque "I see" to acknowledge the fact. "What about our children?" he added, thinking it a rhetorical question.

"Standish will come with me," she said abruptly. Soon it became clear to Frank that his wife had thought it all out. "The girls are old enough to fend for themselves," she said. "They will stay with you. Mrs. Spurgeon will give them and you the support you need." There was no question by this time that Rose Spurgeon could run the household with efficiency and grace. Frank looked at his wife quizzically, anticipating perhaps but disbelieving what was coming next. "Standish will come with me," she repeated.

Frank Burden, past being stunned, now looked overwhelmed.

"He is of strong constitution," she continued. "And he can manage." Their son, Frank Standish Burden Jr., was almost four, and for a number of reasons, some open and some darkly secret, she had decided almost immediately to bring him with her.

"I see," Frank said, nodding his consent, aware suddenly that in the presence of this woman's power of conviction, he had limited choice in the matter.

With Will Honeycutt, she was even more direct. "It is my destiny," she said. "I think you of all people know that, Will."

"I of all people do know that," he said solemnly.

"You will tend to the business."

"Of course—" Will began, but she cut him off.

"And keep an eye on things."

"Of course," he said.

"Good," she said. "I will find comfort in knowing that those dear to me will tend to matters at home."

And so ended this and any further conversation on the matter.

She called Susan and Jane together on the sun porch and told them she wished to have a "family meeting," the name the children had given those times when she and Frank sat down with them to explain some family issue or matter of urgency.

The girls came bursting into the room and sat beside their mother with expectant looks. "Is this dreadfully important," Susan said, "or just something minor?" Her older daughter's directness always made her mother smile.

"It is just that I have something of substance to tell you," Eleanor began. "I will be going to Europe, and I shall be gone for a considerable amount of time."

"But there is war in Europe, Mother," Susan said.

"Are you going to be a spy?" Jane said, bursting forward.

"No, I fear it is nothing so romantic as that. I just need to go see an old friend who has suffered in the war. Now there will be an armistice, and I can travel where one could not before."

"But who, Mother?" Susan asked.

"Yes, who?" Jane joined in.

"Our friend Dr. Jung, in Switzerland. The armistice will allow it, and make it safe."

"An armistice is a peace, isn't it? I learned that in vocabulary," Jane said.

"Yes, it is a peace, and the war will be over. I will be gone for a while, and I am taking Standish with me."

"But he is so little," Susan said.

"He is very brave though," Jane said.

"He will do just fine," their mother assured them. "And your father will be in charge here, and Mrs. Spurgeon will run things." It always gave Eleanor great comfort knowing the degree to which Frank trusted the extraordinary competence of their housekeeper.

"That will be good for Father. He says Mrs. Spurgeon is good at running an organized household, but not as good as you." In this, she sounded like her father.

"I shall miss you both terribly," Eleanor said. "But I know you will mind Rose and do well in my absence."

"You won't need to worry," Susan said.

"We will *cope*," Jane said. "That means 'to make do.'"

Eleanor had always tried to give her daughters all the love and support they needed but at the same time encourage independence. As each of them arrived at age eight, her age when her own mother had died and when her life changed dramatically with the entrance of her severe aunt

Prudence, Eleanor could not help thinking what a tragedy it would be at that crucial moment to lose one's mother. She had marveled at how Susan first and then Jane a year and a half later had each developed her own voice and her unique way of looking at the world. Susan was so much like her father, she thought, and Jane, with her spontaneity and freshness, was so unlike the pair of them. Eleanor loved seeing her two daughters together and found herself constantly amused. And then there was the entrance of young Standish.

A few years previous, when her son was around two years old, she had begun to notice how his sensibilities were shaped daily by his two older sisters. Because of her fateful foreknowledge, she knew from the start that Standish's life was destined to be different, that he was to be set apart from others, but she didn't see how. For a young man, being raised in the presence of strong sisters would have a poignant effect for the better, she concluded.

Some years before, when the world was reading about the extraordinary exploits of polar explorer Ernest Shackleton, it occurred to her that his remarkable leadership abilities were tempered by a kind of connectedness not usually associated with strong men. The reason, she surmised, was the fact that Shackleton had grown up with sisters. Her husband, Frank, on the other hand, who often displayed a stiffness and distance and had become famous in adulthood for his rugged and sometimes quite stubborn opinions, did not have sisters. It delighted her to see the care and attention Susan and Jane gave their now four-year-old brother.

"We shall miss you," Susan repeated when the fact that young Standish would be accompanying her mother on the trip finally sank in. "And we shall miss our brother."

"Yes," said Jane, "he will be all grown up when you return."

Eleanor laughed. "We will not be gone *that* long. And he will miss you. You girls are very good to him."

Eleanor paused and looked at her girls. The visitation of influenza was not far removed, and she could easily fall back into the desperate feeling of loss that it had brought with it. Her eyes began to well up. "I am so sorry that I will be leaving you."

"It's all right, Mum," Susan said bravely, seeing her mother's concern. "You have to go."

"Yes," Jane burst out, "Mrs. Spurgeon won't make us practice our music lessons every day," which brought a laugh from her older sister and her mother.

Serious Frank's contributions to the situation were not insignificant, and typically pragmatic. On the delicate matter of travel into war-torn Europe, he said, "We can book you passage through the bank of London, and enter through Marseilles."

It was, of course and as always, wise and timely advice.

39

AN IMAGE OF PEACE

ravel through Marseilles meant avoiding the war-clogged northern ports, and passing through southern France up to Geneva avoided the southern war zones. The train trip to Zurich would be her first test, a journey "not without its challenges," Frank had said, "but manageable. Passage directly east to the Italian border, of course, would be more direct geographically," he said, reporting his findings from banking colleagues who kept track of international finance, "but traveling up over the Alps to neutral Switzerland is far safer and, of course, easier to arrange politically."

Frank was right. Once safely across the Swiss border and in the protective care of her friend Carl Jung, she and her son could rest a few days, then enter the real test: travel through war-impoverished Austria and Italy.

Eleanor and young Standish traveled easily together, as she had anticipated. In the long hours on shipboard during the crossing, and now on the train, she found him a remarkably calm and self-possessed traveler. And she especially loved having the long hours of reading to him. She had brought with her a number of his favorite books, including Robert Louis Stevenson's *A Child's Garden of Verses*, a child's atlas of the world, and a book of illustrated Bible stories that all three of her children knew by heart and never tired of hearing over and over again. In moments between stories, she would open the child's atlas and point out where they were now and where they were going.

The one book that young Standish wished to hear from over and over, however, was a grandly illustrated children's version of the *Odyssey*. "Read it again," he would say when she finished the last chapter, and at each adventurous moment, such as the encounter with the Cyclops or the drowning of Odysseus's men in the whirlpool, he would stop her reading and ask every manner of question.

She was often amazed by his observations about the stories. During one reading, he stopped her when she got to Odysseus's return to Ithaca. "The people are mad at him, aren't they?"

"Why do you say that?"

"Well, they are mad because he did not bring their sons back from the war. They blame him."

"Yes," Eleanor said, "they do not realize what Odysseus did for them, how hard he tried."

"It's not his fault," the young boy said suddenly. "His men didn't obey. They killed the cattle of the sun, and they opened the bag of winds." One of Standish's favorite parts of the story was when the gods captured all the winds so Odysseus's crew could sail home quickly and safely, but when the ships were just in sight of Ithaca, they disobeyed and opened the bags, sending the ship back to sea for ten more years. "It was his men," Standish said. "It was not Odysseus's fault."

There was something about the purity of that observation that touched Eleanor deeply, and it was a detail we know she shared in a letter to Will Honeycutt back in Boston.

On shipboard, young Standish entertained himself for hours each day by drawing with crayons in the notebook his mother had brought for the crossing.

"This is Poseidon," he would say, and point to a mass of color he had just scribbled onto the page. "And this," he would add with a flourish, turning the page, "this is Circe, the good witch." Eleanor found she was endlessly amused when in the presence of the vivid imagination in all three of her children.

"Wherever do they get those images?" she asked her very practical husband one evening.

"They make them up," he answered with his banker's precision.

Upon arrival in Marseilles, they went by cab from the docks to the train station. While waiting for the train they befriended a young French photographer, who said he was also on his way to the war zone. "You have chosen well to go through Zurich," he said. "It is by far the safest way to make a hazardous journey."

Once in their compartment, when mother and son both tired of reading, Standish would watch the peaceful French countryside out the window, unaware at his young age of the irony, considering the bleak devastation not so many hundred kilometers to the north and east. He would watch the passing farmlands and comment on the various animals he recognized, or fall asleep against her shoulder. Fellow passengers in their compartment on the French train, or earlier on the ship, would smile benevolently at the two of them, the image of serenity and peacefulness, suggesting nothing of what lay ahead for them.

As they approached the Alps, the French photographer found their compartment. "I was hoping for an image of peace, Europe being so consumed by war, and now the aftermath," he said, and in the subdued light from the train window he took a photograph of Standish asleep in his mother's arms, as she read her Henry James novel. "*La Madonna et l'enfant,*" he said in a whisper, as he was framing the shot, "*très sympathique, madame, très sympathique.*"

Some years later, a package arrived at Acorn Street from Paris, a book of photographic images of newly peaceful Europe, and one of the full-page photographs in black and white was mother and son by a train window.

Seeing the French Alps rising off in the distance with their dramatic snowy caps, Eleanor pointed and exclaimed, "Look, Standish. Those are the Alps. Aren't they majestic?"

And her young son looked to where she was pointing, then joined in: "I see them, Mummy, they are indeed majestic," he exclaimed.

As the train approached their destination in the heart of Switzerland, Eleanor admitted to a disappointment that the tranquility of travel was over. The arrival at their destination had brought with it the worry of uncertainty spared them on their long train ride.

Carl Jung met them at the train station in Zurich and took them directly home. He seemed so exceptionally clear-eyed, at the peak of health and fitness, that Eleanor remarked later that both she and Standish seemed to grow in enthusiasm just being in his presence. "I am so glad you are both here," he said with a flourish, and he wrapped Eleanor in an exuberant embrace and then took young Standish's hand as if meeting an important gentleman. "I am pleased to meet you after all this time," he said.

"I am pleased to meet you, sir," Standish replied.

When they had settled into the backseat of the chauffeured auto car on the way to Küsnacht on the lake of Zurich, he said, "We have much to talk about, and the children will enjoy having Standish with us."

"Much has changed in our lives," Eleanor said.

"Yes," Jung said with a smile. "And with change comes growth. Much growth."

She had visited Zurich once before, in the spring of 1913, at a time when she was worried about her friend. Back then she had made plans with Frank for a European trip with the family at summer's end. He would spend time in Berlin on banking business, and she and the girls would stay with the Jungs in Küsnacht. Carl Jung was undergoing a kind of crisis, she knew from the content of the letters. His troubles with Freud and their inevitable separation had brought about an instability not unlike that of the schizophrenics he had spent so much time listening to and studying.

He would spend hours by himself, conversing with the voices in his head, building childlike wooden structures down by the Zürichsee, and writing for hours in his study. He had had commissioned a large red-leather-bound book of blank pages, and he began to fill it with illuminated Teutonic calligraphy and paintings, the result—disturbing, some said—of his conversations with his own unconscious. "Dr. Jung is in the throes of a psychosis," one doctor warned.

"My family worries about me," he admitted to Eleanor in a letter, "but they ought not to. What arises from my unconscious and seems so disturbing is merely healthy exploration of what must be explored."

Finally, in 1913, the tension between the two colleagues had turned to overt bitterness; the insults had gone too far. Jung resigned as president of the International Psychoanalytical Association, and he wrote Freud the final letter, ending with the famous line, "The rest is silence." And it was. The two great men would never speak again.

In dramatic fashion, as was his wont, Freud announced that his association with Jung was over and that his associates should have no more dealings with Jung and Zurich. As much as the split freed both men to go in their own directions and to define themselves and their beliefs more distinctly, Jung at least took the separation as rejection and grieved over it. He retreated to his lake home near Zurich and began spending large amounts of time there in isolation, losing himself in his own thoughts.

During her visit in the summer of 1913, the break all but finalized, Jung was beginning to explore his own unique path. After that his letters to Eleanor seemed to be one among his few anchors. This was a time of intense correspondence between the two. So it was in letters that they continued the discussions William James had begun in 1909, what Jung called "parapsychology and spirituality," which departed starkly from what he was beginning to see as the rigid sexuality-based doctrines of his former colleague Freud.

"Although I greatly enjoyed his approval and was flattered to be thought somehow his worthy successor," Jung wrote to Eleanor in the days just after the final parting, "I knew almost from the beginning that I could not endorse his ideas in their entirety, nor sacrifice my intellectual integrity to a set of dogmas in the way my father had. In time our differences became impossible to conceal. I could no longer pretend to accept, for one, that human motivation is exclusively sexual, and I could not accept, for another, that the unconscious mind is entirely personal and peculiar to the individual.

"These ideas seemed to me, as they seemed to William James, I am sure, reductionist and narrow. To me, the very notion of psychic energy, *libido* as Freud calls it, cannot be wholly sexual. To me, libido is a more generalized 'life force,' of which sexuality is but one part. For me, it became more and more evident over time that beneath the personal unconscious of Freud's repressed wishes and traumatic memories lies a deeper and more important layer that I have come to call the *collective unconscious*. This collective unconscious, in my mind, contains the entire psychic heritage of mankind."

Eleanor had traveled then with the girls to Zurich and followed the Seestrasse along the lake until they came to the Jung house, where they were welcomed with the warmth of Emma's household. Emma was the daughter of a wealthy industrialist who fell in love with both the young man and his ideas. She was for his whole adult life his family stability and colleague, becoming herself a renowned therapist, even if, Eleanor knew, life with the great doctor was not always easy. The second night, after the girls and the Jung children had gone to bed, Jung had arranged that they dine alone together, just the two of them. She expressed her concern for his health, and Jung made light of her attentiveness, commenting that, as he said, "pain and growth come through the door at the same time."

Back then, Jung was still in transition, "in the liminal space," he described it, "on the threshold between two worlds." Now, in 1918, Eleanor found her friend, his split with Sigmund Freud long past, very much estranged from his former world and the international psychological community and left to establish something of his own in Zurich. He found his new situation—she knew from his letters—at once exhilarating and terrifying.

He was now free to take things in his own direction but was also isolated and alone. However it was, it was clear that he found himself now in the grip of a burst of creative energy, the pages of his Red Book serving as proof. One of the most remarkable letters from this period arrived from the Swiss doctor between the time of Eleanor's decision to travel to Vienna and her departure.

My dear Eleanor,

I feel as if I have climbed out of a deep dark hole. In reality, the break with Herr Dr. Freud had actually produced public and professional stability in a form of personal recognition and acclaim that I should have found deeply satisfying at my age and station in life. I had at that time the perfect wife, as my dear Emma was described by everyone who knows her; five healthy and beautiful children, all in awe of their father; a substantial house that attested to my professional success; and a practice that was growing faster than I could keep up with. Nonetheless, I found myself very much at sea, provoked by uncertainty, barraged by inner images, which rather than deny I accepted and examined gratefully. Everything in my life for a time seemed derived from those images, what had broken free of the unconscious, flooding me like a mysterious stream, and threatened to destroy me.

The outward classification, the scientific processing, and the integration of abstract ideas into the events of life was certainly rewarding.

*On one hand they soothed and comforted me, one who at that time
needed a mantra of the facts of my life to keep myself rooted to reality. I
was after all a medical doctor who was absolutely certain of little other
than that I lived at such and such a place, was married to a certain
woman, and had fathered a specific number of children. I recognized
even as I was living in these years that they were the numinous beginning that contained everything. Painful and as disorienting as it was,
I had a premonition that there was enough raw material in those years
to engage if not consume me for the rest of my life. The problem became
how to integrate into some manner of normal life all this amorphous
material.*

*I had withdrawn from the world, and that was not unwholesome.
Determined as I was to stay alert and to work my way through the
morass of what I was feeling, I began very consciously and deliberately
setting aside time each day for child's play. Remembering how much I
liked building blocks when I was a child of ten, I tried to re-create the
activity, this time with sticks, stones, and other materials that washed
up on the lakeshore in front of our house. I realize now that I may have
been in the grip of a psychosis, but I was cognizant enough to confine
my play into a fixed schedule, an organized daily routine, every day
after lunch. Deep immersion in this practice, as bizarre as it may have
seemed to those around me, unquestionably saved my life.*

*The war that raged for those years in the countries neighboring
Switzerland was matched by one that raged inside me. Now that the
end is in sight, the armistice achieved in Europe, I find myself at a
remove from the dark battle, having fought for my own salvation, and
ready to begin again my relationship with the external world.*

*I look forward to your visit more than you can know, and I find
that there is much that we need to discuss and clarify.*

Yours as ever,
Jung

He had taken to spending long hours by himself by the lakeshore,
delving into his own unconscious in what might have looked to others as
a state of depression. It was a time when he needed a friend and he could
have used the perspective of a wise old mentor such as William James,

someone who shared his more Eastern and mythological view of the unconscious and the future of psychology, what the traditionalists such as
Freud had come to think of as parapsychology, mental phenomena outside
the realm of scientific principle. Eleanor knew well the connection the
Swiss doctor made between her and William James, how he did in fact
expect her to speak for the great American philosopher, and she accepted
any pressures that came with that association as a small price to pay for a
friendship that had become both intense and dear to her.

The reception at the Jungs' Seestrasse house was the warm one that she
had expected. The Jungs' children, the oldest fourteen and the youngest,
Helene, just Standish's age, had been prepared by their mother for the
visit and whisked Standish off from almost the moment of his arrival.
Emma Jung met them at the door and offered her spirited greeting. Emma
was warm, outgoing, and engaging, a well-organized mother and an intelligent thinker who would become an analyst herself. "We are truly glad
to see you," she said to Eleanor. "Carl has much to share with you, and the
children have been buzzing about Standish's arrival all week. They have
been calling him their American cousin."

"I too have been greatly looking forward to this visit," Eleanor said, her
smile carrying the warmth she felt from the greeting and the thought that
in this household she would be able to share much of what she had been
carrying secretly inside.

40

"I HAVE EDUCATED MYSELF"

t was not until the late afternoon, after she and Standish were settled in their room and he off playing with the children and Eleanor and Jung were sitting alone in his study, that Toni Wolff entered.

"I do not believe that you have met Fräulein Wolff," Jung said very formally.

The woman approached Eleanor and the two shook hands. Toni Wolff was tall and thin and severe, a strikingly attractive woman in her own way, but markedly different from Emma, who was soft, gentle, and maternal. Barely smiling, the two women greeted each other.

"I have heard much about you," Eleanor said.

"And I you. Carl has been looking forward to your visit."

Toni Wolff was thirty. She and Jung had met when she became his patient in 1910, and soon it became clear that she intended to be more: first a disciple, then a therapist on her own, and then an intimate. Jung was quite open about his relationship with her in his letters to Eleanor, and what he did not state outright, Eleanor could infer. She knew that the Zurich Psychology Society had become accustomed to Jung entering its meetings with the two women, and everyone knew that for some time now Emma had found herself accepting the intimate connection between her husband and this other woman and accepted it, all at least superficially, with grace. But no one ever saw the two women in any form of affectionate exchange. When Jung would retreat to the lakeshore in his afternoons of active imagination and imaginary construction, it was Toni

Wolff who accompanied him, sitting quietly nearby, smoking and reading.

Eleanor had heard that Toni's sharp, penetrating mind had contributed to Jung's thinking more than any other and that he shared more ideas with her than he did with Emma. Years later, she would hear that Jung described the two relationships a man needs from a woman: On the one hand, he needs a wife to create his home, and to bear and rear his children; on the other, a *femme inspiratrice*, a spiritual companion, to share his fantasies and inspire his greatest works. Jung found those two roles to be played by two separate women in his life, and he expected them and the world to understand. Eleanor immediately thought of William James and Pauline Goldmark, and what conditions James's wife, Alice, and Jung's wife, Emma, had to accept in order to preserve their marriages.

On this visit, Eleanor was not certain what form Jung's relationship with Toni Wolff had taken, but she, no stranger to complexity herself, had anticipated encountering this complex relationship, so different from the staid convention of Boston society, with an openness worthy of the trust her Swiss friend had placed in her. "I hope we shall have time to talk," she said to Toni Wolff with a smile.

"I would enjoy that very much," Toni Wolff said, picking up on Eleanor's intention. There was a kind of intensity in her eyes that even Eleanor found compelling.

Later, that evening, when they were alone, Jung repeated to Eleanor his interest in someday meeting this Will Honeycutt, the man who had conversed with the ancient Democritus. "I have told his story often," Jung said.

"You both have much in common," Eleanor said, "your descent, some call it."

"There was a certain descent," Jung said. "I will admit that, but I have passed through it, I can say with confidence. The war is over."

"An armistice," she said, "a blessed relief."

"There is never an armistice with the self. But yes, I have staked out a sort of peace."

They continued on in this abstract manner before they arrived at family. "And Toni Wolff is part of that peace?" Eleanor said.

Jung looked at Eleanor for a long moment, surprised by her new addition to the discussion. "Yes," he said matter-of-factly. "Toni has become a vital part of the equation. One that requires understanding. She provides invaluable insight and inspiration." There was only the slightest hint of apology in his voice.

"I think I understand, but I do not hold a place within your inner circle." Circumstance had certainly given Eleanor an appreciation for the unconventional in marriage, but still she expressed concern. "Were I in that circle, I would find cause for concern. I wonder how it affects Emma and your children."

"My family accept me as I am. And they have for a long time."

"That is asking a lot, or at least from my perspective it is. If I were Emma I would have a difficult time with such attentions to another woman."

"You are very forthright, my dear Eleanor, a most endearing quality. And you have shown great courage in accepting this proposed journey into the war zone."

"And you are changing the subject"—she took a sip of claret—"which I shall allow." And she paused for the subject to change. "As for me," she continued, "I am simply doing what is expected."

"Expected of the hero," Jung said, smiling admiringly. "Your inner strength is very much on display, and very much admired, I might add. It is your inner masculine, I think you have caught me saying."

Eleanor smiled. "Your animus theory," she said. "The inner masculine in every woman, the unresolved father, I believe you have also said." She was quoting him.

"Do you not agree?" Jung said. "Most women spend a lifetime trying to understand the image of their father within them."

"And that is the cause of a certain assertive, sometimes strident tone."

"Well," Jung said, staring with piercing eyes, "is it not?"

"That is difficult to see in oneself. You make it sound fearsome."

"The animus in a strong, high-spirited woman, that uncontrolled masculine force? It is fearsome, something most men cannot handle. It is the Amazon fierceness that makes us cower."

"Like the Medusa, you have said. It turns men to stone."

"Well?" Jung said. "Look at you. You are convinced that the reports of Esterhazy's death are inaccurate, and you have traveled three thousand miles to find him. No one, no evidence, has been able to dissuade you."

She looked serious. "You think my quest is irrational, animus-deceived, as you call it, my unresolved father image."

Jung said nothing, as if her very question proved his point. "Well?"

Eleanor looked uneasy. "You think my strong will is often greater than what is called for. That in strong women this animus, the unresolved masculine, overreacts."

Jung smiled. "Yes, I have observed that."

"But I am also realistic," she said, and she reached way back into her past, to her previous time in Vienna, the city she was now reentering.

"I know you are also realistic," he said. "I have known that for some time, since our idyll at Putnam Camp."

"William James pointed out that my faith was strong, that of a fundamentalist," she said. "He found some amusement, I think, in my 'absolute certainty,' as he called it."

"And you hear that strong, true voice speaking to you from time to time?"

She could not deny it. "I do."

"You know then why you are here."

"I do. I am called, I think you would say," she said. "I believe what I believe."

"Well then, I rest my case." She could see on his face a look of admiration. Not knowing of the journal, he attributed her strength and certitude, she knew, to his new discovery of the animus. "That belief is now taking you on this quest. It will take you as far as the underworld perhaps, and you are not fearful."

"Oh, I am plenty fearful, but I simply know what needs to be done."

"And that you are the only one who can do it?"

"Well, yes," she said. "Can you name another?"

"Point well taken. No, there is no one else who believes as you believe. You see, that is heroic, a perfect example of the animus. You are Marlow searching for Kurtz."

"Ah, *Heart of Darkness* again," she said. "That sounds a little grand. I am simply going into the war zone to find Arnauld. I know he cannot be dead."

"How do you know this?"

"I can't account for it, but I do *know* he is not dead."

"You see, you are very courageous. There is no other way to account for it."

"But still you think it folly? A fool's errand."

Jung smiled at her admiringly. "My dear, it is indeed grand. Grand and admirable, and perhaps even folly, I don't know, and I worry that you will discover as fact what is already accepted."

"That Arnauld is dead."

"That is it," he said. "I do know something in all this, and it is that if I were similarly lost in war, my situation hopeless, you are precisely the person I would want searching for me. And that is why I give this effort of yours my support." He raised his wineglass. "And I salute you, my dear, determined friend."

The next night she and Jung dined alone, as had become their tradition, after Standish had gone to bed with the Jung children, and Emma had left them to their conversations. "You are concerned about me," he said with his usual matter-of-fact directness after raising a glass of claret in toast.

"I thought perhaps you had gone too far—"

"You feared that I was showing signs of a psychosis. You are not the only one with those concerns. It is said that I have internalized the chaos that war has brought."

"And there is reason for that concern?"

"And there is on your part?"

Eleanor took the question with seriousness. "Your writings and your paintings, they have shown a depth and intensity we are not accustomed to."

"They resemble the work of my schizophrenic patients, it is said."

Eleanor laughed. "And for good reason," she said. "The concern seems legitimate."

"And you worry about me the way you worry about your Harvard friend who corresponds with his inner voices."

"I do," she said. "I do worry about my colleague Will Honeycutt, I have to admit, and I do worry about you." She paused, giving the matter some little consideration. "But the presence of voices in your lives, and the responses, do make both of you interesting."

That brought a smile to Jung. "I hope to meet your interesting colleague someday, your Mr. Will Honeycutt. I owe him a great deal."

Eleanor only nodded slowly.

They were alone now in the spacious living room, the Küsnacht air crisp and cool and the house silent. She had asked if she could see the Red Book, the large leather-bound volume he had had made just for the purposes of recording dreams and reflections.

"I do show it," he said. "We shall move to the study."

She stood before the larger volume on its wooden stand beside the settee, and she turned the pages slowly, running her fingers over the beautiful colored drawings and careful calligraphy, each page full of exacting detail.

"These are beautiful," she said, "done so painstakingly."

"I began with the black volumes"—he pointed to a collection of three smaller black leather volumes on his desk—"but then finalized them with the drawings and calligraphy."

"Well, this is just exquisite; I had no idea you were such an artist."

"Nor did I," Jung said with a wry smile.

She had not planned to tell him the whole story perhaps, but in the still quiet of his study, having just been allowed to see his Red Book, a feeling of intimacy came over her. "I have something to tell you. Something I have shared with no one but William James."

Knowing that he had the ability to create such moments of intimate trust with people, especially women, the Swiss doctor would not have been surprised, and he certainly knew how to lean forward and present a posture of welcome. He said nothing except, "Please."

And she began. "In the year 1897, the year after my graduation from college, I traveled to Vienna to write 'something of significance,' my head-mistress called it, about music. And while there, I fell into the thrall of a remarkable American, an older man from San Francisco, one whose presence there involved unusual circumstance, you would say. In the future, the sound recordings of the Victrola will become greatly enhanced and expanded with electricity, so that musicians and instruments can be amplified to fill great auditoriums and athletic stadiums, bringing great popular fame to musicians and performers."

"And this mysterious man from San Francisco is to be one of such great fame?"

"Yes," Eleanor said.

"And he was from another time?"

Eleanor nodded, looking down.

"From a time in the future?" Jung said. There was a warmth in his voice. Carl Jung, this man who understood complexity, showed nothing but acceptance in his eyes.

She nodded again, then continued. "While in this remarkable man's company and under his influence, I experienced the world in ways I had never experienced it before, and I made discoveries about myself—admitted things actually—that changed my life forever. He held back nothing. I lost my innocence, one would say, and I gained much, too much perhaps. When I left Vienna after this experience, much sadder but much wiser, as they say—far far wiser—I carried with me a journal this remarkable man had carefully prepared during his time in Vienna, and I have used that journal as my guide from that time forward. That is how I know certain things about the future and how I have known to take certain actions—certain investments, marriage to Frank Burden, the recruiting of Arnauld Esterhazy to St. Gregory's, all of which have brought about my very good fortune."

"All of that prescribed in this journal you brought with you from Vienna?" There was directness but still nothing judgmental in his tone.

Again, Eleanor lowered her head solemnly and nodded slowly. "All part of the commitment I made back then, all carried out with great purpose."

"It has brought you great good fortune," Jung said, obvious in slowly absorbing what he was hearing. "Your investments."

"Yes, and much consternation, I must add. I have been blessed, and I have been cursed."

After she finished this small exposition, Jung sat without speaking, a look of the deepest compassion on his face. "Oh my," he said finally, in a kind of awe. "That explains a great deal. And it raises many questions, as you know. Many questions."

"I know it is a great deal to take in right now, in one sitting. There will be time for questions. But right now I just wanted you to know the rough outline of the story."

"And why you are here right now?" he asked.

"And why I am here right now."

"It is how you and you alone know for certain that Arnauld Esterhazy cannot be dead."

"It is."

Then he looked deep into her eyes. "And if he is dead?" Jung said, barely able to pose the question.

Eleanor bowed her head in silence. "You may think that I have not confronted that possibility."

"To the contrary, my dear Eleanor, I know of your courage and your integrity."

"If Arnauld is dead—" She faltered, needing to collect herself for a moment. "To answer your question, I would be devastated," she said in a whisper. "It would be devastating, and it would be a relief. I would lose my purpose in life—" She stopped, barely able to continue. "And I could become normal again, like everyone else."

"And you would not have to carry this weight any longer."

"I would not," she said with her head still down.

"And that would be the devastation, and the relief."

"Yes." She nodded, holding for a moment in silence the comfort of being in the presence of someone—one of the few in the world perhaps—who could understand. Then she looked up, a characteristic steely resolve returning to her eyes. "But he is not dead," she said, now with a renewed conviction. "I know he is not dead, and I shall find him."

"And that journal?" Jung said. "It is your holy book, your scripture."

The words caught her by surprise for a moment. "That is funny," she said. "That is what William James called it, when he heard." Then she looked into her friend's intense kind eyes. "Yes, it is my holy scripture."

"In adherence to it, you are a fundamentalist."

"Yes, that is what William James observed," she said. "In that adherence, that is how I am a fundamentalist, about the literal nature of what is written."

"And this man in Vienna years ago, the man from San Francisco, what of him? You believe that he really had traveled in time? Like H. G. Wells," he said.

"Yes, like H. G. Wells," Eleanor said, smiling at the reference, "but with no time machine, and with no way to get back."

Jung looked serious, giving the words some thought. "There was no way to return?" he said, and Eleanor nodded. "Did he die in Vienna?" he asked, and she nodded solemnly. "Were you with him?"

Eleanor did not answer. "It is strange," she said after the moment's pause, "he had long conversations with your Dr. Freud, all recorded with great care in the journal." She paused again and pointed at the red leather volume open beside them. "Not unlike that book."

"And what did Dr. Freud think of this remarkable man, this man from the future?"

"You know what he thought. You do not need to ask."

"Dr. Freud thought him one of his hysterics," Jung said with a slight smile. "He thought him mad."

"You know that he would, and you know that he did. He would have had no other choice. He was, after all, Dr. Freud." She returned his slight smile.

"Indeed. He would have had no other choice."

"And what would you have thought?" Eleanor asked the obvious, point-blank.

Jung gave the question a respectful moment's thought and then said with another slight smile, "I would have thought him a man from San Francisco . . ." He paused respectfully. "A man of music, a famous one, and from another time."

A profound silence fell between them, and they only looked into each other's eyes for a long moment, neither needing to speak. And Eleanor smiled finally, knowing that indeed her friend would have thought exactly that.

Suddenly, she stopped and broke the mood with a troubled look. "Now that you know of my Vienna experience, there is something I must share with you, about what you learned from Will Honeycutt."

"Why? Is there something improper in that?"

"No. But it has started me thinking." Her look did not change.

"I probably would have come to the idea on my own, in another way. But yes, I came upon the power of imaginary dialogue from your description of your friend."

She paused, giving the idea a good deal of thought. "What that means is that I brought the idea, active imagination, as you now label it, with me from Vienna and told it to William James. Dr. James mentioned it in a lecture at Harvard, where Will Honeycutt picked up the idea and used it quite dramatically in his senior thesis."

"He was ripe for the idea, in my view. He was being visited at night in his dreams and wished to explore those visitations. To gain some insight about himself perhaps."

"Yes, he was ripe for the idea, granted, but the suggestion came from Dr. James. His dialogue with the ancient Greek Democritus caused quite a stir at Harvard because the scientific observations appeared to be uncannily accurate, coming from an unnatural or perhaps supernatural source, on levels far beyond what Mr. Honeycutt knew."

"Or thought he knew," Jung said. "Yes, I can believe that."

"I told you about Mr. Honeycutt, and you were intrigued. I remember that. Now, you say that all this, your Red Book, as you call it, has grown out of my telling you about Will Honeycutt's college thesis."

"Yes, that is more or less accurate, although, as I said, I would have come to the technique in some other way, in time."

She frowned again, thinking. "But you did come to it because of what I told you."

"And is that so very bad?"

She must have paused then, pulling together all the strands. "It is not bad," she said. "No. It's just the nature of what I brought back from Vienna back then. It was not the usual kind of information, parapsychological, Dr. James would say. I had knowledge from the future, from the end of this century."

Jung waited expectantly. "I can see now," Eleanor continued, "that is what I learned then in the form of a conversation with Dr. Freud, what purported to be a real conversation, an argument, I think you would say."

Jung now looked anxious. "Go on," he said encouragingly.

"It is only now that it has occurred to me just where the material for that argument between Dr. Freud and the American came from. Dr. Freud argued his side in a way that I think you would say is consistent with his beliefs at the time, exactly what he would have said back in 1897, and probably would say even today, his defense, his *dogged* defense of the whole Oedipus complex."

"And the other side?" Jung said almost breathlessly, sensing what was coming.

"The argument," she said, "would be very familiar to you."

"It is perhaps what I would have said to Dr. Freud?"

"Exactly," Eleanor said. "And that is the part I am just beginning to comprehend."

"This voice," he said slowly. "This voice from the end of the century from this man from San Francisco is exactly what I would have said?"

"Yes," she said softly, sensing what was coming next, what Jung was beginning to deduce. "But not just then." She paused again, not certain if she should continue. "Over the course of your lifetime. He told me that the famous propriety of my Boston upbringing came from the tradition of the Puritans and the repression of an earthy, baser nature. He said that the Greeks worshipped the debauchery of Dionysus as well as the pure reason of Apollo, and that was good for them. All their gods and goddesses had a dark and venal side, and that was far more healthy than my famous propriety."

"Yes, I believe that."

"He said that all of us carried such a dark side within, the shadow, he called it. He said that if we did not confront that shadow in ourselves and our society, we would not arrive at what he called wholeness."

"The shadow, yes, and wholeness. Those are what I believe also."

"That is my point exactly," Eleanor said. "That is what I am realizing."

"The ideas are my ideas." Eleanor nodded. "They were my ideas now, and perhaps extended over the next few decades, used back then to argue with Dr. Freud, to influence him?" Again a silent nod. "To get him to change his mind, vainly it turned out?"

"Yes," she spoke now. "To exhort him to change his mind, to get him to retreat from his rigid adherence to the Oedipus idea. Just as you would have done then, and would most likely do now. But it was 1897, when you were still a university student, before you knew Dr. Freud."

Both Eleanor and Jung sat quietly for a time, another profound silence falling between them. "The man from San Francisco, this man from the future, knew my ideas, had read my writings?"

"Yes," Eleanor said, "I am beginning to see that."

"And those ideas, through the circuitous route you describe, from you to William James to Will Honeycutt back to you to me, have come to inform my current work, my Red Book."

"That is what I am realizing, only now." There was a perplexed look on her face.

"Oh my," Jung said. "This does get complicated. What you are saying is that I have educated myself."

Eleanor nodded and another profound silence fell between them, another interminable moment. Carl Jung paused, reflecting. "And there is more," he said finally.

"There is."

"The journal foretells that you will live to be an old woman," he said. Eleanor nodded. "You will be able to encounter this man from San Francisco as a young man." She looked away but nodded silently. "And at the end of this century, after you and I are gone, he will travel backward in time again and meet you in Vienna." She held her silence and continued to look down, then slowly brought her eyes up to meet his. "And that is the reason for all this," Jung said finally.

"It is," Eleanor said in no more than a whisper, looking into the intense, patient eyes of her friend.

"It is the reason for your unshakable faith, for your fundamentalism?" Still holding his gaze, she nodded slowly. "It is," she said.

41

"I AM HERR JODL"

o now she would be returning to Vienna, with her young son in tow, to find Arnauld Esterhazy. Jung had made the arrangements. She would travel by train. Franz Jodl, the retired policeman who had done the investigation into Arnauld's fate, would meet her at the border. "Jodl is a former Viennese policeman, the interrogator of Italian prisoners of war, so he knows much about what transpired on the Italian front. As you can imagine, he is a little short of imagination perhaps, but highly responsible. Herr Jodl is a widower with two sons lost, one killed in the early days in Galicia, and one not heard from in the last months, one of the thousands of Austrian prisoners taken in the debacle at the end, one hopes."

"He is not too severe?" Eleanor asked, shuddering for a moment thinking of her encounter with the Viennese police twenty years ago.

"He is a little stern perhaps," Jung said. "But I think you will find him extremely loyal, and also very well connected. He knows his way around, I think you say in America. Money will change hands at all the important junctures, and you can trust him to handle that dimension. He understands his administrative duties in that regard. You will be in trustworthy hands. That is what is important."

"He is the one who confirmed Arnauld's death."

"He is, but he knows the task," Jung said. "For you, Arnauld is still alive. He knows not to argue but to share your conviction. He knows that is the only way."

The trip would be long, the food scarce. She would carry with her a large steamer trunk filled with provisions Jung had procured with the supply of American dollars she had made accessible from the Hyperion Fund's Swiss bank account.

"Frau Jung has packed some entertainments for young Standish," the doctor said. "There are some books and coloring sheets that have entertained our children well."

"Thank you," she said, noting a look of concern on her host's face. "You and Frau Jung are wondering why I brought him, aren't you?"

"No," he said. "I understand that you thought him old enough for such an adventure, but there is more."

Eleanor looked at him expectantly. "And that is?"

"You want him to see all this," Jung said. "You are training him to be a hero."

"Oh my," Eleanor said. "That *is* grand." Then she added sadly, "I suppose I am preparing him for his destiny, though it is not what I would have chosen for him."

Jung gave her a curious look, then one of understanding. "Part of what you know," he said, "your faith."

She nodded, then said, "Part of all this is very selfish, of course. I wanted my son with me. Standish is an easy traveling companion, because he loves being read to, and there is plenty of time for that, train schedules being irregular as they are right now."

"You will have to be patient," Jung said as he laid all the papers and tickets and maps on the table.

"You are an excellent travel agent," she said. "I thank you."

In the morning, Eleanor and Standish said good-bye to Emma and each of the children at the door of the Jungs' house. "You will have a safe journey," Emma said, "and the children wish very much for Standish's return." The children all nodded, and one of them stepped forward and gave the young man a full embrace.

"Yes, we do," they seemed to say in unison. "We wish Standish to return."

Toni Wolff did not appear for the good-bye.

He took his guests to the train station in downtown Zurich and saw that Eleanor's two trunks were properly checked in, and then on the platform outside their car he held her for a long moment, she allowing herself the rare reassurance in her friend's large, vibrant embrace.

"I shall be traveling with you," he said, releasing her. "Strength when you need it."

"Strength when I need it," she repeated.

"You will do just fine," he said. "Your animus is strong."

Carl Jung stood outside their train window until the train pulled away. He waved, and both Eleanor and her son waved back.

She felt suddenly, for the first time perhaps, as if she was off on the first leg of an adventure, a very uncertain one.

The trip through the mountains was long and slow. They reached the Swiss-Austrian border in the late afternoon preparing to cross the Rhine at the little town of Lustenau. She asked the conductor of the Swiss train, "What do we do now?"

"I do not know," he said, a bit imperious in the Swiss manner, making obvious his assessment of the conditions she was about to face. "You will be in the hands of the Austrians."

It became obvious that the Swiss train was not going to continue, and all passengers disembarked. When they stepped down from the train car, she looked up and down the platform for the contracted guide Carl Jung had said would be waiting. Suddenly, a man stepped into her path. "You are Frau Burden, I believe," he said in a brusque German accent.

"I am," she said, and pulled her son toward her.

"I am Herr Jodl," he said. "Dr. Jung in Zurich has arranged for me to meet you." He held out his hand.

Franz Jodl was an erect and formal man in his early sixties, carefully dressed and restrained in his posture and movements.

They stood together on the chilly station platform at Lustenau for some time, the discomfort of unfamiliarity evident in both. From this point in the Rhine Valley they could see the Alps rising on both sides, and they were aware of the change just having crossed the border, the train station showing signs of neglect, paint peeling, a few windows cracked, a look of deprivation in the eyes of the railroad personnel around them. What a contrast, she thought of saying to Standish beside her, just one large river separating the two worlds, one neutral and the other fully in the grip of war.

"We will be attended to in a moment," the former Viennese policeman said, keeping a respectful distance.

After the awkward silence had fallen between the new colleagues, an Austrian official emerged from the station office and asked everyone to form a line. A number of similarly shabbily dressed officials came and joined him and sat at tables where they intended to interview each of the travelers.

Soldiers obviously new to their jobs, recently released from war, it turned out, stood awkwardly by as the customs officers opened suitcases and trunks and examined goods. Eleanor's papers from the Swiss embassy were supposed to explain the unusually full trunk, but Jodl's authoritative style interceded to prevent the guards from riffling through the contents.

Finally, aware of the stern authoritative attention of Herr Jodl, the border guards sealed the trunks and allowed them to pass and board the trains.

The change from Swiss to Austrian trains was a rude shock. It did not take long to see in the difference what had happened to the once-grand empire. The guards had dogs which barked loudly but, like their masters, looked thin and unfed. The train cars themselves were in ill repair: leather seats slashed and crudely repaired, window shades that didn't work, windows cracked or broken. Some of the cars smelled of iodine from only recently having carried the wounded back from the front. Eleanor suppressed a shudder as she did her best not to imagine the bloody scene.

"This, like all of Austria, is not the same as you remember perhaps, Frau Burden," Jodl said, "but it will take us to Vienna. Quite a difference from your previous visit, which Herr Jung has explained to me. There is not much left of the empire and its splendor."

"It is quite all right, Herr Jodl," she said, sitting upright in her train seat, pulling young Standish close. "You will not need to keep reminding me. I am quite capable of adjusting to existing conditions."

42

CITY OF GHOSTS

ienna was almost unrecognizable. Of course, the tall, elegant marble façades of the grand buildings of the Ringstrasse for which Vienna at the end of the century had been renowned were unchanged, and the coffee-houses were still open, but all liveliness and vitality were gone. Nowhere to be seen on the wide Ringstrasse was the elegance she remembered: the handsome men in dark coats and top hats, the finely adorned women in long dresses with tightly corseted waists and well-defined *poitrines,* or the workers hurrying off carrying lunch boxes. And if there were military officers on the scene, their uniforms seemed frayed and worn and without medals and embellishments. Rather than loitering on display, soldiers hurried past without wishing to be noticed. Those who were out wandered the broad streets of the Ring as if in a daze. "There is almost nothing left of the old gaiety and bustle of our fabled city," Jodl had said, repeating his theme. "It is a great sadness." Eleanor felt like a visitor among ghosts.

The city that she entered was now struggling for its very survival, now fully aware that the war had been a disaster and the exuberance for it a cruel folly. In the summer of 1914, only four years before, as Arnauld had written, the city was still electric, overflowing with the power and energy of empire, the thrill of going to war. Then, in almost no time, Arnauld wrote, almost as soon as the bodies started coming back from the Russian front, it all began coming apart.

The fall of the great city and the dissolution of the empire, like the war's end, had come with a great suddenness. After the old emperor died in 1916, as the war was dragging on, suddenly, with the armistice in 1918, the empire disbanded and the economy collapsed. The new emperor, the scantily prepared grandnephew of Franz Joseph and younger nephew of the assassinated Franz Ferdinand, had decreed that Austria-Hungary would become a loose confederation of republics. But none of those—not the Czechs, Slavs, Hungarians, Poles, Croatians, Slovenians, or Italians— paid him much attention. They simply ceased their homage to the empire and went their separate ways, taking their life-sustaining natural resources with them. Within weeks of the end of hostilities in the fall of 1918, each of the separate states simply stopped saluting the imperial flag, and Vienna was left without access to the essential imports of fresh produce, meat, coal, and firewood that had fueled the capital city's magnificence for hundreds of years.

In the formerly grand city coal and gas were in desperately short supply; citizens burned wood they had torn from park benches and local trees. The stream of railroad cars from the mines in Bohemia and Moravia ceased to appear. The four hundred trains that had come daily to the city only a few years ago were now reduced to four. Electricity was absent most of the time. Hungary stopped sending the flour, pork, fat, poultry, eggs, vegetables, and meat that Vienna had relied on for generations.

"It is a pity, Frau Burden," said Franz Jodl, her new guide. "The Viennese are becoming accustomed to eating horse sausages, dried fruits and vegetables, synthetic meat made in part with the pulverized bark of birch trees, along with beet jam, and vile-tasting make-believe chocolate."

Chemically produced saccharine had replaced sugar. Cooking and frying was done with fat derived from petroleum residues and plants. Bread was made mostly of cornmeal and more questionable ingredients. Chicory and ground beets were boiled to yield a beverage that served as a very unappealing coffee substitute. Textiles were woven with yarns of nettle fibers and paper. Shoe soles were hydraulically pressed cardboard and sawdust bonded with tar. Some wartime industrialists made fortunes turning out such ersatz products.

Only the wealthy and profiteers were still able to eat in the old manner, but they had to pay in silver coins or currency from other countries. The once-elegant streets were now populated with throngs of haggard soldiers and ruffians in stolen and ragged uniforms without insignias.

Eleanor had written her former landlady Fräulein Tatlock of her arrival. The pension had been reduced to subsistence, and the fräulein had aged more in appearance than the twenty years since Eleanor had last seen her. The old pension owner met Eleanor and her young son at the door, her eyes filled with tears, and she knelt down after embracing Eleanor to embrace young Standish. "Oh, how he resembles you, Frau Burden," she exclaimed. "How marvelously!"

Eleanor was given her old room at the top of the stairs and suddenly found herself back in the scene of the great loss of her life. She had asked that Standish join her on a small cot, so that neither of them would sleep alone in this strange place, what was for her now a city of ghosts. Still, from the very first moment upon entering her old boardinghouse, Eleanor seemed at first somehow invigorated rather than intimidated by the starkness of the new Vienna. From the start she found herself clearly a New England woman rolling up her sleeves and taking on the tasks of restoration. After settling in upstairs, she had the one heavy trunk moved into the kitchen and asked Fräulein Tatlock to watch as she opened it.

Upon viewing the contents, eyes wide with amazement at the provisions from Switzerland that only months before would have been considered essential staples for a well-stocked boardinghouse such as hers, Fräulein Tatlock was speechless. When Eleanor came to the small bag of roasted coffee beans, she handed it to her host, who held it up and buried her nose in it, inhaling deeply. "Oh my," was all she said.

"We shall set up a modest kitchen," Eleanor said. "We may invite guests."

And when she had unpacked, she came downstairs with Standish and said, "Now, I would like to go out and reestablish my bearings." She walked with young Standish out to the Ringstrasse, as she had done so many times before, twenty years ago. "We will circle the city," she said to her son, and he smiled up at her, having no idea what a commitment to walking his mother had just made for both of them. "I want you to see the magnificent Ringstrasse."

Detouring to St. Stephen's Cathedral, she approached the formidable edifice holding her son's hand. "This is the biggest and grandest building you have ever seen," she said to him.

As they entered the vast medieval structure, Standish Burden let out a whoop. "Oh, Mother," he said loudly. "This is the biggest and grandest!" They stayed inside for almost two hours, examining each bank of stained glass and each statue. Standish seemed inexhaustible in his energy and enthusiasm for the building's splendor.

"Look," said his mother. "There is Joseph in his dungeon, and then telling his dreams to the pharaoh." Standish had loved being read Bible stories by Eleanor and his older sisters.

"I see," the boy said with relish. "And where is the Red Sea parting?"

"I think it is that one," his mother said. And she pointed out other stories with which he was familiar.

"Let's come back," he said as they were leaving.

〰

She arranged for Franz Jodl to meet her at Fräulein Tatlock's the first morning. "Please dine with us, if you wish," she said to him, knowing from her preparation that he was a widower whose two sons were lost in the war.

"That would be possible," he said without apology or apparent gratitude, intent on his business. He laid out before her in the sitting room all his notes and papers, going through them all with meticulous care, showing exactly how he had found the witnesses and how each had described the scene in which Arnauld Esterhazy had died. He repeated his findings that Arnauld had attained a position of leadership on the Isonzo River and had witnessed a number of the battles there. After the decisive struggle at Caporetto, when the Italians had been routed, he had been assigned a number of captured Italian officers and along with another younger officer, a Czech he had befriended, Arnauld had been moving them to a railroad yard, where they had received a direct hit from a mistakenly fired Austrian artillery shell.

"The group was torn apart, Frau Burden," he said with a look of respectful concern. "There is no way any of them could have survived." He paused to look into her eyes to see that she understood, then, for her benefit, retreated slightly, as he had promised Jung he would. "At least that is how it appeared," he added.

Then, as before and afterward, Eleanor stared back at him, signaling her steely ability to hear such realism. "I understand the details, Herr Jodl. You do not need to worry that I do not understand the details."

"Shrapnel, Frau Burden," he said solemnly. "That is what those not familiar with this war do not understand." And then he stopped, wishing to spare her anything further.

She knew from confrontation of the facts earlier that the explosion of an artillery shell in this war sent dinner-plate-size fragments of metal flying in all directions, severing limbs and heads where they flew. A direct hit would have been a scene of utter carnage. "There were many witnesses," Jodl said apologetically, as if to finalize the point. "The outcome was unavoidable. There is absolutely no doubt."

Eleanor did not flinch. She paused a moment before speaking. "And yet you know my mission here," Eleanor said, drawing herself upright to signal a change of mood.

"I do, Frau Burden." He did not hesitate.

"And you will assist me, in spite of the apparent outcome you describe?"

"We search for the living," Jodl said. "I will not be the first to abandon that search. You can be assured of that."

"I am grateful," she said, and the subject of uncertainty never came up again.

The review of details by Jodl, the funereal atmosphere of the city, the scene of people scouring for food and fuel all threatened her great resolve, and suddenly, by surprise, she found herself thinking of Will Honeycutt and what he would have done. "We are going to get control of this situation," she said to Fräulein Tatlock, who had already begun to look more animated by her new charge of tending to young Standish. She went back to Jodl. "We are going to get control of this situation," she repeated.

By nightfall, she had made arrangements to travel by train out into the countryside and meet with a family of farmers to bring back, in exchange for some of her store of coins, a supply of flour, eggs, some meats, and even coffee beans, to stock the modest kitchen of a small boardinghouse. Austrian currency was virtually worthless, but she had been told that American bills or coins worked magic. Then, and for the rest of her stay in Austria, Franz Jodl would be at her side, carrying the supply of American dollars in a briefcase and protecting the treasure, it appeared from his constant grip, with his life.

43

BERGGASSE 19

Eleanor had always wondered if she would ever return to Berggasse 19, one of her first stops in Vienna. The place had seemed a part of her destiny. As she climbed the stairs and felt her heart racing, she thought of how much had changed in the twenty years since her last visit here, how much she had learned of the world, how much of it she had seen. She thought also of the Vienna journal's accounts of visits here, of conversations which she had read about over and over to a point of near memorization. It was from those accounts that she had formed most of her opinions of Sigmund Freud and his theories. She arrived at the top of the stairs and knocked, without giving herself time to pause or retreat, then waited for the maid she knew would answer and allow her in.

Nothing had changed in the small, wood-paneled foyer. A couch stood against the wall beneath some etchings of classic Greek figures. Eleanor felt a strangely comfortable familiarity as she sat waiting the second time, recalling the first time twenty years before when she had known nothing of the man she was about to meet and nothing of the fame that would descend upon him during the two decades between her visits.

The door opened suddenly, and she found herself shaking the hand once again of the most famous man in Vienna. "We meet again, Frau Burden," he said in curt but distinct English. "It is my great pleasure."

"As it is mine, Herr Dr. Freud." He ushered her into his study and gestured to a chair beside his desk.

Dr. Freud wore a black armband, as she knew he would, the symbol of the loss of his beloved daughter Sophie to the influenza earlier that year. Just as Vienna was beginning to suffer the deprivations from years of war and the breakup of the empire, the dreaded pandemic that would take fifty million lives worldwide between 1918 and 1920 accompanied the hunger and cold. Gustav Klimt, Egon Schiele and his wife, architect Otto Wagner, and the editor of the *Neue Freie Presse* were among the well-known Viennese to fall along with Sigmund Freud's dear Sophie.

"You have only gained in impressiveness," he said, once both of them were seated, he behind the desk.

"You are kind," she said, pausing. "I am sorry for your great loss. My daughter and I both came down with the dreaded influenza, but somehow we survived it. For a time I thought I had lost her, and my family thought they had lost me."

"Some were fortunate," he said. "And some not. It has been a second war, right here in our homes."

"So it is," she said with a shudder.

He changed the tone. "I am glad to have this opportunity to thank you, Frau Burden. I learned of your part in my invitation to America in 1909," he said. "Much about that visit was vexing to me, and it was not until much later that I learned of your role in the creation of that event."

"I was able to play a minor one," she said quickly.

"Quite the contrary, Frau Burden. I hear that you caused it all to happen, both in its conception and its funding."

"That is exaggeration," she said, "but I am grateful for the recognition of my small part."

"Well, you may know that I had less than favorable impressions of your country."

"You referred to us as savages, I believe," she said with a little laugh.

Dr. Freud looked uncomfortable for a moment. "I overstated. It was not an entirely pleasant experience for me because of stomach problems."

"The impressions were nowhere near mutual, as you probably know. Your ideas were very well received. You are now very highly regarded in America."

"I am grateful for that." He paused and let his eyes penetrate. "I was most honored to meet Dr. James. For me, he was the main attraction in going to America in the first place, and the attention he gave me, in spite of his illness, was most appreciated. You were very close to him, I gather."

"He was my godfather, and very dear to me." She had become accustomed to referring to William James in this manner.

"I wondered, of course, what he thought of my ideas. We had a chance to speak very briefly, but never in much depth, and then, of course, the world lost him."

"He was very impressed," she said quickly, misrepresenting James's impressions a bit. "He said on many occasions that your ideas were the future, and at the very end he expressed regret that he would not be able to see how those ideas played out."

"I sensed that he felt more in agreement with my former colleague Dr. Jung. I know he was interested in the spiritual aspects of our science, what he called parapsychology. I know that he consulted séances."

"Yes," Eleanor said. "The supernatural was always intriguing for him, but never with any certainty. It was always possibilities that intrigued him."

"And, as you know, not an interest of mine, a disappointment to Dr. James, I fear."

"I think you underestimate the impression you made on him, and on all the guests at Dr. Hall's conference."

"Perhaps," the great doctor said, then paused, giving his guest an evaluative glance. "And I gather you and my former colleague Dr. Jung have corresponded." He paused again in such a way as to imply more.

"We have corresponded," she began, then paused herself, long enough to match his implication. "We have become friends."

"Dr. Jung talked about his Putnam Camp conversations with you on our sea voyage home from New York. Of all the influences that caused him to drift away, I believe, that afternoon with you was the greatest."

"Oh my," Eleanor said. "I hope that is not so."

"Dr. Jung is very impressionable. You are a very compelling conversationalist, I gather. I think he was quite influenced, smitten even. He reflected a number of times on our return trip that you were kindred spirits."

"All of us Americans were quite taken by both of you. You made a powerful impression with your visit, as you no doubt heard."

"Dr. Jung is very compelling in his intensity," Dr. Freud said, refusing to be distracted, and she could hear the hint of irritation in his voice. "He is drawn to intimacies beyond what his former colleagues were drawn to. I gather that the two of you have become quite close."

"We have corresponded." The great doctor could most likely hear a defensiveness in her voice. "That is all."

"You need not worry, Frau Burden. I am not one to judge. You are both adults," he said with an attempt at the cold dispassion for which he was famous.

"Our intimacies have been limited to correspondence," she said, now with a bit of irritation in her voice.

"I wish neither to imply nor to pry," he then offered, and she let it lie.

"We are here to talk about Herr Esterhazy," she said. Eleanor had written him as soon as she arrived in Vienna. She wanted to make use of his experience and great deductive capacity.

"That is right," the great doctor acknowledged.

"You are kind to receive me."

"I wish to help. Herr Esterhazy is dead in the war. I am terribly sorry to hear that. We have suffered greatly as a country and as a city. And I fear that our own folly in enthusiastically rushing to war has brought great suffering upon ourselves and upon the world."

"You had much support in that folly."

"I suppose we did. Anyway, many many young men are dead, your Arnauld Esterhazy included."

"I do not believe him dead. You know that."

Freud took a long look at her, measuring exactly how he was going to approach this. "As is your assigned role," Freud said, referring for the first time, she deduced, to his knowledge of her past in Vienna twenty years ago, and the journal. "But you must know that there are numerous very reliable reports and witnesses, too many to be dismissed."

"Yes, I do know that," she said. "And yet I have reason to believe that he is still alive."

For a moment he said nothing.

"Of course. I understand," he said, accepting the stalemate. "Your faith is strong. That causes us to revisit our very basic difference from the former time." He had his reasons to believe the man was dead, and she had hers to believe he was alive. They had accepted this stalemate and armistice twenty years ago, neither venturing to try to persuade the other, each fully invested in believing a contrary version of reality. "You have lived your life according to your faith," he said.

"And you according to yours," she said.

"Nothing has happened to shake either of us from our convictions."

"Oh, you can be assured that I have had quite a bit of shaking," she said pointedly. "There have been predicted events, granted, ones requiring research and execution." She avoided mentioning the one enormous one. "It has not been without considerable complexity and struggle."

"You have carried out your assigned tasks, I assume."

"Yes, the predictions have come to pass, and I have benefited greatly. I have created a fund, as instructed."

"I understand that," he said without emotion, the closest he came to admitting that he had indeed done some research about her and her visit.

"And what you have seen unfold in the world has not caused you to reconsider your original skepticism?"

"Not in the slightest."

"And what then of the events you heard predicted," she said, pressing him, "the ones you have seen come to pass?" She looked into his serious implacable face. "What do you make of the epic tragedies, the *Titanic* sinking and the advent of the great world war? They were both foretold."

"Life is full of coincidences," he said, more as a scientific observation than a defense. "Awful tragedy and coincidence." He paused to gather his thoughts, then continued. "When I was in medical school, on one of the wards there was a mental patient who was so convinced that he was king of Prussia that he convinced others, and he was so persuasive in his claim for a particular investment that one of the interns put a good deal of money into it and made a small bundle. There are coincidences," the great doctor concluded.

"It seems to me that in the case of the *Titanic* alone that there have been more than just coincidences."

Dr. Freud stared at her for a moment. "We are at a standstill, Frau Burden. You take as literal the words in the mysterious American's journal, and I do not. You are like the Mormons in your country who follow literally the words of their Joseph Smith and his gold tablets. I am like the nonbelievers who see him as a charlatan. It is simply a matter of faith."

"Then it is pointless for us to approach this matter in this way."

"It is," he said, with his famous clarity and conviction.

"And nothing more?"

"Nothing more." The certitude in his voice signaled clearly that he had not budged in his opinion of their shared experience twenty years before. "Coincidence, and nothing more," he reiterated, just for good measure.

"And what of the evil child?" she said.

"There was indeed in this city before the war a young man of the name Adolf Hitler, from Lambach," Freud said calmly, trying not to show that he had indeed been keeping track. "I did take notice to that extent. But the young man in question is a failed artist and a lowly corporal in the kaiser's army, I believe, and now lost in the great struggle. Not much earth-shattering significance there."

"I am not here to dissuade you," she said, more vehement with her eyes than with the words. "I am only here to solicit your assistance."

"What help could I, a nonbeliever, give?"

"You could tell me where to find Arnauld."

"You are interested in retrieving his body?" The words came out more coldly than the great doctor perhaps intended.

"Please," she said. "I have come to retrieve *him*."

Dr. Freud, a notoriously stubborn man, looked for a moment as if he might argue. Then he paused. "Of course," he said abruptly. "We will proceed according to your beliefs, not mine. You have traveled a great distance to be here, and I respect that. You have honored me with this visit, and I am duly flattered. I wish to help, as I said in my correspondence. It is your conviction that Arnauld Esterhazy will emerge from this brutal war alive, and we shall honor that conviction."

"Thank you," Eleanor said flatly.

"It is your conviction that Arnauld Esterhazy will emerge physically intact, is it not?" She nodded. "And that he will emerge emotionally scarred perhaps, but physically unmarked?"

"Yes," she said. "That is essential."

"It is your conviction that eventually he will regain his full mental capacity, with no permanent physical impairments?"

She nodded. "Exactly."

"In your version of the story he will become a legendary teacher of schoolboys." She nodded her silent appreciation of the great doctor's acknowledgment of at least a part of her version of Arnauld's story. "He has lost no limb or eye nor sustained any marring physical wound." She nodded again. "Emotionally damaged, I assume, but capable of total rehabilitation."

"Yes," she said. "Of that I am certain."

"Then," Dr. Freud said, "we know exactly where to find him. There is only one possibility. We know now that there is a way to sustain the most horrible damages from war that have little to do with physical impairments. The unrelenting and repeated shock of war can render its victims, although perfectly fit physically, unable to function normally, in some cases totally so. If one could somehow recover from this horrible condition, one would resume life in an absolutely normal manner, the manner in which your version of the story describes Herr Esterhazy in the future. But for the time being, if he were victim of this war trauma, this 'shell shock,' the English call it, he would be totally unable to identify himself or to care for his own recovery, thus causing his disappearance and presumed death."

"You are suggesting that this war trauma is Arnauld's fate?"

"That is the only answer, the only way he could be vanished now, unable to identify himself, and yet emerge intact. Unless he were taken prisoner by the Russians and removed deep into their homeland." He paused. "In such case he would never be seen again, and therefore this is not a possibility." The great doctor had obviously thought it all through. "Were shell shock the case, as it obviously is, we would indeed know at least generally where to find him."

"Perhaps," she said. "So I could use your help."

The doctor looked as if he might have reconsidered his cooperation, but then he moved forward. "He has sustained no permanent physical damage. His limbs are intact. He has sustained no permanent brain injury and has a damaged but still recoverable mind. He has not been taken into the heart of some vast enemy land where there is much bitterness and secrecy. He was on the Italian front, where the fighting was continual and relentless in its horror."

"I know this," Eleanor said, just a bit impatient.

"Very few would return untouched, in one way or another, from that fate. For a sensitive man such as Herr Esterhazy it would have been especially traumatic. So," he said, the fingers of each hand meeting the other in front of his chest, "that means only one thing."

She waited expectantly. "That is why I am here, Herr Doctor," she said, "to hear of that one *thing*."

"There is only one possibility. One place you will find him. The war has taken a horrible toll in human life, and throughout Europe there are thousands of unidentifiable souls, physically alive but so spiritually dead that no one knows their identities. It will take years to identify them all. If Herr Esterhazy is alive, my guess is that he is among those lost souls. But not *permanently*, according to your beliefs."

She nodded her agreement. "Yes," she said.

"If he were to be alive, you would find your Arnauld Esterhazy in one of the many hospitals, both makeshift and formal, filled with the many hopeless victims of the war, caught up in the chaos and confusion of huge numbers. He will have no way of identifying himself or anyone looking for him, or else he would have done so. Lost in the confusion of war. There are no records to help these victims or their loved ones. One hears terrible stories on both sides, of such severe psychological shock that the young men are rendered totally incapacitated. Unimaginable devastation." The doctor shook his head. "We in our profession only wish we could be of more help."

The great doctor paused to see that Eleanor was following. "I understand," she said.

"Do not forget that he might be with the Czechs or the Romanians or the Germans, or even the Italians," he said. "The numbers are overwhelming. The task is too much."

"I am up to the task," Eleanor said, the vehemence returned to her eyes.

Dr. Freud looked into those eyes. "I do not underestimate you, Frau Burden. It will be a very disturbing journey, your descent into the underworld."

"To retrieve my Orpheus."

"Eurydice searching for Orpheus," he said, "a reversal of roles." Dr. Freud, the nonbeliever, reached for a desk drawer and withdrew an envelope. "I have done some research. These are the hospitals where you can begin, a few nearby, but most in the war zone west of Trieste." He reached across his desk with the list, which Eleanor took.

"You can begin here in Vienna, at the huge Vienna state hospital, Allgemeines Krankenhaus, but that is filled mostly with soldiers from the Russian front. Then you will have to travel to our territories north of Italy, near Trieste, to the infamous Isonzo River front. There is one collection place in Gorizia, a requisitioned palazzo, a forgotten place of lost souls, it appears. That seems to be the best possibility. You will look there first," he said. "But if not Gorizia, there are others, all listed here. All the way over to the new front on the Piave River north of Venice, where it all came to a close, and the chaos where the Italians have taken hundreds of thousands of prisoners."

She held the list for a long moment, reflecting on all the great doctor had said. "Thank you," she said in little more than a whisper. "You have obviously done a great deal of research on my behalf." She neglected to add, *and in a cause in which you do not believe.*

"There is no need for gratitude," Dr. Freud said with genuine concern. "In this instance, I hope that you are right and I am wrong. And I wish you the speed of the gods."

44

THE FIRST HOSPITAL

igmund Freud's list of hospital sites for the wounded would eventually take Eleanor and her new partner Franz Jodl to the vicinity of Trieste, at the southernmost edge of the empire, on the Adriatic. "But be prepared for uncertainties," the doctor had warned as she was leaving Berggasse 19. "Both sides have been quite overwhelmed by the management of casualties. There are many makeshift hospitals, some now closed, some in great disarray. Yours will not be an easy search."

Their first visit had been to the large hospital of Vienna, where soldiers had been delivered from the very first disastrous days on the eastern front against the Russian guns, in Galicia. But Freud had not been hopeful about that visit. "Most of the patients here in Vienna have names and are accounted for." And, of course, Arnauld, were he alive, would not be among them. "There are many damaged souls among the wounded here, and in the mental wards, but I doubt he would be one of those. Your Esterhazy would have been lost in the chaos of the Italian war zone."

Their letter of introduction from Sigmund Freud worked well at the huge Allgemeines Krankenhaus. They were greeted by a serious-looking doctor who resembled a younger, taller version of Freud himself, and he introduced them to a nurse, an officious but kindly woman with a neatly starched uniform and thick spectacles.

"I will give you a general tour," she said, "and then we will visit the ward of the unidentified patients, where you may find the man you search for."

She explained that, during the days of battle, wounded soldiers were taken first to field hospitals, then, as soon as they were stabilized, moved by train to the larger city hospitals throughout the empire, Prague, Budapest, Romania, preferably near their homes. But many of the soldiers ended up here, displaced and far from home. The schedule of family visits from all over the provinces alone was staggering. After each large battle, first in Galicia, then in Serbia, France, and finally Italy, there were tens of thousands of casualties, each requiring special attention.

"We will have to be diligent and thorough, I know," Eleanor said. "We must leave no stone unturned, no patient unvisited."

"I am sorry that you need to see this," her new partner said, having not yet learned that he did not need to protect her. "I wish there were another way."

"Be prepared," Freud had warned her. "The Vienna hospital is clean and tidy but shocking all the same. Where you are going the conditions will be unnerving. You will be descending into the awful world of war."

Even after the armistice, the flow continued, every week new patients coming in by train.

"One can only imagine the chaos out in the provinces where the battles take place."

The visitors were ushered through rows of beds, observing patients in all manner of condition, some prostrate, unable to move, some up against the headboards reading, some sitting on the edges of beds, some walking slowly in the aisles, supported by nurses or orderlies. "All of these have an identity," the nurse said. "All of these have families they are writing to."

In the next room patients were recovering from operations. Many of them had survived amputations, and most of them were heavily bandaged. "You can imagine the need for medical supplies. Fortunately, in this hospital, we have what we need. And we are well staffed. In the provinces, they are not so lucky, we hear."

Before entering the room at the end of one wing, the nurse stopped them. "This is the difficult one," she said, "even for those of us who have seen much. Many of these poor souls are alive in fact only."

They entered and walked silently between beds. What they saw defied description, bodies torn apart and sewed back together, some bandaged, some not, some soldiers not able to identify their names or where they came from. "War is hell," the nurse said to them, "and this is the proof."

"Arnauld would not be among these," Eleanor whispered to her companion.

"And how do you know this?" he asked.

"Arnauld will be returning to normal life without physical scars," she said with conviction. "We must travel to the war zone."

As they passed beside the bed of one young soldier, he sat up suddenly and stared directly at Eleanor. "Ernestine," he said loudly, and reached out his hand, as if across a vast expanse. There was a haunting fierceness in his eyes. Eleanor stepped forward and took the hand. "Ernestine," he repeated, and a nurse, hearing his expostulation, stepped up to intercede.

"It is all right," Eleanor said, holding tight to the hand. In a moment, the fierceness began fading from the young man's eyes. "Ernestine, you have come," he said, searching Eleanor's face for some missing element of connection.

"It is all right," Eleanor repeated, this time directly into the face of the young man, and as she released his hand, he fell back in his bed, now staring at the ceiling. Eleanor and Jodl moved on without words. The nurse stepped toward the bed and helped the young man close his eyes.

They passed one bed where a man lay motionless; he seemed to have no arms. Later they passed men whose heads were totally bandaged. "I believe these have no faces," Jodl whispered.

By the time they finished their tour of the military wings of the Allgemeines Krankenhaus, Eleanor admitted to Jodl her fatigue.

"It is overwhelming, is it not?" the nurse said to them as it was clear their lengthy tour was completed. "And it remains so for us who have been here for the duration. Elsewhere," she added, "we hear that the numbers are less intimidating, but the conditions appalling."

"I know," she said. "We shall prepare ourselves."

"You have before you a daunting task, Frau Burden," the doctor said as they parted. "I wish you luck."

"We will press on," she said.

"There is one thing you must know," the doctor said. "There is a great deal of hope within the hopelessness of your mission. There are literally thousands of unidentified and unaccounted-for soldiers in the aftermath of this horrible war. The odds are on your side."

"Thank you," Eleanor said. "Hope in hopelessness," she repeated.

Eleanor and Jodl were silent on their taxi ride back to Fräulein Tatlock's. "One must not be disappointed," Eleanor said in parting. "It was not reasonable to expect to find him so easily. There will be more of this."

45

"VERY MUCH AMONG THE LIVING"

he next task was the visit she was both anticipating and dreading, to Arnauld's parents. The family home was a hillside property some thirty kilometers from the heart of Vienna. From Arnauld's descriptions over the years, Eleanor could visualize it before her actual visit with her young son. As she rode up the long gravel entryway in the motorcar that had been sent for her, the landscape felt familiar. The small vineyard had belonged to the Esterhazy family for generations. "The plot of land has produced for generations some of the best wines in all of Europe," Arnauld used to say, "but no one has tasted them save the Esterhazys and half of Franz Joseph's fabled aristocracy and their fortunate guests." And she knew from the last letters before their abrupt cessation that with the dissolution of the empire the small acreage was now given directly to Arnauld's father, to do with what he could, to share its produce with the world.

"My father is an excellent winemaker," Arnauld would say, "as was his father." And Arnauld would describe accompanying his father in the morning inspections of the rows of vines and the supervision of the harvests in early fall. "There was a seasonal rhythm of my parents' life that always seemed orderly and peaceful."

Arnauld's parents were elderly and genteel, as she knew they would be. They welcomed her and her son with great warmth and humility, treating young Standish with affectionate attention from the start. Frau Esterhazy mentioned immediately that Herr Esterhazy's cousin, recovering from war wounds, was staying with them and would be joining them later.

"Are you enjoying your visit to Vienna?" Frau Esterhazy asked.

"I certainly am," Standish said with an assertive authority that brought from both of his hosts an affectionate laugh.

"There is much for a boy to enjoy in our city," Arnauld's father said.

"Mother and I liked the Bible story windows very much," the boy said, again with authority.

"We spent some time in St. Stephen's," Eleanor explained.

"That is a beautiful place," Frau Esterhazy said, which brought a nod of enthusiasm from young Standish. "Arnauld loved going there when he was a small boy. He too was entranced with stories from the Bible."

Eleanor had decided long before this visit to keep to herself the reason for her return to Vienna. As far as the family was concerned, Eleanor was there to grieve with them and to tell about what an honored presence their son had been at a small New England boys' school thousands of miles away across the Atlantic Ocean.

"Arnauld was considered a great teacher," she said after the affectionate salutations. "He was thought to have a great future."

Arnauld's parents nodded quietly and absorbed the observation. "Much has been lost in this war," Herr Esterhazy said.

"Yours is the loss of a dear son," she added solemnly, "mine the loss of a dear friend." She paused and looked into the grief-worn faces.

"We know of the place you hold—" Frau Esterhazy caught herself. "We know the place you held in our son's heart."

And it was in that moment alone with Arnauld's mother that Eleanor was struck by a depth of feeling she had not anticipated. She felt a rush of what could be described only as guilt, that she had lured this woman's son away from his home and coerced him into feelings and actions beyond what was appropriate.

"I am so very sorry," she said.

"I know that," his mother said, and then as if it were a most natural sequitur, she asked suddenly, "Have you visited Arnauld's childhood friend Alma? I know she would enjoy hearing of his life in Boston."

"Standish and I will visit her tomorrow."

Arnauld's mother rolled her eyes ever so slightly. "Alma is very different from our Arnauld. She has been married twice, you know, and is very"—she paused—"artistic. But they were very close as children, something you might not have guessed. Alma's father and mother were close friends of ours. Oh my, what a painter he was. We have a few of his paintings in this house."

"I knew her slightly in my time in Vienna twenty years ago, and we saw each other in New York and Boston when Herr Mahler came to America."

"Alma has been very good to us," Herr Esterhazy said. "She has visited a number of times since the news."

"You will have to pardon Herr Esterhazy," the mother said when he left the room to bring the wine. "We were opponents of war long before our country's current debacle," she said. "He has lost his dear son, the light of his life, to a cause he did not believe in." She paused.

Herr Esterhazy returned with a tray and three glasses of clear cold white wine. "This is the famous *heuriger* wine," he said with a proud smile, "the new wine that the Viennese are so crazy for."

They talked about Arnauld as they drank the wine, and then Frau Esterhazy rose and gathered up the empty glasses and retired with them.

"You will have to pardon my wife," the father said quietly when she left the room with the tray of glasses. "For her, it is the absence as much of his letters as of his physical presence. There will be no more letters."

"I am aware of the terrible grief in the loss of a son."

"You know the details, I assume, Frau Burden," Arnauld's father said with sudden seriousness.

"I know of some. I would like to hear everything you know."

Herr Esterhazy paused as if to gather strength. "We received a notification from the emperor's chief of staff directly," he continued. "Arnauld had allowed himself to be assigned to the front and had been placed in charge of a group of Italian prisoners, a group of officers to be placed in a train car, when an artillery shell exploded in their midst. It was a horrible scene, we were told, spared the details of course, but a dreadful and hopeless disaster."

"I am so very sorry," Eleanor said.

"There is much loss in this regrettable war," the old man said, his eyes filling with tears. "Ours is but a small portion of it."

She let the conclusion stand, not sharing with either parent her strong conviction that Arnauld was not dead. "Your loss is enormous," Eleanor said, "I know that. Arnauld was a fine and sensitive man, with great promise."

"A fine and sensitive man," Herr Esterhazy repeated slowly, savoring the words, amused. "He was the third son of a third son, far from the primogenitor role in this family, as was I, his father. He wished to be a teacher of history, in America."

"I hope that was not a disappointment to you."

"Oh, no," Herr Esterhazy said. "We were quite proud always of his passionate spirit. To be a teacher is a noble calling."

"And a very good teacher," Eleanor said. "His American school is in mourning."

"I can imagine," the father said, and he looked up as a handsome young man around Arnauld's age entered the room. He had a decided limp. "Oh," said Herr Esterhazy, "here is my nephew, Michelangelo."

The man approached, holding out his hand and smiling broadly. Eleanor, startled at first, reached out her hand reflexively and found it in the vigorous grasp of Arnauld's cousin Miggo Sabatini.

"I thought—" she stammered.

"You thought me dead," he said. "The world thinks me dead. I have a long story to tell, but I am now very much among the living."

At luncheon she sat beside Miggo and he told her at least the rudimentary details of how he was seriously wounded on the first day of fighting, taken prisoner, escaped, and spent the duration of the war there in Austria, "Hiding from both sides," he said with a smile.

"Did no one know you were alive?" she said.

"I was a deserting officer and an escaped prisoner of war. I didn't wish anyone to know."

"And your parents?" Eleanor said with a frown.

"They would have to wait like everyone else. After Caporetto, after the sadness with Arnauld, I wrote them."

After lunch, he pulled up his pant leg and showed Eleanor a deep and jagged scar, running from ankle to knee. "I did not wish to spoil your meal," he said. "A piece of shrapnel from one side or another tore up my calf. I nearly died from the infection."

A single sheet found among Eleanor Burden's papers tells the story of Miggo's experience. It is written on both sides, in Eleanor's hand, probably from sometime after the telling. It is in an attempt, no doubt, to round out the larger story.

> *Lieutenant Michelangelo Sabatini had joined the Italian army, like Arnauld resurrecting his officer commission from his university days, and chose Italian over his other citizenships probably because that choice offered the most flair and the least risk of actually going to war. On the opening day of hostilities in 1915, he found himself at the head of a caravan heading across the Friuli plain in what he thought would be a quick and easy offensive action and then a triumphant entry into Trieste as a liberator, all of this attracting his sense of adventure. And so on that first day he found himself totally by surprise stopped dead by heavy Austrian artillery as soon as they crossed the Isonzo River. The consequence was brutal and bloody, and he spent more than a day lying badly wounded among the dead and maimed, himself nearly ripped apart by shrapnel from an exploding shell.*
>
> *He saw enough of war in those two days, he later explained, to let him know that he wanted no part of it, and that he had made a horrible mistake. He and what was left of his expeditionary group were taken prisoner and carted to an Austrian field hospital, where there was much confusion. When an Austrian medical officer came by with a handful of papers trying to identify the dead and dying, Miggo found himself in possession of a report form and filled it out with his name as one of the deceased and dropped it on the ground, where it was picked up by a nurse who assumed the officer had dropped it. In the quiet of night, he dragged himself across a line in the field hospital, and in among the Austrian wounded he blacked out and nearly bled to death in the effort.*
>
> *That is how he ended up as an "unknown" in an Austrian hospital, and how word arrived at Italian army headquarters that he had been killed in battle. He spent six months recuperating from his near-fatal wounds and then one day simply limped out of the hospital and spent the remainder of the war in Budapest, assuming the identity of a Bohemian poet unfit for military service because of a*

bad leg, and trying to find a way to escape to America, where he would not be identified as a prisoner of war or a deserter. Eventually, he found his way into the company of some Esterhazy relatives, and there was no mention of his having been in the Italian army.

After the armistice, he arrived at the door of his uncle and aunt, Arnauld's parents, where he was taken in without question, still with plans to end up in America, after things settled down. It was from there that his availability would prove to be invaluable.

As Eleanor and Standish were preparing to leave, Frau Esterhazy pulled Eleanor aside, and when the two women found themselves alone, the older woman spoke. "There is something I wish you to have. You may take it with you and return it when you are finished." She handed Eleanor a tin container the size of a small hatbox. "These are Arnauld's letters of the past ten years, from even before the time he first left for Boston. You and your son are featured prominently in them, you will see." She held the box tightly for a moment before releasing it. "There is in here information that you must know, but must hold with the highest confidentiality." Arnauld's mother kept her eyes fixed on Eleanor. Her look was one of the deepest fondness. "I believe that my son worshipped you," she whispered.

"And Arnauld held a special place for me," Eleanor said. "As you perhaps already know."

Later, in the quiet privacy of her old room at Fräulein Tatlock's, Eleanor opened the tin box and read uninterrupted through the collection of simply and thoroughly detailed letters of a loving son to his parents. What she held in her hands was an extraordinary description of Arnauld's life, even during the war. What was remarkable about this collection of letters was the description of Boston and Arnauld's newfound life there, and of course his emotional attachment to Eleanor.

In some ways the letters to his parents were the observations of a stranger in a foreign land, life in one of the oldest of brash young American cities so vastly different from the café culture of Vienna in which Arnauld had grown up. "Americans are confident and friendly, without the reserve of Europeans, and yet well informed and unafraid of depth. I wish to stay here for some time."

Eleanor realized from the start the candid and intimate nature of these letters home and felt honored to have been given them by the author's mother. Over the course of this first reading, she became amused anew by how unlike her husband, Frank, this writer was. Her friend Carl Jung would have found the two of them excellent models for the theory of personality type he was developing. Whereas Arnauld was sensitive and self-analytical, always seeking connection, Frank was abrupt and self-assured, always seeking to be definitive, decisive. Whereas Arnauld embraced change and the excitement of an evolving world, Frank met each day as if yesterday, today, and tomorrow would be the same, "as it is now it ever will be." Arnauld's sensitivity radiated a deep feeling that Jung would have immediately identified with the feminine. As she read the letters, she found herself moved many times. The articulate grace of this extraordinary young man, now in his late thirties, struck her over and over as she read his eloquent descriptions of the life she had shared with him, at least in part, during his time in Boston. But as she came to the last of the letters, the flow stopped first by his return to Vienna in 1914 and then by his disappearance, an enormous sadness began to settle on her. This was the man whose life had become inexorably linked to hers, the man whose physical well-being had suddenly become of utmost importance to her.

And suddenly, while reading, she began to be struck by an unavoidable reality: For one of Arnauld Esterhazy's remarkable sensitivity and astute perception, the experience of war would be absolutely devastating. She read, and she found the experience heartbreaking.

As she read further, she found herself revisiting involuntarily the feeling of guilt she had experienced with Arnauld's mother. What she had engineered over the course of many years and what had come to fruition that one evening on Beacon Hill was required of her. That was her justification. What she felt for him now, what she could share with no one, came back to her in recalling her uneasy moment with Arnauld's mother.

She read with pain and joy knowing that it was she who had caused this talented and sensitive young man to come to the new world of America and open himself to this new experience he described with such enthusiasm. Now, reading each line with affectionate attention, her complex feelings of attachment only increased.

One letter among all of them stood out especially. It was written in the heart of war, approximately nine months after his departure from Boston, and it reflected at the same time heartbreaking naïveté and worldliness. "Eleanor has written of the birth of her son, whose name will be Frank Standish Burden Junior. Since it now appears to me likely that I shall never be blessed by either matrimony or fatherhood, I shall consider this very special child like my own."

When she had finished the letters, she saw at the bottom of the box a simple notebook of the kind used by schoolboys. It was worn and marked with rust-colored blotches that could have been mud or human blood. She opened the book and flipped through the handwritten pages enough to identify them as descriptions of war experiences, and to see that it was filled with graphic descriptions of what Arnauld had been through, his war journal, she would call it later. The pages were written in English, no doubt to elude accidental readings by comrades and the prying eyes of censors.

Wedged within the pages at the back of the notebook was a single photograph, a commercial image perhaps from the Italian cinema printed in the subdued tones of a wall decoration. It was a romanticized representation of a well-dressed man, suave and debonair, a lothario with his hair slicked back fashionably, leaning into the neck, whispering into the ear, of a beautiful and enchanted paramour. On the back, dated from the time of Arnauld's Roman visit with his cousin before the outbreak of hostilities on the Isonzo front, was this inscription:

> *Arnauld,*
>   *Inside every shy man is a great lover trying to get out.*
>
> *Your ever-faithful,*
> *Michelangelo*

She held the photograph for a moment and thought the image a strange one for Arnauld to carry in such a place of importance through his immense ordeal, and it was not until later that Will Honeycutt explained for her its likely significance.

She had put it and the notebook aside, and now gave her attention to the bundled letters and noticed the one last letter that had sat on the bottom of the collection. It was sealed and addressed to her. She opened it and read slowly, this one last letter that answered everything, that caused so much to fall into place.

It was, she knew, the missing piece.

46

A LINGERING CURIOSITY

leanor had postponed her meeting with Alma until after her visit to Arnauld's parents at their family estate and until after she had paid her respects to the cemetery in Grinzing, the section north of the Ringstrasse. She had researched the exact location. The morning she walked there was gray and cold. As soon as she was standing before the large stone column marking the grave, as she expected, a rush of emotion came over her. The art deco lettering at the top of the column read *Gustav Mahler.*

The fact that he was now celebrated as one of Vienna's great musicians and that his grave marker was frequently visited by admirers was supremely ironic given the rude treatment he had been subjected to in the press and anti-Semitic harassment he had endured in his last year at the state opera, before his departure for New York City.

Because of the anonymity she had insisted on, nearly a decade had passed now and no one knew the part that Eleanor and the Hyperion Fund had played in that move to America nor in the authorship of the book, *City of Music,* that had stirred up so much interest in him before his arrival.

In that last visit, when Mahler's heart had failed to near the point of breaking and he and Alma were to sail that last time for home, just before their departure from New York, Eleanor had arranged to meet alone with the great musician for the first time.

"We know each other from your visits to Boston," Eleanor said.

"Of course, I know that," Mahler said, responding as if challenged. "You are a great supporter of music there, and a great supporter of mine."

"But do you remember from before," she asked him, the first time she had mentioned it, "from 1897, when the young American Weezie Putnam fainted dead away in your studio?"

The great musician, by then enfeebled by his grave condition, thought back, with a tired look on his face. Then slowly a spark came into his eyes, and he smiled. "Why, yes," he said wistfully, without the energy to register surprise. "Why, yes, I do. She was a very pretty and very—" He paused. "Very young. It is not every day that one experiences such a dramatic event."

"I was that American girl," she said.

Mahler looked confused, then took a long moment to examine the face in front of him, and then smiled again weakly and nodded. "Why, yes, I see that you are."

"You made an advance." She said it without emotion.

"Oh my," he said, nodding, exploring the memory more deeply. "I hope you have forgiven me."

"I have thought about it from time to time since that day. I am greatly embarrassed that I fainted dead away." Then she smiled gently into his careworn face. "I have always considered it—very secretly, mind you—a great compliment."

"I hope that you have," he said.

"I was in the thrall of your music. I had traveled from Boston to meet you."

"I hope you were not disappointed."

"How could I have been? I had the privilege of hearing you conduct at the state opera. And it was thrilling. When you did allow me an audience, I commented on your symphonies, how I had experienced them only in the sheet music. I said I had never heard anything like it."

"I am sure I was impressed by that."

"You were. You were gracious and charming."

"And still you fainted dead away."

"Had it been later in my life, later in my development, you might say, I would have perhaps responded differently."

Mahler, tired and ill at the end of his life, closed his eyes and smiled, as if he had just taken a sip of his most favorite fresh, cold *heuriger* wine. "The young woman had come to Vienna," he said finally, "to meet me, I believe she said." Eleanor nodded. "To hear my music and 'to write something of significance,' were her words."

"You do remember," Eleanor said.

The great musician looked genuinely interested now. "Did you indeed write such a work of significance?"

"I did, at least to my mind."

"And its name? Perhaps I have heard of it."

For a moment Eleanor thought of withholding the title, keeping it forever a secret, but then she relented. "*City of Music,*" she replied.

Now Gustav Mahler looked really confused for an even longer moment. "I know the work," he said softly. "It is said here to be the work that made my reputation in New York."

"I too have heard that," Eleanor said.

"But this *City of Music,* it was written by a man, a Mr. Trumpp, I believe."

Eleanor said nothing but gave a slight gesture of resignation with her eyebrows and hands, which Mahler seemed to understand. "I see," he said, looking still a little confused and still very serious. He raised his tired eyes to hers and within them flashed a tiny spark of recognition, that finally he was beginning to understand all. "Oh my," he said, and she did not look away. The two held the mutual gaze for a long moment, one that Eleanor would cherish all her life, one that held within it all the depth of this extraordinary man's music and the intimacy of a hundred lovers' embraces.

Then the great musician smiled. "Thank you," he said.

Gustav Mahler died in May of that year, back in his beloved Vienna in the presence of his beloved Alma.

N

Alma's sitting room was like an island apart, untouched by the war and its aftermath. Her fresh beauty radiated as it had always, now with a slight matronly air, positive and glowing still, as if there had been no loss: no

daughter's or husband's death, no war, no influenza. She was still as strik-
ing and vibrant as ever. Eleanor was glad to see her again and buoyed by
her cheerfulness as the two embraced at the doorway. The host reached
down to caress Standish's cheeks and offer, "What a handsome young
man!" Standish smiled roughly at the attention, and the mother could see
in an instant that her son had fallen, like so many men, into the thrall of
this remarkably sensual woman.

"I visited Herr Mahler's grave today," Eleanor said.

Alma paused for a moment, surprised perhaps at such an opening line.
"Oh, I am glad for that," she said. "Gustav would have been greatly
pleased."

"It was a moment of great poignancy for me."

"We both have experienced much since we were last together," Alma
said.

"I was happy for you when I learned of you and Herr Gropius," Eleanor said.

"You do not think it was too soon?" She paused and looked away.
"Some think I was disrespectful."

"Life must go on," Eleanor said, knowing that Arnauld called her actions predictable.

"You were kind to write. Such expression means a great deal, in times
of joy and in times of loss." Eleanor had written her twice. First, when
Mahler died, and then upon the news of her marriage to the young architect Walter Gropius.

"You deserve to be happy."

"We all deserve to be happy, although that is a difficult perspective to
defend in these trying times."

"This city has changed since our time here twenty years ago."

"And we have changed," Alma said with a knowing smile. "We have
matured."

"Still," Eleanor said, "it is impossible not to notice that the city has
become a grim place where there used to be such gaiety and life."

"The war has terrible consequences, something we women would have
predicted perhaps, had we been running things back then."

Eleanor smiled. "That is a truth that perhaps history will record as
tragic."

"The war and the influenza," Alma said, shaking her head. "The toll has been unimaginable. I hear that Dr. Freud has lost his daughter." Eleanor nodded. "Herr Mahler and I experienced that, you know. I think he never recovered. His heart was broken. You can hear it in his music."

"My husband and I nearly lost our elder daughter," Eleanor offered. "She was at death's door with the flu. My husband nearly lost both of us."

"I am so sorry," Alma said. "I did not know."

"It ended well. We both recovered."

Alma looked distracted and distant for just a moment, her beautiful face locked in an instant in a frown. "I am glad for you. And for your husband. You know that we lost Klimt, Schiele, and Kokoschka. Two to sickness, and one to war."

"Oskar Kokoschka?" Eleanor said. "I did not know."

"Yes, on the Russian front. With Arnauld, I lost a dear friend, with Kokoschka, a lover." It all seemed surprisingly easy for her to say.

"I am sorry to hear it. Kokoschka's was a great talent. How exactly did it happen?"

"At the front. He was a cavalry officer, a very passionate and dashing one, you can imagine. In a way it was a relief. I don't think he would have reacted well to my marrying Walter."

Eleanor's breath was taken away a bit by the ease with which her summary erupted and altered the mood of their exchange.

"That sounds cold, doesn't it?" Alma said.

"I know that after a time one becomes inured."

"Inured," she repeated, reflecting, "I suppose that is so."

"Arnauld would say that he loved you."

"And I him. That is not cold."

There was a pause, then Eleanor spoke suddenly. "I believe that Arnauld is not dead," she said. "That is why I have come to Vienna."

Alma looked startled. "Oh my," she said, surprised. "What on earth prompts you to think that?"

"I just know."

"Enough to travel here from Boston," Alma said. "And at a great deal of inconvenience and risk, I should think."

"Yes, *inconvenience and risk*. I just believe he is not dead."

"That would be something, would it not?"

"Something?"

"If they all came back, all the men we have neatly put away in their graves. Just a curious thought, I guess," she said almost wistfully, then snapped back. "I am sorry, I didn't mean to be perverse. Tell me, how on earth did you decide Arnauld is still alive? You have come so far."

"I just have a strong intuition. There was so much confusion and I think he became swept up in it and is still alive out there somewhere."

Alma looked more amused than perplexed. "Lost men coming back . . ." Again, she gave the idea some thought. "That adds a level of complexity."

Eleanor smiled. "I think that is a more complex thought for you than for me."

And this time Alma laughed, accepting the remark with a good-natured and respectful irony. "Imagine if all of them showed up in this room together."

That made Eleanor laugh. Alma suddenly became serious. "I cannot share your optimism, I fear. I have heard too many grim details. But of course, I will do anything I can to assist you."

"Of course, I too have heard the grim details, but I will press on with my search. I have indeed come a great distance, and inconvenienced my family. I could not rest comfortably back in Boston with what I suspected."

Alma was suddenly caught in a reverie: "With so much loss, it is difficult to concentrate on just one. I do miss dear Arnauld terribly. He was my oldest and dearest friend, you know."

"I know that."

"And you have just visited his parents?"

"I have."

"I am curious. Was there any mention of the circumstances of his birth?"

Suddenly in new and unexplored territory, Eleanor gave no indication of the startling contents of the letter she had just received in the box from Arnauld's mother. "What do you know of that?" she said.

"Just a lingering curiosity," Alma said. "I do not know any details, and I never approached Arnauld regarding them. In fact, the subject never arose. When we were very young, our parents were good friends, as you know, fellow artists from the old days, and Arnauld and I spent a good deal of time together. He was always very delicate and proper, and you know how Arnauld always carried himself with an air."

"You don't mean haughty," Eleanor said.

"Oh, no, quite the opposite. Even when he was little, there was an air of shy elegance about his bearing. One that I found very appealing, even then. Father alluded a number of times to some mystery of his birth, his being adopted, and that gave my childish imagination enough evidence to imagine that he and I were royal twins separated at birth from our parents, the king and queen, and raised separately by commoners. But unfortunately Father died before I was old enough to ask anything significant."

Eleanor remained noncommittal. "It will remain a mystery," she said.

"I just wondered," she said. "And I thought that his death might have stirred up something."

Then she paused and without the slightest warning looked squarely at young Standish and just stared for a long moment as if suddenly seeing it all. "And your arrival with your son. To find him, the lost prince." She looked up at Eleanor. "That is why you have brought your son all this way with you, is it not?"

Eleanor simply gazed quietly at Arnauld's oldest childhood friend, this now-famous woman of the world, and nodded ever so slightly.

"His son," Alma said, then repeated with barely more than a breath, "Arnauld's son."

47

TRIESTE

s soon as Eleanor realized that they would have to venture into the war zone, she knew she would have to leave Standish behind, a turn she had not really thought through when she decided to bring him on her journey. Eleanor had felt comfortable leaving young Standish in the company of Fräulein Tatlock as she went about her business in Vienna. The old Viennese loved the company of the child, but for a long absence, the demands would be different. Part of her regretted the impulse to bring him, even though there had been ample reasons to introduce him early to a city which she knew with prescience would later play an important role in his life.

Eleanor waited to make a decision. There was a great new energy in the Pension Tatlock. The infusion of fresh meat and vegetables and the well-prepared table had brought new guests, and all of them had included Eleanor's young son in their dining ritual.

"I have made many new friends," the boy insisted with enthusiasm.

At first, Eleanor had thought of taking him with her, but Fräulein Tatlock interceded. "Where you are traveling," the genial old Viennese landlady said with great concern when she was alone with Eleanor, "it is not safe." From the look on her face, Eleanor knew that she meant it was not safe for anyone, certainly not a headstrong young woman from Boston traveling more or less on her own. But sensing that there was not much she could do about the former, she added, "It is not safe for a young boy."

"You need not worry about my traveling," Eleanor replied to her host's

admonition. "I will have Herr Jodl at my side always. He is very resource-
ful, and very protective." Fräulein Tatlock had come to know Herr Jodl
from his numerous visits for dinner, and a mutual respect had grown between the two, Eleanor noticed with pleasure.

Eleanor explained it all to Standish, leaving him with a long embrace
and a cheery word about how he would be well cared for, an idea the boy
absorbed without alarm.

"We will visit the zoo," Fräulein Tatlock said with a smile.

"We will visit the zoo," he repeated matter-of-factly. "And then every
building."

"Young Standish and I will have a grand time in your absence," she
said in front of the boy. "There is still much of the city to see, and there
are many tasks around the pension that need attention."

"I am going to help Fräulein Tatlock fix things," Standish added help-
fully, and nodded his agreement. "There is much to do," he said with a
tone that over the next trying days made her smile. Young Standish Burden was sounding very much like his mother.

➔

If leaving Zurich and Dr. Jung had felt like the first leg of an adventure,
leaving the relative comfort of Vienna now felt like approaching the
threshold to a netherworld. They would take the train from the Südbahn-
hof south, in the direction of Trieste. "We do not know what we will
find," Jodl said. "Border issues are very uncertain, and the trains are erratic." He shrugged with a sort of resignation. "But we will persevere.
Because you have the rarity of an American passport, we will attract much
attention but should be able to navigate uneventfully. Where we are going, there is much resentment of Austrians." Eleanor did not know him
well enough yet to deflect his seriousness with the good-natured observation that in the presence of a lady from Boston he would be well protected.

They sat across from each other in the compartment that would have
been designated first class in the days before the war, when travelers had
need for such isolation and comfort and before the glass in the door became cracked and the long gash had appeared in one of the backrests. The
passage through the Alpine terrain was long, grim, and indeed uncertain,
and the descent to the coastal plain, like the descent into the uncertainty
Jung had predicted, brought with it a more bleak landscape and more

ragged collection of humanity. Railroads that had been totally taken over by the demands of the war were now suddenly abandoned to what few resources remained. The war had disrupted the rails, and now in the chaos of armistice and defeat, service was sporadic. Trains stood empty in boarded-up stations. Jodl sat stiffly in his place, aware of his position as interpreter and guide, but also as protector, the role that remained implicit only, but obvious always in his bearing.

"You will be a woman traveling friendless in a world like nothing you have seen before," Jung had said with concern the evening before her departure.

"Most everyone on the trains will be soldiers trying to get home," Herr Jodl said, "those fortunate enough to find passage." Most of the soldiers from the empire, those not rounded up as prisoners of the Italians, were left to find their way on their own. "But we are heading into the war zone," Jodl said, "not away from it. The railway stations will be crowded, but with those trying to find their way back from war."

Herr Jodl's first value as a companion came with his handling the irregularity of the train schedules. The train they were riding on would suddenly stop and leave them at a small station. Jodl would begin negotiating immediately and without fail would suddenly find another train for another section of the journey, in what seemed a chaotic business, so unlike Austrian trains of the past. His further value soon became apparent in the security he provided. Always, he let Eleanor pass before him, and always he brought up the rear. Her appearance as a woman traveling alone caused attention, but as soon as anyone approached in anything like a threatening manner, Jodl would step forward with his most severe countenance, and the threat would evaporate.

Once, he had gone to inquire within the stationmaster's office and had left Eleanor alone on the platform. A group of soldiers, "provincial ruffians," Jodl concluded later, approached and began pointing toward her, smiling and speaking in a guttural language completely unfamiliar to her. One of their number staggered further forward than the others, gesturing with his thumb and fingers and calling back to his friends, who seemed to be encouraging him. Eleanor made no eye contact and tried to calm her racing heart. The aggressive one was obviously addressing her, and his friends were obviously encouraging him further. Suddenly, just as he seemed about to reach out to her, her companion stepped out of the station door and with a few quick strides was beside her. Realizing the significance of the former police officer's presence, all stepped back save the one, the most brazen and drunken of the group.

At the first insult from the one obstinate soldier, a reference perhaps to the retired policeman wanting the pretty lady only for himself, Jodl said something in what Eleanor thought was the same Slavic language. The drunken man did not back away. "Why don't you share your bounty?" was a sanitized version of what followed from the soldier, she learned later.

"Step back and retire," Jodl snapped, and the man, heeding nothing of the warning in her protector's German, took a fateful step forward, not back. Suddenly, with an alarming quickness his hand shot out and the retired policeman struck the young offender in the abdomen. As he doubled over with a sharp groan, the others began to step forward to protest, then, seeing the steely look in the attacker's eyes, they thought better of it, pulled on their incapacitated friend, and retreated with hardly a word spoken.

Stunned by the abruptness of his action, Eleanor stared at her companion, about to voice an objection at the use of violence, then reconsidered, realizing in that moment that it was not she and her old-world civility that held sway here, but rather a whole new set of rules. They had entered a world the likes of which she had never experienced, a stark new world in which this retired policeman from Vienna displayed a startlingly sound command. Her new companion seemed to know exactly what he was doing.

"Thank you," she said very simply, collecting herself.

"There will be a train for Trieste within the hour," was all he said, then added, "I trust we shall have no more of *that*."

The ancient Adriatic city of Trieste had an unnatural stillness about it as Eleanor and Jodl walked out into the street from the train station. Not long before the Austro-Hungarian Empire's only seaport, Trieste now found its harbor virtually empty of ships. "This is difficult to imagine," Jodl said. "This, the great port of the empire, has lost its hinterland," he added.

There were few goods being shipped in or out. The proud jewel of a grand empire for five hundred years, Trieste now found itself under new ownership, only weeks before claimed by the Italians. The citizens of Trieste had stood around in confusion when a cruiser from the Italian navy arrived and announced that the port had been liberated. "Liberated from whom?" was the question on nearly everyone's mind. Now, because the occupying Italians already had a thriving Adriatic port in Venice, the once-vibrant docksides sat idle, and the people walked the empty streets more in shock than with any sense of liberation.

"What is most ironic," Jodl said, "is that this city that became the cause of all the fighting bears no sign of the war."

Their immediate business was to find a way to get to the Isonzo River only thirty or so kilometers to the west. It took them most of a morning of searching to come upon a Slovenian truck driver with an automobile in good working order who was willing to drive them, and even he showed little interest until he saw the American dollars. The car was one abandoned by the Austrians, he explained. "Petrol is the problem," he said pointing to the bills, "but those will help."

He delivered them to Monfalcone, the point at which the Isonzo River flows into the Adriatic. "Much death on this river," the driver said in broken German as they stood at its bank. "The Italians wanted to possess it, and the Austrians wanted to keep it. Over there just a few kilometers distant, a horrible stalemate. To what use?" He made a gesture of exasperation with his upturned hands. "Three years, twelve battles, and one million souls lost. To what use?"

"There is no spot on the Isonzo not ruined by the shells," Jodl had said, a fact he knew from his countless prisoner interviews. The closer they got to the river, the more they saw the effects of war, and the more even the hardened Jodl became silent. He shook his head and explained that he had known the area well in his younger years. "I grew up thinking this one of the most beautiful of places, 'the greenest spot on earth,' my father called it. We came here on vacations when I was a boy. My wife and I were here on our honeymoon." He recalled that the Isonzo had been called the Green Beauty for its famous turquoise color as it flowed down from the Alps into the farmlands of the Friuli plain.

It seemed even more ironic to both of them that the land around Trieste, the main reason for the struggle, remained untouched, but now, only a few kilometers away from this seaside city all the way up into the Alps, they were entering the periphery of the devastation. They walked through Monfalcone, the street still mostly abandoned, the buildings pockmarked by the occasional bullet and shrapnel. They stopped one of the passersby, an old man with no teeth, and asked for the first address on Freud's list. The man and Jodl spoke briefly, and the retired policeman nodded with comprehension as the passerby pointed out the direction. Then he thanked him, and they walked away.

"I did not understand one word of that," Eleanor said.

The serious Jodl smiled. "In this region there are many dialects, the meeting point of Teutonic, Slavic, and Latin, the three great cultures: German, Russian, Roman. People in one village sometimes do not understand the language of a neighboring village. It has been this way for centuries."

"Did you understand where we need to go?"

Again Jodl smiled. "What is there to not understand in pointing?"

They walked in the direction the toothless man had indicated, and found an old stone church that had only recently been returned from its temporary manifestation as an infirmary to its peacetime use, although some of the pews were still out of place, and the whole building still carried the telltale smell of iodine. The priest they found in the chancel told them that all patients who survived had either been sent home, "the lucky ones," he said, or moved to a collection further inland, another makeshift facility, a palazzo closer to the fighting.

"Are there other hospitals?" Eleanor asked him.

"A number," he said, "further up the valley, but I think that they too have been abandoned. The region tries to recover." He told them of specific locations, adding that he did not know which ones still held patients.

"The woman is an American," Jodl explained, as if to signal neutrality. "She searches for a friend, an Austrian officer, lost during Caporetto."

"He could be anywhere," the priest said, with a tired look on his face, shaking his head but not questioning the oddity of the travelers. And as they thanked him and turned to leave, he added, "The palazzo at Gorizia, madam. That is your main hope. That is the repository of lost souls." And then he added, "From all sides."

48

GORIZIA

orizia, Görz in its Slavic iteration, the main city on the Isonzo, lay twenty kilometers north of the Adriatic coast. Eleanor recalled that Arnauld had called the area "the Nice of Austria," where Viennese aristocrats spent summers enjoying its warm climate and streets lined with stately mansions and rose gardens. The palazzo, in the old medieval town center, had been requisitioned as a hospital from the first months of the fighting. The family who had owned it going back to the fourteenth century had possessed a number of estates in the region, and so they had moved out into the country, but Contessa Carolina maintained a residence in the vast urban structure and continued to run things before and after the hospital's heavy use before the Battle of Caporetto, at which time the Austrians had taken over control of the region.

With its ancient claim to property, the contessa's family had loyalties on all sides of the conflict, and it was known that many of the patients, especially the badly wounded ones, were both Italian and Austro-Hungarian. "At this stage of desperation," the contessa said, "it doesn't really matter which side one fought on." Then she added ruefully, "It seems that both sides have forgotten them."

The palazzo had been intended originally as a temporary center, requisitioned by the Austrians for their wounded before they were shipped home, but when the Italians overran the city during the sixth battle of the Isonzo, the family's loyalty shifted supposedly to the Italians. The stream of wounded seemed to acknowledge even then no such loyalty, although some now expected to be treated as prisoners of war. With the armistice and the ensuing chaos of troop movements and the uncertainty of borders, the hospital space had been turned into an undiscriminating limbo. "People know to bring the wounded here. Soldiers who had only months before been fighting each other hand to hand, overrunning trenches, facing each other's withering machine-gun fire and hated barbed wire, now lie side by side," Contessa Carolina had explained.

Now that the armistice had been reached, the area would be taken over by the Italians, which seemed to make no difference at the palazzo. She greeted Eleanor and her Viennese friend with a warm politeness, obvious in her pleasure in seeing an American. "I have been to New York many times," she said. And she listened with concern and interest as Eleanor told her their mission, she too not questioning what affair of the heart would bring an obviously well-bred lady all the way from Boston searching for an officer from Vienna.

"We have many badly wounded boys," she said before turning them over to the nurse administrator. "Here and in places like this, you might find the lost man you are looking for."

When they had arrived at the palazzo, the driver had gone off on foot to seek out information about gasoline. There was a great commotion outside. A crew of men, all speaking some unique local dialect that sounded like both German and Italian, some in military uniform and some in workmen's clothes, were conversing intermittently with the hospital staff. It appeared that an unexploded artillery shell that had been partially exposed near the hospital, in the palazzo's garden area, was finally being dealt with. "We have known it was there for a long time, since the barraging of the city," the admitting nurse explained to them. "They will either dismantle it or detonate it on the spot, bury it completely, then set it off. It should not interfere with our day, but they wanted us to be alerted." Then she added for reassurance, "They know what they are doing. There is, unfortunately in this region, much opportunity for such experience."

The nurse ushered them to the first room of patients. "I trust that you are prepared," she said with a grimace.

Eleanor nodded. "We have already seen much," she said, and followed the nurse, with Jodl behind her.

In spite of her preparation, Eleanor had no way to anticipate what was to follow. The palazzo was a large sprawling structure with a spacious walled garden in back, and all the rooms on two floors had been converted to hospital space, including a large living room, a ballroom, and a vaulted chapel on the ground floor. The space once too small to hold all the wounded who came through was now more sparsely filled, they were told, the beds now in neat manageable rows. "All the remaining patients are those too ill to move or those whose identity had not been established," the contessa had told them. "The abandoned ones."

"There are so many of them," Eleanor whispered to Jodl as they entered the first room. "I thought there would be fewer." Jodl only nodded.

"You will hear some groaning, some muttering indistinguishable syllables," the admitting nurse who had taken over their tour said, "but most of them, you will see, are silent."

"Why have they not been shipped home?" Eleanor asked.

"These are the unnamed and unknown, the hopeless cases," Jodl said as they entered. "I have heard about these. They are the detritus, too badly wounded to travel, even if they did remember where home is. You have to remember the numbers," he said. "In even one of the battles of the Isonzo, there were tens of thousands of casualties. Just imagine trying to clean up and restore order."

"I fear that we have been forgotten," the nurse who showed them into the main room said, echoing the common theme. "There is too much disorder. We were already full and then came the Battle of Vittorio Veneto." A look of utter exasperation came onto her face. "Chaos," she said. "Wounded soldiers making their way home, overcome by infection and delirium, unable to take care of themselves. They are brought here. Some die, some linger on."

In a separate room, there were men who seemed physically intact, but who for one reason or another could not speak in such a way as to identify themselves, the "disturbeds," they were called. There were a few dozen of them, some sitting, some wandering around the room, all of them aimless, some mumbling. They looked unkempt, ill shorn, staring blankly, all of them victims of the carnage they had been drawn into unwarily and unable to get back out of, and certainly unable to describe what it was that pushed them over the edge. "The army doesn't know how to handle such cases," Jung had warned Eleanor in a rare dark moment. "Their society doesn't know how to handle them. They are the seriously disoriented, damaged by the horror they have seen and done, most of them beyond repair, some without a single wound on their bodies, some missing limbs, testimony to the horror and the folly of war. They will serve as reminders for generations, out on the streets begging for coins, but very few will heed the message, certainly not the commanders and the politicians who were responsible for sending them into the nightmare to begin with. They are the shadow men."

The religious nurses, doctors, and priests at the palazzo, understaffed and undersupplied from the start, had done the best they could to sort out and calm the patients, a daunting task. "We keep hoping for relief," the admitting nurse said, grim-faced. "In the beginning we looked to the Austrians for our supplies, then to the Italians. Now, who knows where to look. And occasionally someone does come, some messenger from Vienna or Rome. But then more bodies arrive too, coming from both sides, with these." She gestured to the beds in front of her. "Contessa Carolina's family has been most helpful. They have provided the place."

At first, fresh from battle, the nurse explained as they walked from room to room, the wounds had been life threatening because of loss of blood or the compromise of bodily functions, but now, the battles long over, the healthy troops sorted out and shipped home, the main challenges, along with the hopeless task of identification, were those of infection and the complications of amputation and surgery. Throughout the vast infirmary space, as would be the case in all the hospitals they were to visit, there were the strong medicinal smells vying with the stench of urine, rotting flesh, and death.

Eleanor and Jodl had been greeted positively, as if these two visitors from the upper world, dressed as they were in clean fresh clothing, would somehow contribute to the relief the staff prayed for. "She searches for her Austrian brother, an officer," Jodl said, to simplify matters, adding, "She is very determined," as Eleanor passed out of earshot.

"I am afraid that here we are very far past distinguishing between officers and the conscripts," the nurse said. "Very far past any such distinctions," she added, casting a sympathetic eye toward Eleanor.

They were told upon arrival, as they would be at each such hospital, that the casualties had been high, staggering in number actually, too much for the system to handle, and that the suffering and death had mostly gone unnoticed and uncelebrated by the vanquished military of any country. Many of the patients were abandoned and nameless, hopelessly unable to find their way home. The task was impossible, the patients unrecognizable.

Countless boys had died with no one knowing where they were or where they belonged, "unknown soldiers," they would be called later, each one representing a soul dear to someone back home, someone who would perhaps never know the fate of the young man full of promise who had left for war months, maybe years before, maybe even with a sense of adventure. "Some of these are deemed too ill to move," one Sister of Mercy said to them, "but most are the great unknowns. No one knows where to move them. No one cares anymore for which side they were fighting."

As they moved among the beds, surrounded by the suppressed moans of the wounded and dying, Jodl allowed Eleanor to walk in the lead, following behind her at a respectful distance. They both knew her task, to approach each soldier and make what she could of eye contact, to search each contorted face and to leave no face unexamined. Occasionally, when she would come to a face so completely bandaged that it made recognition impossible, she would ask for a name.

Each young man would react to her, some appealing for help, some in a form of anger, some just grateful for the receipt of a warm maternal smile. As she approached one young man sitting on the edge of his bed, he tried in vain to rise on his one good leg. "Oh please, do not rise," Eleanor said.

The nurse said something to him, and held out her hand. The soldier responded by sitting back down.

"He does not wish for anyone to see him like this," she said to Eleanor. "He says he used to play football."

"And I am sure you were quite good at it," Eleanor said. "I hope you will soon be going home." The nurse translated for her.

"He has no home," the nurse said. "He wishes for no one to think ill of him."

"Please tell him that I am sure he has loved ones who are awaiting his return," she said.

"I wish that were true," the nurse said on her own without translating as they walked away from the bed. "I intend no offense, madam. But such thoughts are from a world very far from this one."

"I know it is true," Eleanor said with conviction. "I know he will be going home again." And she turned and left the soldier sitting as he had been on the bed.

"It is heartbreaking," she whispered to Jodl. Her companion did not speak. He looked back at the boy on the bed, and perhaps thought of his two sons.

They moved on to the next room, a spacious one, the grand salon of the palazzo, in which the windows were stained glass. With great purpose, Eleanor walked up to each patient, looked into each face, searching for some strand of recognition, some hope that the blank stare or anguished brow or expectant returned gaze might have the slightest resemblance to the face she so longed to see. When she came to a missing limb or a heavily bandaged upper torso or face, she passed on quickly, remembering Freud's ironclad logic: Arnauld would emerge, if he emerged, without any physical signs of his desperate plight. And yet, with each new soldier, young or old, no matter how wounded, she began with hope before passing on in disappointment, only to come upon another face and another resurgence of hope.

At one moment in the first minutes, she would falter, obviously overcome and light-headed. At those crucial moments Jodl would simply step forward without sound or ceremony and support her arm, holding her firmly until the moment passed and she could continue. In those instances, as if following a predesigned choreography, she would turn and look him in the eye, signaling wordlessly her ability to continue.

As they reached the far end of the room, a sudden and loud explosion shook the windows, and they could hear the sound of breaking glass, and then a deathly silence. Everything in the palazzo hospital stopped. "The bomb squad," the nurse said, laying a firm grip on Eleanor's arm, for a moment reassuring even herself, unable to hide her concern, this woman who had seen so much in the past two years. Then she pulled herself back to calm control. "This is not good." She looked around at her patients, who had flown into wildness, and then she rushed to the window. "Oh, no," she said with despair, and hurried out of the room.

The explosion had caused an immediate eruption of moans and cries from the wounded, startling the two visitors. Men who had been sitting quietly on their beds or in nearby chairs were now on their feet, dashing about, most of them with looks of wild agitation on their faces. An older nun and a male assistant had entered the room in haste and were grasping at patients, trying to restore order. "We apologize," the older nun said to the visitors, barely pausing beside them as she rushed past. "It will take time to regain our calm."

When they reached the room of the "disturbeds," it was clear that the explosion had created more than a little turmoil, and some of the patients had run about, a few even fleeing the room.

"This is exactly what these poor souls do not need," another nurse said, as she rushed past.

"These especially do not wish to hear explosions," Jodl said, pulling Eleanor away. "And the raining of the shrapnel," he added with concern. "Once you have heard the sound, you never forget it."

Then, calm restored, Eleanor stepped forward to continue, having done what she could to calm even her own panic. She walked slowly up to a few stationary patients, the ones who had returned to their places, and made eye contact, smiling at each with motherly concern, examining each face, exchanging a word or two. But obviously their visit was ruined.

As always, Jodl stood silently behind her, at the ready to step forward if there appeared the least sign of need or threat. "These are not the best conditions for your task," he said as she turned from the last patient. "I am not certain it is wise to continue."

"It is as good as can be expected," Eleanor said, now visibly pale and shaken. "And I think we have seen enough."

As they were leaving the palazzo, in the last room there was great commotion. One of the wounded men from the garden had been brought inside and transferred to one of the beds near the door they would pass through. There was a flurry of activity. One tall thin doctor and two nurses were huddled over him, working feverishly, trying to stop the bleeding. To leave, they could not help walking close to the bed.

From what Eleanor and Jodl could see at their distance, the man's arm was gone along with much of his shoulder and fragments hung off the edge of the bed, and his face was bloody and much of one side torn away. His one good eye was open, frozen in terror. One of the nurses was leaning close to the distorted face, speaking words of encouragement to him as the others worked. None of the group looked up as the two guests passed through the room into the hall leading to the reception area.

The nurse who had been on duty when they arrived spotted them and left the side of the injured man, rushing toward them. She had blood spotting the front of her white uniform.

"This has been terrible for your visit," she said. "The war continues its destruction."

"We did not wish to be in the way," Eleanor said, even more pale, obviously disappointed in herself but also obviously in a hurry to get outside.

"I hope you saw what you needed to see."

"We did, and we thank you," Eleanor said quickly.

"Do you know of another such hospital?" Jodl would always ask, and Eleanor and her companion would take careful note of the responses, always leaving with another destination in mind.

"Arnauld is not here," she said quickly as they departed, with a fateful certainty.

Then, when they had passed out of sight of the hospital staff, Eleanor stopped and leaned over, pulling her long skirt out of the way, and retched violently. Showing not a trace of surprise, Jodl stood as if at attention beside her and reached out a hand to her arm until she had finished and signaled with a nod that she was ready to continue. They moved on to the waiting auto.

49

GONE TO UDINE

hey were directed to the large Franciscan monastery only a few kilometers to the north, out away from the destruction of the city, where the imposing mountain range rose sharply beyond the valley, beyond the piles of rubble and the treeless plain and the river, still clear and aquamarine. "It has been heavily damaged by shelling," their driver said as they approached the ancient monastery, "but it still serves as a hospital, I believe."

They drove up a winding road to the large tile-roofed structure. It was sprawling and comprised a number of separate buildings, one of which was nearly demolished.

A number of brown-robed monks were walking around the front of the largest part of the complex of buildings, and one greeted them as they moved away from the automobile. "We are looking for a missing soldier," Jodl said after they had introduced themselves, "an Austrian officer."

"The hospital has moved," the monk said. "We used to have quite an operation here, but it has been moved to Udine."

"Would the wounded from Caporetto have been here?" Eleanor asked.

The monk paused to think. "Yes," he said, "we had many wounded from last October, especially the badly wounded."

"Austrians?" Jodl asked.

"Austrians, of course, and Czechs and Romanians and Hungarians, and then later Italians. And many of those who could not identify themselves and could not be identified. There was much confusion, especially among the severely wounded, those who needed surgery especially. We were supposed to treat the Italians as prisoners, but no one paid much attention to that."

"And there were many of those unidentified?" Eleanor asked.

The monk looked at his two guests as if they were from another world. "Oh my, yes." He stopped and examined the American woman before him. "There were twelve battles here, thousands and thousands of dead and dying. This damage was done in the sixth of those battles, the Battle of Gorizia, it has been called." Then he paused and looked around. "Now it is so peaceful," he said, gesturing to the large monastery building and its now-quiet surroundings. "It is difficult to recall the horror. God's peace has returned."

"And what of the wounded?"

"Little by little, they were shipped elsewhere, those who survived. Some were fortunate and were transported home by train. Some to Udine."

"To Udine?" Jodl said. "You will direct us?"

"Yes, signor, there is a large hospital near the command headquarters. I believe it is still open and still holds many wounded, especially the severely wounded."

That first night, the travelers found a hotel that Contessa Carolina had mentioned being not far from the edge of the city. "Their restaurant still has a well-stocked larder, I am told," she said, "a rarity in these times."

They were happy for a place to stay with a bed and a meal, arriving late in the evening as would become their pattern, too tired and weary to enjoy a glass of wine and informal conversation. Jodl would escort Eleanor to her room, leave her with a word of encouragement and a commitment to awaken her at dawn, which was rarely necessary as Eleanor, having slept lightly, was usually up and dressed before he knocked on her door. "You must get rest," Jodl would say to her each night, always with a look of concern. "Tomorrow will bring better luck."

The day following the journey between hospitals the two companions pressed on, neither Eleanor nor Jodl admitting that their hope could be faltering. During the days, they would spend much time together, and Jodl would explain the conditions. "This is a near-impossible task," he said to her. "This whole area was ravaged by war, and everyone with any sanity moved out. When the Italians occupied territory, they suspected many of the local people of being spies, and there were many arrests, often for no offense at all. Many people suspected of disloyalty have been deported to concentration camps in Italy." There was an unmistakable bitterness in his voice. "For little more than a drunken public statement that Italy might lose the war. The Italians do not trust anyone Slavic, and they use the term loosely."

The whole length of the Isonzo River was the scene of most of the fighting on what was called the Italian front, the battles in the area having raged for nearly the full duration of the war, from 1915, when the Italians entered on the side of the Allies, to the present armistice. Evidence of the enormous toll was everywhere in razed buildings and land now barren of foliage, no trees, no shrubs, no undergrowth.

"The war is over," one town official said in Italian. "Because both sides have lost their will to fight. This town was Austrian. Our young men were conscripted to fight and die for the empire, shipped far from here to fight the Russians in Galicia. Few came back. Few of those came back healthy or unmaimed."

It had been policy in the Austro-Hungarian army for centuries to ship recruits far from their homelands, to areas where theirs was not the native language, to discourage fraternization and desertion. "But the Austrians have lost," he said with no form of joy, "and now we are to be Italian again." He stopped and gave a rueful smile. "Such is fate. Everyone here is too weary to care." Very few of the towns and villages along the river remained untouched or intact. Some of them were destroyed, their important buildings razed by artillery shells from both sides. What had been beautiful, wooded rolling hills were now open treeless, barren land, filled with craters and exposed rock that looked more like the surface of the moon than the former bucolic countryside.

They had a plan. They would follow the course of the retreating Italian army from the mountain town of Caporetto, high in an Alpine valley, down through the mountains to the city of Udine, where the Italian command had been established for three years. They would travel all the way to the Piave River, north of Venice, where the Italian army had formed a line of defense they had held for twelve months, from the previous October until the end of the war a year later. It was from this westerly position that the Italians launched their face-saving attack in the last days just before the armistice, when the Austrian army was in disarray and they were able to round up their three hundred thousand prisoners of war. "The Austrians had stopped fighting, their empire dissolved," Jodl said caustically. "The Italians, suddenly very brave, swept through them and declared victory." On the first night of their journey into Friuli, Eleanor and Jodl stayed in a small town outside Udine.

From Caporetto on the upper Isonzo River, they tried to locate the spot where Arnauld had been assembling prisoners and had been hit by artillery fire. As Jodl had learned from his eyewitness reports, the incident had occurred at a railhead, so if prisoners were taken in the attack from Caporetto, the nearest railway depot was back near Gorizia. Prisoners would have been marched there and put on trains or forced to continue marching to the prison camps in Austria. But first they would be rounded up near the battlefield, and it was there that the shells would still be flying, from both sides. "It would have been anywhere out there," Jodl said as they stood at the side of the road, pointing down into the open plains leading to the flat land of Friuli.

◥

On the way to Udine, they located the site of a second hospital on Freud's list, forty kilometers up the mountains, smaller, less populated than those in Gorizia, in a converted parish hall of an old church, and the third hospital was no more than a large open room in what had been a town hall; once again it had been filled with bodies, in all states of disability and disorientation, always the disoriented being almost as numerous as the wounded and dying. "Everything has moved to Udine," they heard again.

So on they went, and they found the permanent hospital in Udine, an old Roman city important in the region for millennia. Before Caporetto, Udine had become the seat of the Italian high command. "The Italians called this city their *capitale della guerra.*" Jodl said, "Their war capital. After the retreat to the Piave, over a year ago, it was occupied by Austrians until after the Battle of Vittorio Veneto just past, when the noble and brave Italians—I believe they say now—took it over again." The hospital there had been solidified by the Austrians all last year, he observed, pulling together the various field hospitals in the area.

By now they knew what to expect. The men lay or sat up in beds in big open spaces with that unmistakable rank odor, some seemingly unmarked by their injuries, many of them heavily bandaged, some so heavily that they were completely unrecognizable.

Eleanor and her companion were greeted by a nurse who seemed to be the chief administrator, and as before she was impressed and immediately cooperative when she realized that Eleanor was an American looking for an officer. This nurse told a familiar story, with a certain irony. "We were Italian," she said, "then we were Austrian. Now we are Italian again. As a result, we have a collection of war's unfortunates." And, as before, she explained that it really made no difference which side the poor souls had been wounded by. "Some here were wounded by their own artillery. Some merely collapsed trying to get themselves home."

"Are some from the Battle of Caporetto?" Eleanor asked.

"Way back then, yes," the nurse said. "And some from just now."

"Are some unnamed?" Eleanor then asked.

"Oh my, yes," the nurse said. "We try to keep track, but as you can imagine, there is much confusion."

She led them through the first large hall, allowing Eleanor to walk into the heart of the room, understanding from the beginning her purpose. "These are the worst injuries," the nurse said with a tired voice. "They are barely alive and perhaps will never recover."

As had become her habit, Eleanor approached each bed, examined every face. If the patient looked at her and made eye contact, she offered a cheery greeting and then offered a "Please get well soon" as she departed and moved on to the next bed.

And then, as before, there were some with little damage at all, but vacant and distant looks on their faces and little apparent ability to acknowledge the nurses in any way. "These disoriented ones," a nurse said to Eleanor, "will end up in the asylums. There seems little hope for them."

After Eleanor had moved past each and every bed, her Viennese companion close behind her, she turned to the nurse administrator and said, "The man I am looking for is not here."

"I am very sorry, signora," the nurse offered. "We have many visitors, and all of them leave as you are now leaving. I wish you Godspeed in the rest of your journey. May you find your friend. Yours is a difficult and emotionally demanding task."

"As is yours," Eleanor said. "I hope all of our loved ones, and these poor souls, find themselves home soon."

"That does not seem likely," the nurse said in what was probably a rare moment's weakness. "But we shall see."

"We shall see," Eleanor repeated.

On the way out to the car, she stopped suddenly and turned to Jodl, allowing in an instant the deep disappointment to overcome her. "He is not there," she said, the full weight of despair in her voice. "I was so hoping."

Jodl, aware along with Eleanor that this one hospital because of its size and location had held the promise of success, offered special condolence. "I am sorry, Frau Burden. I too was hoping."

"Could he be one of those ghastly lifeless faces?" she said in despair.

"I do not think so, Frau Burden," her partner said, trying to be helpful. "I think you will know."

Eleanor stood motionless, allowing herself to feel, her shoulders bowed as if by a great weight. Then she pulled herself upright and said, "It is just a setback," and strode off toward the car and the waiting driver with her loyal companion in tow. "We still have much to do," she said.

50

A ROUGH BUNCH

hroughout their travels, they passed through scruffy-looking bands of war's human detritus. "These men are stragglers, far from home, left to find their way on their own," he said.

"One has to sympathize," Eleanor said. "They are abandoned, much like modern vagabonds, with no way to get home."

In medieval Europe, she knew, when a peasant army was taken to a foreign land, they were encouraged to live off the land, and in the end, even if their effort brought victory, the king would not provide transportation home, leaving the peasant force to fend for itself and find its return passage as it could, often leaving behind bands of vagabonds living off the land and creating havoc for the local population. In that regard, things had not changed much in five hundred years, it seemed.

"I would not be too sympathetic," Jodl said coldly. "They are a rough bunch. I am not sure they are even trying to get home." But accustomed now to the watchful companionship of the retired policeman and preoccupied by their task, she gave little thought to her personal safety.

They had found a hotel in the center of town that the owner had kept open, in spite of the loss of the back wall of the building, a gaping hole in the bricks, crudely boarded up. The owner, a seedy-looking Italian who walked with a limp, with one eye, in only slightly better shape than his building. He showed no enthusiasm when the pair of guests walked in, but his face lit up when he saw the American dollars, and he was unctuous in showing them two undamaged rooms.

"These will be safe," he said. "My wife will cook you dinner, if you wish."

Eleanor nodded approval. "That would be very generous of her," she said, not wanting to offend the man but from the looks of him and his submissive wife not entirely eager to accept. Jodl nodded only slightly. Weary beyond words, the two travelers would have found moving out to a restaurant difficult, even if they could have found one.

She and Jodl sat for a long time after a dinner of actually quite edible cabbage and sausage and drank the good cheap wine of the region. After the meal, they both seemed content to sit in silence.

"All this must make you think of your sons," Eleanor said after a time.

Jodl looked wistful for a long moment. "Oh, yes, they are never far from my mind." The former policeman was silent, as if finished, but Eleanor said nothing, sensing that her reserved partner might continue. "Ivan, the youngest, went first. Like his brother, he was eager to join the army. He had no idea what he would see. That was in Galicia, against the Russian guns. He wrote a few letters home and described some of the ordeal, but I am sure he kept most of it to himself, sparing his mother. It is hard to describe what one sees at the front, always horrifying. Then an explosion in his area." The stolid retired policeman paused again, tears now coming for the first time. "He was young and naïve. Theodore, his older brother, was more the cynic," he said. "Theodore got swept up in the fury at the beginning; they all did. We all did. But unlike our young Ivan he lived through most of it. He was a cagey soldier. We saw him back home twice, when his mother was dying. He seemed to have grown in years. I think he was hardened and a good fighter. He got all the way to the Piave River, just a few months ago. There was a letter. Then no word. I am glad that his mother did not live to be in this uncertainty. The not knowing is worse in some ways than the sudden jolt of knowing, as we had with our younger son. In the end, we heard, there was much chaos and much retribution. Many died and many were taken prisoners. There were some executions, we heard." He took a deep breath and let go a sigh, one of the few signs of emotion she had seen from him. "I hope my son is among the living," he said finally, "among the prisoners. The Italians have hundreds of thousands of prisoners, you know. Perhaps we will never know the fates of all of them. The Italians are arrogant and resentful, in no mood to cooperate."

Eleanor nodded, not wanting to stop the flow from this man who rarely said more than a few words. "You have lost much," she said. "Too much."

"None of us knew," he said quickly, as if more would open up wounds he did not wish opened.

"I will speak for Frau Jodl," Eleanor said, not wanting to appear too sentimental. "She would want you to retain hope. Your Theodore is with those prisoners. You will see him again."

"As you will see Herr Esterhazy again." There was a kind of weary determination in this first affirmation from Jodl, one dogged combatant talking to another, as if raw determination and action could overcome the obvious hopelessness. It was the first time he had mentioned Arnauld by name. "I do not even know your connection to him," he said.

"I met him in Vienna twenty years ago. We wrote letters over the years, and then he came to Boston to teach at my husband's school. He has been a guest in our home many times, and he is dear to me and to my children."

"But why all this?" Jodl, the expert at questioning, could not help asking. "Why this search?"

"He is close to my family and to me. I know he cannot be dead," she said, making it clear that this was as far as she would go. "It is as simple as that."

"And you are a very determined woman."

She looked down then, and Jodl did not press further, giving no indication in his poker face if to the former police investigator the answer was even close to satisfactory.

Throughout her entire descent into the chaos of the war-torn areas following the path of the retreating Italian army away from the Isonzo River, looking for Arnauld preoccupied her, and at night finding a soft place to lie down was on her mind and then being bone tired caused her to fall off to sleep as soon as she could. *I must get rest*, she thought every night upon lying down. *We must be sharp and attentive for the job ahead.*

That night in the small room of the ruined hotel she had removed her clothes and fallen off to sleep in her undergarments, as always, with the thoughts of her daughters back on Acorn Street with Rose and their father, and young Standish, safe back in Vienna with Fräulein Tatlock.

She did not hear a door open, and the first impression she had was of a rough hand tearing at her and being yanked out of sleep; another rough hand covered her mouth so she had to fight for breath. Terror seized her immediately, rendering her unable to move or to think. She could see almost nothing but could smell the acrid breath and feel the hand brutally at her breasts, grabbing and grasping. She froze at first, then kicked with her legs, but the attacker's full weight was on her, and the sounds were not formal language but guttural animal outbursts. She did what she could to protect herself, but she knew immediately with a kind of horrible clarity what was going to happen. Thoughts of her children leapt into her mind. *You must survive,* a voice within her said, *you must do what is necessary and survive.* With all her strength, she hit at the hand on her mouth, and it slid away so that she could gasp for breath. She kicked and punched, but the weight of the body and the strength of the grip were too much for her. Always, the acrid smell of breath in her nostrils.

In her panic, she thought to lie still, perfectly still, but a stronger impulse told her to keep struggling. The hand now tore at her waistband and grabbed between her legs, and she waited, frozen, self-preservation telling her to struggle with all her might. The other hand was tearing at her clothing, and she was powerless to stop it. *Stay alive!* she screamed to herself. *Stay alive!*

Then as abruptly as the attack began everything stopped. The weight on her shifted, then froze; the guttural gasping changed to something like choking. The weight was off her suddenly and there was a terrible explosion and the sickening thud of the body hitting the floor. Then for a moment nothing.

Everything whirled about her. "It is over," an unearthly voice rasped in the confusion. "You are safe now." And then the dragging of boots across the floor and out the door into the hall, from which a dim light now illuminated the room, and dead silence.

She sat up for a moment, gasping for breath, straining to see in the darkened room, her heart racing, and then she lay back, quieted and still, her undergarments torn and in disarray. *No blood,* she thought. *Nothing broken, no harm.* She pulled the covers up over herself and didn't move. She could hear her heart racing, and for a moment she thought she might explode from it. Then the door pushed fully open again and then clicked closed and she heard the reassuring voice again. "You are safe now, Frau Burden," the disembodied voice repeated. It was Jodl.

"Thank you," she said weakly.

"I should never have left you," she heard, and the sound of a chair being dragged close to her bed. "Sleep, and we will need to leave at dawn. I will be here." She heard him settle into the chair beside her bed. And try as she would, tired beyond description, aware now of her protector beside her, she was unable to fall back into sleep. She lay awake until the first light of dawn.

"We must be gone," she heard beside her, and he left her alone to dress. She rose quickly and dressed to leave. She could see the chair where Jodl had settled and got what sleep he could.

With perfect timing, he reentered the room. "Let me know how I can help," he said.

Leaving the room, she released an involuntary shudder as she saw the splattering of blood on the wall and a dark streak where the body had been dragged out the door.

"I shall not leave you alone again, Frau Burden," Jodl said. "That was my error." And for the next few nights, Jodl slept beside her bed, upright in a chair, she always too tired and too grateful to object.

"It is all right, Herr Jodl," she said on the eve of the third night. "I feel quite able to sleep alone." Her protector said nothing, only nodded. "I feel quite safe," she added, and then paused and looked into his face until his eyes met hers. "And extremely grateful."

51

THE UNIVERSAL LANGUAGE

hat day they had moved further along the path to the Piave. They would be traveling from Caporetto in the mountains down past Udine to the plains and on to the Piave River, where the retreating Italian army had made its stand for almost a year until the armistice.

They had known that they would lose their driver in Udine, and they had spent much of the afternoon after the hospital visit looking for another car and driver. They found another automobile left from the pool of abandoned Austrian equipment. This time the driver was a young man named Paolo who looked barely over eighteen. He walked with a pronounced limp that explained at least in part how he had escaped being swept up in the war. Eventually, in the middle of their first day together, he explained that he was from Udine and had, like so many young men from the former empire, been conscripted. "I wanted to be a writer," he said. "I read a lot." He was sent to the eastern front in 1914, a year before the Italians invaded, where in the first days against the Russians a shell fragment had nearly torn off his leg. "I was the lucky one," he said. "The corporal beside me received his share of that shell in the neck. I nearly bled to death, then nearly died of the infection, but that was on the train ride back from that awful front. I had to limp home," he added, remarkably free from bitterness. "On my own. No one seemed to notice when I took possession of this automobile when the Austrians left." He pointed to the dangling wires beneath the dashboard he now used in place of a key to activate the ignition.

"You certainly deserve it," Eleanor said, "after what you went through."

"I fought for the Austrians," he said. "Somehow the Italians think that disloyal. They suspect me of being Slovene."

"It does not seem to get in your way," the former policeman said curtly, and their new driver only flashed him a devilish grin.

The young would-be driver agreed to accompany them as far as they needed, all the way to the Piave, to whatever they found there. "Gasoline will be a problem," he said, and then thought. "But I suppose you heard that from the other driver."

Jodl nodded. "We were able to help with that," he said, patting the briefcase that remained firmly in his grip.

There had been no fighting in the area west of the Isonzo and north of Venice, but two huge armies, one in retreat and the other in pursuit, had passed through, consuming with the passage everything in their path and wake. There were no crops, no livestock, no poultry, nothing to sustain life. Most of the civilians had evacuated when the Italians swept through in 1915 and now, slowly, the common folk worked their way back. But everywhere was poverty and deprivation. There was no food and no medical attention except for that procured by the armies, and even the armies had been unable to feed and care for their retreating soldiers.

Now, with the armies of both sides disbanded and civilians staggering back to their barren homes, the whole area was sad and depressed. Eleanor and Jodl passed through, finding what they needed, depending on the ingenuity of young Paolo and the supply of dollars to procure the necessities.

The night before their move westward, they inquired about hospitals and followed two unproductive leads, to an abandoned school and an abandoned church, both of which had once served the dying and wounded. Finally, they were told by an old priest that they should move away toward Venice. "We shall press on," Eleanor had said with conviction, never pausing to ask herself just how long she was willing to stay with the depressing task. "We shall press on until we have looked into every face. But tonight we will rest."

They found a run-down café and a grocer on the same block. "Let me try," Paolo said. "We will need that," he said, pointing to Jodl's briefcase and encouraging him to follow.

They entered the store with its meager supply of canned goods. Jodl had extracted some bills and held them in his hand. "Can you find meat?" Paolo asked the portly grocer behind the counter, who eyed the bills.

"Perhaps," he said.

"And vegetables?"

"There are some," the grocer replied. "Everything is used up. But I know a source."

"And paprika?" Jodl said, offering one of the bills.

The grocer, reaching out to take the offering, turned and opened a large cupboard and from deep inside he pulled out a small jar of red powder and beamed at his customer.

Both Jodl and Paolo beamed back. "And you and your wife will join us for dinner next door?" Paolo said. The grocer smiled and nodded.

"You can bring others," Jodl said.

The café owner cooked up a goulash, enough to share with a scattered collection of townspeople, and found some bread and wine.

"Have you noticed?" Jodl said. "They are too tired to see that I am one of the hated Austrians."

"And I a suspected Slovene," the young man added.

Never had simple food tasted so good, both of them agreed. And neither seemed to mind the extreme starkness of the setting. The room was a makeshift barroom, reconstructed with scraps of paneling and molding from what had once been a quaint and inviting café. Four kerosene lanterns provided the only light, giving the space a distinct odor that reminded Eleanor of evenings at Putnam Camp in the Adirondacks. "You will have to pardon our surroundings," the innkeeper said. He was a humble man of Slavic descent. He introduced himself as Herr Schmidt, deferring to the Austrian that had been the language of government his whole lifetime. "We have not had a chance, or the means, to rebuild. You are welcome to what food we have." He seemed to have no interest in money.

"This is perfect for us," Eleanor said with a contented smile.

After the meal, Jodl disappeared and came back with a satisfied grin on his face. "I have a surprise," he said, pulling out from behind his back two well-worn musical instruments: a beat-up violin and a small concertina-size accordion, scarred but in playing condition. "I have found something for you," he said. Then he moved over behind the bar and pulled out an equally well-worn cello and a bow. "It is missing a string, but you can make do."

"Where on earth did you find those?" Eleanor said.

"Frau Schmidt has quite a collection," he said. "I wish to hear you play."

"Oh my," she said, surprised and deeply touched. "You have been talking with Fräulein Tatlock. She remembers me from many years ago. I am very rusty."

"And you?" Jodl turned to the youthful Paolo, who had watched Frau Schmidt lay a number of assorted musical instruments on a nearby table. He looked at the motley collection and picked up a stringed instrument that looked like a Russian balalaika and plucked at a pair of strings, frowned, then immediately set to tuning.

"From many years ago," Jodl said, drawing the concertina out to its full expansion and pushing it closed with a deep groaning sound. "I too am rusty."

Eleanor ran the bow across the strings and began the simple strains of a melody Jodl followed with rough notes. "You know this?" she said.

" 'Plaisir d'Amour,' " he said with a satisfied smile. "It is a universal language."

Herr Schmidt came to attention and walked to a back room. He reappeared with two old violin cases and laid them on the bar. "There was much music here before the war," he said.

Two patrons stepped forward and opened the cases and suddenly their simple melody was joined by the two violins, and they played through one whole rendition of the song and began it over again. Another patron joined them, this time with a clarinet, another with one of the violins. Before long there were ten instruments, all playing the familiar "Plaisir d'Amour," gently and beautifully. They came to an ending, and the group fell silent, each player smiling softly, remembering other times, peaceful times. Jodl and Paolo, both with instruments in hand, smiled at each other, then at Eleanor, who had been the one to signal the final bars. She had lowered her bow and looked around at the ragtag group and the rugged, beat-up collection of instruments. She nodded silently and smiled back at her two companions.

Then she picked up the bow and began playing a melody from her long-ago past, from her time in Vienna twenty years before, from another improvised group. "It is from Haydn," she said.

Since the melody was unknown to the other players, but with vaguely familiar classical origins, they waited, listening to the deep rich strains of the cello. And then one by one the musicians found enough familiar to latch on to that soon the ragtag dream orchestra was playing together the song that more than half a century later in 1975 would be played before a hushed crowd in a football stadium in California and would become the most famous song of a decade. On and on the makeshift orchestra went, and they played until all the players, Eleanor leading and Jodl and his accordion right behind, all found tears running down their cheeks. Each witness, like the players, was lost in the rapture of the perfect harmony, each transported to an earlier, happier time.

It was, Eleanor told Jodl later, one of the most sublime moments of her life. "And of mine," the retired policeman said.

52

THE TROUBLE BEGINS

he trouble began almost the very moment they crossed the Piave River near Treviso. They had been asked for their papers when they crossed, and although a few remarks had been made sotto voce, they were allowed to pass, and at least one young soldier wished them well. At the Piave River border, the place where only weeks ago the Italians had made their desperate stand, Jodl exerted his forceful presence. They encountered a definite change of mood. This was Italy and resentment of Jodl and suspicion of Eleanor were obvious. "We are going to have a difficult time here," the retired policeman said. "The American woman is searching for her brother," he said through an interpreter, and the border guard nodded that he had seen a number of civilians passing through on similar quests. "He is among the 'disturbeds,' she fears."

The guard acknowledged that there had been Americans mixed with the Italians coming through on the medical trains. "It has been madness," he said. "There are even Austrians. No one seems to care; the hopeless are the hopeless."

Jodl gave him some American bills.

"Good fortune to you, Signora American," he said to Eleanor, as he let them pass.

But as they were sitting at a bus stop trying to work out directions, a group of four uniformed men approached, and Eleanor could see from Jodl's expression that this was to be the trouble he expected. Jodl had told her to be prepared. "These Italians were greatly humiliated by the retreat from Caporetto," he said. "And in the last days, when the Austrians were in disarray, they attacked and claimed a great victory. There is now much chaos in their ranks, and much face-saving. You can expect a mixed greeting, as you are traveling with one of the hated enemy." Then, as an afterthought, he offered rather unconvincingly, "But we should be safe."

The men were different from what they had seen before, dressed in new brownish uniforms unlike the threadbare look they were accustomed to. "This is the new Italy," Jodl said under his breath as they approached. "The trouble begins."

The leader of the group walked up to Jodl as if he were looking for him specifically. "Papers," he said curtly in Italian, snapping his fingers with impatience. Jodl handed him his passport, and the officer barely looked at it before handing it to a short, rat-faced man beside him. "Military?" he said abruptly.

"I am Viennese," Jodl said, hoping that the clarification would mean something. "I am a policeman," he added. "Retired."

The rat-faced man handed the passport back to the thin officer. "Deserter," they heard him say barely loud enough to be heard.

"I am not military," Jodl said, stiffening.

The thin officer stared at him for a long moment and then looked back at the passport, holding it up as if weighing its authenticity. "We get many deserters," he said with a snide smile. "You will have to pardon us if we are a little suspicious."

Jodl did not flinch. He looked directly at the rat-faced interrogator, who looked down, but the officer only stared back. "There were many deserters," he said, "from your ranks."

"As there were from yours," Jodl said, in a momentary and uncharacteristic lack of discretion, this staunch man who seemed to judge human nature so well.

The officer looked them both over until the smaller man had a chance to collect himself. "Many cowards on your side," he snarled. "Not much to crow about." He looked at Paolo, the young driver, for a long moment. "You, the Slovene," he said slowly, and Paolo showed no expression. "I suggest that you take your contraband automobile and depart at once."

Paolo looked at Jodl, who stood grim-faced, then he looked at Eleanor. She was doing her best to appear unmoved, but her eyes betrayed fear and concern.

"I am sorry, signora," the young man said, looking into her eyes, hoping for some kind of reprieve.

"It is all right, Paolo," Eleanor said. "You have served us bravely and well. Now you must go."

Paolo nodded his gratitude, then backed away slowly, still looking at her. "It has been an honor serving you."

"You have done so very well," she said. He turned and walked quickly to his contraband automobile, his limp more pronounced than ever before. No one seemed to notice as he grabbed the protruding wires and started it up. All attention was back to the Viennese as the car drove away.

The rat-faced officer gave a silent signal with his hand and the two other soldiers stepped forward, and each grabbed one of Jodl's arms. Jodl reacted with a stiffness that Eleanor had seen before, and she watched in fearful anticipation as she remembered the hand that had shot out at the drunken man at the train station only days before. But Jodl did not budge.

"Are you arresting me?" he said.

At first, the officer said nothing, only looked him over again. Then he said, "We cannot have enemy residue wandering freely through our country as spies, can we?"

"We are not spies," Eleanor said, her first words in the encounter. Jodl tried to silence her with the movement of a hand, but it was too late. The rat-faced officer spun around to face the affront and glared as if surprised to hear a woman speak. "I am an American," she continued, "and I am searching for my brother who was lost in battle, on *your* side. This man is my assistant and interpreter."

The officer looked at her coldly. "We are not arresting you," he said as if issuing a warning.

"This man is not military," she had the audacity to say. "He is not your enemy."

Now the rat-faced officer held up his hand to silence the impudence and signaled to the men, who tightened their grip. Again, Jodl did not move but stiffened further.

"Wait," he said suddenly, and he held out the indispensable briefcase. "This is the lady's," he said. "It contains her personal effects."

The officer said, "Well, we shall have to have a look," and he reached for the briefcase, the briefcase that held the American dollars, the lifeline. Time seemed to stop in that moment. Eleanor stood frozen.

Jodl's fist was tight on the briefcase handle. "Her personal effects," he said distinctly. "Personal feminine effects." Again, everything stood still. And with that the officer stared at the briefcase for a long moment. Everything froze. Then he pulled back his hand and gestured to allow the transfer from Jodl's hand to Eleanor's.

"The American lady will have to be escorted safely to Venice," Jodl said with an authority that certainly did not come from his current position as a very compromised prisoner, and the officer said nothing. They led Jodl away to a waiting automobile, and one of the soldiers stayed beside Eleanor as she watched the door close and then the automobile drive slowly away.

A new sense of peril seized her in that moment. Ever since leaving Trieste they had become aware of the martial law that seemed to sweep up soldiers and stragglers at random and try them and execute them on the spot, even now since the armistice. "What one does not wish to be in this hellish countryside," Jodl had said to her grimly back in Udine, "is a military prisoner."

Who these supposed officers were and where they were taking this man she had grown to depend on so was now totally uncertain. She collected herself enough to speak. "I need help getting to Venice," she said, obviously trying to be strong.

The soldier beside her looked her over with a salacious smirk. "We shall see," he said in a way that did nothing to diminish her feeling of vulnerability.

I must get to Venice, she thought, and raised herself to her full height, allowing as little of her feelings of desperation as possible to show. "I am an American," she said suddenly with an assertiveness borrowed from her brave companion who had now disappeared. "Are you the one who will help me, or do I need to find someone else?"

Everything froze again. The officer, startled again no doubt to hear such authority from one in her position, stared for a moment. Neither Eleanor nor the officer breathed.

"You are right, madam," he said suddenly, and then snapped an order at an enlisted man standing some distance away. "Corporal, bring the automobile, and see that this American lady gets what she wants."

The corporal rushed away and soon an Italian automobile had driven up and she was ushered into the backseat. "This should serve you," the officer said, "and you will tell the driver to take you to the train station. The trains will take you where it is you need to go." Her feeling of immense relief could barely suppress the companion feeling that she was abandoning Franz Jodl.

∾

Considering all she had to worry about, she gave little thought to being a woman traveling alone. At the train station in Venice, a porter told her that a gondolier would take her to a hotel for a tip. "In Venice," the cheery man said, "you can find anything for a tip."

And so she found herself out of harm's way, in a gondola on the Grand Canal in Venice, probably the most romantic location in the world, on her way to a tourist hotel, an irony not lost on her in her dire situation. *Just imagine that you are Henry James*, she told herself, and she formed a plan.

After she had been delivered to a small hotel and had parted company with the soldiers, she did her best to settle in and take care of her disheveled appearance. With her companion's life in the balance, she could hardly enjoy the essential short but very warm bath or the thought that she now found herself in one of the world's most beautiful cities.

She stood at the window for a moment, transfixed by the vista of narrow streets, canals, and in the distance a piazza she had read of in novels and heard described by countless visitors.

She did what she could to clean and press her dress and to straighten her hair, to regain at least some proximity to a woman in charge. She knew she had to act quickly if she was to save Jodl, who might already have met a terrible fate. Then she asked to be shown the American-owned Bank of Italy, the largest bank in Venice, and was granted an appointment with an official, a well-dressed Italian man with what she thought was the proper arrogance. "Can you cable New York City?" she asked.

"Of course, madam," he said, heartily making clear his surprise that she even needed to ask.

"I must send this message." And she handed the man the words she had carefully written out on a piece of bank stationery.

"Are you sure of this address?" the man asked suspiciously, as if her careful handwriting was not completely clear and legible. "And the addressee?"

"I am certain," Eleanor said, nodding, without apology, as if her position and request were a natural part of the clear crisp Venice morning. "That is correct. He is a personal friend," she said to add a note of authenticity. And the banker looked her over for an instant, not certain that he believed her or that he would proceed. Then he turned and disappeared into a spacious side room.

The New York cable was to the most powerful man in America, son of the most powerful man in the world, Mr. John Pierpont Morgan Jr.

53

A VERY WELL-PLACED
NEPHEW

t was late afternoon when she received the message at her hotel.

She had spent the day by herself in her room, uncertain what to do, sure that at least for the time being waiting for word from New York was the only course of action available to her. If nothing came within twenty-four hours, she would try something different, but exactly what that would be she had no idea. How, in these moments of anxious waiting, she felt the split in her personality, the logical and systematic thinking of Dr. Freud and the innovative and spontaneous impulses of her friend Jung, caught between the two, always wondering how each would handle the situation, always wishing for their great skill of detached objectivity, always aware of her weaknesses of being overly anxious and connected.

Twice during her long wait, aware of the extraordinary setting in which she found herself, she went out for a walk, once along the Grand Canal and once into the Piazza San Marco and into the basilica, which in other circumstances would have been for her a source of awe and wonder. There in the darkened space, surrounded by candles lit by penitent Venetians, she sat alone on a cold wooden pew, trying to assuage the feelings of helplessness. In that moment in the cavernous basilica of San Marco in one of the most beautiful and historic cities in the world, she prayed that her mission would end successfully and soon, that she would rescue Herr Jodl from his predicament, find Arnauld in one of the Italian hospitals, and return home speedily to Boston and her family.

Always in her past, when in the presence of such symbols and rituals of European Catholicism, she felt a kind of deep envy of that simple connection to religion that the candles and iconic images of saints and the Virgin represented. Now she admitted to a desire to submit to it all and allow the Virgin and the saints to intercede for her. How simple and affirming that would be, an end to the independence and inner strength that had been her blessing and the weight she carried all these years.

She thought of her children, the girls on Acorn Street and Standish safe with Fräulein Tatlock. So many times while on this journey, far from home, she dreamed of them. She worried about them, but she also carried deep within her the confidence that each of the three of them had developed internal strengths that would get them through this ordeal of separation from their mother. But now, in this ancient and sacred space, she allowed the image of them—Susan the scientist, Jane the poet, Standish the mythic athlete and hero of countless games—to come to her, and in a welcome reversal to comfort her, children comforting mother. She closed her eyes, and in the flickering light of the votive candles she savored each image, they and the woman in white of so many of her dreams. *Oh, Mother, you are well!* she heard Susan exclaim to her as they emerged from the dark night of the dreaded influenza. *We have survived after all*, she heard herself respond. And she was able, as her friend Jung recommended, to hold the image of that joyous scene for a long moment before opening her eyes and rising and walking back to her hotel for more of the interminable wait.

She asked at the hotel desk if there had been any messages during her absence, then returned to her room and waited. When the word finally came, she hurried through narrow streets to the address she had been given back near the Piazza San Marco, on the Grand Canal.

After a short wait beside a secretary in the reception area, she was ushered into the large wood-paneled room of the American consul, who greeted her with a broad welcoming smile. William Hardy was a lean, fit American with prematurely gray hair. He shook her hand vigorously with an obviously studied and firm grip. "I am glad to see you, Mrs. Burden. You will have to pardon the tentativeness of our office. We have just arrived, obviously."

"I am relieved to find your office open, Mr. Hardy," she said.

"We can be of service, Mrs. Burden, I hear."

"I am so glad you could see me," she said with the greatest relief.

"There is someone who can be of great help to you," he said, and ushered her into an adjoining room where a handsome young Italian in his twenties awaited, unlike the type of Italian soldier she had grown accustomed to in the past few days. His uniform was tailored and neatly pressed, something new in her experience in Italy, and he smelled of fine cologne.

"Lieutenant Sonino here will be assigned to you. We have a car and a driver waiting outside Venice. Lieutenant Sonino has the full authorization to give you all you need." The Italian smiled. "Come with me," William Hardy said, and led her into his office.

The American diplomat folded his hands on his spacious desk. "Your mission has the fullest cooperation of the Italian military. You know Mr. Morgan, I gather." He paused. "Personally."

"His father was a personal friend," Eleanor said without pause or further explanation, allowing any inference that could be drawn.

"Well, that friendship will be of great service now. Italy is in great disarray, and Lieutenant Sonino is very well placed."

The young man joined them. He had the polished look of aristocracy about him. He nodded his complete agreement when the American described his full cooperation. Eleanor smiled her gratitude at the American diplomat and then the lieutenant.

"You are on a mission to find a missing officer, I hear," he said, "an Austrian." He paused and looked down at the paperwork in his hand. "And your colleague has been taken into custody." He was not very successful in suppressing a frown. "A compounding of the problem, for sure."

"Yes," Eleanor said. "My companion is a retired Viennese policeman who is helping me in my quest. He was taken prisoner by a group of soldiers near Treviso yesterday. It was a dreadful mistake."

Eleanor proceeded with a complete description of her crossing the border with Herr Jodl and their encounter with the Italian military, including the actions of the rat-faced officer. "I was sent on to Venice," she said in conclusion. "I am very concerned about the fate of my colleague."

"We will find him," the lieutenant said. "You need not worry. You have the full weight of the Italian government behind you." Even though there was something very glib about the handsome lieutenant, there was reassurance in his brash confidence. Where Eleanor saw disorder and chaos out there, the self-confident Lieutenant Sonino saw a new purpose and meaning.

Lieutenant Sonino shook the American's hand and smiled graciously in his good-bye. "I must make a few telephone calls on your behalf," he said, taking his exit.

"The lieutenant has connections," Mr. Hardy said when they were alone, "the nephew of a famous general. He represents the new Italy." The last of the comment carried weight. "And if I might add a bit of a warning," he said, "there will be no talk of defeat or humiliation of the Italian troops. The war effort has been one of great purpose, and a united Italy has emerged stronger from the experience." The American diplomat looked at Eleanor for long enough to see that she understood.

"I understand," she said. "I have been in Italy long enough to know how to behave."

"I was not suggesting that you did not," he said. "I am only being cautious, perhaps overly so."

"And I appreciate that," she said.

"You are in good and safe hands," he added.

"As long as everyone remembers that it is the new Italy," Eleanor said, smiling.

"Exactly," the diplomat said. "You do understand."

The smartly tailored lieutenant rejoined them. "I believe that I have found your Austrian policeman," he said with a smile.

❧

When they had left Venice and were alone in the car, the young lieutenant inquired further about Eleanor's mission. "The man you seek is named Esterhazy. Is that true?"

"Yes," Eleanor said. "Arnauld Esterhazy."

"His is an old family. Hungarian nobility, I believe. In former times he would have been a guest of state in our country. Now you seek him in the most humble of hospital wards. Such is the irony of war."

The driver took them back toward the river Piave outside Treviso, to the small military station Lieutenant Sonino had been able to locate from the details Eleanor had related. When they walked in, she found the atmosphere completely different. The motley collection of officers who had been rude and disrespectful before now stood at attention and addressed

Lieutenant Sonino with efficiency and officiousness, with many a "Yes, sir" and "Yes, Signor Lieutenant." The rat-faced officer had converted his manner to one of total unctuousness.

It took no time for the crudely organized band to locate their prisoner, with the young lieutenant watching unsympathetically the whole time, tapping impatiently on the countertop of the small office. Suddenly a door swung open and there was Jodl, standing beside two of the men who had taken him away with so little respect just one day previous.

"Here is your man," said the rat-faced officer Eleanor knew well from her previous experience, and Lieutenant Sonino said nothing but merely looked over at Eleanor to see her silent approval.

Eleanor was so glad to see her companion, alive and unmarked by abuse, that she stepped forward quickly and suppressed an urge to embrace him. She burst out, "Yes. Yes, this is Herr Jodl."

Jodl, for his part, retained his stiff rectitude but could not suppress a smile. "I think you came just in time," he said to her in a whisper. And then he turned to the young lieutenant. "I am very glad for your arrival," he said. "There was a mistake in identity. These gentlemen are convinced that I am a spy."

Lieutenant Sonino said nothing but extended his hand and gave Jodl's a vigorous shake. "I am pleased to be of service," he said finally.

Then after the lieutenant had signed a few papers, Jodl said, "Now we have our Esterhazy to find," and the trio walked out into the sunlight.

On the way to the auto, when they were alone, Jodl released a loud sigh. "Things did not look good," he said. "I had become convinced that they were preparing an execution. Then everything changed. They started racing around."

"I came as quickly as I could."

"How did you find this Lieutenant Sonino?"

"I prevailed on Mr. J. P. Morgan Jr. in New York." Jodl nodded. "This Lieutenant Sonino is the new Italy, you know," she said quietly so that only he could hear, and Jodl nodded his understanding.

"So I gather."

"We shall be hearing much about the glorious Italian victory and the glorious liberation of the territories," she added.

Jodl nodded again. "The glorious liberation," he said without any audible irony. She nodded, and they walked on to the auto.

54

THE CONFESSION

irst, we visit the Scuola Grande of San Marco. It is the Austrian hospital," the confident young lieutenant said.

The beautiful old building in the heart of Venice was built at the height of the Renaissance, its façade a masterwork with delicately decorated detail in white or polychrome marble. "You would never guess such a magnificent structure to be a hospital," he said. "Almost exclusively the enemy," he added, "a great irony of war."

Perhaps because of its urban setting, the Scuola Grande was cleaner and newer than the military hospitals they had seen before. Sonino waited outside as Eleanor and Jodl entered and were escorted around by a nurse. The party made pleasant conversation as they passed from bed to bed, chatting informally with the patients from time to time, always in German. When they came to the last bed, Eleanor thanked the nurse and the pair walked outside to meet the lieutenant.

"You have not found what you were looking for?" he said as they approached.

"It is a small hospital and very well ordered, but the wounded are all from the past few months, all accounted for by name." And she led as they walked away. "Not what we are looking for."

Later, when they had left Venice and found their car, Eleanor spoke. "There are prisoners of war," she said to the lieutenant, once they were back driving again. "Will we be visiting their wounded?" She was asking for Jodl.

"If that is your wish," he said, "my assignment is to see that you get it."

"It is my wish," she said.

"Yes. We will go there first. I understand what you search for," the young lieutenant said. "There are three places for us to look into. We will drive you there."

They were heading back to the northwest of Venice to the large military hospital at Treviso in the region of the Piave River, where the last horrific battles had been fought.

As they were accustomed to seeing, there were beds of the severely wounded, and then a special room for those without physical wounds, the ones unable to identify themselves. They wandered through, walking up to each bed, looking into each face, smiling warmly, offering a word of comfort, reaching out a hand when appropriate, receiving the attention they were used to. Jodl could see the mechanical way Eleanor had applied herself to the task, missing no patient, no matter how maimed or pathetic, but also resigned to the impossible assignment she had been given by fate. "Do not give up hope," he had said to her. "You must keep his rescue in front of you always." But his words had little effect. Facts were facts. They both seemed to know that they were running out of possibilities.

They were leaving the Treviso hospital on the grounds, having passed through the endless rows of beds, without success. "This last wing is for officers," the lieutenant said, "the ones with family connections. I doubt that you would find your misplaced Austrian here."

"With such confusion on all sides," Eleanor said, "we desire to look everywhere."

They walked through this last room, a less crowded room than the others, the patients more severely wounded, but receiving more personalized care. "These are all Italian men," the guiding nurse said.

"Nonetheless," Eleanor said, "we will look at all of them."

Jodl and Sonino no longer eyed each other, simply went about their duties with grim-faced determination. Any disappointment they both experienced in the biggest of hospitals, this one well within the boundaries of Italy, they kept to themselves.

"We are ready to move on to the next location," Eleanor said.

The Italian nurses, of higher training perhaps than their counterparts in the villages, had done their best to keep the rooms clean, but their task too was near impossible. In spite of the best intentions and the liberal use of disinfectant, the whole place smelled of feces, urine, and despair. They had become accustomed to the task but also to refraining from evaluating the situation at each departure. But Jodl could sense now, as they passed the last cot and stared into the last haggard face, that it was over. They had passed into the last row and looked into the eyes of the last patient. Eleanor looked at Jodl and sighed deeply. "He is not here," she said with finality.

Lieutenant Sonino, following some distance behind them, always alert and looking fresh, shook his head. "I am sorry, Signora Burden," he said in one of his only moments of humility.

"And this is your last suggestion?" she said.

"I am afraid so. The other hospitals are near Rome, very far to the south, and they have received no patients from the Caporetto debacle or directly after." When to accept? When to object? There was, she knew, no science to it. Dr. Freud had advised looking for the unusual: "Do not forget the counterintuitive," he had said. But this time the observation seemed undeniable. No wounded from Arnauld's time had been shipped south to Rome. They were looking too far from the war zone where the explosion had happened.

Eleanor said nothing but turned with her head down and walked past Jodl without a word and out toward the entrance of the hospital. At the door, the nurse who had received them offered her consolation. "I am sorry, signora. We have many visitors who come looking and nearly always they leave without any news. I fear there have been many souls lost in this war."

Eleanor reached out her hand and laid it on the nurse's arm, as if she were the one bereaved. "I know," she said softly. "I know that you have seen much misery."

As they walked away and Jodl saw the look of resignation on Eleanor's face, he approached her. "Might we have a word in private, Frau Burden?" he said.

At a good remove from the others, out of earshot, Jodl stopped, and she noticed immediately the severe look on his face, something she had not seen before from one with whom she had shared so much. "I have something to tell you," he said solemnly.

"Please," she said, unable to imagine that any words of consolation could help in this moment.

"I was not honest," he began slowly. "I thought it would do no harm since the situation was dire anyway, but when I wrote my report, I did not tell all I knew. My apology now is abject."

"Go on," she said, suddenly looking puzzled.

"When I interviewed the witnesses of the carnage of Herr Esterhazy's end there was not the agreement that I represented."

"Go on," she said cautiously.

"They all agreed that the shell had exploded nearly on top of the group of prisoners and Austrian officers, but their descriptions differed. One was certain that the decapitated man was Herr Esterhazy, but one said it was the young Czech officer, and the third said it was an Italian prisoner." The words hung in the small space between them, and neither spoke. "There was not the decisiveness I reported."

At first, Eleanor could not speak. "But why, Franz?" she said finally.

"I was bitter, Frau Burden. I had lost my sons. I wanted some kind of balance to things. So I made up the report and turned an ambiguity into a certainty." He had his head down. "I am deeply sorry."

Eleanor said nothing. She could not speak. The look she gave Herr Jodl was more questioning than angry, but then it softened and she looked into his downcast face. She reached out and touched his arm. "It is all right, Herr Jodl. I understand." And still stony and now resolute, she turned and walked away toward where Lieutenant Sonino waited by the automobile.

She walked in silence, the two men following. She opened the door by herself, not waiting for the Italian lieutenant. She let herself in and sat in silence while the two men found their seats. When all four of them—Eleanor, Jodl, the Italian lieutenant, and the driver—were in their places, and before Lieutenant Sonino, who had turned in his seat, could ask his "Where to now, Signora Burden?" she looked up, as if passing from deep reflection into determination.

"I wish to return to Gorizia," she said.

55

"WE HAVE COME TO THE LAST"

hey drove through the night, the passengers sleeping as they could. It was eight in the morning when they pulled up in front of the ancient palazzo where Eleanor and Jodl had been the morning that the bomb-disposal crew had made their miscalculation with the unexploded Austrian artillery shell. She stepped out of the car, and as usual Herr Jodl followed. "This is where he must be," she said, expectation in her voice. "This is our last hope." And her companion said nothing, only followed grim-faced, aware along with her that they had reached the end of the line.

As they walked in, the reception nurse on duty recognized them. "We have returned for a second look," Eleanor said with a friendly assertion.

The nurse, who like her counterpart in Piave had seen many fruitless visits and had learned to withhold her opinion, said, "Of course," and rose to usher them into the center of the hospital.

Lieutenant Sonino waited behind in the reception area as Eleanor and Jodl walked into the first large room of patients, the room where just days ago they had seen the man who had been torn apart by an artillery shell. They walked past the beds and remembered some of the most severely wounded from their first visit. But true to their original mission, Eleanor walked up to each former soldier and made the most intense of eye contact, and Jodl walked beside her, offering the taciturn support to which they both had become fully accustomed.

When they came to the large room that held the most desperate of the cases, she did not flinch or look away, and Jodl did not leave her side. Both of them were aware of how orderly the room was now after the mayhem of the morning of the bomb explosion. They approached each forlorn case, performed their function, and then walked on. When they finished with the last, Eleanor gave her companion a final resigned nod, and they turned to leave the room and perhaps the final group of disturbeds.

"He is not here," she said with a finality that her partner had not heard before.

"I am sorry, Frau Burden," Jodl said.

They had visited scores of hospitals, it seemed, looked into hundreds, maybe thousands, of faces. Now there was a finality to their return to Gorizia, a sad culmination. With her eyes alone, Eleanor said to Herr Jodl, "This is the end. We have come to the last." For perhaps the first time in their long journey, there was bitter resignation in her voice. "It is over."

As they approached the door of the large room, a young woman in a novitiate's habit, who had seemed to appear from nowhere, called out to them. "Signora, signor, wait please."

They turned and found her pointing into the center of the grim space they had just left. At the far end of the room, standing in a corner they had just recently walked past, stood one neglected patient, gaunt and harrow-eyed, one without a trace of physical injury, now raising his hand toward them. A loud moan came from his twisted lips and filled the room. He was staring after them, his arm raised, as if he had seen a vision.

"He is one who hides, signora," the novitiate said, her voice almost in panic. "He does not wish to be seen."

Eleanor took a few tentative steps toward the pointing man. He appeared a ghostly figure, a man older than the others, with matted hair, deep-set and hollow eyes, a haggard face. He opened his mouth to speak, but only a deep mournful and guttural moan escaped, and the hollow eyes stared at her. She came across the room to him, and for a long moment the two just stared at each other.

He spoke the words now with unmistakable clarity: "Bay-ah-tree-chay." The beloved Beatrice.

"It is what the Italian boys say," the novitiate said. "There are many reports of this."

Eleanor Burden stared into the ghostlike face for a long moment, then turned suddenly to the retired Viennese policeman who had moved up to her side. Eleanor released a sigh from the depth of her being. She spoke in a barely audible whisper. "Our search is over," she said. "This is Arnauld Esterhazy."

56

REBORN

rom there the task was simple, a plan worked out well in advance. "Now we must get Arnauld to Dr. Jung without mishap," Eleanor said. They would take him by train back through Trieste to Vienna. In fresh clothes, cleaned up, shaven, well shorn, except for the haunted vacant stare, their newly resurrected companion looked almost normal and would attract no unusual attention. And they had the official papers provided by Lieutenant Sonino, although Italian, establishing him as an Austrian citizen.

"Is there anything else I can do for you?" the young lieutenant asked Eleanor, as he helped her out of the automobile at the hotel near the train station in Trieste.

"There is one more favor, actually," Eleanor said, and she handed him an envelope she had prepared. "This is the name of a prisoner I very much wish to find. Among so many defeated Austrian prisoners of war."

The young lieutenant frowned involuntarily and then looked down at the envelope and accepted it as he knew was his obligation. "If you wish it," he said, "it is my command. It will be my personal project," and then he added, "among the many Austrians."

"You are kind to do it," Eleanor said, as Herr Jodl came around from the other side of the automobile. "Lieutenant Sonino has asked if there is any more he can do for us," she said to her companion.

"With these papers and forceful explanation," Jodl said, patting the briefcase, "we ought to make it through." "Forceful explanation," of course, meant Jodl's strong presence and the use of American dollars. Without speaking, Franz Jodl would eye their silent companion from time to time, wondering if they had indeed found the right man or if intense expectation had shaped the hapless soul now in their custody into what his determined companion from Boston desperately wanted to find. "You are absolutely certain, Frau Burden?" Jodl had asked more than once shortly after the moment of discovery, and she answered that she was.

"Absolutely," she had said each time with her ferocious conviction. "This is Arnauld Esterhazy."

"Is there perhaps some identifying characteristic?" the former policeman said.

"There is," Eleanor answered, but offered no more.

But still, silently and involuntarily, Franz Jodl could not help his scrutiny of their mysterious travel partner from time to time, and his wondering.

Lieutenant Sonino and their driver had agreed to leave them at a hotel near the train station in Trieste, where they would stay for the night and be traveling in the morning. "I have completed my assignment then," the young Italian said in parting from them.

"And well," Jodl said.

"I have given you a way to reach me," he said, "should you be needing more." He handed Eleanor a folded sheet of pale blue stationery. Eleanor was silently grateful for her connection to the house of Morgan.

"You have been kind," Eleanor said. "Herr Jodl and I can manage from here."

And when they had found the hotel room, Jodl had gone out to find new clothes, giving Eleanor some time alone with their new companion. She insisted on giving him a bath.

Alone with this man she had missed so powerfully—yearned for even—over four years, she undressed him slowly. He did not resist, nor did he cooperate any more than moving as she suggested with gestures. Once naked, he stepped into the warm bath and sat, as if recognizing the familiar action.

She was reminded of the story that circulated in Vienna in the aftermath of the tragedy of Mayerling. The empress, fully devastated by the apparent death of her son, would not accept the reports, it was rumored, until she was able to be alone with the body and to see for herself the birthmark she knew her son bore, one identical to that of his father, the emperor. And so, Eleanor thought, she would not be able to accept the identity of this man until a moment like this, alone.

Having seen the birthmark for herself, knowing now for certain that this man was Arnauld Esterhazy, she began slowly sponging his nakedness with loving attention and found herself curious and aroused and touched, more deeply than she could express. Unlike his soul and mind, his gaunt body, beautifully untouched by the horror he had experienced, bore no traces of war, his flesh, smooth and unblemished, carrying no trace of the violence and flying metal that had surrounded him all those months, tearing apart the lives of so many in his presence.

He submitted to the attention of her gentle sponging with a neutral gaze, resisting none of her stroking, but showing no sign of resistance or pleasure, except a small smile from time to time as the warm water flowed over his torso and limbs. He made no sound as she talked to him soothingly. "It is all right, Arnauld. Everything is going to be all right."

Jodl had left her alone with this man they had rescued from obscurity, as she had asked, and it would have been easy now to lead him to the bed in the adjoining room and to lie with him in her arms, a memory that had been with her for the past four years. But with each stroke of the large sponge, she calmed any yearning and inched toward that sacred distance she would keep from this moment on, that her friend Jung had advised her to maintain. "It will be different now," Jung had said, "if you find him. There will be a line you must never cross. He will need you as his untouchable inspiration, his Beatrice."

She caressed his nakedness now, as a mother and a lover, dissolving with each intimate stroke any doubts in her own mind. She took her time in the ceremonial process, practicing what she knew must be her new role, watching over her charge but with the detachment of a temple priestess. So much seemed to come together for her in that moment, so much memory, so much longing, so much fulfillment. She was back in Vienna with the great love of her life, each stroke of the sponge carrying with it the memory of fulfillment and connection, the memory of complete physical gratification that had come to her then in Vienna and had been rekindled briefly and poignantly that night four years ago on Acorn Street. Quietly and calmly, without emotion, this man seemed willing to represent the other, this moment encompassing all other moments of deep love and connection in her life. The moment was sublime and timeless, and Eleanor gave in to it completely.

The man before her submitted to the attention, closing his eyes as the sponge and Eleanor's gentle strokes worked over his body. When she had finished, she paused for a moment and pulled herself back to the present, and then at her suggestion, he stood and allowed her to towel him with careful thoroughness and then wrap the towel around his waist. "There you are," she said with a warm satisfied smile, his face remaining without expression. "Reborn."

Moments later, as if fully aware of the timing, Herr Jodl returned with the new clothing. As he entered the bedroom and saw the man supposed to be Arnauld Esterhazy wrapped in a towel, Jodl looked at Eleanor and asked his question. "Now," he said, "are you absolutely certain?"

"I am now absolutely certain," she repeated to her protector after they had dressed their patient. "Our search is over."

As with their trip from Vienna, more than once they found their train stopping and going no further. In one small Austrian village, they had to disembark and sit in a small station. Jodl left the other two travelers sitting on a wooden bench while he talked with the stationmaster about the schedule, if there was one, to Vienna. The station man only shrugged. "We shall see," he said in German.

When their train arrived, they boarded and continued their journey back through the impoverished countryside until the next stop and then stood patiently on platforms together waiting for the next connection, none of the three seeming to tire. Finally, at one last small Austrian town, the conductor said the magic words, "Through train."

The three of them now sat in silence as the Austrian countryside rolled past, on their way north to Vienna. The man chosen by fate to be reborn as Arnauld Esterhazy, legendary teacher of St. Gregory's School, stared vacantly, only the deep recesses of his eyes betraying that hint of terrified alertness that signaled his not being an ordinary traveler.

Oh, my dear Arnauld, Eleanor wondered at one point when Jodl had gone to find coffee, *where have you been? What have you seen?*

57

ODYSSEUS AND ACHILLES

leanor and Jodl thought it wisest that they travel directly to Zurich, without stopping in Vienna for more time than necessary to pick up young Standish from Fräulein Tatlock and for Eleanor to say her good-byes, informing no one of their extraordinary discovery until they had arrived safely in Switzerland. "We shall wait until we are secure in Dr. Jung's sanctuary," Eleanor said, "before we try to sort all this out," and Jodl nodded his taciturn consent.

They had planned that Jodl would wait at the train station with his secret charge, the man they assumed was Arnauld, while Eleanor went on to Fräulein Tatlock's.

As anticipated, the reunion at Fräulein Tatlock's was emotional, joyous on young Standish's part. He ran to his mother and threw out his arms. "Oh, Mother," the almost four-year-old exclaimed, "I thought you would never come," and she hugged him with a fierceness that surprised both of them.

"We have made the best of our time," the fräulein said, "but he missed his mother." She had tears in her eyes now, already anticipating the parting. "He is a brave young man."

Eleanor paused with her news, as she knew it would be poignant for this old woman, who had known the family from long ago. "I have found Arnauld," she said. "He was in a hospital in Gorizia, among the unidentified."

The old woman took a long slow moment to absorb what she had just heard. "He is alive, then?" she said faintly.

"He is alive. He and Herr Jodl are waiting for us at the train station. We are taking him to the hospital in Zurich, to Dr. Jung's care."

"Have you told his parents?"

"No," Eleanor said. "I wish to get him safely to Switzerland before I tell them. You must tell no one until then."

And Fräulein Tatlock, who held the secrets, only nodded. "It will be a shock to them."

"I know," Eleanor said.

Fräulein Tatlock looked at Standish for a long moment. "There is much you need to know of his birth," she said suddenly.

Eleanor searched Fräulein Tatlock's face. "I know the story," Eleanor said. "Frau Esterhazy has told me in a letter."

"It is only a story from long ago, not mine to confirm or deny." Eleanor had known twenty years ago that Fräulein Tatlock had known Arnauld Esterhazy's family, and now she was aware for the first time that the old lady knew dark secrets.

"You know the whole story?" Eleanor asked.

"It is not mine to tell."

"I will see his parents in Zurich," Eleanor said. "We will share the story then."

The old woman nodded. "Perhaps then," she said.

Eleanor ushered Fräulein Tatlock and her son to the train station, and they approached Jodl and his companion sitting on the bench in the large central hall. Fräulein Tatlock approached cautiously, her eyes filling with tears. "It is he," she said in little more than a whisper. She reached out her hand and touched his arm. Arnauld did not move or acknowledge her in any way, only stared straight ahead. "It is he," she repeated, obviously stunned.

"I will wait for you to inform Herr and Frau Esterhazy," Fräulein Tatlock said as they bade good-byes there in the spacious sitting room.

Eleanor repeated her intentions to keep shipments of food coming from Switzerland. "Things will get better for Vienna," she said with confidence.

"That is our prayer," the old Viennese said.

N

During the whole trip to the Swiss border, the four travelers kept silent company. Arnauld sat across from Eleanor and her son, and he could only stare. Young Standish was fascinated by the man, finding it difficult to keep his eyes off the face that showed so little of the animation the boy was accustomed to.

"Why does he not speak, Mother?" the boy said, noticing that whenever the man became agitated and tried to form words, his mother calmed him with a movement of her hand, and with a comforting smile.

"He has been in the war," she said, as if that would be enough explanation for her young son.

"I see," Standish said, "like Odysseus and Achilles."

"Like Odysseus and Achilles," the mother repeated, and at the words their passenger gave the hint of a troubled look.

"It is all right, Arnauld," she said gently. "You do not need to speak." And then she added for good measure, "Everything will be all right." And that seemed to calm him.

58

A SAD PARTING

leanor was unable to rest until she had delivered her charge to Carl Jung deep in neutral Switzerland. "We must get him there," she had announced to her companion Jodl, "and only then announce to the world and his family our remarkable discovery." She sank as comfortably as she could into her seat, allowing herself to drift into sleep, her attention fixed on the beautiful but vacant face across from her, fully assured that her companion would watch over them both. She thought of Arnauld's letters to his parents she had received only recently and recalled one in particular, the last fully detailed one from the Isonzo war zone, the last fully coherent one.

Dear Mother and Father,

The tension is palpable as we await the next move of this Italian enemy that a very short time ago was our admired friend. The stench and discomfort of the trench becomes so routine as to be bearable, the uneven moments of rest and sleep now regular. Nerves that have gotten the better of me, I fear, can now be hidden as I look out for the betterment of my men. They don't complain, the conditions of daily life so awful as to appear deadeningly normal. One of the most vocal, a seventeen-year-old from Moravia who has seen two of his teenage friends blown to pieces has concluded, "Don't pick off the lice until they're the size of cockroaches; they're easier to see."

Be on the ready, I tell them all. Always be on the ready. I steady myself through meditation, like a Buddhist monk. I try not to let anyone hear me talking to myself. My boy-men need me; they need someone to tell them what to do: to stand fast in the middle of the deafening artillery fire.

One dream keeps me going, one image sustains me. My last night in Boston, with my beautiful Eleanor, whom you will someday meet perhaps when this nightmare has passed. We were alone at dinner that last night. She told me with great confidence of her vision of the future. Years before in Vienna an older gentleman, an American, had given me the same vision. "You will need to know this," Eleanor said. "You will be a great teacher. You will be revered and long lived. I hope to have a son, she said, and you will be his Mentor, as Mentor was the great teacher of Odysseus." She looked into my eyes with great intensity. "You will have a great ordeal, I fear, and you will have to keep this certainty before you, but you will return. I know you will return." She seemed emphatic, desiring that I absorb without question what she was saying. I could not understand the urgency of her words then, but you can imagine now how comforting that simple prediction becomes in my present state.

We sat in her beautiful drawing room, and we talked leisurely and at length. The memories of that last evening fuel me now, carry me past my despair, allow me to escape this hopelessness. It is in that moment that I see and feel, in all her tenderness and power, my beautiful Beatrice.

Your loving son,
Arnauld

The other letters, the ones that followed, only a few of them, were short and increasingly disconnected, written in an increasingly faltering and trembling hand. And then they stopped altogether. That last letter was very much on her mind now as she looked into the face of the man who had been lost and now perhaps could be restored to life. She found herself grateful that her words of confidence had carried such weight for him during his ordeal, and she searched within herself now to find that faith once again, this time for herself.

It was then that she felt especially grateful for the friendship of Carl

Jung. *How fortunate we all are to have him,* she thought, *how complex and challenging, if even possible, his task is to be, leading this ruined human being back up into the real world.* If anyone could do it, she reckoned, Jung and his clinic could.

Jodl had agreed to accompany them to the Swiss border, providing that final measure of support. She knew that their parting at the border would be difficult. Ever attentive to his responsibilities as protector, Jodl had arranged for an associate from the Swiss national police, also retired, to accompany Eleanor and Arnauld and young Standish until they reached the care of Dr. Jung in Zurich. Although he never mentioned his concern, he knew that those disturbeds returning from the war, such as this man they were returning to civilization, had the capacity for aberrant behavior or even violence, and he wanted a watchful eye kept on their companion at all times.

"My counterpart from the Swiss national police will be at your side," he said. "He is a good man. You will have an easy go from here, Frau Burden."

"Come with us to Zurich," she said in a burst of spontaneity to her steadfast companion. "You can meet Dr. Jung."

"Thank you," he said, trying to maintain his reserve. "But my assignment is completed. I will return to my own city, to my other duties."

For a moment she entertained teasing him for his staunch rectitude, but thought better of it. How she had grown to love this man of great strength. Again, wordlessly she looked into the retired policeman's face. "We shall miss you," she settled for. "This is a sad parting."

Jodl nodded. And now, for the last detail of closure, he held out the suitcase he had guarded carefully during their whole time together, the lifeline of the operation. "And now this," he said dutifully.

She paused, eyeing the offering, and then held out her hand, palm first. "No," she said softly, and Jodl began to protest. "You keep it."

"You must take it," he said.

"No," she repeated, looking him square in the eye, this time with supreme tenderness. "Fräulein Tatlock's kitchen," she said. "It will need support, and a treasurer."

Franz Jodl paused before he spoke again. A man who weighed his words carefully, he weighed these words with special care. "I wish that my sons had had such an advocate."

Eleanor held the man's eyes for a long, sacred moment. "They had it," she said finally. "In their father." She moved to him and kissed him on both cheeks, then held on for a long moment. "Be well, my trusted champion."

"Be well," he repeated.

No further words were exchanged, and Jodl, ever the watchful sentinel, stood in his place on the station platform as Eleanor, her charge, and her young son disappeared through the doorway of the train car. She watched him through the cabin window as the train began to move and at the last moment waved, then she turned to the two passengers beside her, one small and one grown, but both totally dependent on her alone now.

PART
FIVE

59

BECAUSE OF THE BOY

arl Jung had arranged for Arnauld to be admitted under his specific care to Burghölzli, the psychiatric hospital of the University of Zurich, where he had begun his career and made his name. The hospital had been founded in the 1860s as a facility specifically for the humane treatment of mental patients, one of the first and best in Europe. "Your Arnauld could not have landed in a better place," the doctor said.

"That was the intention," Eleanor replied.

Eleanor had arranged to stay in Zurich with Standish until she felt a proper diagnosis had been made and a path toward restoration had been established, a process, Jung assured her, that would be accomplished in just a few days. She was eager to return home to her daughters and Frank as soon as possible, but she awaited one more crucial step.

To her great relief, Eleanor found a message waiting upon her arrival in Zurich that all was as it should be in Boston, and the girls were well and eager for their mother's return.

"I shall stay until the staff has had a chance for a thorough evaluation and you are able to report," she told Jung, who agreed to the wisdom of the plan, and indeed within a few days he was ready. "Your friend Arnauld is an extreme case, as you know," he said seriously. "He has lost his ability to relate to the world. It is, as you suggest, a case of severe repression of war experience, what the English call shell shock. There was perhaps head trauma, brain damage at its root that caused his present state, one from which some poor souls never emerge. He has dissociated, unable to sleep and unable to return to full consciousness. His reaction to the horrors of war is extreme, granted, but not highly unusual. He has gone deep inside, and it will be our task to try to entice him back to our world. He is a deeply tormented man, not shut off from feeling, as it appears, but feeling too much."

"There is hope?" she said, halfway between a statement and a question.

"It is too early to establish that one way or the other. We can only progress one step at a time. The first step is a thorough neurological examination."

"And is there no way to establish a prognosis and a schedule of recovery?" Eleanor asked, openly concerned.

"You have brought him this far, and by so doing have saved his life. You did your job, and heroically. Now we and time will have to do ours."

"You can lead him out of this?" Eleanor said.

"We begin with that premise. Full recovery will always be our goal. The human mind is complex, and it protects itself in complex ways. Your friend Arnauld has sealed himself behind a great door. We will now attempt to untie the Gordian knot securing it. It will be done strand by strand. That is the only way."

When she visited that first day, Arnauld had been moved to his own private room. "This will be his arena," Jung said, "the place where he will find himself."

She returned every day, and on the last she placed in his hand a single slim black volume and pressed both his hands around it until he had it firmly in his grip. "I must leave you," she said. "I must tend to my family. But I leave you with this book, as part of me," she added with firmness. "It will be your guide out."

Still unable to speak or acknowledge much from the outside world, Arnauld took the gift and clutched it tightly, pulling it to his chest. His lips moved and he seemed to mouth once again those syllables that had become familiar to anyone who had spent time with him. The book that from that moment onward was rarely out of his hands was titled *City of Music* by Jonathan Trumpp. She took her young son by the hand and led him out of the room.

Eleanor knew from a telegraph message from Jodl that he had been successful in his last task and that Arnauld's parents would be arriving in

Zurich on a train from Vienna in the early afternoon, the final step she was waiting for. She arranged for a driver to take her and Standish to the train station so that she would be there to greet the couple when they disembarked.

Herr Esterhazy and his wife looked expectant and somewhat awed by the whole turn of events. "This is an extraordinary surprise," he said to Eleanor once they had said their greetings and the driver was loading their bags into the car. "You will have to pardon us if we are a bit out of sorts."

"We had lost our son," Frau Esterhazy said. "Now, we hear, he is found."

"He has been found," Eleanor said with calm authority. "I can only guess what you are feeling. He does not express much right now, you realize."

"But he is alive," Herr Esterhazy said. "That is the miracle."

They talked quietly about how Eleanor and her companion Herr Jodl had searched through the war zone, and the parents had many questions. "Did you know," Frau Esterhazy said, "when you were with us?"

"I knew that I had to search for him," Eleanor said.

"By what inspiration?" Herr Esterhazy said with a look of profound puzzlement. "The rest of us accepted the reports."

"I know it is difficult," Eleanor said, "and I didn't wish to give you false hope. But somehow I just knew."

"Was it because of the boy?" Arnauld's mother said. "Was it because of your young Standish?"

Eleanor smiled at her, not missing the full depth of implication in the question. "How do you mean?"

"Was it because of your son that you wished that Arnauld be alive?"

"Yes," Eleanor said, considering the question. "Yes, I suppose it was."

"Well," said the father, reaching out with his hand and touching Eleanor's for just an instant. "We are overwhelmed with gratitude for what you did." He looked into her eyes. "You alone."

Eleanor paused for a moment to acknowledge the father's sentiment. "Our sole purpose now," she said finally, "is to make him well again."

"You believe it is possible?" the mother asked with a look of deep concern. Obviously, Jodl had given them a frank description of their son's condition. "It is almost too much."

Eleanor smiled again and nodded. "Yes," she said gently. "I do believe. And he is in extraordinary hands with Dr. Jung."

Eleanor walked with the parents to the door of Arnauld's room, as a white-coated doctor opened it and ushered them in. For a moment, the parents kept their distance and looked stunned, not moving, not daring to accept what they were seeing in this shell of a man sitting in pajamas at the edge of his bed. Eleanor could feel the tension from the unspoken fear that all of them carried but did not acknowledge: that this might be a horrible and cruel mistake. Without breathing, she watched the faces of the two parents, in that moment thinking, *What if they recoil with "This is not our son"?* Time stopped.

Then the mother stepped forward toward the man who looked vacantly and straight ahead, with no sign of recognition in his blank stare. For a moment she scrutinized the empty stare. Then she spoke in no more than a whisper.

The father came forward and stood close to his wife. "Arnauld," the mother said, and hesitated before laying the back of her hand gently on his cheek. "My son."

The sitting man did not move. He looked up in the direction of the voice, and it would not be exaggeration to say that he gave no sign.

60

THE MISSING PIECE

t was late afternoon when they were together at the Burghölzli. Frau Esterhazy approached Eleanor and asked if there was a place where they could be alone, and the two of them walked together to a small garden area out a side door. They sat on a small bench, and Frau Esterhazy spoke. "When I thought we had lost our son, I wrote you that letter. I thought you needed to know Arnauld's extraordinary origins."

"You were kind to include me," Eleanor said. "I found the revelations very powerful. They are for me most assuredly the missing piece."

"We thought our son was dead." Her voice faltered, and Frau Esterhazy paused to collect herself. "You were vitally important to him. We thought that at the very least you should know."

"And now that he has been found, do you wish you had not written the letter?"

"No one knows," the mother said. "It must remain that way. But I am not sorry that I wrote it all to you."

"I understand."

"At the time of his birth, we thought it a necessity. For his safety. The baby was being searched for. You understand."

"Yes, I understand. The situation was very precarious."

"Now—"

"Now you wish his secret to remain secret." Frau Esterhazy nodded silently. "You think it sacred information." The mother nodded silently again. Eleanor waited until the older woman's eyes rose to meet hers. "I know of that sacredness, and I will share what I know with no one. You can trust that."

Arnauld Esterhazy's mother nodded. "Thank you," she said. "I suspected that I did not need to mention it now, or later. Herr Esterhazy and I know that our son will never be the same again, but still we are happy to have him alive."

"I believe that he will return in all ways."

"You have strong faith, Frau Burden. That has brought you here in the first place, and we are grateful beyond words for it. Now that faith tells you that he can be brought all the way back."

"It does," Eleanor said.

"We do not have your faith perhaps, but we are still happy that he is alive."

"There is more—" Eleanor began, and stopped. "There is something you can share with me now. When you told me, back when you thought Arnauld lost, did you have a reason?"

"I think you know the reason," the mother said.

"It was because of Standish? Because of my son?" Again, Frau Esterhazy said nothing, only nodded with the slightest movement of her head. "Arnauld is to be very important in my son's life. I know that to be true."

"I hope that is to be true."

"It is," Eleanor said. "It absolutely is."

"We shall cling to that hope then," Arnauld's mother said with a profound sincerity. "We shall cling to your faith." Then she went quiet, lost in thought for a long moment. "Your son," she said. "Your Standish. He reminds me so—"

"Arnauld will return to Boston. I just know that. He will be the great teacher of my son and others."

A gentle calm had come into Frau Esterhazy's face. "We can all wish for that," she said. "It is something to hope for."

And as the two women sat quietly together in the garden of the Zurich hospital, Eleanor could not help reconstructing in her mind the remarkable letter from Frau Esterhazy that explained so much, and would remain a secret between them.

My sister, Madeleine Arnauld, and I were raised in Vienna, by
artistic parents, I think you would say. Our father was Viennese and

our mother French. *Our home was very cultured, and my sister and I studied music with great seriousness. I pursued the study of opera, while my sister chose the theater. Madeleine was very outgoing, and I was the quiet one. She was also very beautiful, which brought her much attention and success, but in the end caused more trouble than good, I fear. But that beauty and her skills as an actress did serve to earn her a prestigious position in the Hofburgtheater. In the meantime, I pursued music and ended up in the fascinating world of the Paris opera.*

Madeleine Arnauld became a name quite well-known in Vienna, as a young actress and a colleague of the famous Katharina Schratt, consort to the emperor. I pursued my opera career and met Herr Esterhazy, Emil, who was an artist of some ability but also a history student and an aspiring opera librettist, convinced that he could write the definitive opera of the French Revolution. We fell very much in love and lived a life of some romantic Bohemian appeal, not unlike the characters in Murger's Scènes de la Vie de Bohème, *discovered by Puccini. We would have been good material for an opera ourselves, Emil always said.*

My sister's life was very different from mine. She had found a home in the pension of a family named Tatlock, a humble one, but her theater life was very grand, I think you would say, with a great deal of money passing from hand to hand. In those days, the Hofburgtheater was popular in the court, and I fear that my sister had much opportunity to consort with aristocrats of name. She became swept up in the high life there, being, as I said, very beautiful, and very lively. She caught the eye of many of the nobility and eventually the crown prince Rudolf himself, who, although married and with children, had quite a nightlife. Soon, it became generally known, she and the crown prince spent time together. And then she discovered that she was pregnant.

At this point, the crown prince disappeared from her life and the representatives of the court interceded. My sister became an outcast and lost her position in the Hofburgtheater, and she even feared for her own safety, and the safety of the unborn baby.

In the meantime, Emil and I had decided to marry, he a starving artist from an aristocratic family, and I a promising soprano with a chorus position in the opera. Madeleine moved to Paris and Emil became concerned that she needed to disappear. He prevailed on his family to make discreet arrangements so that she could move in all secrecy to Paris to have the baby, all of us fearing what the officials of the court would do when the baby was born. The Esterhazys, by the way, are very good at secrecy. Only they and Fräulein Tatlock knew of her whereabouts.

The pregnancy went well, but the delivery was problematic, and, after a long tortured labor, my sister hemorrhaged and died, leaving a healthy son behind. It was without question the saddest and most joyous event in my life.

I was with my sister during the labor and when the trouble began and she was near death, and I pledged to care for the baby and to guard with my honor and my life the secret of the child's identity. Emil, with the help of his powerful family, saw to it that the report was spread that both mother and child had not survived. And, having exhausted our desire to live the life of artists, we decided to return to Vienna, where Emil could take up the position he has held all these years at the family vineyard recently made vacant by the death of his father's cousin.

So we returned to Vienna and moved to the family estate with our adopted baby, everyone, including the court officials, accepting the fact that my sister's baby had died tragically with her at the birth and that the birth of our own baby boy had been the natural outcome of the artist's life in Paris.

We named him as our own, and all of us who knew agreed to keep the details of his conception and birth in the deepest secrecy, not knowing what the court would do with the true story. I think you can see our reasoning. There were always rumors in Vienna that a secret imperial son had been born, as there were always rumors of a search for the fabled lost prince.

With the suicide death of the crown prince at Mayerling in 1889, a devastation from which the empire would never recover, and the line of succession very much in question and doubt, we feared even more the possible discovery, and did not want known the details of my dear dead sister's pregnancy and the identity of our dear son, Arnauld.

We and the Esterhazys, with all their traditions and power, kept the whole story as the darkest of secrets. And we never told our son.

The boy, our son, Arnauld, was heir to the Hapsburg throne, the empire's lost prince.

61

A LESS-THAN-SANGUINE REPORT

nd indeed, with Arnauld now safely in the care of Dr. Jung and the Burghölzli, his parents informed of his return from the dead, and there being no more she could do, Eleanor knew that it was safe to return to Boston. Sometime after her return, she received this letter.

My dearest Eleanor,

I am sorry to offer here this less-than-sanguine report on Arnauld. Since we both concluded that his recovery would take the better part of a year, we should, I suppose, be encouraged by his progress over these months. Although he is not ready to return to society, he has taken great strides in recovering some of his faculties. In ways, he has recovered a great deal, and in others he has recovered very little of what it will take to return to ordinary life.

He carries with him constantly a small book, his "little book," the doctors call it. Some of the staff conjecture that it is not with his own history that he will be filling the empty vessel of memory but rather with the contents of this remarkable book, that out of the reflections in this small volume he will structure a new self. For matters of therapy and pure curiosity, most of us have read it, at least in portion, when he will part with it, and it is indeed quite an extraordinary description of Arnauld's old world.

As for how he passes his days, he listens to music, mostly a now—

well-worn gramophone recording of the first movement of a Mahler symphony, his third I believe it is. He also has been constructing his imaginary city, which he began almost from his first day here. He loses himself in the project for hours, using scraps of paper and cardboard and wood to construct streets and buildings and parks and monuments, a model of the city he reconstructs in his memory, no doubt, the building, one hopes, of his sanity.

We will probably never know what dreadful experiences brought him to the desperate condition in which you found him, but we do know that even the most extreme trauma can be overcome with care and patience.

He is a very pleasant and well-mannered patient, highly dignified. The staff enjoy working with him and are very hopeful that he will regain the functions necessary for independent life. But he is still not able to sleep, and there are concerns that he is not progressing. He has reached a plateau, and can go no further. "We are waiting for a break-through," one of the staff says. "He is stuck in no-man's-land between light and dark. He is polite and compliant, but he seems to have no personal affect." One suspects that he is developing a persona with nothing beneath it.

As always, I wish that I could be giving you a more sanguine report. I will keep you informed about his progress, but for the time being you can rest assured that Arnauld is receiving the very best of modern med-ical and psychological attention. As always, I look forward to your next visit.

With deepest fondness,
Jung

She had been back in Boston for six months, back to her role at the head of the Burden household, being the mother for her girls and Standish. The household ran efficiently in her absence, but she could see a few ragged edges of inattention. "We did well," Susan said. "We got off to school every morning on time, and Mrs. Spurgeon served dinner every evening on time, and Father tucked us into bed each night."

"We missed you awfully," Jane cut in.

"It was the little things," Susan said. "No one read to us at night, and no one played music with us. Those are the things that matter."

From almost the moment of her return, she was aware of a change in her very being. Arnauld's rescue and rehabilitation were now out of her hands and in the experienced care of Carl Jung and the doctors at the Burghölzli, the very best in the world. Naturally, she should have been able to relax and to reflect on all that had happened, but she felt captive to a residual nervousness and sleepless nights in which she was visited by images of violence and terror, some directly related to her time in Italy, some not. All of this she had to bear alone.

The music with her daughters helped. Nearly every day, they gathered in the music room and played together, piano, recorder, and cello. And she was aware of the healing power of the sessions, how she had always felt a wholeness while playing music, and now more than ever she felt a connection with her daughters and with the world. She wrote to Jung, "I don't think I ever thought before how music for me causes the parts to come together. It is for me my connectedness of all things."

One afternoon she found a copy of the familiar Haydn piece, and they played that, bringing back images for her of both Vienna and her evening in Italy. Standish would sit and listen to them with great attentiveness, and she would become aware how important those moments were for him and for his sisters. "Listen, children," she said, "there is such beautiful harmony in this music."

But as the anxiousness persisted, she found herself more and more in a reflective mood, worrying that something permanent had taken her over, until one evening a month after her return, a thought occurred to her. She was experiencing in a minor way what soldiers do after the horrific experiences of war. She could feel happening in herself what had happened to Arnauld.

That night, she wrote out her thoughts in a letter to her friend Jung. "How curious," she wrote her friend, "that I should be experiencing, even in small portion, the devastations of those who return from war. Those around me would not understand, and would think me a malingerer were I to complain, but I feel the disturbances nonetheless." And as soon as she mailed it, she noticed the anxious symptoms diminishing. "Simply acknowledging the effects," she wrote later, "seemed to be part of the cure."

The week's demands for charities and public appearances as the com-
petent and poised wife of the prominent banker Frank Burden resumed
immediately, as if there had been no interruption and as if Eleanor had
never been gone and had experienced nothing while away. The vestry of
Trinity Church was planning a renovation of the meeting hall and had
postponed doing the initial solicitations for the "significant gifts," the
rector called them. "We were waiting," he said. "Everyone wanted you to
do the initial asking. No one felt comfortable proceeding without you."

And the Museum of Fine Arts was busy planning the spring tulip sale,
and even with something as trivial as that, she seemed to be the only one
who knew how to order the tulips. No one asked where she had been or
what experiences she had survived.

Dr. Jung and the staff at the Burghölzli had notified the world of the
return of Arnauld Esterhazy and had arranged for the continued visits of
his parents. The milieu he had known growing up in Vienna knew the
news that, in the midst of all the loss from war, at least Arnauld had been
spared and was alive and recuperating in Zurich. Eleanor had seen to it
that the people at St. Gregory's received the notification. They were over-
joyed.

To her great pleasure, a few weeks after her return, Eleanor received a
letter from Alma, who obviously was thrilled at the news of Arnauld's
resurrection and was planning a trip to Zurich for a visit. "It will be invaluable for him at this time to visit with old friends. He needs very much
to be reminded of the past he seems to have forgotten." And in her letter
Alma presented the remarkable news that Kokoschka had also returned.
Though reported dead, he had been only severely wounded and had recovered in a Russian hospital. "He is now back in Vienna and causing a
good deal of embarrassment. He has not responded well to my marriage
to Gropius. My friends say that in his anguish he has rendered a sensational painting of himself with me in a tempestuous bed, wild with swirls
of bright color. It is causing quite a stir."

62

"YOU ARE JONATHAN TRUMPP"

n the month following her return, as she adjusted to the reactions to her experience abroad and returned to the myriad details neglected during her absence, she could not avoid feelings of apprehension, waiting for word from Jung and the Burghölzli. During that time there were three events that happened concurrently as far as we can tell: Will Honeycutt found out the full story, Jung's letter arrived, and Eleanor had her dream. There is no way to determine the order in which the three events occurred, so we will assume them to be simultaneous. Jung had a theory of such a simultaneity, which he called synchronicity, a moment in which the physical and nonphysical worlds come into concert.

One day at the end of an afternoon of planning out investments, Will Honeycutt looked up at her and said suddenly, "I think it is time."

"Time?" she said, genuinely not understanding his request.

"I think it is time you told me."

"Told you what?" she said flatly.

"The whole story," he said. "What happened in Vienna twenty years ago, where you are getting your investment information, how you knew Arnauld was alive, the whole story."

"My," she said, caught off guard, looking for a way out. "That is presumptuous, Will. You must know that I cannot talk about this."

"I know it is presumptuous, but I think I need to, and deserve to, know. I have been your most loyal employee over the years. I have shared

everything with you. You know everything about me. You have been my
one constant friend ever since that day I signed on. It goes beyond business arrangements—" He stopped, searching for words. There was now a
familiar wild look in his eye. "You believed in me when no one else did. I
have served your intentions devotedly, with increasing ability—you must
admit. I have no other life. I am not very graceful in my dealings with
people, but I am very good at keeping confidences. You will have to grant
me that. I am very good at serving as your secret accomplice. And now—"
He paused. "I think I deserve to know." He stared at her in a way that
always made her feel uncomfortable.

"Well," she said quickly. "That is quite a compelling argument." She
pulled herself together and she rose. "I shall give it consideration," she
said, heading for the door. "But believe me, Will, this is not information
that you want to know. It is knowledge that has tormented me for twenty
years, and I do not want it to weigh on your mind as well."

The next day she arrived at the office early. Will was looking remorse-
ful as she made her way to her desk. "Come in here, Mr. Honeycutt," she
said formally, and he walked in, about to offer apologies. But she began
before he could say anything. "I have given your request the serious
thought I promised. In fact, I spent a rather sleepless night thinking about
it. I do think of you as my most loyal and even devoted partner. I suppose
I had not thought about it before, but I did last night. There have been
times when I could not trust you, but I have come to believe that now I
can, completely."

She lifted a well-worn leather volume from her desk. "And it is time.
This is, you will see, the most confidential of documents. No one must
know of its existence or its contents. It is from my time in Vienna, and I
have added to it over the years. It is the 'full story,' as you say. I have
shared it with only one person since my return, and he has now died. You
will be the only living person to know the story."

She handed him the volume, and, sensing somehow its significance, he
hesitated a moment before he took it.

"Prepare yourself, Mr. Honeycutt," she said, and she walked past him
and left him alone with the leather-bound book that had for twenty years
controlled her life. "Even you are in for a surprise."

The next morning they met again. He had a disheveled look she had seen before, as if he had slept in his clothes. "Well?" she said.

"I have read it all," Will said. "A number of times. I stayed here late and returned early."

"And?" she said finally.

"There is so much to take in," he said.

"I know," Eleanor said, looking down.

"You wrote *City of Music*."

"I did."

"You are Jonathan Trumpp."

"I am. Actually, Johnny Trumpp was the janitor at my college dormitory. He was Slavic and spoke broken English. I stole his name for an article."

"The *New York Times* published your article and then sent you to Vienna, and you wrote the book."

"More or less. Going to Vienna was my headmistress's idea."

"And you met this Wheeler, who wrote this journal, and you fell in love."

"Yes."

"He was killed and you wrote *City of Music* based on what he told you about Vienna."

Eleanor nodded. "More or less."

"And his ideas he had gotten from his teacher at St. Gregory's School, and that teacher the boys called the Haze was Arnauld?"

"That is correct."

"And the Haze also taught your son, Standish."

Again, Eleanor nodded. "Yes."

"And from this journal you knew, at least in part, how you were to invest the monies from the Hyperion Fund, monies obtained from selling a ring of the crown prince Rudolf."

"Yes," she said quietly.

"You know that one needs time to absorb all this," he said, pausing for a long moment before changing the subject.

"I know." She nodded. "It is overwhelming. You are not the first to encounter it all in one sitting." She was thinking of her own first encounter with the journal twenty years ago, and then that of William James.

"As a result of this experience in Vienna," he continued, "you made certain that Arnauld would be invited to teach at St. Gregory's because you were certain that he was destined to become a great teacher of both Standish and the Wheeler of the journal. You knew that the war was coming and you knew that Arnauld would be drawn into it on the side of the Austrians, but you also knew that as terrible as the war experience was for him, he is, he was, destined to survive and return to Boston and his position at St. Gregory's. And that is why you knew that it was up to you to go find him, and it is why now you are the only one who is certain that he will recover from the sorry state in which he finds himself at Dr. Jung's hospital in Zurich, although you do not know how."

The stream of words came forth from Will Honeycutt without a break. Eleanor listened without reaction, no affirmation, and no denial. "I do not know how," she said.

Will's tone changed to one of reverence. "This is amazing, overwhelming, and you can be sure that I will hold it in the strictest confidence. And that I understand, I think." He paused, looking deep into her eyes. "You do not need to fear. I know the weight of this."

"It is very complicated," she said wearily, "and indeed overwhelming."

Will Honeycutt smiled, something new in his eyes. She had become impressed by how stable he had seemed over the past months, completing a mysterious transition that had begun back in the Loeb office during the Northern Pacific business. Suddenly, for this moment, it was not only she who bore the weight of her knowledge alone. He sat before her, armed now with the full import of the journal. "You forget," he said. "I am a scientist. I like to think about complications and complexity."

"What you hold in your hand now has determined the course of my life."

"I can see that. And I know now why you sought me out at Harvard, intruded in my life."

"I am sorry," she said. "I had to be—"

"No, no," he interrupted firmly. "You don't need to apologize. You have caused great and positive changes in my life, unbelievable ones, actually. It is all foretold here. I know now why our interactions must be as they are. I see all that now." He held up the journal.

"You know now that it has been both a blessing and a curse."

"I do. You think it is a curse because you must work hard to make things come about."

She said nothing.

"Has it occurred to you that this is destiny, that you need do nothing?"

"I can't believe that," she said with a grim certitude that caught Will by surprise, causing him to think hard for a moment.

"No," he said. "I guess I can see that. And in your position, come to think of it, I could not either."

"And now you know everything."

"I do. Of course." He paused and looked deep into her eyes. "All except that one part, when you found out about the other T. Williams Honeycutt, the right one. Why didn't you—"

"Why didn't I abandon you?" she interrupted.

"Yes, that," he said. "Why didn't you abandon me?"

She had now fully returned to the present, looking him square in the eye. "You know why."

"Tell me," he said. "I want to hear it."

"Because," she said. "Because I had grown very fond of you."

"That was not in the journal."

"No," she said. "I improvised."

He stared for a moment, absorbing all that was there. "Well," he said, signaling his discomfort. "I am very glad for it." And then he changed his tone, becoming businesslike. "You went to Vienna just now because you *knew* Arnauld was alive."

"Yes," Eleanor said softly. "I knew. From what had to be, I knew."

"Because of this." He held up the journal again.

She nodded, a seriousness returning to her face. "You know that to be true now."

"Fortunate for him." A silence returned between them. "His return means a lot to you, doesn't it?"

"It means everything."

"And he is trapped now in his inner world, and there is fear he will never come out."

She nodded silently, acknowledging the seriousness of his probing. "Yes," she said. "And you know something about that isolation, don't you, Will?"

It was shortly after that conversation that the letter came from her friend Jung in Zurich.

My dear Eleanor,

I have waited to write until I had received the final report from the third doctor. Now I can deliver the conclusion with confidence that it is accurate and not merely defeatist. After a month of examination, and from three different points of view, my own in addition, I must tell you that the conclusion is that although Arnauld has received enough shock to produce psychological trauma, he has most definitely received physical injuries to his brain, of the kind that are, most unfortunately, considered permanent. One always hopes with war trauma that the emotional distress is causing the problem, not the neurological damage, and that the proper therapy will bring the patient back to normal. In the case of neurological damage, one hopes that the effects can be reversed by healing.

Emotional damage is difficult to assess, but neurological damage is not. After extensive analysis and examination, the staff have concluded that Herr Esterhazy's primary injuries are neurological after all. The diminished state in which you found him in Gorizia will be with him for the rest of his life. In the opinion of the doctors here, the damage to Arnauld's brain is irreparable.

I know the shock for you this message brings and if there were any way to avoid telling it to you so directly, believe me I would. I am only telling you now what everyone who cares for him must know.

Very sadly yours,
Jung

Eleanor stayed away from the office for a day, trying to think of what to do. She told no one but kept running the letter through her head. Carl Jung was a vibrant and optimistic man full of ideas. For him to reach a negative conclusion was the worst news she could imagine. "If Dr. Jung cannot see a way out," one of the Burghölzli doctors once said to her, "there is no way out."

When she finally did appear at the office, she found Will Honeycutt sitting at his desk. She told him she had news from Zurich and handed him Jung's letter. Will took it and with concern on his face read it over several times.

"This is terrible news," he said after a long silence. "The best doctors in

Europe have reached a dead end. If they give up, no one will pick up his case, and he will be done for. I now understand what this means." She nodded, still looking down. "I know what this means to you."

At first Eleanor said nothing, then, "I am for the moment without words."

"Dr. Jung has told you that there seems to be no way to get Arnauld past the state in which he hears and sees and smiles but shows no sign of any of his former intelligence or personality." There was now a look of intense curiosity on Will Honeycutt's face.

"This comes from a man who always sees possibilities," Eleanor said.

Will Honeycutt sat with her in the Hyperion Fund office for a long time. "You know there is one thing in all this"—he held up the journal—"one thing that has troubled me."

"And that is?"

"And that is that you believe you have chosen in me the wrong person, and have had to compensate for that choice over the years."

"I know that," Eleanor said. "And I thought that I have eased that troubling aspect for you. I have become happy with my choice."

"But it was the *right* choice," he said suddenly and with conviction. "Don't you see, it was the *right* choice."

"Oh?" Eleanor said. She had noticed the return of a wild intensity to his eyes, and she had learned in those moments not to get in the way.

"Your son, Standish, is to grow up to be a great hero, and to play a part in saving others. I know that from my reading." Eleanor said nothing and only nodded. "Arnauld is destined to return from the war and be his great mentor, an indispensable piece of the story. . . ." Again she only nodded. "Your son is to have a son who is destined to become another kind of hero in his time, and seventy years from now, in 1988, he is to become dislocated in time and show up in Vienna twenty years ago and write this journal." Again, he lifted the volume.

"I know it is hard to understand," she said now with compassion. "But, yes, that is true."

"This journal upon which you are going to base the rest of your life, it is an accurate description of how things will turn out."

"Yes, all that is true."

"The list of investment. That is what you will do, all that you will bring about."

Eleanor looked at him for a long moment, then said very slowly, "Not what I will do. What I *did*."

Will Honeycutt looked puzzled for a moment, then showed with his eyes that even this most profound point was sinking in. "I understand," he said tentatively. "That means that eighty or so years from now, you are going to return from Vienna and search for a T. Williams Honeycutt again because the name is written in this book, and once again you are going to find *me*, the wrong one," he said in conclusion.

"Apparently so," she said. "Yes."

"It is so. It is destiny. But, don't you see, you will do the same thing again. It is the right choice. It was in the past and will be in the future. Over and over. The right one."

"Yes," she said, now hesitantly, having followed his scientist's logic and perhaps acknowledging it for the first time. "The right one."

"And Arnauld," he said now with a clear confidence. "Arnauld is the key to the whole thing. In order for the whole story to repeat itself, as it must, Arnauld needs to be back here, back at St. Gregory's, back in our life."

"Yes."

"That," he said, "is why you risked so much to go find him. And that is why you were successful."

"Yes," Eleanor said, now clearly shaken by this continued barrage of logical interpretation. "But then it is destiny. It should happen by itself."

"No," Will said quickly. "Not by itself. Don't you see? You have had to act within it. That's the whole point." If possible there was now an even greater intensity in his eyes. "*We* have to act to make destiny unfold. This is a partnership."

Eleanor shook her head quizzically. "It is a lot to absorb, I know," she said finally.

"We must create our own destiny. We must act to make the preordained happen. That is our obligation. I must tell you this," he said, his eyes wide with revelation. "I know my role here. I know that I am not normal." She tried now to stop him, holding up her hands. "No, no," he protested. "I must finish. I know that I do not feel empathy or connection the way others do, and I obsess about details. You have been right in pointing out that I am good with the ticker tape but do not care about the people, that I know all about the parts in the automobiles but don't care about the drivers. I am not able to care." He was waving his arms. "I am not able to love."

"Oh, Will," she said, trying to intercede.

"No, no," he said again. "I live in my own world of systems. Systems, systems, always systems. I know this. It is my tragic flaw. But now, just this once, I can do something. I care about you," he said. "And I care about Arnauld. It is hard to describe or explain, but it is true. Just this once."

"Oh, Will—" she began, and again he held up his hands, stopping her.

"Therefore," he said with absolute intensity and absolute clarity, "that is why I must go now to Zurich."

63

ELEANOR'S DREAM

t was right about that time, perhaps even that night, that Eleanor had the dream. When she awoke from it, she took care to record it in the most minute detail.

The scene seemed to be a number of years in the future, around 1926, when Standish was eleven. Arnauld, now fully restored and teaching again at St. Gregory's, had agreed to travel to Dexter School, Standish's school, to watch the closing activity of the fall boys' competition. Eleanor had scheduled a car and driver to pick Arnauld up at St. Gregory's, and they would travel together to the game. She found herself looking forward to a rare moment alone with him, acknowledging the pleasure of being near this man who had secretly meant so much to her for so long.

They were sitting in the backseat of one of David Dunbar Buick's limousines, and Arnauld, looking mature and poised, was telling her about his new appointment at St. Gregory's, European history teacher for the first class, the most prestigious assignment on the faculty.

"It is a great honor," she said. "And one well deserved."

"They think me fully recovered," he said. His eyes were clear; his hand was steady.

"I am happy to have this moment alone," Eleanor said on their way to Dexter School. She felt a great warmth sitting beside him.

"I was lost," he said. "You came to save me."

"You remembered that?"

"I remember," he said. "I remember that the war was folly. We have lost so much. The world as we knew it fell apart."

"And that is what you will teach the boys?" she asked.

"I shall teach the boys what we lost."

"And you remember your time here, the night before you left, that summer of 1914?"

He put his head down. "I remember," he said in little more than a whisper. "I remember," he repeated, and then shook his head. "The thought of it kept me alive during the war. But I fear."

"You fear what?" she said.

"I fear I violated the trust, I intruded myself."

"Oh, no," she said with an unrestrained burst, breaking through the formality for a moment, her hand shooting out to touch his arm. "Oh my, no, dearest Arnauld. It was completely and utterly my wish. You must always know that."

And suddenly they were at Dexter School. "And what is this event?" Arnauld asked. "I know it is important to Standish."

"It is the treasured Iroquois Cup, the most important event of a Dexter boy's year," Eleanor explained. "It instills in them the spirit of competition."

"It is what the older boys at St. Gregory's engage in," Arnauld said. "I wondered where they learned it."

"From an early age," Eleanor continued. "There are two teams here, the Mohawks and the Oneidas, and at the end of the fall the winner in points will be given the Iroquois Cup. Standish is an Oneida, as was his father, Frank Burden, before him."

"American boys throw themselves into these rivalries," Arnauld said. "It is superb."

Eleanor and Arnauld were then standing on the sidelines, watching. The boys, fifth and sixth graders, were dressed in the colors of their teams, blue for the Mohawks and red for the Oneidas. Each boy had tucked into his waistband a yellow sash. The game was tied. "One play remaining," came a cry from the bench. At first there seemed to be only chaos, and then from the middle of the confusion of flying bodies one red-shirted boy emerged darting and twisting and dancing from side to side.

"It is Standish," burst from Arnauld.

The boy kept spinning and dodging, and then with what seemed like a superhuman burst of speed, he threw his arms into the air and crossed the goal line. What followed for the Oneida team was absolute bedlam. They swarmed toward the victorious runner and enveloped him in hurling and flying bodies, all chanting.

"What is it?" Arnauld said.

"They are saying, 'Dilly, Dilly,'" Eleanor said. "The boys have begun calling him Dilly."

Arnauld and Eleanor watched in delight and amazement as young Standish Burden was tossed about in the middle of the pile. Eleanor reached out then and patted his arm and felt again the warmth of closeness. She saw that Arnauld was completely absorbed in watching the boy in this glorious moment.

"Dilly," he said. "The boy will be called Dilly."

And Eleanor concluded her description of her dream with the observation that she woke up with a feeling of great contentment. "That is the vision," she wrote, "but I have no idea how to bring it to fruition."

64

ROWING HOME

efore Will Honeycutt left for Zurich, he discussed details with Eleanor. "The Hyperion Fund will cover the expenses, I assume," he said.

"Of course," Eleanor said. "This is exactly what all we have done is for."

"I have a plan," Will said with a newfound authority, "and I will execute it myself. But when I am finished, I will be coming home, and someone will have to follow through back in Vienna. Someone will have to be with him day and night to reintroduce him to the full life he had in Vienna, and to guard against his slipping back."

"I understand," Eleanor said. "And I know the perfect person, after you have done your part."

And Will Honeycutt asked that he be able to take some special items. "I will need some supporting tools. I would like your copy of Chapman's *Odyssey*," he said. "And Standish's picture book of that story. And as many of Arnauld's letters as I may have." She agreed and made a packet of the requested items and added it to his baggage.

"And that romantic Italian photograph?" Will said at the end of the packing process. She had nearly forgotten about it, but found it among Arnauld's papers.

"I have not been able to understand this image," she said, handing it over.

"This photograph is very important," he said. "He kept it in a place of honor."

"And its significance?" she asked.

"Don't you see?" Will Honeycutt said, as if explaining some obvious but important point in atomic science. "It is his image of himself, his ideal self, the archetypal lover, the one trapped inside, as Miggo says. And this"—he pointed to the beautiful fashionable woman—"we all know who this is."

She went silent for a moment, and then suddenly it all became clear and she stared at the image of the lovers in stunned silence. "His Beatrice," she said in little more than a whisper.

"Of course it is," Will Honeycutt said, oblivious to her reaction, lifting the photograph and adding it to his packed materials. "And it will come in handy, added to my other tools," he said in conclusion.

When the United States entered the war in 1917, like many men his age, Will had been too old to volunteer, so he dedicated himself to reading a good deal about the war and about the ordeals of those who did go. When he discovered that his friend Arnauld was suffering from what he deduced was shell shock, he found in his research a relevant report by a British psychiatrist. A soldier who suffered a battle neurosis, the report said in essence, had not lost his reason, but was laboring under the weight of too much reason: It was not that his senses were not functioning; they were functioning with painful efficiency.

Armed with that simple notion, he met with Dr. Jung when he arrived in Zurich and explained that he wanted to work with Arnauld, that he thought he had an answer, and Jung was impressed by his determination.

"I am not a physician," he explained, "I am a physicist. I want to know how systems work at the atomic level. I am like the medieval alchemists, always looking for the *prima materia*."

"I understand," Jung said, with great seriousness. "And you believe that you know how your friend Arnauld's system worked in shutting down, at this, the *prima materia* level?"

"I do, sir," Will Honeycutt said with the unearthly intensity in his eyes.

"The human mind is very complex," Jung said, cautioning the neophyte.

"I relish complex problems, sir," Will Honeycutt said.

Jung wrote Eleanor. "Young Honeycutt's intervention, as it were, can do no harm," he said. "At first we all balked at his lack of psychological training, but then, his manner won us all over, and no other avenues in sight, we acceded, admitting that the rest of us are stuck. He sees through to what none of us are able to see, ventures where none of us are willing to venture, to what he calls the *prima materia*. It is fascinating to watch. He pursues like a fox after a rabbit, descending at times into the abyss to rescue his friend. Arnauld is fortunate perhaps that his friend has come along. One of the doctors is writing a paper. Arnauld's case could well become renowned in the treatment of battle trauma. Everyone was impressed by your Will Honeycutt's bearing. He seemed to have taken on the persona of an experienced aged and wise practitioner." And back in Boston, when Eleanor read that last sentence, she smiled and knew exactly what was happening. Will Honeycutt was having conversations with William James.

It was on only his second day, after he had read the medical report and assessed the arrangements at the Burghölzli, that Will Honeycutt announced that he intended to have Arnauld Esterhazy rowing. He set out to find a source of a single shell somewhere between the Zurich waterfront and Jung's house at Küsnacht, where he was told by a number of sources that there were possibilities. He found by the end of the day a friend of the hospital's director who rowed on the lake regularly.

Mornings on the Zürichsee, he observed, were usually glassy smooth, the wind and waves not picking up until midafternoon. So on his third morning, he drove with Arnauld Esterhazy and an accompanying doctor, a neurology resident named Knoffler, who seemed to be in charge of Arnauld's "recreation," to a small boathouse and dock five kilometers from the hospital.

"We'll get him into the boat," Will said, not revealing what he hoped would transpire. "We'll just see what happens."

Arnauld approached the excursion as he did everything, with a genial half smile and a blank gaze. Will Honeycutt helped him out of his clothes and into shorts and a rowing jersey. The patient did not resist. Then the two observers carried the single-seated boat to the dockside and dropped it into the water, Arnauld following behind, watching with no apparent interest or emotion.

The two observers got him into his seat in the shell and placed his hands on the oars. "We will just let him sit and get accustomed," Will said, again revealing none of what he hoped for. Will gave the shell a little shove, and it drifted away from the dock, bringing a look of alarm to Dr. Knoffler's face.

"Don't worry," Will Honeycutt said, pointing to the dinghy tied alongside the dock. "We have that."

Arnauld sat without moving, hands on the oars, as the shell drifted out onto the lake. Then, ever so slightly, he began moving his hands, first one, then the other, lifting each oar from the still, clear blue Alpine water. In a slight, uncoordinated effort the movement propelled the boat forward, then gradually his legs pushed forward and then retracted in the seat until both oars began pulling up and then hitting the water at the same time. The shell began to slide away out into the deep, and Dr. Knoffler made a quick movement toward the dinghy. Will Honeycutt reached out a hand to stop him.

"Don't worry," Will said, as both men could see the shell picking up speed, and the rower beginning to slide up and back in the seat and the oars beginning to move in rhythm. Now, a good thirty meters from where the two observers stood, the rower and boat seemed to have found an easy fluidity that propelled the shell across the glassy surface.

"We must follow," the doctor said, now making a move toward the automobile.

Again, Will held out his hand to stop him. "Don't worry," he repeated. "Arnauld knows what he is doing." And Will looked at his watch. "We have forty-five minutes."

"I need to call the hospital," Dr. Knoffler said, fully agitated.

And Will said he could do that if he wished, but it was not necessary. "Let us go find a coffee."

Dr. Knoffler got into the automobile to do what he could to follow the small speck of oars and rower along the lakeside, and Will found a coffee in a nearby café.

On schedule, Will was back on the dock, where Dr. Knoffler was joined now by another doctor from the hospital, both frowning and looking alarmed.

"Look," Will said, pointing off across the glassy blue lake. There coming toward them was the tiny speck of a two-oared boat, gliding across the surface. As it came closer, they could see the smooth muscles of the rower in totally synchronized movements. Will Honeycutt looked at his watch and said coolly, "Forty-five minutes." The two doctors watched, now in a combination of relief and approbation.

As Arnauld approached the dock, they saw on his face the same blank look they all were accustomed to, but this time it had the slightest hint of something new beneath it, something like euphoria.

When Will met with Dr. Jung that afternoon at his house in Küsnacht, he was the one with the look of euphoria on his face.

"There is life in there," he said in a burst of enthusiasm, recounting the details of the morning boating exercise.

Dr. Jung looked concerned for a moment, obviously reluctant to deflate the younger man's hopes. "Muscle memory," he said finally. "It is not what it appears to be." And then he looked serious. "Did you read the reports?"

By then, Will had begun reading to Arnauld. "That is my plan," he had said to Jung the day he arrived. "Arnauld has gone into a deep introverted paralysis." The American used language he knew the Swiss doctor would understand. "His feminine has been severely wounded, his anima. It has been imprisoned deep within, and it is my job to go in and retrieve it. I intend to read to him until he comes out. I think you will find me tireless in that regard."

Jung smiled at him patiently, not rejecting what Will had to say but not accepting it either, having in his hand by then a letter from his friend Eleanor, a full description of this "eccentric genius," Will Honeycutt from Boston, who ought to be given a chance.

"I intend to read to him day and night, from his own writings, his beloved Homer, and from that small black volume he has been clutching in his hands ever since Mrs. Burden left."

"Ah," Jung said, "*City of Music.*"

"Yes," Will Honeycutt said, "*City of Music* by Mr. Jonathan Trumpp."

So Will Honeycutt read to his Viennese friend every day, all day and into the night, reading over and over the man's letters to his friends and his parents, the works of Homer in an English translation, and the work from his cherished little black book *City of Music,* and on the rare occasions when he did tire, he found a Burghölzli intern to keep up the pace. Arnauld seemed to listen attentively to whatever was being read, responding to none of it.

On the third day of this reading regimen, Will Honeycutt said to his unresponsive friend, "Now, I have a treat for you." He held out the child's picture book of the *Odyssey* that was dear to Eleanor's son. "This is from Standish," Will said. "He thinks you will like it very much."

He opened the book slowly and laid it in Arnauld's lap. Arnauld did not move, and Will began turning the pages, looking for some sign of attention. "Look here," he said, as he came to young Standish's favorite page. "Here is the Cyclops," the reader said, and Arnauld's eyes seemed to flicker for just an instant. "And here is Odysseus escaping under the belly of one of the sheep." Again, just the hint of a recognition. It was an exercise that would be practiced every day.

"Herr Esterhazy seems to follow with special care the pages of the children's book of the *Odyssey* as Honeycutt turns each page and points out the story behind each drawing," one of the nurses reported to Jung in the second week. "One can almost make out a smile on the patient's face as he follows along with the mythic adventures."

But Jung remained unimpressed.

It was during these first few days that Will Honeycutt introduced his friend Arnauld to the three-ring binder and the typewriter, which he had acquired from the Burghölzli administration. "You will write," he said to his friend, as more of a command than a suggestion. "Every day. You will write a page and then use this hole punch"—he held up the hole punch he had found—"and place the page in the binder. If you rewrite a page, adding more detail, you will drop the former page into this box. And you will call this expanding and evolving volume your Random Notes." Will left nothing to chance.

Arnauld barely acknowledged the commands, but we do have evidence that he began the process in a very rudimentary fashion. Since none of the pages are dated, we do not know the timing, but from the complexity of thought expressed alone, we can establish the sequence. The very first page, the one at the very bottom of the box of discarded pages, contains only two words: "ARNAULD WIEN." The next sheet in the pile reads, "ARNAULD WIEN MUSIK MALEN SKULPTUR CAFÉ." And on what we can assume was the third day, on the third typed page we read, "MY NAME IS ARNAULD. I GREW UP IN VIENNA, A CITY OF MUSIC, PAINTING, AND CAFÉ LIFE." And from that page forward, all the entries were written in English. And finally, after a few more

rudimentary pages found in order in the box, there is the page that remained permanently in place at the front of the volume, as the second
page of what was to be called, per Eleanor's instructions, his Random
Notes.

> *My name is Arnauld Esterhazy, and I grew up in Vienna at a*
> *time of cultural fulfillment for this magical city. During my young*
> *adult life, all manner of human endeavor had evolved and flour-*
> *ished to a point of what we would consider later a zenith, and much*
> *of this cultural zenith came to life for my friends and me in the cafés,*
> *which in our city were abundant. My personal choice and that of*
> *many of my friends was the Café Central. During that time, a*
> *group of my associates—painters, sculptors, musicians, historians,*
> *and thinkers of all sorts—formed a movement we called the Seces-*
> *sion, and it made our city one of the centers of intellectual life in*
> *Europe, certainly the most—we believed—original and creative of*
> *all Europe. For myself personally, I was more of an observer than a*
> *participant, and I shall use these pages to describe what I witnessed*
> *during this extraordinary time, so that others might benefit as I*
> *have from the brilliance of the era.*

When asked later by one of the doctors, "Why do you write in English,
Herr Esterhazy?" the patient Arnauld responded, reportedly, "Because
Korzeniowski wrote in English."

At some point in the early days of the binder, his Random Notes, he
typed the first page that remained at the front of the collection for the
remainder of its life, and remains today. The page is yellowed and worn
because it is the only one that was never revised and replaced. It says simply, "To my son."

Similarly, the back page was placed in the early days and never removed. It was the photograph of the debonair lover given to Arnauld by
his cousin Miggo. Will produced it one morning and held it up to Arnauld. "Do you recognize this?" Will said, and his friend only stared
blankly, perhaps showing the most minute hint of a smile. "I believe this
is your alter ego, and it belongs in your Random Notes." Will took the hole
punch and made three holes, the photo then took the binder and put the
photo in place, where it too would stay permanently. Some days when Will

arrived in the hospital room, he found his friend sitting silently with the binder open to that last page, simply staring at it and showing that hint of a smile. "Inside every shy man," Will would say as he took up his position in the nearby chair preparing for his daily readings. Even in the early days in the Burghölzli, it appeared that the photograph brought great pleasure.

During those early days also, at Will's request, the doctors found at the university a graduate scholar of ancient Greek, and she came every day and read for an hour, mostly from the *Odyssey*. It was during one of these hours of Greek two weeks into the routine that Will Honeycutt noticed something that the ever-realistic Dr. Jung agreed was a more than slightly significant sign of hope. On that special afternoon, after seemingly endless days of nothing even close to progress, Will Honeycutt saw an almost imperceptible change as the young woman from the university read a passage near the end of the Greek *Odyssey*. Will called Jung and had him sit in on the next afternoon, and the two men watched and listened. Arnauld Esterhazy's lips were moving as he listened. He was reciting from memory the words of Homer.

"Now," Dr. Jung said as he and Will left the hospital room, "we have something." And that evening the Swiss doctor wrote his friend Eleanor in Boston, "There is life in there. Our friend Mr. Honeycutt has indeed gone in deep and found his Eurydice."

The next day, Will Honeycutt had changed his strategy. When he arrived in the morning, the hour before they left for the boathouse, Will handed Arnauld the Chapman translation of the *Odyssey* and said, "Here, you read."

At first Arnauld only stared at the open book in his lap, the familiar blank look on his face, then when Will Honeycutt tapped a place on the page and said with firmness, "Here, begin here," slowly the miracle happened. Arnauld Esterhazy began to read. Will smiled but showed no surprise. "Keep going," he said, "we have the better part of an hour." The passage Will Honeycutt selected for Arnauld was chosen not by accident. It was, it turned out, one of great significance.

The selected passage described how the gods had captured the winds in a bag and left them on deck so that Odysseus could sail home to Ithaca directly and without incident, and then how his men, suspecting that their leader was keeping treasure from them, opened the bag, released the winds that blew their ship way off course and away for ten long years of adventure from which only Odysseus would return.

Later that morning when the single shell glided away from the dock of the boathouse on the Zürichsee, Will Honeycutt did not move from where he stood watching. He remained there for the full forty-five minutes, watching the boat glide away until it was a tiny speck in the distance and then waiting with total confidence until it reappeared, again as a tiny speck, rowing home.

65

TO TELL STORIES

y design, the readings had shifted to the *Iliad*, in both the Chapman translation and the graduate student's Greek. "We will talk about the war," Will had said to the patient one morning when there was a break in Arnauld's reading. Will's tone was gentle and respectful, but firm. "Very scientific," one of the doctors said in his first report, "surprising from one untrained."

"We will talk about the shelling and the mangled bodies and the rats and the lice and the blood." Arnauld looked at him blankly and blinked, giving in the subtlest of facial expressions his permission. At first Will was guessing, reconstructing from reports he had read, and he admitted later from a good deal of imagination. He knew nothing of war firsthand, but he had read voraciously. He knew of the appalling conditions of a military whose strategies had become hopelessly outdated with the advent of heavy artillery, barbed wire, and machine guns. And he knew from Eleanor the descriptions from her companion Jodl, who had interviewed countless Italian prisoners and knew as much as most survivors about the grueling and pointless campaigns and the horrifying conditions.

"My goal," Will told Jung in one of their frequent meetings, "is to keep Arnauld supplied with his own horrific images from his own notebook. Details that he can attach his own specific memories to, and I need to keep them coming, to bombard his denial system with the brutal truths."

Interspersed with passages from the *Iliad*, Will had his patient read to him from his own war notebook. The entries in his notes begun in 1914 were candid and painfully vivid in their description of the horrors of the war his country had embraced with such zeal. Arnauld would read through it, and then Will would command coldly, "Read it again."

And in between the readings Will Honeycutt would take on the role of interrogator, forcing his listener to confront and to listen and to respond. In that role, he was relentlessly direct, even heartless in his questioning, but ever patient, he never lost the attention of his obedient if not willing subject.

"It has been thought that men in Arnauld's condition need to forget," Will Honeycutt said with his patented directness in his afternoon summary to Dr. Jung, "that they need to be soothed into some kind of forgetful serenity."

"And you do not believe this to be the proper treatment?" Jung responded, not entirely comfortable with the American's abrasive assertion and its implied criticism.

"It is quite the opposite," Will Honeycutt said, oblivious to any skepticism from his Swiss host. "They need to *remember*, not forget. Until he speaks of the horrors, he is going to carry them inside forever." But the horrors were as yet unspeakable, and through relentless, sometimes heartless interrogation, Will intended to get his patient to describe them. As was so often the case in this "talking cure" that Dr. Freud had developed, once the unspeakable became spoken, it left the troubled mind of the patient forever, or so the theory went.

"From what I have been able to deduce," he often began when talking to Jung, and the Swiss doctor listened with his own patented forbearance, "the mind organizes the random impressions it comes upon in daily life into what one might call meaningful clusters, and it uses these clusters to tell of the impressions. A chaotic experience with a hurricane or an earthquake becomes in its aftermath a logical series of events, a hunting accident is explained as a reasonable combination of circumstances, an investment in the stock market is told later as a series of planned and intelligent guesses."

"That is very interesting," Jung said, "and certainly aligned with my thinking."

"These clusters are what make meaning of life," Will Honeycutt continued. "At first, I could not understand why people at Harvard, intelligent people, took such interest in football, and told such grand stories about those who played it. A football game is a chaos of collisions and strategies and counter strategies, that the observers tell about in a cluster of details in such a way as to give it all order and meaning, creating along the way heroes and villains, martyrs and sacrificial lambs, winners and losers."

"I am following this," Jung said, his skepticism and irritation, he admitted later, beginning to fall away.

"And in war, think of the horror and the chaos, and yet the people engaged in it, those fortunate enough to survive, find themselves making meaning of it all."

"Hence the *Iliad*," Jung said.

"Exactly. Hence the *Iliad*. The human mind tells stories to bring order and meaning to what otherwise would be terrifying randomness," Will said, now obviously wound up. "Without stories, don't you see, we stare out into the vastness of the universe and lose all sense of order and connectedness."

"This is very good, Mr. Honeycutt," Jung said, now genuinely impressed. "Where do your ideas come from?"

"I took William James's course at Harvard College, and I've been thinking ever since."

"These clusters of yours, these stories, give meaning to life," Jung said.

"Yes," Will said. "That is my conclusion. They structure randomness and chaos to create meaning." Then he thought for a moment. "The human mind cannot stand randomness, don't you see? Randomness makes one distraught. It means that anything can happen." It did not occur to him at this moment that he, neophyte in this arena of the unconscious mind, was lecturing the world-famous Swiss doctor. "Randomness is insanity," he concluded with a flourish.

Jung listened with interest and now not in any way irritated or demeaning. "The stories, small, such as a game at Harvard, or grand, such as in the battles of the Isonzo River or Homer's *Odyssey*, they are then your definition of sanity."

"Yes," said Will, delighted that he was being taken seriously. "Stories give meaning to life," he repeated, now with urgency, "They bring life-saving, life-affirming order." Then he added almost as an afterthought, "As you say."

"Then," the great Swiss doctor said, as if questioning not so much a graduate student as a respected colleague, "how does this relate to our friend Herr Esterhazy?"

Will paused to collect himself, to calm his racing mind, Eleanor might say. "It relates totally," he said, gesturing with his hands, "don't you see? War destroys the process. Prolonged exposure to terror and savagery ruins the ability to create meaningful clusters, overpowers it, the way that exposure to electrical shock ruins the body's flow of energy. Randomness remains randomness."

"And for our patient?" Jung asked calmly.

"Arnauld has become lost in randomness."

"And therefore?"

"He has lost his ability to tell stories," Will said simply.

66

AN EXQUISITE FRIENDSHIP

ill had pieced together what he could of the details, mostly from Arnauld's war notebook, but also from his extensive research, and from what he knew through Eleanor of Franz Jodl. The war had been one of attrition on many levels—manpower, resources, national unity, the credibility of governments, and the individual sanity of its most sensitive participants.

One can read in Arnauld's war notebook the thoughts that must have been on the mind of every halfway-intelligent observer of the fray: Going to war was a disastrous idea and a horrific mistake.

"Here," he wrote, "we encourage young men, many little more than children, to match the enemy, to indulge in behavior and to live in conditions abhorrent to the civilized mind. To give in to all sorts of previously forbidden and hidden impulses, cruel, sadistic, murderous ones. Impulses which had been subdued before by means of what Dr. Freud called repression are now reinforced as normal, and the young men are compelled to employ them now under the totally different code of behavior."

And he began to see the effects on the officers, the well-educated civilized former denizens of the coffeehouses of Vienna, Budapest, and Prague. "For those not killed," he wrote, "the shock and strain, their hidden stammering, disconnected talk, their old, scared faces, their haunted nights, their subjection to the ghosts of friends who died, often torn apart in front of them, their dreams that drip with murder, broken and mad."

In time, Arnauld was put in charge of an attachment of young Czechs, like him, recently recruited and new to both army life and battle, some of them no older than fifteen. "I have become fond of them," he recorded, "and distressed by how the fatigue has worn them down in numbers. It is all I can do," he continued, "to hide the trembling of my hands and the hollowness that sleeplessness has brought to my eyes. They, these young recruits, of course, are no better off, the tension of waiting having taken its toll on them as well."

There was simply no relief, and the frequent shellings and the deadly raining down of shrapnel make for the most perilous of surroundings. In the beginning months, all soldiers were issued traditional soft caps, and it wasn't until more than one year into the grim stalemate that those caps were replaced with steel helmets to protect from the deadly assaults of exploding artillery shells.

"We are all certain that an attack is coming on our position," he wrote, "and if it does not come here, we will be moved to the location on this river where it does come." One way or another every soldier on the Isonzo front was guaranteed to be in the thick of the slaughter, much of which was hand-to-hand combat of the worst sort, killing and being killed with bayonets, knives. One Slavic division was famous for its use of war clubs. "It is the waiting and the daily not-knowing that weighs so heavily on the men, and their officers. Theirs is not the only commanding officer whose hands shake. It is awful business."

It was not uncommon to have to work around the dead and parts of the dead, never knowing from which side of the battle lines they came. "One has to be disciplined not to think of what that remnant of human life had been before this or that a shell took life away. An unfortunate soul, one has to think, certainly not a friend or a loved one. One has to try not to think." And the lice and vermin were everywhere. The food, what there was of it, was rotten, and the shellings incessant, often the percussion rendering those below temporarily or permanently deaf.

"One can see just from simple observation," Arnauld wrote, "that life for the enemy is the same. On those occasions when we have advanced and overrun their trenches, we find the identical conditions, or even worse. It is for them as it is for us, a terrible way to live. The most distant of memories, now nearly extinguished, is the opportunity to sit beside a quiet river with a dear friend and talk of things sublime, far away from this horrible mistake that has become endless and meaningless slaughter."

And the last entries, short, choppy, only a few scattered words, contain what were probably the final sane moments. Arnauld's Czechs had been moved north up to the town of Caporetto, where a huge force was amassing. Then came an October day of the heaviest bombardment yet, and Arnauld noticed shells being loaded with a new material.

"Gas," came the dreaded word. "All we are awaiting is for the winds to be right."

And then the word came to charge, and he urged his men forward, across the river, into the heart of the suddenly ineffectual enemy who had begun a disorganized retreat.

> *With bayonets fixed, we rushed into the void of the retreating enemy. We came to trenches where the gas had drifted. There were dead Italians everywhere, their faces drawn into the most horrifying grimaces, mouths frothing. Some dead reaching for the masks—some crawling over one another trying to escape.*
>
> *My Czechs stood on the edge of trenches horrified, and we, the officers, had to scream for them to carry on. The Italians retreating— total disarray—some reversing their direction and coming toward us, hands raised, calling out praise for our side.*

At a moment of quiet, with the enemy in disorganized retreat before them, Arnauld had been assigned the group of Italian prisoners, ordered to escort them to the trains, where they would be shipped to the prisoner camps near Vienna. For the task, he wrote that he had recruited as his assistant a sensitive young officer who had frequented the Prague coffeehouses. "We have formed an exquisite friendship," Arnauld wrote, "of the sort possible only in war. He was a philosophy student at the university in Prague, with an especial affection for the music of Mahler, who he insisted was really a Czech. A poet of unusual sensitivity. We have spent long hours together in the quiet before battle. We have become very close." The next morning the two officers would go about, as was their assignment, rounding up the Italian officers and directing them toward the trains. That was the last entry.

The last details Will Honeycutt obtained not from Arnauld's war journal, but from Jodl's original report to Eleanor, the observations of witnesses. "While they were organizing Italian prisoners in a rail yard, an enemy shell exploded nearly on top of them, and the whole group was obliterated, pieces of bone and flesh everywhere. It was, by all accounts, a horrifying mess from which for certain no one survived. It is clear from the reports that one body, identified as Arnauld Esterhazy, had been decapitated by a large piece of shrapnel."

67

A FEW MORE DAYS

escribe for me the trench life," Will Honeycutt would say, accepting even the smallest detail, but asking the question over and over, expecting more and more painful details with each asking, so different from the approach that tried to make the patient feel comfortable.

Later, when asked how he knew how to proceed, the American said simply, "I am a scientist. I know how systems work. I have read with some thoroughness about the extraordinary lengths the human system employs to protect itself and to avoid."

"The Czech officer," Will Honeycutt said, homing in now. "What was his name?"

Arnauld looked back with the blank stare his unconscious had been using as a shield. "Pietr," he said quietly.

"He was your friend?"

"Yes. Yes, he was."

"And when you began to regain consciousness, he was beside you. You saw him. He was beside you." There was a calm insistence to the question, one Arnauld could not dodge.

"Yes," he said quietly.

"And his head was gone?"

Again the stare and the silence, but a memory began forcing itself to the surface. "Yes. And his—" The dread returned and stopped him.

Will Honeycutt paused, waiting, but no more came, so he said it. "It was his brain material that covered your face."

"Yes," Arnauld said, almost whispering.

"And you lapsed into unconsciousness. The Italians found you and thought you one of theirs. They took you."

"I suppose."

"That is what happened," Will said with authority. "They heard you muttering about Beatrice, and they thought you one of theirs."

"I suppose."

"That is what happened, Arnauld. I am not making it up." Suddenly, Will stopped and looked at his friend. "Arnauld, dying in battle is horrible. Those Italian soldiers, those horrible faces. Think of the deaths by infections you had to witness in your men. Your friend Pietr," he said. "He was very dear to you." The patient nodded. "You had become *companions of the heart*, I believe you wrote."

Arnauld showed no objection to the term and remained unmoving and silent for a long moment, then looked up slowly and gave the slightest nod.

"The Czech Pietr was the best of humanity," Will said. "He was a beautiful man." Another nod from the subject. "And the explosion, it was devastating." Another nod. "You came back to consciousness surrounded by blood and pieces of flesh. There were bits of flesh covering your face. You had seen it before, many times before." Arnauld said nothing, only grimaced.

"Arnauld, look at me," he said, and waited for the patient to look up, now he the one losing control. "Pietr the Czech poet, your friend, his death was horror."

"It was all horror," Arnauld said softly, with almost no emotion. "So much horror."

"Descending from Caporetto you came upon men, gassed, scores of men grotesque, frothing at the mouth." Again a grimace from the patient, but no response. Arnauld looked paralyzed. Suddenly Will Honeycutt broke the silence. "It was your fault," he said, raising his voice now, accusing. "Eugene of Savoy came to you, told you, talked you into it. You were supposed to emerge as the charismatic leader. You were supposed to get them to stop, and you didn't. It is all on your shoulders, all your fault."

A glassiness having come over him, Arnauld seemed to fall back into the abyss in which he had been for the past few months.

"Arnauld, look at me," Will Honeycutt insisted, and he waited. "You think it is your fault," he said. "Prince Eugene of Savoy, the great hero, came to you, spoke to you, and you could do nothing, and it is all your fault."

Will Honeycutt stopped, looked hard into the blank stare. Suddenly he was aware that he had pushed too hard, gone too far, his old bluntness with people resurfacing. The blank look had returned to Arnauld's face. There now existed between the two men an empty silence. And all seemed ruined.

In his meeting with Jung the next day, the doctor expressed his concern about reports he had received from the Burghölzli. "Our method with this patient, as with all patients, has been to wait things out and allow the unconscious to reveal its secrets as it will." He had assumed a kindly, fatherly tone. "You have gone on the attack, pursuing what you think is right. But, you have to appreciate, it is a method many at the Burghölzli find counterproductive."

"They think I am bullying," Will Honeycutt said, and Jung nodded. Will stared at him for a moment. "I think I can make it work."

"You attacked and attacked and won't retreat—"

Will Honeycutt interrupted. "Until he confronts the horrors he has seen and experienced firsthand."

"Yes," Jung said, "that would seem the case. It is just not our way. I am sure you understand."

"But you had reached an impasse," Will offered in protest.

"I will grant you that," Jung said. Even this brusque American could see that the Swiss doctor was retreating. "For the time being, perhaps—"

"But I am getting past that impasse," Will said, his brusque manner now fully surfaced. "Don't you see?"

"Perhaps we need to discuss this later," he said, pulling back in his chair.

Will Honeycutt, usually not one to notice even obvious language of body posture, sensed that he was losing. He stopped and tried to compose himself.

"Dr. Jung," he began, "I know I am an abrasive man. I know I offend people with my manner. I know I am offending you now. It has been that way all my life. But this time I am right, don't you see?" He stopped and looked for some kind of affirmation in the intense eyes of this man who knew so much about human nature, but there was none there. "Dr. Jung," Will repeated. "Can I just have more time?"

Jung eyed him silently. "The doctors will do what I ask."

"And will you ask for more time?"

Jung thought for another long moment, again assessing, and then said, "A few more days. I can ask for a few more days."

68

THE FOLLY OF MEN

he next morning when Will Honeycutt walked into Arnauld's room and placed a copy of Chapman's *Iliad* in his lap, the patient only stared at it blankly and said nothing.

"I would like you to read to me," Will Honeycutt said, impatient, tapping the spot on the page, and there was still nothing. "Very well," Will said. "I will read," and he proceeded to read scenes of battle in the *Iliad* until it was time to leave for the boathouse on the Zürichsee. In the auto on the way, Will feared that the regression was complete and that Arnauld would not row. Perhaps his brusque manner had ruined everything.

But after the usual routine and Arnauld, in his rowing shorts and jersey, was seated in the shell and pushed off from the dock, he began to row and headed out onto the mirrorlike smoothness of the lake. Exactly forty-five minutes later he was back at the dock.

For the rest of the day and into the evening, Will Honeycutt, patient again, read to his friend and got no response. The doctors at the Burghölzli avoided them both. The next day the same thing happened, and it was late at night, just as Will was thinking of calling it quits till the morning, that the change came.

They were back to reading the *Odyssey* and had arrived at the end, after Odysseus's men had been drowned, and the hero had sailed home alone to Ithaca. There was a passage in which the citizens of Ithaca blamed their leader Odysseus for not bringing their sons safely home from war. Will read the passage and then stopped. Then he read it again, and looked up into the face of his friend.

"Arnauld," he said, "look at me. For God's sake, look at me." The persona of any mentor far gone, it was now just the very fallible Will Honeycutt himself, alone with his friend. And he might have been imagining it, but for just an instant he thought he saw a flash of recognition in those vacant eyes. "It is not his fault," Will said, and there was nothing. "It is not his fault. Don't you see"—and he enunciated each word slowly—"it is not his fault."

And then, after more excruciating silence, he saw the lips move in what might have been *It is not his fault.*

Quickly, Will turned back in the book and found the passage about the bag of wind, and he read it aloud. "Did you hear?" he said when he had finished. "They were in sight of land, in sight of home. Odysseus had done all he could. He had convinced the gods to seal up the winds so that they could come home, all of them. Safe and sound from the war." Will saw the eyes move and definitely saw a flash of life in them this time. "Whose fault was it?" he said, and then stared into the face. There was another long, painful silence.

Will Honeycutt saw the lips move first, then the words came. "The men," Arnauld said.

"Arnauld," his friend said, "it is not your fault."

"It is not my fault," came in little more than a whisper.

"Whose fault is it?" Will said.

There followed a silence, and then Arnauld Esterhazy uttered a single word, in little more than a whisper. "Men," he said, and Will Honeycutt repeated his question.

This time the words came out with clarity. "Men," Arnauld said, and then added very distinctly, "The folly of men."

And the next morning when Carl Jung heard of it, he had tears in his eyes.

69

HOMECOMING

BOSTON, 1919

n a late summer afternoon, Eleanor stood on the plat-
form at Back Bay Station waiting for the 3:50 train from
New York. She was accompanied only by her young son,
Standish, having decided that the girls and her husband, Frank, would stay home and offer their greeting
there. She had also decided that it would be better if Will Honeycutt
traveled to New York and met the ship from Le Havre and arranged for
the train to Boston. She would be waiting at Back Bay Station.

She had been nervous and anxious all day, as the time seemed to pass
with excruciating slowness. As there had been no word from New York,
she judged that everything had gone smoothly, and she gathered Standish
and left for the station much earlier than was necessary.

In the time that had passed since her return from northern Italy and
Zurich, much had transpired. Will Honeycutt's treatment had brought
about what Carl Jung considered a near-miraculous breakthrough, one
that the doctors at the Burghölzli believed would affect greatly the manner in which battle trauma would be viewed and treated.

"Once Arnauld could express outwardly the extremity of his trauma,"
her friend Jung wrote, "his unconscious mind permitted full access to
memories which had been denied. This change in turn brought about his
near-complete return to normal, a return from the underworld."

The change became so thorough that before Will Honeycutt left his post at the hospital to return to Boston, it was concluded that the patient was fit to leave and continue his rehabilitation in his native Vienna, a step Will had prepared for by assigning the patient's cousin as his companion and helper. He had very carefully recruited Miggo Sabatini to the task and to live at his cousin's side for the months of the return to his former life there, including life at the university and in the cafés. Miggo had very detailed instructions on exactly how he would conduct his assignment, serving as Arnauld's "extroverted alter ego, the perfect guide for the last part of the journey out," as Will said. "Miggo knows not to stop the readings."

"Be relentless," Will Honeycutt had said, as if the impossible cousin needed coaching.

"Don't worry," Miggo replied. "I know the value of the letters and the readings and the memorials. I shall give him no rest."

When Eleanor heard of this turn in the tale of the restoration of Arnauld Esterhazy, she smiled, thinking it a brilliant move, and she enjoyed receiving letters during this phase of the rehabilitation from both the mentor and the subject.

During this rehabilitation period, she also received a letter from Fräulein Tatlock and read with great pleasure that Herr Jodl had become a regular visitor at the pension and that he had heard word from the Italian government that his son was definitely among the many Austrian prisoners of war detained near Rome during the complexities of postwar negotiations.

She also heard from Edith Hamilton, from her girls' school in Baltimore. Edith was overwhelmed by the news of Arnauld's being found alive and then by the reports of his restoration and his need for further rehabilitation. "I shall bring him down here to the Chesapeake," she wrote, "and take him up to Maine. We shall rediscover ancient Greece together and renew our work on our catalogue of the classic myths. I shall give him no rest until he is back to his old self, as good as new."

And then as Eleanor waited with her own son on the platform of Back Bay Station, she heard the sound of the approaching train and Standish's exuberant, "Oh boy. Here it comes," not really clear on who it was exactly they were there to greet.

She knew the position in the line of cars where they would be disembarking, and she watched as a few passengers appeared in the doorway and then stepped down onto the platform, the conductor watching to see that there were no missteps. Then suddenly Will Honeycutt stood in the doorway, and her heart began to race, and Standish burst out with, "Here he is!" thinking his mother's longtime business associate the reason for their long wait at trackside. And immediately behind Will Honeycutt, the cousin Miggo appeared, now exercising his American citizenship, looking from side to side a little nervously from the train car doorway, then stepping down into the world of Boston.

And then time stopped. As the two men stepped down onto the station platform, behind them in the train car doorway a handsome and distinguished European appeared. He was tall and alert, with a clear-eyed presence that might have caused anyone to stop and notice. He looked down to where Eleanor and her son were standing. For an instant he flinched as if his eyes were adjusting to the light or he was unable to absorb immediately what he was seeing. And then he smiled, a smile of such radiance that it should have been captured by a great photographer or painter. He was looking straight into the face of Eleanor Burden, and she returned the gaze for a long moment.

"Oh, look," Standish said. "Look who it is."

It was Arnauld Esterhazy.

Arnauld's smile in the doorway of the train car contained for her the whole world. As she stood rooted to her spot on the train platform, watching as his focus shifted from her own radiant face to the boy, she did not move. And then the moment he descended the steps and touched foot on the terra firma of the station platform in her Boston with his arms out, her son responding by rushing toward him, the sight crystallized the myriad thoughts coursing through her mind. She found herself overcome, transported to the dream of a few nights before, of standing with Arnauld, the fully recovered teacher, the Haze, a few years hence watching Standish perform heroically in his football game. Everything seemed to fall into place. She had done her job.

This lost prince returned, saved from the horrors of war, would resume his role at St. Gregory's and become the Haze, the legendary teacher he was supposed to be. The boy, her son, Standish, growing up under his tutelage, would rise to become Dilly Burden, the great hero of countless campaigns at Harvard, and go to war himself. In this role as a warrior, in pre-Blitz England, he would meet the love of his own life. She, already pregnant, would deliver a son, whom Dilly would accept as his own son. This boy would grow up—after the death of his father in war—and, acquiring the name Wheeler as a result of his prowess in baseball, become a legend himself, a musician, one of the most recognizable faces of his generation. And then, through a miracle, he would end up in Vienna in 1897 at the same time as her sojourn there, right after her graduation from college. All of this would now fall into place.

And now, standing on the train platform in Boston's Back Bay watching Arnauld Esterhazy and her son embracing, she could for the first time in twenty years transport herself back there to the scene that had for years been too painful to recall: Wheeler Burden, the love of her life, standing surrounded by beautiful Secessionist paintings. In an instant, something broke loose, something permanent she was to discover, and she found herself able to travel there now in her mind, and for the rest of her life relish, rejoicing in what she found, content with the role the experience had given her on into the future. Suddenly it all fit together, all the parts: William James, Sigmund Freud, Carl Jung, Will Honeycutt, the Hyperion Fund, Franz Jodl, even Miggo Sabatini.

In retrospect, it would amaze her that the one simple event of Arnauld's return from war, healthy and in full possession of his faculties, had caused such an explosion in her. The world was now, because of this return, as it should be: The past was what it was, the future would be what it would be. "We meet each other in dreams," her great love had said to her, and she herself had repeated. Now, suddenly, in a rush she could see it all. Now suddenly she believed.

And even Frank Burden played his part willingly, oblivious to much of what went on, missing out on much because he did not wish to "engage the world at their level," as he had stated proudly, referring to Freud and Jung, and perhaps even William James, but also to much of what she had done and believed. Always the literalist, as he called himself, Frank would watch his son grow into the great hero with whom he could identify, watching him be sacrificed in war and finding a kind of steely pride in that sacrifice.

She revisited Vienna now and would comfortably into the future, welcoming the poignancy of the memories and their powerful gifts to her.

She watched Arnauld and Standish, man and boy, embracing, and she approached them smiling. She reached out to join in the embrace, not as a lover or even as a mother, but with the objectivity of a temple priestess, not so much with the power of Athena now, but with that of the Egyptian goddess Isis.

She allowed herself to drift back to that time, felt herself back in the artist's studio in Vienna, back in the arms of the love of her life, feeling as he called it then "the connectedness of all things." She reached out and touched this restored and healthy man Arnauld Esterhazy, who meant so much to her life, and she touched her son. The *two* princes.

And, for the first time in more than twenty years, she allowed herself to hear the music.

It was the music of Vienna, the music of the waltz.

AUTHOR'S NOTE

Like its predecessor *The Little Book*, this novel is a work of imagination, but it derives much of its context from actual history. Sigmund Freud and Carl Jung really did go to Clark University and then Putnam Camp in the Adirondacks in 1909; J. P. Morgan actually did miss, for some unknown reason, sailing on his White Star liner *Titanic*'s maiden voyage; the World War One scenes really did play out in their horror on the Isonzo River in northern Italy; and the Spanish Flu added its devastation to that of the world war in 1918.

A number of sources were essential from the story's beginnings, particularly *The White War: Life and Death on the Italian Front 1915–1919* by Mark Thompson; *Jung: A Biography* by Deirdre Bair; *William James: In the Maelstrom of American Modernism* by Robert D. Richardson; *Reminiscences of a Stock Operator (Annotated Edition)* by Edwin Lefèvre, Jon D. Markman, and Paul Tudor Jones; and *Putnam Camp: Sigmund Freud, James Jackson Putnam, and the Purpose of American Psychology* by George Prochnik.

A number of people served as invaluable readers, adding constructive and critical support along the way. Principal among these were Meghan Tally, my Princeton roommate Louis Sanford, the invaluable Pat LoBrutto, and, of course, my wife, Gaby, the consummate English teacher, who lent careful attention to every page. Bobbi Wolf, Cathy Frantzis, Jano Tucker, Dave Raphael, and David Agnew also read and made timely suggestions.

A number of people helped with research. Invaluable resources among these were Paolo Valdemarin and Monica Loredan in Gorizia, Italy, and

Dietmar Steinbrenner in Vienna, all three of whom devoted valuable time hosting and generously sharing locations. It was Aaron Edelheit who pointed me in the direction of Jesse Livermore and the bucket shops that proved so instrumental in the development of Will Honeycutt's passions. Brock Brower lent his expertise on William James. And, as before, I am grateful for my years at Pacifica Graduate Institute for filling in details of depth psychology, Jung's active imagination, and the significance of dreams.

There is no question that this novel would not exist if it were not for two extraordinary colleagues in the book business: my agent, Scott Miller, and my editor at Dutton, Ben Sevier. Scott and Ben, both superb at their jobs, prodded, goaded, and cheered me on during the difficult gestation period of this second novel.

Also I am grateful for the remarkable support team at Dutton: President Brian Tart, Christine Ball, Carrie Swetonic, Liza Cassity, Stephanie Kelly, Susan Schwartz, Rich Hasselberger, Monica Benalcazar, and Kirby Rogerson. All played their parts well.

On a personal note, I cannot express adequately the significance of the friendship shown to me over the past four years by Pat Conroy in the development of my own journey as a writer. Pat has been as supportive as he is an inspiration. Also this time around I wish to thank Seattle writers Jennie Shortridge and Garth Stein. What a luxury to have such writers as friends.

And finally a word about my dedication page: my three children, Nan, Bruce, and Paula, readers all, have chipped in over the years to help with ideas and plot points. They along with their mother have been the ideal family for a late-blooming author. To all four of them I extend my deepest love, gratitude, and admiration.

ABOUT THE AUTHOR

A graduate of Princeton and Stanford, Selden Edwards is a former English teacher and was headmaster at several private schools during his career in education. His debut novel, *The Little Book*, which he began writing in 1974 and worked on over the course of thirty years, was published in 2008 and became a national bestseller. He lives near Santa Barbara, California.